Together the two men gently rolled the captain onto his back, lifted his head, and trickled a few drops of water down the man's throat. The effect was instantaneous and shocking. A violent tremor shook the captain's body and wrenched his bloody eyes open. No intelligent awareness remained in his dark gaze, only the fevered terror of madness.

A gasping, raw scream tore from his throat. "Go away!" Fresh blood oozed from his mouth. "Don't touch me!" he shrieked, thrashing away from them.

Rolfe dropped the flask and scrambled away as if punched, his face creased with fear.

The harbormaster placed his hands on the captain's shoulders and tried to ease him back.

The sick man would have none of it. "No. No, no, no. Don't touch me," he screamed again. Blood dripped from every orifice, turning his blotched face into a hideous death mask. "Poison . . . death . . . everywhere," he panted, his eyes wild. "Stay away!"

THE CROSSROADS SERIES

The Clandestine Circle
Mary H. Herbert

The Thieves' Guild
Jeff Crook
(Available December 2000)

CROSSROADS

The Clandestine Circle

MARY H. HERBERT

**In loving memory of
Richard M. Herbert
1914 – 1999.
An engineer, an officer, and a gentleman.**

THE CLANDESTINE CIRCLE

©2000 Wizards of the Coast, Inc.
All Rights Reserved.

Cover art by Mark Zug
First Printing: July 2000
Library of Congress Catalog Card Number: 99-69333

9 8 7 6 5 4 3 2 1

ISBN: 0-7869-1610-9
620-T21610

U.S., CANADA,	EUROPEAN HEADQUARTERS
ASIA, PACIFIC, & LATIN AMERICA	Wizards of the Coast, Belgium
Wizards of the Coast, Inc.	P.B. 2031
P.O. Box 707	2600 Berchem
Renton, WA 98057-0707	Belgium
+ 1-800-324-6496	+ 32-70-23-32-77

Visit our web site at **www.wizards.com/dragonlance**

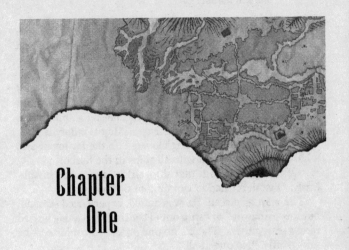

Chapter One

The ship sailed into Sanction Harbor on the morning tide, her sails billowing in the hot breath of the coming summer day. She was a three-masted merchantman, wide-hulled and shallow-drafted, flying the flag of Palanthas, and from a distance, there seemed nothing wrong.

The pilot, at his station at the mouth of the harbor, signaled the ship to lower her sails and wait for his approach, but the vessel glided serenely onward, totally ignoring his order. The pilot grumbled an oath and reached for his farseeing glass. He'd get the name of the ship and report her captain to the harbormaster for that insubordination. But when he trained the glass on the decks of the strange ship, his mouth fell open and his weathered skin lightened several shades.

"Cabel!" he yelled to his assistant. "Signal the harbormaster. We've got a runaway!"

The young man named Cabel hurried up the ladder of a high wooden tower that overlooked the teeming harbor.

From a wooden box that held a number of signal flags, he drew one made of red and yellow fabric, one so seldom used it was still creased and brightly colored. Quickly he ran it up the signal pole.

His master came puffing up the ladder to join him, and together they stared across the water toward the distant tower near the piers where the harbormaster's apprentices received and acknowledged messages. Almost immediately a matching red and yellow flag bloomed on the far tower and a horn signaled a warning to all ships in the harbor.

"What's wrong with that ship, sir?" Cabel asked breathlessly. "I've never had to run up that flag before."

The pilot grimaced. He was an old, experienced seaman, but the "runaway" or "ship out of control" was a flag he had rarely seen either. "There's no one on deck I could see," he said gruffly. "No one at all."

Cabel's eyebrows rose. "A ghost ship?"

The pilot stifled a shiver at the mention of a ghost. Like many seamen, he was superstitious and firmly believed in omens and portents. "Can't say who's sailing her, but she's real enough," he replied. "Maybe the ship lost its anchor or slipped its cable. Maybe they're all belowdecks dead-drunk."

"With their sails out?" Cabel asked, his tone dubious.

The pilot grunted a noncommittal response. He raised the glass to his eye again to watch the strange ship cruise blindly into the bustling harbor. "A ghost ship is a bad omen, boy," he muttered. "A bad omen. So don't go talking about it again."

The red and yellow flag on the harbormaster's tower was visible to everyone in the harbor, but not everyone knew what it meant. The horn signal, though, blared from one end of the busy docks to the other, and those who heard the warning blasts paused at their work and glanced anxiously at the sky or out toward the harbor entrance.

Sanction was a city constantly alert to danger, and her citizens rarely took warnings complacently. But there were no dragons in the sky winging in to attack, no fleet of black ships at the harbor's mouth lining up to fire a barrage. There was only one lone vessel sailing silently toward the docks. Only those who recognized the danger flag craned to get a glimpse of the runaway and, if possible, get out of its way.

Pushed by the morning wind, the ship cruised by a cluster of small fishing boats, two pleasure craft, and a large war galleon being outfitted for the city's harbor defenses. An ore freighter, already under sail, eased out of her way. The crew of one galley floating at anchor managed to haul on the anchor chain and pull the stern of their boat out of harm's way. They stared openmouthed as the lifeless ship slipped by their own with inches to spare.

As the Palanthian ship slid closer to the docks, the breeze in her sails dropped and the canvas sheets collapsed to slap against their masts like limp laundry. The merchantman's course slowed but became erratic as it approached the crowded docks.

All around, heads turned to watch the ship, and those close to her held their breaths. The first impact came with a loud thud and a splintering, grinding noise as the ship sideswiped another large merchantman. She began to slow, then a gust of wind caught her sails in its clasp and sent her rushing forward directly toward the long southern pier and an Abanasian trading vessel tied alongside to unload its cargo of cattle and sheep.

The crew of the trader, *Whydah*, gaped at the ship bearing down on them and scattered wildly just as the runaway rammed into the broad midsection of the trader, with a crash of splintering wood. The ship's bell clanged crazily. The impact jarred both vessels and raised a cacophony of bellows from the terrified livestock.

"Look out!" someone yelled just as the bowsprit and the foremast of the runaway crashed to the decks, bringing down yards of canvas and a tangle of ropes and shattered spars.

"Great galloping sea dragons!" roared the Abanasian captain. "What in the name of Chaos do they think they're doing? Come on, you lot, get over there and teach them some manners."

His crew climbed swiftly to their feet, grabbed the nearest truncheon or cutlass, and swarmed over the debris of mast

3

and sail onto the offending merchantman. Once on board, they paused and stared around at the lifeless deck in surprise. It was hard to vent anger on people who weren't to be found. Slowly they spread out to investigate.

The first mate made his way cautiously toward the upper aft deck and the ship's wheel. Something large lay in the shadow at the base of the big wheel, something that didn't look right. A bundle of laundry or bedding perhaps.

"Sir!" called one of his sailors from near a large hatch that led down to the crew's quarters. "Over here!"

The first mate hesitated, then switched around to see what the man had found. He hadn't gone more than five paces before the stench hit him. He clapped a hand over his nose and mouth and fought the desire to gag. His sailor looked green. Pale as the sheets, the two men lifted the hatch and peered downward.

The first mate glimpsed a row of supine bodies, all hideously dead, before he knocked the sailor's hand away and slammed the hatch shut. The sounds of retching behind him told him his own man had succumbed to the stench of rot and death, and he had to swallow hard to stifle the nausea in his gut. He wiped his streaming forehead. By the gods, it was hot.

"What about the rest of them?" he shouted.

"There are bodies over here," replied another sailor from the doorway into the galley and captain's quarters. "The officers and the cabin boy!"

"And here!"

"Over here, too," other voices responded from other parts of the ship.

"Rolfe," bellowed the captain to his first mate. "What's going on over there? Where is the crew?"

Rolfe scratched the back of his balding head as he looked around at the wrecked merchantman. "They seem to be dead, Captain."

There was a stunned pause, then, "All of them?"

"So far, sir."

"I think there's one still alive up here," shouted one of the sailors. He waved from the aft deck and bent over the pile of clothes Rolfe had noticed earlier by the wheel. The first mate hurried up the ladder to the deck to see for himself.

A man lay by the ship's wheel where he had collapsed, perhaps after a last desperate effort to steer his ship to safety. His skin was a ghastly yellow, like ancient vellum pulled tight over the bones of his long frame. Livid blotches of red and purple, like bruising, mottled his face, neck, and arms. Dried blood caked his nostrils and ears, and more blood oozed from his mouth and the corners of his sunken eyes. Bloody vomit stained his clothes.

It seemed impossible that this wreck of a man could still be alive, but Rolfe and his companion leaned closer and saw the faint flutter of the man's chest. Their eyes lifted and met with a mutual look of fear.

"Is this some sort of plague?" asked the sailor nervously.

The first mate shook his head. "Not one I've heard of, but the absent gods only know what has spawned since their departure. We need a healer." He rose to his feet, propelled by a sudden decision. "All of you," he shouted to his crew, "off the ship, now!"

Relieved to get away from the death ship, the crewmen hurried back to their vessel and reported to the captain. Rolfe hesitated, torn between his desire to get off this frightening death ship and his compassion for the sick man. After a moment of indecision, he left the sick man where he lay and went in search of water and something to make him more comfortable. To his surprise, the water barrels on deck were dry. No amount of compassion would drag him into those lower decks to look for water, so he returned to his own ship to fetch a bottle.

The captain met him on the deck of the *Whydah*. "The harbormaster's coming. Is it that bad?"

The look on his first mate's face was all the answer he needed.

Meanwhile a crowd had gathered on the pier to view the accident and lend a helping hand if needed. Humans, dwarves, minotaurs, a few gnomes and elves, and a swarm of wide-eyed kender waited in loudly talking groups to see what would happen next. Their shouted comments and chattering conversations combined with the lowing of the distressed cattle and the general ruckus of the docks to make a steady din of noise.

A wave of movement through the crowd caught the eyes of the captain and the first mate. They saw the tall, slender figure of the harbormaster approaching down the long stretch of the pier, followed by a contingent of the City Guard in their scarlet uniforms. The onlookers parted before them.

The first mate waited patiently while the harbormaster greeted the captain of the *Whydah* and briefly surveyed the damage. Carrying a flask of water, Rolfe escorted the harbormaster over the ruin of the mast and sails and onto the Palanthian merchantman. The City Guards stayed at the dock to keep the crowds off the ships.

Shaking his head in dismay, the harbormaster climbed the ladder to the aft deck and knelt by the sick man. "Is this how you found him?" he asked the waiting sailor.

Rolfe nodded without reply.

The harbormaster's piercing eyes filled with sadness when he tilted the dying man's head just enough to recognize his face. "I know this man. Captain Southack. One of the best."

Rolfe was not surprised. He knew, everyone knew, the harbormaster of Sanction, and the harbormaster made it his business to become familiar with every ship and captain that plied the waters of Sanction Bay. He was a half-elf who, many years ago, before the Chaos War, had worked in the harbor as a slave under the Dark Knights of Takhisis. Now a member of Hogan Bight's government, he was free and master of his domain.

Together the two men gently rolled the captain onto his back, lifted his head, and trickled a few drops of water down the man's throat. The effect was instantaneous and shocking. A violent tremor shook the captain's body and wrenched his bloody eyes open. No intelligent awareness remained in his dark gaze, only the fevered terror of madness.

A gasping, raw scream tore from his throat. "Go away!" Fresh blood oozed from his mouth. "Don't touch me!" he shrieked, thrashing away from them.

Rolfe dropped the flask and scrambled away as if punched, his face creased with fear.

The harbormaster placed his hands on the captain's shoulders and tried to ease him back.

The sick man would have none of it. "No. No, no, no. Don't touch me," he screamed again. Blood dripped from every orifice, turning his blotched face into a hideous death mask. "Poison . . . death . . . everywhere," he panted, his eyes wild. "Stay away!"

"There's something sensible," Rolfe muttered under his breath. He wanted to bolt back to the *Whydah*, to get away from this terrifying apparition, but his pride would not let him leave the harbormaster alone.

All at once the captain's voice fell silent. A second tremor shook through his ravaged body and left him limp and deathly still, his mouth open, his face slack.

The first mate looked at the harbormaster as he checked the captain's pulse. "Is he gone?" A nod answered his question. Fearfully he wiped the captain's blood off his hands. "Gods beyond, did they all die like this? What is wrong with these men?"

The half-elf stood up, his expression grim. "Do not disturb anything on this ship. I will send a healer to investigate this strange malady."

Rolfe stood, relieved to be able to turn this tragedy over to someone else. "What about our ship?" he inquired worriedly. "We've got to get those cattle off, and Gilean only knows what damage has been done belowdecks."

The harbormaster nodded his understanding. "Go ahead and unload your cargo and do any necessary repairs. The dry dock is available at the moment if you need it. We'll check this ship and move it as soon as possible." Leaving the dead man beneath a shroud of canvas, he strode to the damaged rail and passed on his instructions to the captain of the *Whydah*. Then he called to the City Guards' leader. "Sergeant, send word of this accident to Lord Bight. He may want to investigate this himself."

The leader of the patrol saluted smartly. He snapped an

order to his patrol, and a slim, attractive, woman with short-cropped red hair stepped out of rank. "Lynn, you have a horse stabled nearby. Take the harbormaster's message to Lord Bight. He's in the eastern fortifications, surveying the lava dike. Find him, then report back to me."

The woman masked her pleasure of the unexpected task behind a stiff salute and a deadpan expression. Lynn of Gateway, a sell-sword, ruffian, and newly trained member of Sanction's City Guard, would not show much enthusiasm for saddling her horse and riding all over Sanction to find the governor, Lord Hogan Bight, after a long, hot night of walking patrol through the tavern alleys of Sanction's waterfront and harbor district. But as soon as she turned her back on the sergeant and marched up the long wharf toward town, Lynn relaxed her stiff facial mask and allowed herself to smile. Meeting Lord Bight was something she had wanted to do for a very long time. Filled with anticipation, she broke into a jog toward the stables where she boarded her horse.

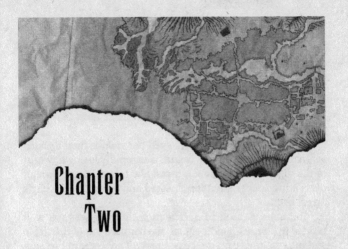

Chapter Two

Apleased nicker greeted Lynn as she opened the stall door. Windcatcher, a powerful bay mare, pranced excitedly in place while Lynn buckled the bridle on her shapely head. The woman ran a hand down the horse's silky neck.

Keeping a horse in Sanction on a guard's meager pay was an expensive luxury. Prices were high, hay and oats were often hard to come by, and it was difficult to find time around her new duties to exercise a horse every day. Lynn, however, considered her mare not only a pleasurable indulgence, but also, in her line of work, a necessity.

She had been living in Sanction for almost eight years and was well known to many people there as a cutthroat alley-basher named Lynn of Gateway, who managed to worm her way into the City Guards and put her skills to a more legitimate use. Only a few people, a very few, knew the redheaded, freckle-faced alley cat with a temper was more than she seemed, and if anyone outside of that small circle learned her true identity, Lynn knew a fast horse could be her only chance of survival. So she scrimped and saved to keep Windcatcher fit and well housed, and she silently prayed that the day she had to flee Sanction would never come. In the meantime, the mare had proved useful for other tasks as well, and this morning, unknowingly, she had helped obtain Lynn's first chance to meet Lord Governor Hogan Bight himself.

Humming to herself, Lynn eyed her saddle, then decided against it. The day, newly begun, was rapidly losing any hint of the night's cooler temperatures. She tossed a light blanket over Windcatcher's withers instead and sprang to the bay's broad back.

The mare danced in anticipation, but she was too well trained to bolt. At Lynn's signal, she bounced out of the stable and into the traffic on the busy streets. The sergeant had said Lord Bight was somewhere in the fortifications on the eastern side of Sanction, the opposite side of the city from the harbor, so Lynn guided her horse toward Shipmaker's Road, the main east-west thoroughfare that bisected Sanction, and nudged her into a comfortable jog trot. It was impossible to travel faster than that. Although it was early morning, the streets were full of carts, wagons, and pedestrians, and the shops were already bustling with people trying to do a day's work before the heat became unbearable.

This summer in Sanction was the hottest in memory since the Chaos War over thirty years ago, and one of the driest. It had altered the routines of daily life in the city by making early risers out of everyone and virtually closing down the town by noon. Only dogs, kender, gully dwarves, and the City Guard could be found moving about outside in the middle of the afternoon. By evening, the intense heat relaxed its grip just enough to give some relief and bring the city back to life.

In the lower end of Sanction, where the taverns, inns, offices, and warehouses jostled for space along the waterfront, most of the people Linsha saw on the streets were connected with the city's burgeoning sea trade: sailors, sail makers, carpenters, rope makers, caulkers, oar makers, and blacksmiths. There were minotaurs, dwarves, humans, and elves all working together to load and unload cargo, refit ships, repair sails, and build new businesses. Only the taverns were quiet at this time of day, until the heat drove everyone indoors or to the nearest shade and a cool drink.

As Windcatcher drew closer to the upper city and the massive walls of Sanction's inner fortifications, the character of the streets changed from docks, taverns, and mercantile offices to new apartments, shops, and tall, narrow houses clustered along cobbled streets. Here were many of the service industries such as laundries, bakehouses, bathhouses, massage parlors, and herbal shops, all showing signs of prosperity and healthy business. Skilled artisans had many shops here, too, and painted their storefronts in bright colors to advertise their wares. Awnings shaded the wooden sidewalks, and scattered about were small gardens that added splashes of green to the timber and stone edifices.

Above it all reared the tall towers and stone battlements of Sanction's fortified walls. Here, facing the harbor and the threat of seaborne invasion, was the main western gate, where Shipmaker's Road left the lower city and plunged into the heart of Sanction. The gateway was a massive doorway wide enough for two loaded wagons to pass side by side, and it was flanked by two round guard towers. The City Guard had its headquarters here and flew their scarlet flags emblazoned with a flaming sword for all to see.

The wall was a fairly recent addition to Sanction's defenses, built by the lord governor to protect the city from a long list of enemies. In the years before the Chaos War, Sanction had been under the control of the goddess, Queen Takhisis, and her Dark Knights. It had been an encampment for dragonarmies and a nest for piracy and slavery. All that changed, though, at the end of the war with the departure of the gods. The Dark Knights lost control of the city, and what was left of the slums and slave pens and temples was in danger of being buried under molten lava spewed out by the three volcanoes, the Lords of Doom. At some time, and no one could remember exactly when, a stranger named Hogan Bight had entered the city and proclaimed himself governor. Using a power beyond anyone's understanding, he tamed the volcanoes and diverted the lava, ash, and smoke away from the city. He built a government where there was none, banished the slave trade, formed the powerful City Guard to keep the peace, and brought prosperity far beyond anything the inhabitants of Sanction had ever imagined.

One of Lord Bight's first major accomplishments had been the fortification of the city through a network of earthworks, stone walls, high towers, and most impressive of all, moats of lava created from the flow of the three giant volcanoes that hemmed in the city to the north, east, and south. The moats began at Mount Thunderhorn, the eastern volcano, and flowed in a horseshoe pattern around the city to Sanction Bay, encompassing the city, the harbor, and most of the wide valley.

The defenses were impressive and, so far, successful. The Knights of Takhisis desperately wanted their city back, but moats of lava and the earthworks kept their land forces at bay to the north and east. The harbor defenses protected the port from pirates and the Dark Knights' seaborne forces, and the great wall guarded the inner heart of the city. Unfortunately the fortifications were not enough to protect Sanction from all her enemies. There was something more at work in the city, something unseen and subtly powerful that kept even the great Dragon Lords at bay. Something that rested in the hands of the mysterious Hogan Bight.

It was because of Lord Bight, this unknown man and his growing influence, that Lynn, known to her family as Linsha, had come to Sanction, sent by the Grand Master Liam Ehrling to serve the Solamnic Knighthood as an undercover agent in Sanction's Clandestine Circle. To her, and to others like her, fell the task of learning all they could of this strange man and the forces that influenced the development of Sanction from a dying slave port to a boomtown. Linsha did not really like the subterfuge and devious dealings of the assignment, but she was good at it and she had grown to genuinely like the people of Sanction in the time she had lived there.

As she saluted the guards at the West Gate and rode through, she felt her pulse quicken at the prospect of meeting Lord Bight. She had joined the City Guard almost a year ago with the hope of working her way closer to his inner circle, but so far she had only managed to see him from a distance on the parade grounds at the guard camp and during official visits to the city council.

The traffic became heavier on this section of the Shipmaker's Road, and Linsha was forced to slow Windcatcher to a walk. This part of Sanction had once been an old slave market and slum until Lord Bight allowed a group of gnomes to experiment on some new construction techniques. Of course, the foul tenements burned to the ground, allowing Lord Bight to rebuild the entire area. The land was divided into orderly lots and streets and portioned out to new owners, guilds, and businesses. The sound of construction was everywhere as new houses, shops, guildhalls, and craftsman shops filled in the vacant lots. Near the center of the city, a huge area had been set aside for an open-air market called the Souk Bazaar, where farmers from Sanction Vale brought their produce, livestock, and goods, and merchants from as far away as Palanthas sold their wares in rows of stalls, booths, and carts.

When Linsha approached the bazaar, she took an appreciative sniff of the smells wafting from the vendors' carts. Her stomach reminded her she hadn't had breakfast yet, so she kneed Windcatcher close to an old man selling cheese turnovers and pasties.

"Morning, Calzon," she greeted him.

The old man's face cracked a black-toothed grin. "Lynn, you gorgeous thing. Get off that bag of worthless bones and give us a kiss!"

She chuckled. "Sorry. I want to keep my breakfast down. Just give me a turnover. One of your good ones. Not the ones you've shorted the cheese with extra flour." She flipped him a coin.

Cackling to himself, Calzon caught the coin and handed her a warm turnover from his cart. Before she could move out of his reach, he ran his hand down her knee. "One of these days, Lynn, you'll see the error of your ways. Marry me and I'll make an honest woman out ye."

"When gully dwarves rule in Sanction, I'll think about it," she replied, well used to his banter.

"So where're you off to this fine morning? Shouldn't you be off duty? Looking for a little action?" He cracked the knuckles on his fingers to add emphasis to his words and topped them off with a suggestive leer.

Linsha deliberately took a large bite of her turnover and buried any chance of a reply in a mouthful of pastry and cheese. With a gentle nudge, she urged Windcatcher back on the road, leaving Calzon to his customers and his speculations.

Calzon had been her first lesson in looking behind the masks people wear, for beneath the ragged gray hair, tattered clothes, and lecherous leer was a very talented member of the Legion of Steel, whose mission in Sanction was much like hers. Although Linsha had known Xavier Kross, the leader of the Legion, when she arrived, Calzon and many of the other Legionnaires had not known about her. It had taken her several months to gain his cautious confidence. He did not know her real name and rank any more than she knew his. All they could ever know was their mutual membership in the thriving underground of spies in Sanction. They traded bits of news once in a while and acted as liaisons between their respective leaders, but because the Knights of Solamnia and the Legion of Steel did not trust each other's motives, they were not allowed the opportunity to work together.

Linsha thought that was inefficient and a shame. She had spent many visits with her grandparents in Solace, where the Legion had its first headquarters. She still harbored the respect she learned for the secretive organization, whose sole purpose was to serve justice and help where they were needed. With better communication and less self-serving motives, she felt the Knights of Solamnia and the Legion could make formidable allies against the Knights of Takhisis. Unfortunately the last time they tried to work together in Sanction, their incautious zeal allowed the Knights of Takhisis to wipe them out and caused Lord Bight to ban both groups from the city forever. Another union did not seem promising.

Eating as she rode, Linsha guided her horse around the market grounds and toward the East Gate that led out of the city to the guard camp, the outer fortifications, and the roads into the Khalkist Mountains. To her left sat a low range of hills skirted by imposing residential homes. The nearest hill was crowned by the newly built luxurious palace of the lord governor, while its neighbor bore the Temple of Huerzyd, an old relic of the departed gods now renovated and refurbished for the mystics from Goldmoon's Citadel of Light in Schallsea. The city wall curled around the hills and ran for some distance beside the lava moat as it cut through the flank of the northernmost volcano, Mount Grishnor, the first of the three Lords of Doom. From there the wall continued east to Mount Thunderhorn, then curved south toward the third of the active volcanoes, Mount Ashkir.

Not far from the gate, the road rose over an old stone bridge that once spanned a glowing river of lava. Now the lava lay hard and cold, and its old course served as a foundation for a new aqueduct that Hogan Bight planned to carry water from the mountains' geysers and springs into the city. The aqueduct had been completed from the reservoir between Mount Grishnor and Mount Thunderhorn to the edge of the city wall. All that remained was the distance from the wall to the public cisterns near the Souk Bazaar and the difficult section needed to cross the lava moat. Dwarf engineers were already hard at work at the city site, building the scaffolding and chiseling blocks of local red granite to construct the next span of supporting arches.

Saluting the guards at the East Gate, Linsha rode through and quickly approached the edge of the sprawling guard camp. A sentry immediately stopped her.

As soon as she stated her rank and business, he pointed to the peak of the second Lord of Doom. "See the smoke on

Mount Thunderhorn? The governor and his men are up on the northeast observation tower studying the volcano. Rumor says its going to blow again," he added with the stoical resignation of a man born and raised in Sanction.

On a clear day, with wind from the west, the volcanoes and the Khalkist peaks that barricaded Sanction were visible with startling clarity. Their stark red peaks, many topped with a mantel of snow, formed a palisade that helped protect the city from many of her hostile neighbors. The active peaks also provided their own form of trouble, and this morning Mount Thunderhorn brooded under a new nimbus of smoke and steam, spewing from a tremendous lava dome that had appeared near the summit only a few days before.

Linsha waved her thanks and nudged Windcatcher into a trot along the outskirts of the camp, past neat rows of tents, horse pens, and practice fields. The first training period of the day had just commenced, and groups of guards and recruits marched, drilled, and practiced swordplay. Linsha paid scant heed. Her eyes were focused on the distant tower perched on the great earthen wall.

Four stone towers had been built along the eastern siege works to stand guard not only over the eruptions from the volcanoes but also the forces of the Knights of Takhisis, who remained poised on the two roads through the Khalkist Mountains. Armies sent by Governor-General Abrena watched from their positions in the northern and eastern passes for any sign of weakness. Lord Bight made sure there were none.

At the base of the northeast tower, a sentry took Linsha's reins and pointed to the top of the tower, where flew the pennant of the City Guard, flaunting the emblem of the flaming sword in the eyes of enemy observers. She bent her neck to look up, wiped the sweat from her forehead, and began to climb up the long flight of steps inside the round tower. By the time she reached the top, she was dripping with sweat again from the exertion and the building heat.

Five men leaned over the parapet, gazing toward the smoking mountain. Two wore the scarlet tunics and black boots of guard officers, two were dressed in elegant official's robes, and one was garbed in a simple gold tunic and pale leather pants that fit him like custom-made gloves. Four of the five appeared to be engaged in an animated conversation, while the fifth man, in the gold tunic, remained silent. His gaze was fastened on the far volcano, which loomed steep and red against the hazy summer sky.

Linsha paused, intrigued by the tableau in front of her. She did not want to interrupt the conversation, so she stood at attention and waited for the men to notice her, giving herself a few moments to catch her breath and to study the interaction of these five.

"I'm telling you, I've seen these things before. That dome is going to blow any minute," one of the officials said forcefully. "And if that lava follows the easiest course, it will burn right through those eroded sections in the moat and ruin three of the finest farms in Sanction Vale."

That man, Linsha knew, was the elected leader of the newly formed Farmers' Guild, a group dedicated to helping the farmers in the reclaimed lands outside the city.

Until the Chaos War and the coming of Hogan Bight, there had been no farmers anywhere near Sanction. The region had been constantly besieged by lava, ash, and occasional pyroclastic flows from all three of the volcanoes. Once Lord Bight had tamed the Lords of Doom, the results had been miraculous. Free of ash and the danger from lava, people had spread out into the fertile valley and up the mountain slopes and turned the land into small productive farms that specialized in dairy cattle, wine, and wool.

The second official, a portly man who served as head of the city council, vehemently waved a thick hand at the volcano. "Chan Dar, I doubt the lava will endanger your farms. I've already sent professionals to study the possible paths of flow from the dome. It is their considered opinion that the lava will come south down into the guard camp and overwhelm the breastworks. If that happens, we could lose part of the city wall and the guild district. You, as a guild master, should be concerned—"

Chan Dar snorted and interrupted his esteemed colleague.

"I hardly think one dwarf and an overbearing draconian constitute a professional opinion."

"And what makes you think your opinions are any better?" Lutran the Elder said heatedly. "At least they have experience working in the mountains."

"Gentlemen," soothed a tall man in one of the scarlet uniforms. "Farm or city, we are all part of Sanction, and wherever the lava goes, we will be there to fight it."

Chan Dar refused to be placated. "But it's going to explode any minute. We need to evacuate—"

"It's not going to blow for at least a week or two, you idiot. There's plenty of time to . . ." began Lutran, clearly exasperated.

"Says who? Your so-called experts?" said Chan Dar scathingly. He suddenly turned to the man in gold. "Lord Bight, you must do something immediately."

Lord Bight stirred slightly, as if drawn from a deep meditation. He turned his head, and Linsha caught her breath at the sight of his profile silhouetted against the backdrop of the smoking volcano. Hogan Bight was a tall, powerfully built man, with chiseled features that stood out sharp and elegant against the red of the volcano and the blue of the sky. His hair and beard, both golden brown, were closely trimmed, and his eyes, framed by curved brows, glowed like sunlight through amber.

"The dome on the side of the volcano is not going to bother us in the next day or two," he said in a voice deep and resonant. "Do not worry. I have already ordered crews to the dike to strengthen the erosion damage. I will monitor the activity, and when the time draws near, I will be here to control the flow." His manner toward them was tolerant, patient, like a parent calming fussing children.

The city officials exchanged glares, then bowed low. Linsha gave her head an imperceptible shake. Those two were so involved in their petty arguments, they did not care how a mere man subdued a volcano, nor were they dazzled by the wonder of it. All they wanted were their walls and their cows kept safe.

As if he had seen her movement, Lord Bight turned completely around and gave her the full regard of his piercing gaze.

She returned his stare openly, frankly, her own eyes as green as spring grass. "Your Excellency," she said in as steady a voice as she could muster.

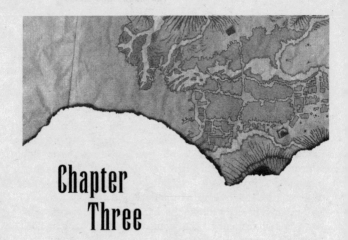

Chapter Three

The other men noticed Linsha for the first time, and she quickly saluted the two officers, Commander Ian Durne and his aide, Captain Alphonse Dewald.

"Sir," she addressed Commander Durne. "I have a message for Lord Bight from the harbormaster."

"Tell me," Lord Bight demanded.

Linsha felt sweat trickle down her backbone. She was sweltering in her heavy red tunic, and nervous excitement only added to the heat. Now she was face-to-face with the controversial Lord Hogan Bight, and she did not want to make a fool of herself. She turned slightly toward him and repeated the harbormaster's message.

Loud voices of consternation burst out from the other men and cut her off before she finished.

"A runaway!" Lutran the Elder cried. "In our harbor?" How did such a thing get past the defenses?"

The farmer looked grave. "And everyone on board dead?

An ill omen!"

Captain Dewald demanded, "Who is in charge of your patrol? Are they still on the dock?"

Linsha pursed her lips, annoyed that she was unable to finish her message over the noise. She raised her hand and said, "Excuse me, gentlemen," very loudly. The men were startled into silence. With a bland expression, she said politely, "First, the ship was under sail and steered a straight course. It wasn't until she passed the pilot that anyone noticed anything amiss. Second, I do not know if everyone is dead, because the ship had not been carefully searched when I left. Finally, Sergeant Ziratell Amwold is commander of my patrol. He is guarding the dockside and the wreck so no one may board without the harbormaster's permission. Now, Your Excellency," she went on, looking back at Lord Bight, "if I may continue?"

He hadn't said a word or moved during her speech, but his intent gaze and the coiled tension of his stance revealed his close attention. Perhaps she was mistaken, or were those laugh lines around his mouth and at the corners of his eyes?

"Sir, the harbormaster has sent for a healer and has sealed off the runaway. He sends you word of this mishap in case you wish to inspect it for yourself."

Lord Bight considered the message, and the message bearer, for a long moment before he turned to the city officials and said, "Good day, gentlemen. I will keep your concerns in mind. Commander Durne, ride with me to the docks. I want to have a word with the harbormaster."

Muttering between themselves, the two officials bowed and withdrew, leaving Lord Bight with his guards.

"What is your name?" he asked Linsha. "You look familiar."

"Lynn of Gateway. You probably don't remember, but I brought several saddlebags full of crystals from the Valley of Crystal to your palace some time ago. One of your agents bought them from me."

"Ah, yes. Lonar's friend, the enterprising alley-basher. I see you've turned your sword to serving the city."

Linsha was surprised he remembered her. Then again, Lord Bight was known for his phenomenal memory, and Lonar, one of his top officials, hadn't returned from that fatal trip to the Valley of Crystal. She pushed an auburn curl from her brow. She had wanted Bight's attention for some time and now she had it. How to make the most of it without being too pushy? "Sanction has taught me a good deal, Your Excellency." Which was true. "I have found more opportunities here for my abilities than anywhere else. I find I like this work."

Lord Bight nodded approvingly, his eyes still appraising her from polished boots to feathered hat.

Commander Durne and his aide waited silently, their expressions watchful.

Linsha took a deep breath, rested her hand lightly on her sword hilt, and took a plunge. "Sir, I'd like to do more. If I may serve you in some way—"

Commander Durne cut her off with a short bark of irritation. "The governor does not need ambitious female mercenaries offering vague services."

Linsha bristled at his insinuation. "My services are strictly limited to sword and horse, Commander."

Hogan Bight raised his hand to cut off Durne's reply. "I appreciate your initiative, young woman. I have nothing to offer at the moment, but if you serve my city well, we will keep you in mind for the future."

Well, she had tried. Linsha knew there was little to gain by pushing the issue. She bowed to Lord Bight and respectfully stood back to allow the men to descend the steps of the tower. At the bottom, the two officers and Lord Bight called for their horses but watched appreciatively while Linsha sprang lightly to the back of her mare.

"Do you keep your own horse?" Commander Durne asked her.

"She was a gift from my father," Linsha replied. "I enjoy her company."

Commander Durne mounted his own horse, a stallion similar in color and conformation to Windcatcher. "I believe your patrol should have gone off duty at sunrise. Do you have orders to return to Sergeant Amwold?" At her affirmative reply, he waved Captain Dewald on to ride beside Lord Bight, and he reined his own horse over beside her mare. "Then accompany us back to the harbor. I would like to talk to you."

Linsha felt her nerves go bowstring tight, though whether in wariness or anticipation, she wasn't certain. Commander Ian Durne, captain of the governor's personal guards and commander of the City Guards, was Lord Bight's trusted aide and probably the second highest-ranking man in Sanction's government. Not only was he extremely capable in his duties, but he was also well liked. Charming, charismatic, and roguishly handsome, he seemed almost too perfect sometimes to Linsha, who would have preferred someone a little less efficient and a little more approachable. His pale blue eyes had an unnerving clarity and icy acuity that made others feel as if he could strip away social facades with a mere glance. Few people could look Commander Durne in the eye for long without feeling self-conscious.

Fortunately Linsha did not have to face the test of his eyes at that moment, for the four riders were too busy guiding their horses across the busy parade ground and camp toward the East Gate.

"I apologize for my abruptness earlier," Durne said. "We are constantly bombarded by requests for service in His Excellency's name, and not all of the petitioners are motivated by altruism."

His tone was light and casual, but Linsha sensed the steel behind the velvet. She snorted indelicately, like a crude mercenary with few social skills. She had toned down Lynn's wild and crude character the past few months to make her persona more acceptable in the guards, but it didn't hurt to maintain some of the appearance. "Petitioners like me, you mean. Cheap self-seekers looking for an extra coin, or an infiltrator from the Knights of Takhisis who'd sell his own parents for the job."

He cocked an eyebrow at her and began to tick off more

names on his gloved hand. "Not to mention those pesky Legionnaires, the infuriating Solamnics, the minions of the black dragon, Sable, the ogres of Blöde . . ."

She suddenly laughed and finished the list for him. "As well as spies, pirates, con men, thieves, assassins, and snitches who would love to replace or depose or kill Lord Bight."

"Working for Lord Bight isn't easy. He demands courage, skill, and complete loyalty."

"I see that. But keep me in mind anyway."

"Why?" he demanded to know.

Linsha hesitated, searching for just the right words that would not sound too arrogant or false. She waved her hand at the city around them. "I like what he has done here. I want to see it continue."

He nodded. "Fair enough. We will keep your offer in mind, Lynn of Gateway."

And that, says he, is that, Linsha thought to herself. Oh, well. It was worth a try. She wiped her sweating forehead again and realized for the first time that morning how tired she was. It had been a long night on patrol. She sighed and wished she didn't have to sit so straight on horseback. She would have liked to relax, but Commander Durne rode beside her, arrow-straight from the waist up. He was a natural rider, one of those born to sit in a saddle, and she would be fried alive before she would allow this officer to prove himself her superior on horseback.

They rode quietly for a while through the gate and into the city proper. It was midday and already growing quite hot.

"Were you born in Gateway? Or did you just take the name?" Durne asked suddenly.

Linsha's heart skipped a beat. It was a casual question, but coming from Commander Durne, it could hold a hundred pitfalls. Assuming a casual air, she yawned and waved nonchalantly toward the north. "I was born there. Didn't stay long, though. I felt the itch to travel. Caergoth. All around the Newsea. Khuri-Khan. Spent some time in Neraka."

"Neraka," he repeated. "I assumed you didn't like the Dark Knights."

She shrugged. "I don't. Too many rules. Too intent on their dark goddess. If you ask me, a goddess who abandons her minions in the middle of a deadly war is not worth the spit it takes to polish her altar. No, I didn't stay in Neraka for long."

The commander's mild tone continued. "How long have you been here?"

"I came over with a caravan from Khur about eight years ago." Which was the exact truth. Linsha had learned early that the best lies were those intertwined with as much truth as possible. She cast a sideways glance at Durne's profile and asked, "So where are you from?" She already knew from the meager Solamnic profiles on him, but she had also learned that it was safer to listen than continue to lie.

His cool blue eyes continued to scan the road ahead as he answered cryptically, "Port Balifor, before the war."

Linsha saw a spasm of anger flit across his face. It seemed the iron commander harbored some feelings within his controlled exterior. Not that there wasn't good reason. Durne had seen more than thirty-five years, so he was old enough to remember Port Balifor, before the Chaos War and the coming of the great dragons, when it was a peaceful, thriving port on the Bay of Balifor. The arrival of the red dragon, Malystryx, had changed all that, and now the remains of Port Balifor scraped out a poor existence under the merciless claws of the dragon overlord. She considered asking him more about it, if he had lost family or fortune in Port Balifor, but the chill of his eyes and the bitter set of his face persuaded her not to. She didn't want to alienate the commander at this particular moment.

She was about to change the subject when the warehouses and buildings around them opened out into the teeming wharves and the shimmering smooth waters of Sanction Harbor. Activity on the waterfront had increased with the coming of midmorning, and in spite of the collision at the southern pier, several new ships had arrived and tied up at the smaller northern piers.

One, Linsha recognized, was a galley carrying passengers

from various ports in the Newsea. She knew some of the people would most likely be refugees fleeing the depredations of the great dragons and seeking new lives in the comparative freedom of Lord Bight's domain. Refugees had been flowing into Sanction for years, forming one of the most diverse populations on Krynn. The other two ships flew the flag of Solamnia and probably carried foodstuffs to exchange for Sanction's widely acclaimed cheeses, volcanic products, and wool.

At the southern pier, the crowd of gawkers beside the runaway and her hapless victim had grown, impeding the work of the dock laborers and blocking Lord Bight's progress. Fortunately, Sergeant Amwold had anticipated this difficulty and called for reinforcements. A signaler stood at the head of the pier, and at the first sight of Lord Bight and his party, he lifted a small horn to his lips and blew a single clear note. Heads turned and people quickly moved aside to make way for the lord governor. A second patrol moved in and formed up at the head of the governor's party to escort him to the ship. The riders dismounted, leaving their horses with the signaler.

Linsha fell in behind Commander Durne and followed the men down the pier, past the curious onlookers. She noted the respectful demeanor of the mixed crowd and the way people watched Lord Bight avidly. Even minotaurs and kender tended to pay attention when Lord Bight was near.

As soon as the lord governor reached the ships, the captain of the *Whydah*, the first mate, and the harbormaster hurried to meet him. Agitated and fearful, the captain had his say first, punctuated by broad gestures and an overly loud voice. Lord Bight listened patiently. When the captain was finished, the harbormaster led the governor aboard the *Whydah* and described what he had seen so far on the runaway.

After a brief nod to Sergeant Amwold, Commander Durne and Captain Dewald hurried after Lord Bight. Linsha fell in at their heels. Nobody had bidden her to attend, but they hadn't dismissed her yet either, and she was eager to stay in Lord Bight's sight as long as possible.

In a group, the governor, the harbormaster, the first mate, and the three guards climbed over the splintered wreckage of the ship's railing and rigging and onto the deck of the merchantman. The *Whydah*'s captain stayed behind.

Linsha gazed around at the empty deck, her eyes wide. Already the heat of the day had increased the stench rising from the dead in the holds to a nearly unbearable level. She clamped a hand over her nose and tried to breathe only through her mouth. To still the stirrings of nausea in her stomach, she walked to the broken foremast and leaned against the fallen timber.

"I've sent for a healer to examine these bodies," she heard the harbormaster say as he climbed up to the upper deck. "This sickness that has afflicted them is unlike any I have seen." She turned and saw him lift the shroud from Captain Southack's body to show the men the ravages of the disease.

Lord Bight's expression was unreadable, yet his voice became oddly gentle. "They died hard. It is a fate I do not wish on any man."

The half-elf nodded, his slim hands reverent as he replaced the shroud. "I recommend we burn this ship as soon as our investigations are complete."

Lord Bight agreed. "Do it. The bodies, too. Haul it out beyond the harbor and douse it with oil so it burns well. I want nothing left to wash ashore. We'll deal with the owners later."

From her position on the lower deck, Linsha was the first to hear the strange sound. It came, soft and pitiable, from somewhere near her feet. She stiffened and listened closely. It came again, like the terrified whimper of an anguished child.

"Sir," she called. "I think there's someone still alive down there."

"But they're all dead," the first mate exclaimed in surprise.

Without reply, Linsha clambered over the tangle of ropes and splintered wood to a hatch she could see near the bow of the merchantman. She wasn't an expert on ship design, but she knew most vessels had sail lockers near their bows, and it seemed possible the sad, miserable moaning that reached her ears emanated from there.

She heard someone behind her, pushing aside debris and coming to join her. Just as she cleared the hatch and bent to pull it open, Lord Bight reached to help her. In a combined effort, they pulled open the hatch and let the full light of day fall on the dismal gloom.

As Linsha guessed, the hatch revealed a short ladder that led down to two large compartments used for storing sails. At the foot of the ladder crouched a young man in tattered pants and shirt. He threw his arms over his head when the bright light touched him and screamed as if in mortal pain. With the speed of desperation, he yanked a cutlass out from a dim corner and swarmed up the ladder like a frantic beast.

Linsha had barely a few seconds to draw her own weapon and throw herself in front of Lord Bight to fend off the sailor's wild swing. Their blades met with a ringing clash. She realized immediately the young man was too sick to put up a fight. Skillfully she caught his blade with hers, twisted it, and sent the cutlass flying into the water. His eyes bulging in terror, the sailor scrabbled past her and leaped to the port rail.

Linsha blanched at the sight of his face. Once he had been a comely man, but the disease had withered his form and brought the livid red and purple blotches to his skin. Blood oozed from his eyes and mouth, and vomit stained his clothes. She sheathed her sword and reached out to him, but he fled from her to the standing rigging of the mainmast that still rose upright above the deck of the ship. Swift as a squirrel, he climbed up to the crow's nest near the top of the tall mast. The nest was little more than a round platform and a safety rope, and it looked too precarious for a man sick with fever.

Linsha didn't hesitate. She followed as quickly as she could up the rope rigging toward the crow's nest in the hope that she could comfort the sick sailor and talk him down from his dangerous perch.

Rolfe, the *Whydah's* first mate, hurried to help her. He climbed up the rigging on the starboard side, intending to cut off that avenue of escape.

The sailor was beyond reason. Infected by the disease, his mind crazed with fever and hallucinations, all he saw were enemies trying to reach him.

"No!" he screamed down at them. "Leave me alone!"

His terror tore at Linsha's heart. "It's all right," she called softly. "We don't want to hurt you."

"Hurt me?" he cried, almost hysterical. "How can you possibly hurt me any more?" He clung to the mast and glared wildly at the two people approaching him.

Linsha slowed her ascent and gripped the ropes so she could lean back and let him see her better. "Please come down. We're here to help you."

"No help left. No water. No medicine. All gone. All dead." He was babbling, spitting drops of spittle and blood from his mouth as he flung his head back and forth.

Rolfe was close now, almost within touching distance of the crow's nest. He looked across at Linsha as if to ask, "What now?"

She swiped her sleeve over her forehead to wipe away the sweat on her face and slowly took another step up until her head was level with the planking of the crow's nest. "Easy," she said quietly. "We only want to help you. Do you want some water?"

His bloody eyes blinked rapidly at her. His breath came in short, panting gasps. "Help me," he repeated in a voice hoarse with dread. "Water."

Linsha saw Rolfe step up the ropes and slowly reach his arm over the platform to grab the sailor's ankle. She did not think that was a very good idea until he caught her eye and pointed downward. On the deck below, she saw Lord Bight, the two guard officers, and the harbormaster. They had found a length of sail and stretched it out like a net to catch anyone who fell. Perhaps that was for the best, she thought. If she and the first mate couldn't talk the sailor out of the rigging, they might have to knock him down. Meanwhile, the guards, the sailors, and the spectators out on the pier watched the unfolding action in noisy excitement. A few prayers were said and a few bets were made, and one enterprising youngster came out to sell cupfuls of water to the spectators.

Up in the crow's nest, Rolfe's hand suddenly clamped around the young man's ankle. With a shriek, the sailor wrenched away from him, leaped over Linsha's head, and crawled out onto the yardarm.

"Wait!" Linsha cried. "Please . . ." She pulled herself up and onto the wooden yard and crawled slowly toward him. The yard, heavy with drooping sails and the weight of one man, swayed beneath her. She clung to it with all her strength, her eyes on the sailor.

He crept away from her until he could go no farther, and there he perched, where the end of the yard leaned out over the water. His arms and legs trembled and his body swayed.

Linsha carefully eased her hand out toward him. "Come on. Come off there. We'll find medicine and water for you. We'll find a place where you can rest."

A deep, racking sob shook his entire body. For just a moment, Linsha hoped she had convinced him. His hand lifted toward hers, and his face relaxed into a semblance of peace. The hope lasted only a heartbeat.

Abruptly the sailor's bloody eyes rolled up in their sockets, his muscles failed, and his body slipped off the narrow yard and plunged toward the water below.

Linsha threw herself toward him, but his hand slid beyond her grasp. Then, in an instant, she had herself to worry about. Her balance, already unsteady on the swaying yard, rocked forward with her sudden movement and tipped sideways. Her upper body slid off the beam, and she found herself hanging upside down from the yard by her toes.

Rolfe gasped and scrambled toward her.

Shouts rose from the crowd on the dock as the sailor's body hit the water and disappeared in a splash of white foam, then all eyes turned back to the woman dangling over the deck of the runaway.

Linsha tried frantically to grab a handful of sail. She

could feel her feet slipping. Her boots were made for walking, not gripping the smooth sides of a wooden beam. There was no time to find a convenient loop of rope or dangling lifeline. Her feet slipped free and her body dropped, its weight wrenching her grip loose from the heavy sails. She fell, tumbling, toward the deck nearly thirty feet below.

The fall happened so quickly Linsha barely had time to draw a deep breath and force her body to relax before she landed with a hard *whump* in the middle of the canvas sheet. The four men grinned down at her, pleased at their success. The spectators burst into raucous applause.

"Th-thank you," Linsha said breathlessly.

"Lynn of Gateway, you are either incredibly brave or incredibly foolish," Lord Bight commented as he offered her his hand to help her rise.

Linsha climbed to her feet and looked over the rail where the sailor had disappeared. There was no sign of him in the warm, dark waters under the ship.

"That was a brave attempt," Commander Durne said from beside her.

"But a vain one," she replied sadly. The rush of excitement had ended abruptly and left her exhausted and drained. She stood limply, drooping in a weariness that seemed to deprive her of thought and energy. She glanced back at the lord governor and saw he had already moved away and was talking to the harbormaster about the damaged *Whydah* and the best way to separate the two ships without sinking the freighter. She sighed gently. Her meeting with him had certainly taken an unexpected turn, but it was over. It had been a long day and a very exciting morning. What she wanted now was her own lodgings, where she could drop the pretense and be herself for a little while. Time to think, time to rest.

Commander Durne understood her exhaustion. He, too, had felt the loss of strength and will after a heartfelt struggle. He bowed slightly to her, a mark of respect for an underling. "I will tell Sergeant Amwold you are dismissed. You may return to your horse."

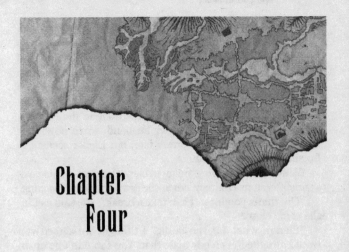

Chapter
Four

Linsha's lodgings were small and run-down and, best of all, inexpensive. They also had the advantage of being close to Windcatcher's stable on a side street halfway between the West Gate and the harbor. Although she could have chosen to get a free bed in the billets at the guards' camp, being one of the few women in the guards prompted her to look for her own place. Besides, as Lynn, she would have much preferred a room closer to the action of the gaming houses and taverns.

With a tip from her leader, Lady Knight Karine Thasally, she found an elderly widow seeking to rent the top floor of her house. Despite Lynn's uncouth, uneducated manners, the widow Elenor took the wild Lynn under her wing and did her best to care for the young woman. Perhaps she appreciated having a member of the guards under her roof; perhaps she was lonely. Whatever the reason, Elenor reminded Linsha of her grandmother, and she was not loath to return the regard.

After stabling and rubbing down Windcatcher, Linsha walked gratefully home. The house was a narrow two-story timber-and-stone edifice with a tiny garden in the back and leaded windows that looked out toward the harbor. Elenor's husband had built the house for her shortly after the arrival of Hogan Bight, and for over twenty years, she had lived in the house while her husband plied his trade in the Newsea. Time and illness had taken her husband, worn down her house, and aged her once pretty face, but Elenor seemed to Linsha to be indomitable.

Elenor was standing on a ladder, slapping whitewash against the stone chimney, when she saw Linsha approaching.

"Oh, thank goodness, I can take a break," she said as Linsha came closer.

"Elenor, what are you doing? I thought we agreed you would hire the Kellen boy to do that! You shouldn't be up on a ladder in this heat."

Elenor came carefully down her ladder one step at a time. "He was busy. But I think you're right. I'm parched. And you look all wrung out. You're late! What did they have you doing today?"

Linsha gave her a weary smile. She was tired and wanted to get out of her sweat-soaked clothes, but Elenor loved to hear the news and gossip of the city and counted on Lynn to spend a few minutes to tell her all about her duties and activities. In return, she plied the young woman with ale, tea, or cooled juice, and honey cakes, tea cakes, cookies, shortbreads, or whatever she had taken from the oven that morning. Linsha thought it was a fair return. She crossed her arms and said casually, "I had to take a message to Lord Bight."

Elenor's creased face lit up. "My dear, come in the kitchen and tell me all about it. We'll hang that tunic of yours in the breeze to dry and share a pitcher of cold cider." She rubbed her whitewash-speckled hands on her apron. "Do you know, old Cobb down at the Dancing Bear contrived to bring some ice down from the mountains. Oh, my stars, you should have seen the crowd there this morning! When I took the order of tea cakes to his kitchen, he gave me a bowl of ice in thanks. Come have some before it melts."

They walked through the small house down a central hallway to a kitchen attached to the rear and finished several glasses of icy cider and a stack of tea cakes. Linsha thought she had never tasted anything so delightful. It was nearly noon before she reached the end of her tale and exhausted all of Elenor's questions.

Drooping with weariness, Linsha trudged up the narrow stairs to her room. Elenor had opened the two small windows wide for ventilation and cleaned the room as usual. The largest room contained a bed covered with a faded quilt, a chest, a few pegs for clothes and weapons, a small table and chair, and a lamp. The furnishings were plain and simple and showed little of the occupant's personality. The second room, hardly larger than a pantry, was used mostly for storage. The little apartment was hot, but after the oppressive heat outside, the shade and the slight breeze were a relief.

Out of habit, Linsha inspected the room for things or intruders that were not there when she left. Then she stripped down to a light linen shift and collapsed gratefully on the bed. Her eyelids slid closed.

"Don't get comfortable," a soft, raspy voice said from the window above her head.

Linsha groaned and cracked open one eyelid. "Varia, you're out late."

There was a sudden whisper of air through feathers, and an owl, russet and cream-colored, landed lightly on the bed beside her knees. With deliberate care, the bird sidestepped up the quilt until it could peer unblinkingly into Linsha's sleepy face.

The woman opened both eyes and stared into two agate-black orbs only a few inches from her face. The owl's deep-set eyes were surrounded by ovals of cream-colored feathers circled by narrow lines of deep brown that made the bird look as if she was wearing spectacles. Linsha stroked the back of a forefinger down the bird's softly spotted chest. She still could hardly believe her good fortune that a bird such as this chose to be her companion. Varia was similar to the rare and elusive giant talking owls of Krynn, but whether she was one of a kind or part of a species related to those Darken owls, she never told Linsha. Smaller in size than the giant owls, she nonetheless had their abilities to communicate with humans and to judge the true worth of a person's character. Varia had found Linsha during a search mission into the Khalkist Mountains and, after a careful scrutiny, had decided to attach herself to a friend worthy of her companionship.

Linsha had been riding hard and fast through heavy woods with a patrol of Dark Knights close behind when Windcatcher swerved to avoid something lying on the ground, and Linsha found herself flat on her back, winded and furious. The something proved to be an owl about eighteen inches high, delicately patterned with creamy bars and spots, flapping in agony with a broken wing. In spite of the danger behind her, Linsha couldn't bear to leave the owl without help. She bundled the bird into her cloak and took off running after her panicked horse. Chuckling a throaty owl laugh, Varia had squirmed out of the wrapping, revealed a miraculously cured wing, rounded up the horse, and scared off the Dark Knights with a spine-tingling chorus of demonic screams, barks, yowls, and maniacal screeches. Then she led Linsha out of the woods and had been with her ever since. It was only later that Linsha learned the talking owls often used such tactics to test the mettle of possible companions.

The owl bobbed her round head a few times and said, "I would have been back earlier except Lady Karine left a message. You are to check in with Lady Annian immediately." Linsha felt a stab of annoyance. "Now? What's so important?"

"I did not see her, just the message."

Linsha's annoyance turned to mild apprehension. What could be so important that the commander of the undercover Knights of Solamnia needed her to meet with her contact immediately? Usually Lady Karine preferred to keep contact to a minimum with all her Knights—for their safety and hers.

"What did she leave?"

"A dead chipmunk on her window ledge."

Linsha's eyebrows rose. "A chipmunk?" Lady Karine, one of the few people who knew of Varia's existence, had suggested using the owl as a messenger and had devised a system using some of Varia's favorite delicacies. A chipmunk meant "Come at once. Most secret." Despite her usually cool and regal demeanor, Varia did not seem to mind "playing pigeon for the spies," as she called it. In fact, Linsha thought the owl fancied the intrigue. To Varia, it was just a game played by humans.

To Linsha, the game could turn all too deadly, and no matter how tired or hot she was, a dead chipmunk on the window ledge of a certain house was an order she could not ignore.

She rolled off the bed to her feet. Her guard's uniform was too damp and too conspicuous to wear, so she pulled out an old short-sleeved blue tunic, dry pants, and soft boots to wear. She also slipped her daggers into her belt and strapped on her sword.

"Hurry back," Varia called. The owl was ensconced on her favorite perch by the window, where she could watch the street. But she wasn't watching street this noon. Body hunched and eyes closed, the owl settled down for a nap.

Smothering a yawn and a grumble, Linsha slid past the vigilant Elenor, back on her ladder, and slipped into a narrow back alley. In moments she swaggered into the pedestrian traffic on a busy street three blocks away and melted into the crowd.

Linsha's contact, Lady Knight Annian Mercet, like Linsha, preferred to have her domicile outside the city walls where the chances of escape were greater. She ran a small perfume shop ideally situated between a bathhouse and a jeweler near the Street of Courtesans. Her shop was small but well known in Sanction, and her business, like so many others, prospered in the growing fortunes of the city.

When Linsha reached the perfumer, she stopped outside. Before her lay a small open courtyard formed by a low stone wall. Inside sat a domed oven, an open fire, and several braziers tended by one very busy youth. As Linsha watched, he thrust a heavy clay pot of resin into the oven and dashed around to stir pots on the braziers. She inhaled the rich fragrances of spices, heated fats, herbs, and oils that issued from the pots. Annian did not need a sign to advertise her wares. All she had to do was fire her braziers to heat the oils and scents and open her door.

Linsha went inside the workshop. Glancing at the shelves that lined the walls, she saw countless vials, pots, stoppered jars of stone and glass, and exquisite hand-blown bottles filled with liquids of every color. A woman was busy grinding spices with a pestle and mortar at the back of the store.

"I'm looking for something to repel chipmunks," Linsha said loudly.

The woman chuckled, a deep, throaty sound of amusement. She broke off her grinding and dusted her hands. When she stood up, she towered nearly a head taller than Linsha. Slender, fair-haired, and pale-skinned, the woman hardly looked the part of a Solamnic Knight, and that was part of her success as an operative.

"I'm afraid my wares are to attract, not repel. If you're interested in an unguent for those calluses on your hands, I have just the thing." She pulled a squat stone jar of glossy black from a shelf and placed it on a counter. Casting a quick glance out the door to check on her apprentice, she rubbed some sweet-smelling unguent on Linsha's hand.

"The Circle wants to see you. The sooner, the better," she said softly.

Linsha tried but could not entirely stifle a groan. The Clandestine Circle, the commanders and planners of the Solamnic covert operations, never met their agents face-to-face unless it was imperative. In all the years she had been in Sanction, she had never met them. The fact that they wanted to see her now was not reassuring.

"Do you know why?" she asked Annian with foreboding.

The Knight shook her head. Straightforward and practical, Annian rarely wasted words. "Need-to-know basis only. They just told me to send you. Same place."

Linsha nodded once and thoughtfully rubbed the unguent

into her skin. "Nice. I'll take some." She smiled a brief grimace. "It reminds me of my mother's roses."

While the transaction was made and Karine wrapped the jar in a small cloth bag, Linsha asked, "Have you heard about the ship full of dead men that crashed into a galley at the south pier?"

"One of my customers mentioned it earlier. It caused quite a stir."

"I wonder what was wrong with them. . . ." Linsha's voice trailed off and she shivered.

Lady Annian handed her the bag. "I hear you impressed the governor and his commander."

Linsha's eyebrows lifted. "How do you know?"

An enigmatic smile danced on Annian's pale face. "I have my contacts."

Shaking her head, Linsha took her purchase outside, past the fires and the sweating apprentice, and walked into the street. The noon sun shone hot and fierce, like a dragon's eye, and the heat had grown oppressive. Already the people were slowing down and street traffic was beginning to thin out. Reluctantly she turned her steps back toward the stable. Once again she bridled her startled mare and rode out into the streets. Instead of entering the inner city, she skirted the wall and rode north into the outlying district where many of the city laborers and dock workers lived. The housing was poorer here and consisted mainly of apartments and little houses crowded together. But even here, in what used to be a huge slum, city services kept the streets clean, water was available in city fountains, the houses were in good repair, and the inhabitants looked healthy and busy. There were fewer taverns and gaming houses on this side of the city and more small businesses. Most of the city's population of kender lived here, too, on a lively broad avenue aptly named Kender Street. Perhaps half a mile from Kender Street, the neighborhoods came to an abrupt end in a strip of small orchards and gardens, and the road turned to a dirt path that led out into open fields and gently rolling hills of the vale.

Just to the north of the road sat the refugee camp run by

the mystics of the Temple of Huerzyd. The camp was built on the far side of the city wall on the long slope of a hill that rose to meet the great ridge jutting out from Mount Grishnor. It had been established years before to handle the influx of refugees fleeing from the terror of the dragon overlords, and over time it had gained an air of permanence. Newcomers in need of shelter and aid were sent to the camp and, under the auspices of the temple, were given a chance to build a new life in Sanction. Under Lord Bight's rule, anyone was welcome as long as that person obeyed the city laws and did not harass the citizens. That open-door policy had drawn folk from all over Ansalon, and while it created interesting problems for the city council, it also gave Sanction an open-minded, multicultural population.

Linsha glanced up at the camp as she passed by and saw that the place looked busy. A new group must have just arrived. Her attention turned back to her mare, who sniffed the open grassy stretches ahead and fidgeted for a canter. Linsha let her have her head. Stretching out her neck, Windcatcher happily threw herself forward into a smooth, fast-paced canter. She ran along the path toward the mountains and slowed only to cross the stone bridge that spanned the wide lava moat.

Narrow and heavily guarded, the bridge served as a link between the city and the increasing number of small holdings and farms that nestled in the protective shadow of Mount Grishnor. The guards recognized Linsha and waved her on. She had made a practice of exercising Windcatcher out this way for that very reason. North of Sanction lay one of the safe houses of the Clandestine Circle and one of the few escape routes from the city open to horses.

Past the bridge, Linsha trotted her sweating horse slowly up the road. It rose into the pine woods and scattered fields that grew on the volcano's skirts. As soon as she was well out of sight of the guards, she reined Windcatcher into a copse of pine and cedar and stopped where she could watch the road. They waited quietly in the green shadows until Linsha was sure they had not been followed. Satisfied, she turned the mare onto a narrow path that wound its way up for nearly a mile past the road, through dim woods and meadows dry in the summer heat. A few flocks of sheep lifted their heads and watched as she rode by; a solitary shepherd waved. Only another covert Knight would know that shepherd was a fellow Knight standing guard near a small croft used as a meeting place and safe house by the Clandestine Circle.

Linsha found the croft with no trouble, having been there twice before for different reasons, and she tethered Windcatcher out of sight in a narrow lean-to barn. Three other horses stood contentedly in the shade and nickered to the mare.

The lady Knight walked around to the front door. Although no one was in sight, she knew other sentries watched silently out of sight. She hesitated only a moment in front of the closed door before she squared her shoulders, took a deep breath, and went inside.

Two small windows were open to catch the breeze, but after the hot afternoon sunlight, the croft's single room seemed dark and cool. Linsha closed the door behind her and paused to let her eyes become accustomed to the gloom.

Three men sat around a low table near the fireplace and ate stew from trenchers of dried bread. They were dressed as travelers in coarse, light tunics, high boots, and breeches. Although it was difficult to see their faces clearly, no pilgrim's clothing, no matter how travel-stained and ragged, could disguise the balanced, self-assured manner of all three men, men accustomed to authority and power. They raised their heads in unison to observe Linsha. For a moment no one said a word.

As her eyesight sharpened in the low light, Linsha realized she had never seen these three men before. She didn't know their names or their ranks, and she probably never would. The identities of the leaders of the underground Clandestine Circle were a closely guarded secret. She couldn't even be completely certain these men *were* Solamnic Knights.

Then, "State your name, by the order of Sir Liam and the oath you took," came a resonant voice.

At least they had the coded greeting right. She took one step forward. "Rose Knight Linsha Majere."

The three men rose from the table and raised their hands in salute.

At that moment, the persona of Lynn fell from Linsha like a discarded cloak. She was Linsha Majere, granddaughter to two heroes of the War of the Lance, daughter to two heroes of the Chaos War, and the first non-Solamnic woman to be a Knight of the Rose. Shoulders thrust back, chin up, she saluted the three Knights, not for who they were, but for what they represented: over two thousand years of honor, tradition, and service.

The men returned to their seats and resumed eating. They did not offer a seat to Linsha.

Clasping her hands behind her back, she stayed where she was and waited for them to speak first.

The man on her right, a well-built man of middle height and middle age, broke the silence. "We understand you had a meeting with Lord Bight this morning."

News travels fast, Linsha thought to herself. "I had to deliver a message for my sergeant," she replied.

"Tell us."

Linsha described briefly her experience earlier that day while the Knights ate and listened without interrupting.

"You did not mention you asked to serve the governor in some capacity," the first Knight said pointedly.

The lady Knight started. She had left out that unprofitable exchange. "How do you know that?"

"Do not concern yourself with our sources," replied the second.

"Well, yes, I did, but I was turned down."

The third Knight, an older man with a grizzled beard, responded this time. "We believe that after the incident on the ship this morning, you will be accepted. We do not know yet what employment they have in mind, but we order you to take what is offered."

Linsha crossed her arms and stared at the men. "What makes you think Commander Durne is going to change his mind?"

"Not Durne. Bight. He has apparently taken a liking to you," said the Knight to her left.

"How do you know this?" she insisted. This was incredible. She couldn't believe someone as cautious as Lord Bight would take a liking to her in such a short period of time, nor would the governor or his commander change their minds so soon about accepting her. How had the Circle found out so quickly?

"It is our business to know this," said the first Knight. "Once you move closer to Bight, you will learn all you can of him. We want to know about his strengths, his weaknesses, his friends, his plans for Sanction, his dealings with allies or enemies, anything you can find. Look for ways to undermine his authority."

She shot them a narrow glance. The gist of these orders was what she had been doing all along, investigating Hogan Bight and keeping a watch should he ever reveal a secret treaty with the Knights of Takhisis or an alliance with the Dragonlords, particularly the black dragon Sable, whose realm bordered the southern Khalkist Mountains and stretched as far as the mouth of Sanction Bay. But undermine his authority? What was this supposed to mean? She knew the leaders of the Clandestine Circle, who often worked without the knowledge of the Solamnic Council, had long-range plans for Sanction. Ideally they wanted to oust Lord Bight and turn Sanction into a Solamnic stronghold, something she did not necessarily agree with. Did this group have some new plot hatching? Were they working with Sir Liam's blessings or on their own? What were they up to?

Linsha pursed her lips. A thousand questions crowded her mind, yet she knew from experience that covert leaders were not usually forthcoming with answers. She decided to try a few anyway. "What about the Legion? How do they fit in right now?"

The third Knight spoke. "The Legion's presence in Sanction

is weak at the moment. There are a few legionnaires in the refugee camps around the Mystics' temple and in the city. There are none that we know of in Bight's closest circle of advisers. Unless you learn something of importance, avoid the Legion. They are incompetent."

Linsha bit back a retort. That statement was uncalled for. The Legion was as incompetent as the Solamnic Knights. They had all made mistakes; they had all had successes. But the Circle did not even try to cooperate. A small tendril of frustration began to curl around in her mind.

She tried another question. "Do you know any more about the runaway ship that crashed this morning?"

"Little more than you. No one knows where it came from and no one yet has recognized the disease that claimed the crew. One of Bight's healers is examining the dead this afternoon."

A grimace crossed over Linsha's face. She didn't envy the healer that task. The smell of the dead had been bad enough in the morning. In this heat, it would be horrendous by now.

Well, the Knights seemed to be fairly informative this time, so Linsha asked the question that bothered her the most. "Why do you want to discredit Hogan Bight?"

Although she could neither see it nor hear it, Linsha felt as if a door had slammed shut. The Knights did not move, did not show any reaction, but there was a tension in the cool air around her that was as palpable as a gathering storm.

"It is not necessary for you to understand. Do your duty, lady Knight. Dismissed."

Linsha knew she had little choice. The Circle's orders were inviolable, and no matter how she might question them, she still had to obey. Duty came first.

She kept her face impassive as she saluted the motionless Knights and strode out of the croft. After fetching Wind-catcher from the lean-to, she rode thoughtfully back to the city and stabled the tired mare. The small root of frustration remained in her thoughts, delving deep into buried resentments and feeding on her stifled sense of injustice. Under normal circumstances, perhaps she would not have let the

Circle's orders bother her so much, but this afternoon she was hot and tired and had little patience. Still brooding, Linsha made her way back to her lodgings, slipped by Elenor, and returned to her room. While she did not slam her own door, her agitated entrance was enough to wake Varia.

The owl opened her eyes in time to see a boot go sailing across the room and slam into the wall. "Unless you want Elenor up here checking on you, you'd better find something quieter to throw around," the bird suggested.

Linsha pulled off her tunic, threw it silently on the floor, and opened the chest by her bed. From it she withdrew three small leather balls. One by one, she tossed them in the air and began to juggle. Up and down sailed the spheres, rhythmical and soothing. Her brother had taught her this trick, and whenever she felt agitated or confused, she juggled. As long as the balls were in the air, she had to focus on keeping them there, giving her body time to relax and her mind a moment of distraction from her problems. She often combined the motions with a meditative spell she had learned from the mystics that soothed away the worst of her tension and calmed her furious thoughts.

"Your meeting go well?" Varia prompted.

"I had to meet with the Clandestine Circle," Linsha replied between gritted teeth.

The owl hooted softly. "The three Lords of Stealth?"

Linsha ignored the bird's flippant tone. "They think Lord Bight will favor me with a job."

"Oh? Why?"

Flipping the balls in their constant circle, Linsha told her friend everything that happened that morning and finished with her interview with the Knights of the Circle.

Varia squawked a note, a noise like an out-of-tune psaltery. The owl was a virtuoso of sounds. "You've had quite a day."

Linsha's balls moved faster. "You know, this shouldn't bother me. I agreed to this duty when Sir Liam assigned it. He explained to me the importance of my task and the inherent honor in the goal. I knew what I was getting into."

"But you don't like it."

"No. I don't like it! Oh, I tolerated it at first. It was fun pretending to be someone else. Now . . . there is something tainted about living a constant lie. Est Sularus oth Mithas. My honor is my life. Huh! What honor is there in this subterfuge? How will I ever bring honor to the Knights of Solamnia or my family name by acting like a street-tough, unscrupulous sellsword in a guard's uniform the rest of my life?"

Abruptly Linsha snatched her juggling balls out of the air and banged them down on the table. "They called me up there to tell me they want to find a way to discredit him, to undermine what he has done here," she growled, her anger growing by the moment at the Circle's unfeeling, self-centered attitude.

"Why?"

"They would give no reasons."

"What if you don't find anything?"

"They did not mention failure," replied Linsha. She flopped into one of the chairs and stared wearily into space.

Varia hopped from her perch. Her wings rustled softly when she flew to land on the table, her talons clicking on the wood. She gazed up at the woman with her large black eyes unblinking. "Since owls are generally wiser than humans, I will give you my advice, and you may do with it as you will. Watch and wait. If your offer is accepted by Lord Bight, take it. You will be obeying orders, and perhaps taking the path Destiny has ordained for you. You are a good woman, Linsha Majere. You will follow your heart."

Linsha pulled her lips into a wry smile. "The gods are gone, Varia. Destiny is only what we make it to be."

The owl hooted a gentle laugh. "Your gods are gone. Who can say with certainty that there are not others?"

A sudden yawn took Linsha by surprise.

"Sleep now," Varia suggested gently. "You are due on patrol in just a few hours."

"Thanks for the advice," Linsha said, standing upright. The juggling had helped, and so had Varia. Her heartbeat had slowed, and the tension was gone from her back and shoulders. The tendril of frustration was still there, but

Varia was right. Lord Bight, the Circle, the guards, everything could wait, at least until after a few hours of sleep.

Linsha scratched the owl's shoulders in her favorite itchy spot, then she stretched out on her bed and was asleep before her head sank into the pillow.

Varia fluffed her feathers. Silently she swooped to the bedpost, where she settled down as still as a carving to watch over the sleeping woman and wait for night.

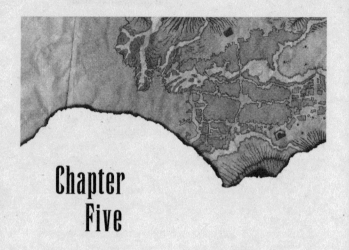

Chapter
Five

L insha reported for duty at the West
Gate just before sunset, about eight
o'clock by the new clock in the mercantile building by the harbor. The headquarters building, built flush against the city wall and the northern tower, was busy with patrols reporting in, the night guards forming for evening duty, and throngs of traffic passing in and out as the city came back to life. The day's heat loosened its paralyzing grip on the city, and the population was making up for lost time.

The night passed as usual, with only the normal drunks and bar fights to liven the patrol. In the harbor, the runaway ship sat at anchor not far from the Abanasian freighter. Both ships had been temporarily patched and left in place for further repairs and investigation. Linsha's patrol checked them several times on its beat, and each time the guards stared at them, rocking silently in the moonlight. They needn't have worried. No one went near the death ship.

At dawn the following day, Manegol, an elderly healer

sent by the city council, came to examine the death ship. He had started the day before and wished to finish the examination before the heat, and the smell, became unbearable. A few complaints from nearby boats had already reached the harbormaster. Quickly the healer completed his examination of each body and made his notes. By noon, he reported to the harbormaster to give his conclusions.

Shaking his gray head, he said, "Everyone on board suffered the same symptoms, and I have no idea what disease killed them. The combination is something totally unfamiliar to me."

The harbormaster had a scribe make a copy of the report and sent it to the palace. Then he ordered the City Guards to burn the ship.

Linsha wasn't on duty when the merchantman was towed out into the harbor and set alight, but she watched the smoke of its burning rise slowly from the harbor and ride the afternoon breeze over Sanction. Eventually the trail of smoke mingled with the fumes and steams of Mount Thunderhorn and slowly came to an end as the ship sank below the waters of Sanction Bay. Everyone breathed a sigh of relief and hoped that would be the end of it.

The elders of Sanction went back to worrying about the volcanic dome, and Lord Bight supervised the strengthening of the lava dikes. The *Whydah* unloaded its cargo of sheep and cows, took on a load of ballast, and made preparations to leave Sanction as soon as the crew had finished a few days of shore leave.

* * * * *

Three nights after the runaway vanished below the water, Rolfe, the *Whydah's* first mate, woke to a terrible thirst. He stumbled to the barrel nearby and ladled out a cup of water, then another and another. He drank until he felt bloated, and still the thirst raged in his mouth and throat. It was then the cramps struck—terrible, piercing, racking cramps that drove him doubled over to the head. By the time Rolfe was drained, he was so weak he could barely stagger back to his hammock.

A sailor found him a few hours later, raving and burning with a high fever. Vivid red blotches covered his weathered face. Appalled, the sailor ran to find the captain. The captain worriedly ordered a search of the ship and discovered three more men in the crew's quarters who were ill, all of them feverish and complaining of a raging thirst and all of them men who worked the same watches with Rolfe and had boarded the death ship with him.

The *Whydah's* captain was stunned. He took a mental head count. Most of his crew was on shore leave, and of those, at least six had also gone on board the galley. The remaining crewmen gathered around him, looking grim and scared.

"Send word to the harbormaster and the healer," he ordered. "I want the rest of you to find the others on shore leave. Look everywhere you can think of. Find them and bring them back here. But be quiet about it! We don't want to start a panic!"

The sailors hurried to obey. By morning's light, two sailors had been found in nearby taverns by the *Whydah's* crew and two appeared on their own, helping each other along the dock and singing bawdy songs. Those four seemed well enough, but to be safe, the captain quarantined them on the ship until the healer arrived.

The healer came soon after, and everyone realized with a pang of dread that this healer wasn't the same one who had examined the dead days before. This one was a woman, lean and sinewy and kindly. She introduced herself as Kelian and confirmed their worst fears.

"The healer, Manegol, is suffering from intestinal cramps, high fever, and dehydration," she told the captain, her concern obvious on her thin face. "The harbormaster is also ill. Whatever this illness is, it is starting to spread."

Swiftly she examined Rolfe, the most ill of the sick sailors, then checked the others. Her expression grew pale. "Keep them comfortable as best you can," she ordered. "Give them water for now. I will bring something to help ease the pain and fever." She shook her head. "I must get help from the healers at the temple. Meanwhile, keep the others on the ship."

The captain groaned. "We still have five men on leave. Part of my crew is looking for them."

The healer's eyes automatically turned to scan the busy piers, and her thoughts filled with dread. "Get them back here and keep them here, Captain. I will send word to Lord Bight." She nodded her thanks for his cooperation and hurried down the plank to the pier.

The captain watched her stride away through the piles of crates and bags, the crowds of busy sailors, dockhands, and merchants, and the general throng and clutter of a prosperous harbor. He would not blame her at all if she did not come back.

* * * * *

Linsha had already been relieved of duty and was about to walk to the stable to check on Windcatcher when Sergeant Amwold caught up with her. His grizzled face looked more strained than usual and he barely acknowledged her salute.

"We've been recalled. Form up by the gateway," he ordered and hurried away to find the others before she could ask questions.

Linsha grumbled under her breath at this change of plan. She was tired from her long night, and she was looking forward to a morning of rest. Rest was the last thing she got.

As soon as Sergeant Amwold rounded up his puzzled patrol, he told them about their new orders.

"The *Whydah's* captain is missing five members of his crew. We have been ordered to search the taverns, pleasure houses, and gaming halls to find them. They are to be returned to their ship immediately. I have a list of their names. We will begin at the Street of the Courtesans and work our way south to Snapfinger's Alley."

While the others grumbled, Linsha felt her instincts come alert. This was unusual. The City Guard did not normally go on searches for lost crew members unless there was a crime involved or some type of emergency. She glanced around the gateway and noticed that all of the night and day patrols were forming up and marching down into the harbor district. Her eyes narrowed as she put two and two together.

"Does this have anything to do with the illness on board the runaway?" she asked.

The sergeant rolled his eyes. He plainly wished no one had asked him that question. "We have only been told that the men could be sick and that they need to be returned to their ship. That is all."

Without another word, he led the five guards back to their patrol route among the back street taverns and alehouses along the southern rim of the harbor district. They searched for hours without success until noon, when Sergeant Amwold found a young man matching the name of a *Whydah* sailor happily drunk in the gutter behind an alehouse. The sailor seemed healthy to the patrol, but Amwold took no chances. He ordered a litter brought and had the giggling man tightly bound in a blanket and pushed onto the litter with a pole. Then he sent two guardsmen to carry the sailor to the *Whydah*, with the added injunction not to touch him and to return immediately. With luck, the other sailors had been located and the patrol could knock off for the day.

The guardsmen came back shortly with an empty litter and frightening news. The harbormaster had died, the first mate of the ship was near death, and seven of the *Whydah's* sailors were ill. Only three of the five missing crewmen had been found.

The guards exchanged uneasy glances and went back to their search. Through the long, hot, miserable day, they went from alley to tavern to inn to house, searching every room, kitchen, shop, common house, and privy for the last two sailors. News of the search and of the harbormaster's death spread like locust on the wind, so by midafternoon, half the population of the harbor district was out looking for the two men. The other half offered advice and criticism but preferred to stay indoors, away from possible contagion.

Sergeant Amwold would have preferred the criticism to the help. More often than not, the citizen volunteers attacked their self-appointed task with too much enthusiasm and ended up antagonizing the owner of a house or tavern. The patrol spent as much time soothing angry feelings and settling arguments as conducting a search. By late afternoon, they were exhausted, hot, and thirsty, and their patience was wearing thin.

Twice Sergeant Amwold sent messengers to the West Gate to check on the progress of the search, and both times they returned with bad news and orders to keep looking.

It was four in the afternoon, by the mercantile clock, when a runner caught up with the patrol and told Sergeant Amwold to stand down. The harbor-wide search had produced all but one sailor, and the night patrols were being recalled to get what rest they could before dark. Drooping with exhaustion, the five men and Linsha trudged back to the West Gate to report in to the day commander. The patrol waited in the shade of the city wall while their sergeant made his report. He came back shortly, carrying a large pitcher brimming with beer. They hastily dug out their horn cups.

"Compliments of Lord Bight," he said with a tired grin. "Be back here at sunset."

They gratefully filled their cups and drank to the governor's—and their own—health. They turned to leave, when the sergeant suddenly added. "Oh, except you, Lynn. There's a messenger here for you. He's been waiting for several hours."

Linsha was too tired to wonder or to catch the fleeting look of puzzlement in the sergeant's eyes. She had no thought of who could have sent a messenger to her, only a desire to be left alone so she could soak her aching feet and sleep. So it was with real surprise that she walked into the shadowed hall of the Guard Headquarters and saw a powerfully built young man dressed in the scarlet uniform trimmed in black that denoted the Governor's Guards.

He bounced to his feet in relief and hurried to meet her. "Finally!" he exclaimed. "I thought they'd keep you out there all afternoon."

The lady Knight felt an immediate warmth for this young man whose sincerity flashed in his ready grin and open countenance. Some of her irritation changed to curiosity. "So did I," she replied. "It's been a very long day."

"Well, come with me. His Excellency wants to see you. Your day is about to get longer."

Linsha looked down at her dirty, sweat-stained uniform in dismay. The rest of her wasn't any cleaner. "Do I have time to change my uniform or clean up a little?"

He twitched his head in a negative reply. "Better not. He sent his orders nearly two hours ago, and the governor doesn't like to be kept waiting."

He led her outdoors, and together they walked rapidly up the Shipmaker's Road toward the inner city and the intersection of the major north-south road. In this part of the city, the news of the sickness in the harbor district had not yet disturbed the peace, and the citizens remained quietly indoors, away from the fierce heat.

"Odd business, that ship sailing in here," the guard said as he made a left turn onto Temple Hill Way. "His Excellency is very upset about the harbormaster's death. They were good friends."

"If this is a plague of some sort, the harbormaster won't be the only one who dies," Linsha said quietly.

"Paladine forbid!" muttered the guard.

In silence, they wended their way past the homes of wealthy merchants and government officials, past the governor's old residence, to the stone-paved road that wound up the hill to Lord Bight's new palace. Many years ago, the low line of hills had been blasted by the volcanic activity of its neighbor, Mount Grishnor, and later stripped bare by the slaves and armies of the Dark Queen. Soon after Hogan Bight diverted the ash and lava, however, he chose the highest hill for the site of his new lavish palace and began a replanting project to stop the severe erosion, take advantage of the fertile volcanic soil, and to add some beauty to the austere hills. The result was an artist's blend of flowering shrubs for color, tall pines for shade, and groves of silver beech for delicate contrast. Other native plants and trees quickly filled in the gaps and spread from hill to hill. The mystics from the Citadel of Light on the next hill took the planting one step further and added exquisite gardens on the grounds of their temple. In the spring, the hills were a tapestry of color and life and one of the most popular places to take a stroll.

The shade trees continued about three-fourths of the way up the hill, then came to an abrupt end. Groves of pine and beech gave way to short-cropped grass that flowed in an open, gently sweeping slope up to the high walls surrounding the governor's palace. Lord Bight's appreciation for trees lasted only so far when it came to the defense of his house.

Linsha stepped out of the trees and into the brassy heat of late afternoon. With a gasp she stopped in her tracks and stared up the huge palace. She had always admired the edifice from afar but never as close as this.

The young guard grinned at her astonishment. "Beautiful, isn't it? His Excellency designed it himself, they say, and brought in a colony of dwarves to build it. They haven't finished it yet. They're still working on some of the outbuildings."

"It's so big," she breathed.

"And built like a fortress. Don't let the size or the beauty fool you. The place is a castle in disguise. We have a full company of the City Guards stationed there, plus the Governor's Guards and the dwarves who stayed to handle the siege weapons. About the only thing that might flatten that house is one of the great dragons."

Linsha studied the massive white stone walls of the palace and asked curiously, "Have any tried?"

The guard gestured toward the house. "Not yet."

They continued up the road to a towering pylon gateway that marked the entrance onto the palace grounds. The governor's red flag flew from the gate, and seven City Guards stood watch at the opening. They merely saluted the Governor's Guard and motioned the two in through the gate.

Linsha lagged behind, drinking in her fill of the magnificent palace. Its main building stood four stories high and was roofed with silvery gray slate. Five huge towers stood, one at each corner and one in the center, where a tall, broad staircase climbed up to the main doorway on the second floor. She noticed there were no windows on the ground floor and only narrow ones on the second. The only visible entrance was the one in the front tower, and that was probably heavily guarded. Looking closer, she saw the glint of weapons in the sun along the roof line and in the tower battlements. More guards patrolled the grounds outside. This place was a fortress indeed.

Feeling impressed and a little overwhelmed, Linsha followed the guard up the stairs and through two tower doors. The doors were massive slabs of polished oak, strengthened with iron fittings, and as she guessed, very well guarded. They passed into a wide hall where more men stood guard at strategic locations. Narrow bars of bright light shone from the western windows and formed golden rectangles on the pale green marble floor. Brilliantly colored tapestries in blues and greens hung on the walls, and a row of alabaster columns marched in single file down the center of the hall. The big room was cool after the heat of the road and strangely empty.

"This is Lord Bight's audience chamber for public officials and petitioners, but he has sent everyone away today. Come this way. He will be in his private office." The guard led her to a set of stairs against the far wall and up to the third floor. From there, she became totally lost. Corridor after corridor that branched away in every direction. Numerous small hallways and countless rooms formed a maze that Linsha guessed was all part of the palace's defenses. She followed the guard and tried to keep track of the left turns and the right turns and the number of doorways, but all too soon she was thoroughly confused and simply hurried to keep pace with his swift stride. The only detail she remembered with clarity was the fact that the upper floor was as richly and beautifully decorated as the audience hall.

Finally he came to a set of broad double doors of polished cedar, ornately carved with tree designs. He knocked twice, and the door was pulled open from within.

Linsha noticed two heavily armed guards at the door,

several officers in scarlet uniforms inside the room, and Lord Bight sitting a huge table before the messenger pulled her beside him and snapped a salute.

Lutran Debone, the head of the city council, stood by the table, thumping his pudgy fist on the polished top. "Your Excellency must agree that this crisis is growing by the minute. What are your plans for the inner city? What if this plague breaks out within the walls? You must do something to contain it."

Lord Bight lifted his eyes to the man's face with a cold stare. His patient tolerance was obviously at an end. "Thank you for wasting my time, Elder Lutran. I have already set plans in motion to contain this disease. When they begin to concern you, I will let you know. Come back when you have something more constructive to say."

Lutran opened his mouth to say more, then thought better of it. His hands fluttered in a disconcerted farewell, and he left the room, pulling the tatters of his dignity behind him.

"Now, Commander Durne," Lord Bight went on. He stood up, pulled a rolled map from a pile on his table, and flattened it. The commander and his aide, Dewald, moved close to see it. The three men bent over the parchment while Linsha and the guard quietly waited at attention.

"Latest reports tell us the sailor from the *Whydah* is still missing. It could be that he is too ill to move or is already dead. The first mate died this afternoon." Lord Bight stabbed a finger at a place on the parchment. "There is a warehouse here, not far from the southern pier, that is nearly empty at the moment. I want it totally emptied. My authority. We will make a hospital out it, and the entire crew of the *Whydah* is to be placed there, as well as any man, woman, or child who shows the slightest symptom of this disease. I want them placed in total quarantine. The healers from the temple have already offered to help. We will need supplies, water, blankets, whatever medicines the healers need, and guards. No one will go in or out without the healers' agreement and permission from the officer of the watch.

"Next, I want all the bodies of the dead placed on the *Whydah*. Tow the ship out into the bay and burn it as well. If the captain argues, charge him with malicious conduct."

"What about the harbormaster? His family is making plans for his burial," Commander Durne pointed out.

A fleeting glimpse of sadness crossed Hogan Bight's face. "His body will have to be burned, too. We cannot let this sickness get out of control."

With a startling change of subject, the governor looked past the two officers and said, "Morgan, what took you so long? I sent you after her hours ago."

Linsha lifted her eyebrows, wondering if she should say something, but the guard beside her replied, "She was on patrol, Your Excellency, in search of the sailor."

"I see." Lord Bight came around from behind the table and stood in front of Linsha. His eyes sized her up carefully, from dusty boots to sweat-damp hair. "Do you still wish to serve my government?"

Linsha tilted her chin and unconsciously stood a little straighter. So the Clandestine Circle was right. But what did he have in mind? She met his gaze with a level stare of her own and answered, "Of course, Lord Governor."

"Good. I would like to offer you a position on the Governor's Guards. Will you accept?"

Linsha rocked back on her heels. The Governor's Guards! She hadn't expected that. The governor's bodyguards were the elite. They had to go through intensive training and were expected to serve Lord Bight with unswerving loyalty and obedience.

She paused a moment to savor his question. Yes, she wished it; she wished it very much. Entering Lord Bight's private circle was something she had been striving for a long while, not only because of her duty to the Solamnic Knights but because she had come to respect this man and his abilities. And therein lay her dilemma. How could she serve both the Solamnics and Lord Bight with honor when her presence here was a lie, when her leaders ordered her to accept this commission solely to deceive and possibly discredit him? How could she give him her oath of fidelity when her first loyalty was to the Oath and Measure?

Of course, this was the only chance she would ever have to be close to him and perhaps learn his secrets. If she turned the opportunity down now, she would never be given another chance. She would have to go back to the City Guards and spend the rest of her days in Sanction patrolling the harbor alleys and taverns, and she would have to go back to the Clandestine Circle and tell them she had failed. Which rankled more? Deception or failure?

"Yes, Your Excellency. It would be an honor."

Linsha's fate was sealed.

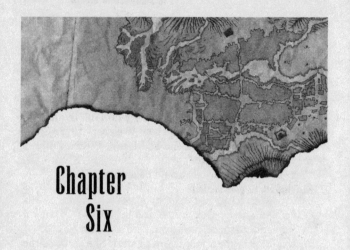

Chapter
Six

A s soon as the words were out of
her mouth, Linsha knew, for good
or ill, she had done the right thing. Without a qualm, she bore
Lord Bight's scrutiny with a passive regard of her own and
waited for his response.

She wondered briefly if he had trained with the mystics
and could read her aura. Many years ago she had spent time
with Goldmoon at the Citadel of Light and had studied the
basics of mysticism before she convinced her parents that she
wanted to join the Knights of Solamnia. Since then she had
used the powers she learned to aid in gathering information
for the Knights. Her strongest ability was to read a person's
aura, or to sense the true nature, good or evil, of an individ-
ual's character. She was tempted to try it now on Lord Bight,
but she immediately dismissed the thought. There were too
many others in the room, and it was quite possible that Lord
Bight or one of his soldiers was sensitive to the power of the
heart and could discern what she was doing. It went without

saying that Lynn of Gateway would not have the trained talent to use mystic powers.

Instead, Linsha forced her thoughts into a silent, calming meditation that would reveal little to an aural scan. She focused her attention on Bight's face. This mystery man, sometimes shady, sometimes cruel, often proud and arrogant, was fascinating to her. She felt no desire for him, only a wish to know him better, to understand what made him who he was. The fan lines in the corners of his eyes and around his mouth bespoke a sense of humor and warmth, yet his golden eyes were deep set and often brooded on the memories of things both glad and sorrowful. His face was ageless, neither young nor old, and alight with wisdom. His skin was tanned to a dark bronze and his . . .

"Commander Durne, my sword," he said abruptly.

The sudden request made Linsha start. She froze as the tall commander of the Governor's Guards brought forth a large sword in a jeweled scabbard that hung behind Lord Bight's chair.

Lord Bight drew the sword in a deliberate motion that sent the rasp of metal against metal scraping through the silent room. All eyes were on the lord governor and the woman.

"Kneel," he commanded.

She obeyed, intensely aware of the shining blade hovering over her head.

"Lynn of Gateway, I accept you as a squire in the company known as the Governor's Guards. Will you train your mind and body to my service? Will you vow to devote your strength to this corps and your obedience to my will?"

"Yes, Your Excellency," she replied in a clear voice.

"You will be allowed six weeks to learn the duties of the guards, train in weapons and martial arts, and study the company you wish to join. At the end of that time, you will have the choice of returning to the City Guards or taking an oath of fealty into my retinue. Is that acceptable?"

"Yes, Excellency. Thank you."

He tapped her once on the chest with the tip of the great sword. "Rise then, Lynn." A smile crinkled the lines on his face. "You may not have time to rest and change your uniform before you begin your duties tonight."

Tonight? Linsha thought with chagrin. Would no one let her sleep? Aloud, she said, "Lord, if I may ask, why did you choose me for this duty?"

He shrugged. "We had an opening. One of my guards was killed last night in an unfortunate accident. I liked your courage and ability, so I will give you a trial."

An accident? she wondered. Had it been happenstance or fate? She climbed to her feet and bowed to the lord governor.

Commander Durne returned the sword to its resting place, saluted Lord Bight, then turned to the guard still standing behind Linsha. "Morgan, you have duty at the training hall. You are dismissed. I will take her downstairs."

Flashing a grin at Linsha, Morgan saluted Durne and Lord Bight and hurried out.

"You have lodgings and your horse in the outer city, I believe," Durne said, escorting Linsha out the door. "You may take two hours to gather your belongings. Quarters and a stall for your horse will be given to you here for as long as you stay. The governor requires his guards to be available."

Linsha hesitated a step. She hadn't thought of that. What would she do with Varia? What about Elenor?

Commander Durne seemed to understand her hesitancy. "I know this is short notice," he said in a surprising note of sympathy. "We're not giving you time to draw breath, but if circumstances get any worse, we will want all the guards on duty tonight."

Linsha was resigned. "Including me?"

"Absolutely. The governor plans to supervise the burning of the ship. You can begin learning the duties of a bodyguard by observing the detachment tonight."

That surprised her. She was guessing she'd have to endure sentry duty or armor polishing her first few days as a recruit.

The commander hurried her down the stairs back the way she had come, but on the ground floor, he took a different turn and brought her through a large corridor to a back entrance that opened into a huge courtyard surrounded by service buildings, stables, barracks, and a high wall. The yard was busy with servants and guards bustling about their tasks. In the northern corner, a crew of dwarves climbed about the scaffolded roof of a bakehouse, laying slate shingles. Horses neighed from a corral by the stables; dogs ran about or slept in the shade. Smoke rose from the chimneys of the big stone kitchen.

"This is the home of the Governor's Guards and the company of City Guards that is stationed here," Durne told her. "The barracks are there." He pointed to a long stone building built over an undercroft used for storage. "The armory is to your right. Meals are available in the kitchen from daybreak until midnight. Don't ask for anything after that or the head cook will put you to work scouring pans."

Linsha crossed her arms. "Huh. I don't do kitchen work."

He laughed, a deep, rich sound of amusement. "Then stay on Cook's good side. He's a mean one with a carving knife. Captain Omat is in charge of recruits. He'll show you to your quarters when you return and issue you a new uniform. Be prompt. We have a great deal of work to do tonight." He slapped her on the shoulder, turned on his heel, and was gone before she could think of anything else to ask.

Linsha took a deep breath. This was happening so quickly, she hardly knew what to think. The lack of sleep didn't help either, and neither did the heat nor the nearly eighteen hours on patrol. She felt sluggish, as if someone had smothered her in a hot, heavy cloak. She couldn't think of more than one thing at a time, so first she decided to collect her gear and Windcatcher. Food and rest could come later.

After asking directions several times, she found her way out to the pylon gate and the road down to the city. First she stopped at the livery stable and retrieved Windcatcher and her saddle. The stable owner, seeing her uniform, insisted on chatting with her about the search for the missing sailor and the growing apprehension along the docks. Linsha said nothing about Lord Bight's plans. She listened to the owner's talk, nodded at the appropriate places, and paid him for the unfinished week of the mare's care. He told her to come back anytime.

Leading the mare, she hurried to Elenor's house. She didn't look forward to this parting, but at least she would still be in the city and could stop to see the old lady once in a while.

Elenor felt the same way. She was both delighted for Linsha's change of fortune and sad to see her go.

"I will miss you so. You have been such good company," Elenor said while she helped Linsha pack. "Now, you must stay and have a quick meal with me. No, don't argue. You look all done in. Food will do you good."

As soon as she bustled downstairs, Linsha sat with a thump on the chair. "What am I going to do with you?" she groaned to Varia when the owl slipped out of her hiding place.

The owl didn't seem the least bit concerned. "Is there a stable?" At Linsha's affirmative, she nodded her head, and her small feathered "ears" popped up, a sure sign of the owl's excitement. "I can make myself at home in the stable. No one needs to know you are with me. People here consider owls to be good luck."

Linsha nodded wearily, glad that problem was easily solved. "We'll meet in the woods if need be. Will you fly to Lady Karine and tell her what has happened? I won't have time."

"Of course."

The lady Knight gathered her meager belongings together and loaded the bundles on her mare. Elenor had a simple meal fixed for her—cold meat, warm bread, cheese, and vegetables from the small garden.

They chatted quietly while they ate until after supper, when Elenor wrapped a few honey cakes for Linsha to take with her.

"I missed you this morning. I baked these cakes for Cobb's order and saved some for you. I took the rest to the Dancing Bear this morning. You should have seen Cobb. My lands, he was all in a dither."

Linsha tried to pay attention, but she was too tired. The proprietor of the Dancing Bear was often in a dither.

"One of his serving girls didn't show up, and the other

kept running upstairs and down to take care of some sailor she had her sights set on. Cobb said the young man was sick, and he was most annoyed that the boy took ill in his inn."

A cold chill crept through Linsha's thoughts and brought her fully alert. "Elenor, did anyone say what was wrong with the sailor? Or where he came from?"

The older woman pursed her thin lips. "Not that I recall. Cobb was busy serving customers and taking deliveries. He barely had time to pay me."

"Elenor," Linsha said, jumping to her feet, "I must go. Listen carefully. Don't go back to the Dancing Bear or anywhere near the harbor until you hear from me or the town criers that all is well."

Elenor put her hand to her mouth as the same horrid suspicion occurred to her. "The missing sailor? Oh, you don't think . . ." Her soft eyes blinked rapidly in growing concern. "But why wouldn't Cobb tell someone?"

"I don't know. Fear, I guess. Didn't want to frighten off his customers. I know one patrol checked there in the afternoon and didn't find the sailor."

Although Elenor looked nothing like Linsha's tall, fiery-haired grandmother, at that moment Linsha saw the same determined, self-assured, don't-worry-about-me expression she had seen many times in Tika's face. Elenor pressed the wrapped cakes into her hand and walked with her toward the door. "I know you must leave. Keep a sharp eye out for Lord Bight and yourself. I'll miss our morning teas."

"Remember what I said."

"Of course, dear." Elenor paused and gave her hug. "There will always be room here for you."

Linsha waved once and mounted Windcatcher. The mare, eager for exercise, broke into a trot and maintained her pace all the way back to the Governor's Palace. When Linsha finally reined her to a walk by the gateway into the courtyard, the mare was sweating but breathing normally.

Torches burned on the walls and at the gate, and the court seethed with activity. The sentries let Linsha pass, directing her toward the stables. She glanced around, wondering what was happening. Horses were being saddled, and mounted guards in their red and black uniforms were forming into squads. Grooms ran back and forth carrying equipment and more torches. Could all this be for Lord Bight's visit to the docks?

Before she reached the stable, Commander Durne intercepted her.

"Lynn, You're late," he growled.

"Commander, I think I know where the lost sailor might be," she said hurriedly as she dismounted, and she told him quickly of the conversation with her landlady.

"By Takhisis!" he snapped. "If this is true, we may have to quarantine the entire inn staff. They won't like that!" he added dryly.

At his command, a stableboy appeared and helped Linsha unload her horse. "Take her gear to her quarters. Second level. Beside Shanron," ordered the commander. "Mount up, Lynn. We're riding with the governor."

He mounted his own horse, and together they rode to join Lord Bight, who sat astride a large, muscular sorrel. The governor had donned a light mail shirt and a golden cloak but had refused any armor. The only weapon he carried was his sword, a broad, double-bladed battle sword big enough to decapitate a small dragon.

His lack of weapons was not copied by his guards, Linsha observed. Two squads of six riders each fell into formation before and behind the governor's party, and each rider was armed to the teeth with spears, short swords, and daggers. Two in each squad carried crossbows and two had axes. All wore breastplates, greaves, and helmets. A flag bearer carried the governor's flag.

Commander Durne, with Linsha in tow, joined the governor and two other officers, and he told Lord Bight the gist of Linsha's information.

"Good. Send two squads to the docks to prepare the ship for firing. We'll go to this inn first," Lord Bight told his captains. "If a body is there, it will have to be burned."

At his signal, a horn blared and the horses sprang forward.

With a clatter of hooves and the rattle of armor, the governor and his escort trotted down the hill into the city. A bronze dusk was falling over Sanction. There was no wind to stir the dust on the roads or the smoke from a thousand dying oven fires. The smell of dung and refuse was strong. Steam and smoke from the smoldering volcano hung over the peak like brooding storm clouds and glowed in the setting sun with a fiery patina of copper.

The streets were busy with evening traffic. Although the crowds quickly made way for the governor's entourage, many people stopped and gawked at the squads passing by, for Governor Bight didn't usually travel about the city with so many soldiers. Rumors and gossip were already spreading through the city about the strange ship and its deadly cargo, and this new development only added leaven to the rising speculation.

As soon as the riders left the city gate behind, Lord Bight motioned Linsha forward. "You know the fastest way to this inn, young woman. Take us there."

After years in Sanction and a year in the City Guard, Linsha knew the streets of the outer city like her own bedroom at home. In short order, she led the squads to the Dancing Bear just as the stableboy was lighting the lamps by the entrance. Swiftly the guards moved to block the front door, the back door, and the small stable yard where the innkeeper kept a few horses for rent.

The door was wide open on such a sultry night, and sounds of merrymaking spilled out with the light. A few patrons came to the door to see what was going on. They took one look at Lord Bight and the soldiers and ducked back inside, yelling for the host.

Cobb came on their heels. His face was pale, and he wiped his hands on his apron and forced a wan smile. "My lord governor, how—"

"You had a sick sailor here this morning," Lord Bight said without preamble. "Where is he now?"

The innkeeper visibly blanched. "He went back to his ship, my lord."

"Which ship?"

"The, uh, oh . . . I've been busy, my lord. I don't remember."

"Call out the serving girl that cared for him," Bight demanded in a tone that allowed no refusal.

Cobb eyed the guards with increasing nervousness. His eyes widened when he recognized Linsha among them, but he knew there was no help there. "Angelan," he called over his shoulder. "Come out here."

Angelan appeared, pretty, blonde, and trembling.

"Are you the one who cared for the sailor?" Lord Bight demanded. He glared down at her, and she seemed to wilt before his eyes.

The blood drained from her face. She looked at Cobb, then back at the Governor's Guards. "I . . . uh, yes, sir. It's like Cobb said, sir. He—"

"Stop dithering, girl!" Lord Bight bellowed. "Where is he?"

Angelan burst into tears. "In the back garden," she wailed. "He's dead." She sagged against her employer and sobbed.

Commander Durne barked commands to three guards, who hurried into the inn.

Without another word, Lord Bight and his men waited in the gathering darkness. Cobb and Angelan remained where they were, too afraid to move without the governor's permission. More customers gathered at the door behind Cobb or hung out the windows; pedestrians, drawn by the sight of the mounted soldiers, clustered at a discreet distance to stare.

The quiet dragged into a tension-filled silence until even the horses grew restive. Abruptly the three men returned, pushing their way through the crowd at the door.

"There's a newly dug grave in the back, Your Excellency. They tried to conceal it under some flagstones, but we dug into it and found the body," one guard reported.

Angelan sobbed even harder.

"Your Excellency, I—" Cobb tried to explain.

Lord Bight cut him off. "Innkeeper, you knew the City Guards were looking for this man. It was your responsibility to notify them of his whereabouts. We are trying to contain this illness before it sweeps through the city. Your lack of judgment has endangered this entire area. Now it is necessary to burn the inn. You, your servants, and anyone who had contact with the dead man will be put in quarantine at once."

Cobb nearly choked. His hands wrung themselves into his apron. "Lord, please. Not the inn. It's all we have."

"Commander Durne," the governor said flatly.

The commander slid from his horse and gestured to his guards. Smoothly, efficiently, he sent the soldiers into the inn and amid an outcry of complaints and sobs. The guards evicted the customers, closed the inn, and soon had Cobb, Angelan, another serving girl, a cook, and Cobb's wife standing huddled in a shaking group with a few belongings in hand. The customers were gone, after giving their names to Durne's lieutenant, and the body of the *Whydah's* sailor had been exhumed, carefully wrapped in a tarp, and loaded on a horse. In moments, flames licked at the timber walls and began to rise toward the roof. The innkeeper turned away, his face stricken. The women cried harder.

Lord Bight watched impassively for several minutes, then left a squad to keep a watch on the fire so it didn't spread and turned his horse back to the road. Pushing Cobb and his group before them, the guards followed.

Darkness was complete by the time they rode to the warehouse set aside for a quarantine hospital. Linsha was impressed by the progress already made by the City Guards and the healers. The warehouse had been emptied as ordered, and dozens of people hurried about by torchlight setting up pallets, carrying supplies, and hauling barrels of water. A makeshift kitchen sat to one side, where a large fire burned under a caldron and several women chopped vegetables for soup.

Lord Bight looked over the facilities with approval. He pointed to the kitchen. "There, innkeeper, would be a good place to ply your talents. We will need everyone's help."

Cobb and his family stared around at the huge area with trepidation. The crew of the *Whydah* was already there, looking disgruntled, as well as about a dozen other men, several women, the harbormaster's wife, and the minotaur repair crew who had patched the freighter after the accident. The door had been roped off, and City Guards stood at the entrance.

The idea of a central healing facility and even of quarantine to fight a widespread disease was something new to Sanction. Before the Chaos War and the disappearance of magic, healers were able to stop disease with spells and enchanted potions. They never had to learn to deal with an epidemic—until their magic was gone. Since then, most epidemics had been allowed to run their course, wiping out hundreds of people, mostly because no one knew what caused them. The mystic healers trained by Goldmoon were beginning to take the place of the old sorcerers, but there were rarely enough in one place to stem a widespread contagion. Lord Bight knew all too well there were too few healers in Sanction to help the population if this strange disease spread as quickly as it appeared to. He hoped quarantine would contain the plague to a small area and to numbers his healers could cope with.

From within the warehouse came the healer, Kelian, who gestured to the newcomers to enter. The innkeeper and his companions didn't move. In the dim light of the torches, the large space loomed over them as black and frightening as the grave, for none of them knew if they would ever come out of that warehouse alive.

"Lord, how long will we be here?" Cobb asked hesitantly.

"Until the contagion is over," Lord Bight replied. For the first time, he looked down from his horse into the faces of the people gathering at the roped entrance to see him, and his expression softened. "I'm sorry to force this on you. It is all we know to do thus far. But I promise you that we will do everything we can to fight this sickness so we can release you as soon as possible."

The captain of the *Whydah* pushed his way forward, his face red and sweating. The guards tensed for trouble.

"Lord, I ask a boon. We were removed from our ship too quickly to settle our affairs. Now I hear the *Whydah* is to be burned."

Lord Bight inclined his head. "You know the reasons."

"Aye, I know," he replied, resigned. "Before you do, will you have someone find the ship's log so it can be sent back to the owner? And bring out our cat. She doesn't deserve to die like that."

The other sailors around him nodded.

The governor's eyebrows lifted in surprise. Of all the arguments or demands he expected to hear, he hadn't guessed that one. "You have my word," he promised.

The troop wheeled their horses and continued along the darkened streets down to the southern pier, where the *Whydah* was tied up. City Guards stood watch on the pier to keep the curious, the looters, and the irrepressible kender away. The governor and his troop dismounted.

The news of the burning had already reached the ears of many of the citizens, and a large group gathered at the foot of the pier to watch. They moved aside to make room for the Governor's Guards, then closed in quickly behind them.

A captain of the City Guard saluted the governor as the soldiers approached the *Whydah*. "Sir, preparations are nearly complete. We have placed the dead on board and have prepared the ship to be fired. We are awaiting the arrival of the rowboats to tow this one out into the bay."

"Good. We have one more body to add," Lord Bight informed him. "The missing sailor was found." When he turned to gesture to the guard leading the burdened horse, his gaze caught Linsha in the middle of a yawn.

"Squire Lynn," he demanded. "You need some activity to help you stay awake. See if you can locate the ship's log and the cat before the towboats get here."

Linsha's face grew hot at being singled out in such a way. She gave a rueful salute before walking to the gangplank that led to the *Whydah*. She was not enthusiastic about going on board a ship whose crew had lost members to an unknown contagious disease, but the thought came to her that this could be a test of her willingness to obey the lord governor, so she squared her shoulders and marched on board.

Two men carried on the shrouded body of the young sailor behind her, stowed it on deck beside a row of other wrapped bodies, and hurried off, leaving Linsha alone on the silent ship.

The ship's log was easy to find. It sat in a niche in the captain's sea desk in his cabin, leather-bound and well cared for. She thumbed through it and noted that the last entry had been made that afternoon:

Kiren and Jornd died this noon. Three more are ill. Orders to abandon the ship. Whydah *is to be burned. May the High God keep our souls.*

Neat. Concise. Full of sadness.

The captain's last words echoed through her mind. *May the High God keep our souls.* She wondered if the dying captain of the merchantman had time to write a last prayer.

She lapsed into thought. In fact, the ship's log from the Palanthian ship might hold some clues that could shed some light on the origin of this plague. The log would list the ports the ship had visited and should contain notes about the onset of the crew's symptoms and deaths. Perhaps Lord Bight would let her read it.

With the book tucked under her arm, Linsha searched the cabin for the cat. There was no sign of it in there or in any of the small cabins under the aft deck. She looked through the crew's quarters, the sail locker, and the galley to no avail. Finally she took a small hand lamp and climbed down the ladder into the hold, where the cargo of sheep and cattle had been contained in two rows of pens. The pens had been cleaned and washed down after the animals were unloaded, which held the odor down to a tolerable level. Thick, hot darkness filled the hold and hid a myriad of places a cat could hide. In the aisle that divided the two rows of pens, a few bales of straw gleamed pale gold in her lamplight. Barrels of oil, ready for the fire that would consume the *Whydah*, sat close to the curving wooden sides of the ship.

Linsha walked several paces down the aisle and shone her lamp around. There was no cat in sight. Something moved in the darkness behind her, a small pattering something that dived into the bales of straw. A furry form flew after it.

"There you are," Linsha said under her breath.

She turned around, and suddenly a heavy weight slammed into her back. She lost her balance, and she fell heavily to the planked walkway. Her lamp smashed into the floor and went out.

Hard and heavy, the weight pressed into the small of her back. A blade nicked her throat.

"What in the name of Reorx are you doing down here?" growled a voice in her ear.

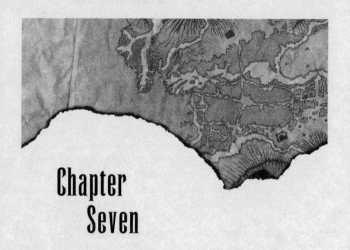

Chapter Seven

Linsha considered her options for a moment, then decided to lie quietly and try to placate the opponent on her back. If that knife hadn't been there, she could have flipped him off and kept him at bay, but an armed enemy she couldn't see in the intense darkness, who had a sharp blade so close to her jugular, was too great a risk.

"I said, what are you doing down here?" he repeated fiercely.

"I am with the Governor's Guards. I'm looking for the cat," she said as calmly as she could.

The voice snorted behind her. "You're wearing a City Guard's uniform, and a stinking one at that. Why were you sneaking around down here? All the guards have been ordered off."

"Lord Bight sent me to look for the ship's cat. Now get off!" Linsha insisted.

The knife moved away from her throat. "The governor's here already?"

Linsha realized her eyes were growing more accustomed to the dark. She could see faint shapes amid the deep shadows, and the glimmer from the hatch above seemed to grow brighter. She turned her head slightly and saw a gleam of light flicker on the long blade of a dagger, now pointed toward the floor and away from her neck. That was enough for her. As quick as a striking snake, she reached behind her shoulder, grabbed the wrist with the dagger in both hands, and wrenched it toward the floor. At the same time, she rolled in the same direction, dislodging her attacker and knocking him into the wooden walls of a pen. Linsha sprang to her feet, a back-alley curse on her lips, and she pulled her own dagger and crouched, ready to attack.

With a disgusted grunt, a short, stocky figure pushed himself upright and spat into the straw. "I suppose I deserved that," he said. "But you startled me. The ship is supposed to be empty. I thought you were a looter."

Linsha relaxed slightly. She could see well enough now to make out the face and form of a dwarf. "Now it's my turn to ask. What are you doing down here?"

"Governor's business," he growled.

"Well, he's right outside," Linsha responded irritably. She was really too tired to be polite to grumpy dwarves, especially ones that put bruises on her back and stuck knives at her throat. She returned her dagger to its sheath, picked up the logbook from where it had fallen, and turned her back on him to search through the straw bales. As she hoped, a slender calico cat was there, sitting behind the bales and staring at a hole where a rat was hiding. Linsha scooped up the cat and, without a word to the dwarf, climbed up the ladder to the deck. She could hear him come up behind her, but she didn't bother to turn around until she had crossed the ship and stepped off the plank onto the pier.

In the light of the torches, she could see the dwarf clearly now as he walked down the plank. She gave him the barest nod of greeting.

A hint of amusement lightened the frown on his face, and he returned the nod. "I am Mica, healer to the Governor's

75

Court and priest in the Temple of the Heart."

So, he was a mystic healer from the newly refurbished temple on the hill. Interesting. "I am Lynn of Gateway, newest member of the Governor's Guards," she replied.

He stood barely four feet in his handmade leather shoes, yet he still managed to look down his nose at her sweat-stained uniform. "You must be very new. Had a busy day?"

The lady Knight examined the dwarf's immaculate brown jacket, linen shirt, and beautifully tailored pants and rolled her eyes. Even after the tussle below deck, he was fastidiously clean and unwrinkled. She felt like a pile of worn-out, discarded rags beside him. "You wouldn't believe it," she muttered and was about to walk away when Commander Durne joined them.

"Ah, Mica. You're still here. The governor would like to talk to you."

The dwarf inclined his head to them both and walked to join Lord Bight at the end of the pier, where he and his officers waited for the rowers.

Commander Durne looked at Linsha, then took a closer look. "You have straw in your hair and a cut on your neck that wasn't there earlier." He grinned. "Did the cat put up a fight?"

To her surprise, Linsha suddenly became very self-conscious of her dirty, smelly clothes and her grimy face and intensely aware of how close Commander Durne was standing to her. She clutched the cat and the logbook close to her, like a shield, and sidled a step away. Fortunately the cat was perfectly comfortable where she was and made no effort to squirm away. A purr rumbled contentedly from her furry throat.

"Ah, no," Linsha said quickly to hide her discomfort. "The dwarf ambushed me in the cargo hold."

"Mica?" said Durne, surprised.

"He thought I was a looter."

"I didn't think he had it in him. He's usually too fussy about his appearance to bother attacking people."

Linsha heard no derision in his words, only an observation. "He said he's the healer to the Governor's Court."

"Yes. He's very good. He read the previous healer's report and insisted on examining the *Whydah* for himself."

"Have any of the healers recognized this illness?" Linsha asked.

Durne crossed his arms and stared out into the darkness of the harbor. "No," he said briefly.

They lapsed into silence and stood together, gazing into the night. The darkness was velvety black, heavy with heat and haze. The moon had not risen yet, and little could be seen beyond the scattered lights on ships and pleasure craft anchored beyond the piers. There was still no hint of wind, and the water rested quietly under a gentle swell.

"Good night to burn a ship," Linsha said softly.

They heard the splash of approaching oars, and two large towboats appeared out of the night. Quickly and efficiently, ropes from the *Whydah's* bow were attached to the sterns of the two boats while the plank was drawn aside and the freighter's moorings were cast off. A chanter on the foremost towboat began a slow, rhythmic song, and the oars on both boats bit deep into the water. The *Whydah* began to move.

Lord Bight and his bodyguards, the City Guards, Mica, and Linsha watched without speaking as the doomed vessel began her slow journey to the funeral pyre. They watched her glide slowly into the darkness until she was little more than a vague shape against the distant lights, then she vanished completely. Minutes ticked by.

In Linsha's arms, the ship's cat lifted her head and pricked her ears. A yellow light flared far away in the inky blackness, followed by a second burst. Two lights, like tiny dancing flames, faded, then brightened and spread into two glowing balls. Suddenly there was a muffled explosion, and the two lights soared into one furious column of flame that consumed the ship and cremated the dead in one last glowing conflagration that could be seen from all sides of the harbor and as far as the city walls.

When the flames at last began to die, a loud, sonorous horn blew a farewell call from the harbormaster's tower. A boat anchored in the harbor responded by ringing its bell, and in moments people on every craft in the bay were ringing bells or blowing horns to pay their last respects to the harbormaster and the other dead. The sounds mingled into a long, wild dirge that carried the grief and fear of a city high into the night sky, where the gods no longer dwelt to hear.

When at last the horns and bells fell silent and the flames died down into the water, Lord Bight passed a hand over his eyes and turned away, his face stony. He gestured to his men to follow. Subdued, the Governor's Guards took their places and began the walk back up the pier toward shore.

Linsha, with the cat and the ship's log still in her arms, walked behind Commander Durne. The dwarf, Mica, stalked beside the lord governor. As the troop approached the boardwalk at the end of the pier, Linsha became aware of a large crowd of people blocking the way. It was a mixed bunch, drawn mostly from the taverns, gaming houses, and sheds along the harbor, men and women, a few minotaurs, a draconian or two, some rambunctious barbarians, and the ever-present kender, who were drawn to crowds like flies to cider. They were quiet at first, but as the lord governor approached, they started shouting questions to draw his attention. Behind them, a few City Guards shifted nervously and waited with the horses while another thin line of guards was all that stood between the press of people and the governor.

He slowed as he approached them, drew to his full height, and swept them with a raking regard.

"Lord Bight, what's happening?" shouted several at once.

"Why are you taking people away?" a woman cried.

"We've heard hundreds have died. They say the illness is a curse!"

Another angry voice shouted, "How many more ships will you burn?"

More people joined the throng, sailors and merchants, pickpockets and servants. Their voices rose, confused and angry, and muddled together until there was only a babble of noise that assaulted the ears and made no sense.

Commander Durne and Captain Dewald, without apparent

concern, sent soldiers to bolster the line of the City Guard and to surround the governor.

Lord Bight climbed onto a pile of crates and raised his arms to the crowd to ask for silence. Gradually, with much squabbling and muttering, the onlookers grew quiet.

Using a loud voice and succinct words, the lord governor answered the questions fairly and fittingly and explained the disaster as best he could over a renewed barrage of more questions, comments, and drunken heckling.

Linsha watched, impressed by Lord Bight's unending patience. He seemed to radiate calm in his voice and in every movement of his body, and his words were chosen to comfort as well as inform. The noisy crowd slowly subsided under the hypnotic quality of his deep, even tones. So powerful was the effort he exerted to sway the mob that no one who stood within hearing remained unmoved by the enchantment of his voice.

Linsha and the guards were so intent on watching Lord Bight, they didn't notice a gang of boisterous youths who had joined the crowd late and were hovering along the fringes, laughing drunkenly and whispering conspiratorially among themselves while they passed several large bottles of ale around.

A stocky man, clothed in a nondescript tunic and leggings, eased into their midst and handed them a jug of dwarven spirits. A smirk and a laugh crossed his face as he whispered something to their leader, a gangly fisherman's son. The boy choked with mirth as at a joke and leaned over to tell his friends. In the middle of their guffaws, the stranger slipped away into the shadows of a dark alley.

The boys passed the jug around a few more times for courage, then one by one they picked up small items from the ground, the wharf, or nearby piles of cargo and eased their way toward the front of the crowd.

The fisherman's son took the last swallow from one of the bottles of ale. "Help, we're under attack!" he bellowed at the top of his lungs, and he hurled the bottle in the general direction of Lord Bight's guards. His friends threw their ammunition, and a virtual rain of bottles, rocks, bale hooks, and broken boards fell among the guards.

Several guards fell, bleeding and dazed. The rest drew their weapons with shouts of fury.

The crowd gasped like people startled out of a dream. They saw the fallen warriors, the drawn swords, and pandemonium broke loose.

Furious City Guards charged into the mob to capture the boys. Most of the people scattered, terrified, in all directions, but a few of the more observant ones jumped on three of the miscreants, and several others gave chase to the rest of the boys. The guards' horses reared and neighed in fright at the noise and rushing people. Officers shouted orders to their men.

The lord governor leaned forward, his hands on his knees, and drew a deep breath. His strength was temporarily depleted by his effort to calm the mob and the sudden shattering of his enchantment. His bodyguards, those still on their feet, immediately surrounded him in an impenetrable wall.

But Linsha saw little of this.

The heavy brown jug, crafted from red clay and fired to a rigid density, sailed through the air and crashed with unexpected accuracy on Commander Durne's head.

Stunned, the commander staggered back between two stacks of barrels, caught his heel on the edge of the pier, and toppled backward into the darkness.

Linsha shouted an oath. She put the cat and the ship's log on a barrel, then stripped off her sword and boots while peering over the edge of the pier. Fortunately for Durne, the tide was full and enough water swirled around the pylons to have saved him from a crushing fall. Unfortunately she couldn't see his body.

Before she had time to think about her folly, Linsha took a flying jump off the pier into the night-black waters of the harbor. Thank the gods, she had learned to swim well in both lake and river, and the water here was fairly smooth. There were no currents, undertows, or heavy waves, since the tide was about to turn. Nevertheless, it was very dark, and it stank of refuse.

She treaded water for a short time, looking frantically for the commander. She had landed close to the spot where he must have gone in, so she hoped to find him quickly. She didn't relish diving underwater in what was little more than a treacherous, submerged trash dump. And who knew what might lurk under that great pier? Linsha hated swimming in water she couldn't see through.

She pushed herself a little higher out of the water and scanned the dense shadows under the pier. Suddenly a yellowish gleam of light reflected on the water around her. Several guards leaned over the pier and held their torches at arm's length for her. It was enough. At the edge of the faint illumination, beside one of the large pylons, she caught a hint of red. Four strong strokes brought her to a body nearly submerged, clothed in red, and floating faceup in the slight swell. Blood oozed from a deep gash at his hairline, and his eyes were closed and unresponsive. She checked him quickly and was relieved to see a faint rise and fall in his chest.

"He's here!" she yelled. She cradled Durne's head in her arms and kicked out away from the pylons, where the other guards could see her. Thank Paladine, he wasn't wearing his armor. With fumbling fingers, she unfastened his belt and let his sword and dagger fall to the harbor bottom. She would apologize for that later.

"He's injured," she replied to anxious inquiries. "I can't see a ladder close by. I'm going to need a skiff or a rowboat. And hurry!"

The noise above had abated considerably, and more guards joined those on the pier with torches. Linsha concentrated on treading water and holding Durne's face above the surface. As worried as she was, she was grateful he was unconscious and not thrashing around in a drowning panic. All too soon, though, her arms and legs grew tired and her lungs ached from the struggle. She clasped him tighter and willed the men to hurry.

A loud splash nearby sent her heart racing, and she turned

as best she could to see what was in the water with her. Torch-light shone on a wet head and a pair of arms pulling toward her, and with a sigh of relief, she recognized Lord Bight.

The water seemed to rejuvenate the lord governor, for his eyes gleamed with strength and pleasure, and he swam about her like a creature born to the waves. Wordlessly he took Commander Durne's weight from her leaden arms and began to tow the soldier toward the dock. Linsha followed wearily behind.

Help came at last in a small rowboat someone finally found tied to a sloop nearby. Mica and Captain Dewald rowed out to Lord Bight, Linsha, and Durne and hauled them, dripping and smelly, into the boat.

Linsha crawled to the bow and collapsed on a small seat. "What took you so long?" she grumbled. "There're things under that dock bigger than I am."

Although she hadn't said what those things could be, she hid a small smile when Captain Dewald threw a startled glance at the darkness under the pier and hurriedly bent his back to the oars.

Mica leaned over Durne, his short, thick fingers surprisingly deft in their exploration of the commander's injury. "Lucky for him you got to him so quickly," the dwarf said to Lord Bight. "Stupid thing to do, falling off a pier," he added.

"I don't think he did it intentionally," said Linsha testily.

Mica ignored her. He placed the fingers of both hands on Durne's temples and closed his eyes. He mumbled a spell in his native tongue to help focus his effort in coaxing the healing magic from his heart.

Linsha soon saw why he was the healer to the governor. He was quick and he was good. By the time Dewald brought the boat to a small floating dock not far away, Durne was already conscious and his wound was closed.

The commander stared around in surprise at Linsha, soaked and bedraggled, at his governor sitting in a dripping tunic, at Mica leaning wearily against the gunwale of the small boat, at the water so close by, and at the concerned guards gathered on the dock. He put his hand to his head.

"What, what happened?" he wanted to know.

Lord Bight laughed heartily, as if jumping into the black waters of the harbor was something he did every night. "This young woman," he said, pointing at Linsha, 'seems to make a habit out of trying to save people. Tonight it was you."

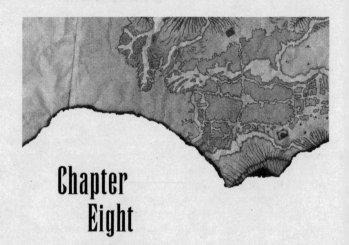

Chapter
Eight

The confusion was over and the crowd had dispersed by the time Linsha and Durne were helped back to the pier. A few guards nursed bruises and cuts from the rain of missiles, but only Commander Durne had been seriously hurt.

Linsha walked back to the barrel where the ship's cat still sat complacently on the logbook. She bent over to pick up her weapons, but she felt her legs begin to tremble, and before she could stop herself, she slid down with a thump and sagged back against the barrel. A reaction to what she had done settled into her bones and left her cold, shivering, and utterly spent. The cat jumped down into her lap and began to sniff her uniform tunic with great interest.

Meanwhile, five of youths had been caught, being too drunk to run far, and they knelt in a terrified row with their hands on their heads in front of a squad of angry City Guards. Their ringleader, the fisherman's son, knelt with the rest and bore a darkening bruise on one eye and a look of frightened defiance. He sank back onto his heels in obvious relief when the commander walked unsteadily to the pier.

Lord Bight wasted no time. He strode to the fisherman's son, grabbed his shirt, and hauled the youth bodily to his feet. The boy's jaw went slack and his eyes bulged in fear; any hint of defiance fled his broad face.

"Boy," the lord governor roared, "my guards tell me you are responsible for this fiasco. You will tell me in twenty words or less why you and your friends did something so stupid. And it had better be the truth, or you will spend a week in the stocks on top of your punishment for disturbing a public meeting, assaulting my guards, attempting to murder my commander, and inciting a panic."

The boy made one feeble attempt to speak, then his eyes rolled up and he fainted, from fear or spirits no one knew.

The governor dropped him in disgust and stepped to the next young man, a scrawny, dark-haired boy of about seventeen in the rough-weave clothing of a farmer. He stood over the youth, his brow dark and his eyes like a furnace.

"It was supposed to be a joke," the boy blurted before the governor said a word. "Just a joke! We didn't intend to kill anyone."

Lord Bight looked down at his prisoner like a lion about to pounce. "A joke?" he said in a voice as rough as a growl.

The boy blinked and plunged on. "Yes, my lord. We were laughing and roughhousing among ourselves when this man came up to see us. He had a bottle of dwarven spirits— smelled like mushrooms, you know. And he, uh, talked to us and gave us that jug."

"He said the speechifying had gone on long enough. How about a laugh to break it up?" offered another boy of about eighteen.

"A laugh?" repeated the governor harshly. He planted his fists on his hips and glared at them. "I almost lost two of my guards."

A younger boy started to snivel. He was so hunched over he looked like he wanted to melt into the planks of the pier. "We're sorry, Your Excellency. Really we are. We didn't think."

"Well, you'd better start thinking now. Who suggested throwing things?"

"The man did," said the third boy, eager to be helpful. "He said we should give the guards a scare."

"What did this man look like? Did any of you know him?"

They all shook their heads. "Kinda tall," offered the youngest.

The others pitched in, hoping to assuage the governor's anger.

"And black hair."

"No. Brown. And he had a beard."

"You dolt. Those were just heavy sideburns."

"Enough!" Lord Bight's order cracked like a whip. His voice took on a relentless certainty no one could disobey. "You will give your statements to the City Guards, including the names of the rest of your accomplices. The magistrate will charge you for malicious conduct and inciting a riot, and the guards will hold you in the dungeons for one week, which should give you plenty of time to think."

The five boys looked appalled, but not one said a word.

"If I ever catch you doing anything like this again, I will send you to the volcanic mines. Is that clear?"

There was a chorus of "Yes, sirs!" and the City Guards took the boys away.

Commander Durne grinned wearily at his governor. "I don't know what scared them more, you or the thought of the dungeons."

Lord Bight sighed and rubbed his jaw. "Both, I hope." He took a deep breath and as quickly as it came, his anger disappeared, to be replaced with a sad resignation. "This has been a hard day for us all. Perhaps I was a little hard on them."

Durne touched the newly healed gash on his aching head. "One week? I thought you were very fair." He looked thoughtfully at the empty boardwalk, the dark side streets, and the wharves stretching away on both sides. "Who do you think this mystery man could be? Is he just a troublemaker, or did he have a darker purpose?"

"Good question to ask, if you can find him."

"I will see what we can do." His eye came to Linsha, sitting by the barrel with the cat in her lap. "Did she really jump off the pier to rescue me?" he asked, still amazed by the courage it must have taken to leap into the harbor at night to save a drowning man.

A faint, knowing smile played over Hogan Bight's face and was gone before Durne noticed it. "Aren't you glad I did not take your advice?" he said lightly.

Together they walked to Linsha's barrel, and Lord Bight offered her his hand to help her to her feet. "Once again, you impress me, young Lynn. Not bad for your first day as my bodyguard."

Linsha managed a bow without falling over. She was so tired she could barely stay on her feet. "Thank you for your help, Your Excellency." She looked down at the cat in her arms. "What do I do with her?"

"Ah, yes. She seems to like you well enough. Take her to the palace stables, and if the captain of the *Whydah* survives, he can reclaim her."

Linsha chuckled. "I fear the cat likes me because I smell of rotten fish."

Lord Bight shot a glance at his own clothes and at Commander Durne's wet and rather fragrant uniform, and his eyes twinkled. "What an excellent way to begin a friendship." He wheeled around, calling for his horse, and strode off to prepare to leave.

Durne paused before joining him and said, "Thank you, Lynn." He stopped there, not knowing what else to say. It wasn't often he was obligated to another person for his life, especially to a lovely, bedraggled woman.

Linsha merely nodded, her eyes fastened on him. She noticed for the first time that beneath that wet uniform the commander had broad shoulders. Intrigued, she let her eyes roam lower and noted his wide chest, a trim waist . . . she suddenly coughed, and her cheeks grew hot. Good gods, what was she thinking about! To hide her unexpected embarrassment, she saluted and said, "You're welcome, sir. And I am sorry about your sword." Ducking her head, she picked up the logbook and hurried to find Windcatcher, leaving Durne looking perplexed.

The squads re-formed as before and rode off the pier into the quiet streets. As they clattered onto the paving stones of the road, a dark shape glided serenely overhead and slid into the darkness between two buildings.

"Did you see that?" one guard said to Linsha.

She smiled to herself and patted the cat sitting on Windcatcher's withers. "It was just an owl."

* * * * *

The day had turned into the furnace of midmorning when Linsha finally awoke. For a time she lay in the strange bed and stared at the strange ceiling and wondered where she was. Sleep still clung to her mind like a hangover, and her body felt too lethargic to move. She dozed a bit in the increasing heat, and the next time she opened her eyes, she remembered where she was and why.

The room she occupied was painted white and shone in the bright sun that gleamed through a narrow window across from her bed. The brightness helped to disguise the fact that the room was very small, hardly more than a cell. At least, she thought, rolling over and sitting up, she didn't have to put up with roommates. In a barracks full of men, that was a blessing.

Someone knocked at her doorway and stuck a head past the thick curtain that served as a door. "Oh, good. You're awake," said a fair-haired woman. "My name is Shanron. I was sent to see if you wanted something to eat."

Linsha put a hand to her empty belly. It had been a long time since her supper with Elenor. "Yes, that would be fine," she said gratefully.

"Good. There are clean clothes for you over there. We, uh, took the liberty of burning your old uniform for you. You'll get a new one this afternoon."

The lady Knight laughed at the expression of disgust on Shanron's face. "Thank you. I was going to bury it in the refuse pile." She looked down at herself and saw she was wearing an old shirt that once belonged to Elenor's husband. She vaguely remembered shedding the wet and reeking uniform and pulling this shirt on before she fell asleep, but nothing else. Her hand went to her hair.

Shanron interpreted her motions correctly. "No, you didn't have a chance to clean up last night. We have a bathing room downstairs, if you're interested."

Linsha stood up. "Show me the way," she said, the relief clear in her voice. Taking her clean clothes and an old linen towel, she stepped out of her room to follow Shanron.

Once in the corridor, she was able to see the whole woman, the only other woman who served with Lord Bight's personal guards. Shanron's mother had been a slave in a house of pleasure just before the Chaos War; her father was anybody's guess, although from the gold of her hair and the pale skin that refused to tan, Shanron guessed he was a southern barbarian. Like the warriors from the south, her body was taut with long tendons and smooth muscles, and of a height that enabled her to look down on quite a few men. She had a pleasant smile that she used often, and she seemed pleased to have another woman in the barracks.

Shanron set off down the hallway in a long, swinging stride and talked as she went. "Commander Durne told me you are to have the day to settle in and learn the schedules for duty and training. Tomorrow you will be evaluated by the weapons master and the horse master so you can be added to the duty roster." She ducked through a doorway and headed downstairs. "The main barracks are down here. Our rooms are on the top floor, under the roof really, with the rooms for the cooks and servants. It gets hot, but it's more private."

Linsha caught a quick glimpse of a long corridor with rows of partitioned cubicles before she had to hurry on after Shanron down another flight of stairs.

"In there," Shanron went on, pointing to the wall to their right, "is the undercroft. Mostly storage, but it is my favorite place." She stepped outside through an arched entry and gestured broadly toward a narrow gate in the high wall behind the barracks.

"A gate?" Linsha said in confusion.

"No. What's beyond it." Like a child with a secret, Shanron waved at her to follow and strode toward the gate.

The blare of a horn startled Linsha, and she wheeled around to look across the parade ground toward the governor's palace.

"That's just the horn to change the sentries on the upper battlements. They can't stay up there too long in this heat. Come on before you burn your feet," Shanron called.

Linsha realized the other woman was right. The parade ground was grassy, to cut down on the dust around the palace. But the paths around the big courtyard were stone, which held the heat like an oven. Already her bare soles felt the effect. Quickly she hopped after her guide across the path and through the gate. From hot stone, her feet stepped onto warm grass, and she slowed to a stop and looked around in wonderment.

They had entered a garden redolent in the morning heat and filled with the heavy scents of gardenias, jasmine, and roses. Thick vines covered the walls, and groves of acacias, golden raintrees, and birches offered scattered oases of shade. A reflecting pool sat in the center, cool and inviting, and rimmed with a wall of blue granite. White lotus flowers floated on its surface. To the right sat a small domed building, its entrance shaded by a loggia of carved wood.

"This is one of Governor Bight's gardens," Shanron told Linsha. "Being a bodyguard has its privileges, and this is one of them. That is the bathhouse," she said, pointing to the stone building. "Enjoy. I shall be out here lounging by the pool and guarding the door until you are finished."

The lady Knight walked under the loggia and stepped into the stone building. Beyond the door was a lattice of carved wood that matched the loggia, and behind it was a pillared room with a domed ceiling and a sunken pool perhaps ten feet around, three feet deep, and filled with gloriously clean water. The room was light and airy, hinting at windows somewhere, but Linsha couldn't see them through the curtains of white gauze that hung between the pillars. A light breeze played through the building and danced with the gauzy hangings.

Linsha couldn't believe her luck. She hadn't had a real deep-water bath since her arrival in Sanction. She'd always had to make do with a basin of water or a quick, and expensive, rinse off in one of the public bathhouses offered by some of the inns.

An attendant came to help her undress and to find the scented soaps and oils, then withdrew at Linsha's request and left the Knight to her bath in solitude. To Linsha, after days of heat, humidity, dust, toil, and last night's dunking in the dirty harbor, the cool water was blissful. She soaped and rinsed and soaped and soaked until her skin wrinkled and her hair was squeaky clean.

Reluctantly she left the pool at last and dressed in the loose, flowing robe and baggy pants someone had left in her room. The clothes were lightweight and comfortable for hot weather and fit her well enough. And they were much more feminine than anything Lynn usually wore.

She walked out of the bathhouse into the brazen sun and stopped so fast she almost stumbled. Commander Durne had one foot on the low wall surrounding the reflecting pool, and resting his elbow on his bent knee, he leaned forward to talk to Shanron. His pose was casual, friendly, and relaxed; his smile was full of humor and charm. Shanron reclined on the wall in front of him, her long legs stretched toward him, her weight resting on one arm as she dangled a hand in the water. They laughed together as friends, but were they intimates?

Linsha was amazed and dismayed by a pang of jealousy that flared out of nowhere. It was no matter to her what their relationship happened to be. She was too busy, and in too precarious a position, to even consider harboring feelings for anyone, let alone her commander. She fixed a smile of tranquil welcome on her features and joined the two by the pool.

The commander turned his pale aquamarine eyes to her.

Linsha had seen those eyes convey many emotions, but it surprised her to recognize the pleasure, surprise, and interest she saw there while he slowly appraised her.

"There is more beneath that rough exterior than one would imagine," he said.

The remark sent a chill sparkling down Linsha's spine. Should she be flattered or wary? Did he simply mean she cleaned up well, or could he see beyond the disguise of Lynn the alley-basher to another woman? She had to remember he was a potential threat, a stranger and a loyal official in the government of a man her order had sent her to investigate. Just because she risked her life to save him didn't mean there could be any emotional attachment.

Linsha abruptly twisted her fingers into her linen towel and tore her eyes away from his face. "Did you say something about a meal?" she said to Shanron. The words came out too quickly to her ears, but she hoped no one else would notice.

Shanron lifted her long frame from the wall and climbed to her feet. "A little better than a bath in the harbor, isn't it?"

The sincere smile that warmed Linsha's face brightened her eyes and brought a rose blush to the freckles that dotted her cheeks. "It was utter paradise."

Ian Durne blinked and looked at her again thoughtfully, disarmed and diverted by a loveliness he hadn't noticed before. His mouth opened as if he wanted to say something, then snapped shut with a second thought. Abruptly he drew himself together. His light eyes turned away. He nodded to the two women. "I will leave you to your duties."

Shanron returned his nod. Since she wasn't in uniform, she wasn't required to salute. If she noticed anything unusual about Linsha's or Durne's behavior, she kept it to herself. As she led her companion toward the big kitchens and the eating hall she told Linsha the functions of some of the other outer buildings, the granary, the smithy, and the brewing house. She pointed out the location of the privies, the training hall, and the central well and introduced Linsha to the half a dozen guards they passed. She dropped no hint of a friendship with Durne, and Linsha didn't ask. The lady Knight was happy to let the subject drop.

The eating hall was filled with guards coming in for the noon meal. They made Linsha welcome and had her repeat the story of her jump into the harbor in her own words. Her reputation, under scrutiny as a new recruit, rose several notches, for Commander Durne was liked by his men and commanded their respect.

Linsha hungrily ate of the simple but hearty food, and afterward she begged a plate of scraps from the cook to take to the cat. He grumped about feeding useless strays, but after listening to several of Linsha's heartfelt compliments, he gave her a bowl of stew meat and some fish scraps.

Outside the hall, Shanron took her leave. "I'm on sentry duty this afternoon," she explained, "but I will see you tonight. Go to the armorer, over there, to see the tailor about your uniform and talk to Captain Dewald. He's filling out the duty roster. Oh, and squires may not leave the palace grounds without permission and only in the company of another guard. So no shopping without me." She waved and hurried off to don her own uniform.

Linsha carried her scraps to the stable and was pleased to see Windcatcher happily settled in an airy stall with a full hayrack and fresh water.

An old groom ambled up to greet her. "She's a fine mare. Glad to have her. That for the cat? No wonder the captain wanted to save her. She's caught three rats already. She's up in the hayloft. And go quietly! We have an owl up there. Just appeared, so don't scare it off." He winked at her and ambled off without waiting for a reply.

Bemused by the groom's rapid-fire announcements, Linsha chuckled to herself. She found the ladder to the hayloft on the far right of the long row of stalls and climbed slowly up, balancing the two bowls of food in one hand. The loft was hot, dusty, and close. Stacks of hay filled the loft almost to the roof beams in some places and made intriguing hills and valleys where it had been forked into racks below.

Linsha moved deeper into the interior and peered around

in the dim light. She whistled softly, the cry of a mourning dove, and from somewhere in the shadowy rafters came a reply. She tried to spot the owl, but Varia's russet coloration and barred feathers made her very difficult to spot in poor light.

A shape detached itself from a beam and came floating down toward her. "There you are at last," called a whispery voice. "I have been waiting for you."

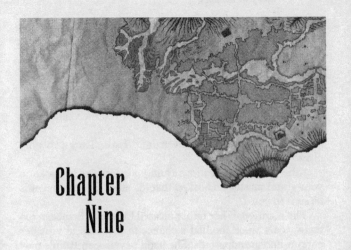

Chapter Nine

Linsha made herself comfortable in a pile of hay and put the bowls on the floor. She was about to ask the owl for her news when something rustled in the hay nearby. The calico cat walked sedately around a mound, a mouse in her mouth, and padded up to the owl.

Linsha watched warily in case the bird or the cat threatened the other, but the cat laid the mouse by Varia's talons and meowed softly.

If the owl could have grinned, Varia would have been smiling from ear tuft to ear tuft. Her golden eyes blinked, and she delicately laid a foot on the gift. "I like this cat," she told Linsha with a soft hiss.

The woman's eyes widened. "She's bringing you mice?"

"We have an understanding. I was supposed to ask you to bring fish for her because that's what she prefers, but I see you've already anticipated this."

Linsha, who had not anticipated any part of this, pushed

the bowls of stew and fish scraps toward the cat and watched, amazed, as each animal enjoyed its meal.

As soon as the last bit of mouse disappeared, she leaned forward and whispered, "What news do you have? Did you see Lady Karine?"

The owl hopped to a pile of hay close to Linsha. "I did. She is pleased and will pass on the word to the Clandestine Circle."

Linsha couldn't help but grunt. "Huh. They probably already know."

"She passes on greetings from your father. He spoke to your grand master and asked that his affections and regards be sent to you."

The mention of her father pleased Linsha. It had been too many years since she had a chance to go home to visit her parents and grandparents. She hadn't even seen Palin's new Academy of Sorcery that he built in Solace.

"She also told me to tell you to be careful," the owl went on. "You have been on the death ship, in town, among the dead. She is afraid you could become sick."

A cold, crawling fear rolled in Linsha's belly like a snake rousing from sleep, a fear made more uncomfortable by her long absence from her parents. What if she never saw them again? "I have thought of that," she responded slowly, "but I don't know what I can do." She paused when another painful thought occurred to her. "Lord Bight was on the ship, too. What if he dies from this plague?"

That event would certainly shake the state of affairs in the eastern half of the Newsea. Who would move faster to claim his authority, the Dark Knights, the Solamnic Knights, or the black dragon, Sable?

Linsha was quiet for a time, lost in thought. "I saw you at the harbor last night," she said after a while.

"Yes. I saw you, too, jumping off that pier after a man you hardly know." The owl chuckled deep in her chest. "I almost sent some pelicans to fish you out."

"Did you see the man who incited those boys?"

"I didn't notice him until he left, and even then I regret I did not know the significance of his departure until he was already well on his way. I lost him in a street of busy taverns."

"Would you recognize him again?" Linsha asked.

"Maybe. He had dark hair and a distinctive gait. Do you think he may be important?"

"I don't know." Linsha absently pushed the curls off her forehead. "Watch for him, Varia. Keep listening. Something doesn't feel right."

"Of course," the owl replied. She was quite good at hiding in trees or rooftops or making herself invisible in the shadows. She had become Linsha's eyes and ears in the night-filled streets of Sanction. She hooted softly. "Always trust your instincts."

Linsha slapped her hands on her thighs and pushed herself upright. "Well, my instincts tell me now I'd better go before that groom wonders what I'm doing."

The cat licked the last of the drippings from the bowls and curled up beside the owl.

"Don't forget to bring more fish," Varia trilled as Linsha made her way to the ladder.

* * * * *

The captain of the *Whydah* never had a chance to reclaim his cat. Shortly after the sun rose and the steaming heat returned, he collapsed from fever and dehydration and was laid upon a pallet. Kelian, the woman healer who had visited his ship and returned to organize the sick house, used her mystic power to sooth his fever and tried to still the raging sickness in his abdomen that caused the deadly dehydration. It dismayed her how much energy it took to give him ease, yet most of his symptoms seemed to disappear and the red blotches on his skin faded. She fed him herbal infusions and beef broth to give him strength and kept a close watch on his progress. But all too soon the rest of his crew began to fall ill, and then the harbormaster's wife, Angelan, and others who'd had direct contact with the *Whydah's* crew succumbed. Some fell into feverish delusions and violent hallucinations and had to be forcibly restrained. Kelian didn't know which symptoms were harder to treat, the rapid decline from dehydration or the delirious terrors.

The rest of the patients in quarantine were terrified and would have fled if the City Guards had not forcibly detained them. Before long, the healer and her assistants were exhausted, their powers spent, and those like the captain, who'd had a remission, slipped back into fever and delirium. Kelian held back her tears and summoned more help.

Shortly after noon the next day, a decree came from the governor's palace in both a written proclamation that was nailed to special notice boards set aside for city information and in a verbal announcement that was spread by the town criers all over the city. The decree detailed the Sailors' Scourge, for that is what the healers called it, and its symptoms and ordered all those with any health problems to report to the healers at the warehouse.

For the first time, the inner city took this plague seriously and the outer city began to panic. No one knew how the contagion spread, so how could anyone defend against it? It could have been caused by evil spirits, foul air from the volcano, insects, or even a curse spoken by any one of Sanction's numerous enemies. The streets boiled with rumors. The sales of amulets and herbs that were reputed to ward off disease escalated like a gnome's skyrocket.

In the manner of all frightened populations, different groups reacted in their own ways. Some people stockpiled food and water in their houses, locked their doors, and refused to come out, while others went to the nearest tavern to indulge as much as possible before death found them. A few packed their goods and left the city by the first available ship. A few more thought of the long-departed gods and wondered if this wouldn't be a good time for them to come back. Although the harbor continued to function as usual, there was an underlying tension in the faces of everyone who ventured out. Only the kender and the gully dwarves seemed unbothered by the currents of fear around them.

Some of those who knew they'd had contact with the

death ship, or the *Whydah* and its crew, appeared at the warehouse to talk to the healer. Kelian was weary and feeling overwhelmed, but she did her best to examine and reassure everyone who came. Six were already showing the early signs of the disease, and they were immediately quarantined. The ones that concerned the healer the most, though, were not those who came to see her but those who'd been with the *Whydah's* crew and kept their mouths shut. If they became ill and stayed away, they could help spread the contagion among the unsuspecting.

By day's end, new healers and more supplies arrived at the sick house for those in quarantine. There were now twenty-seven people in various stages of the illness, the captain and the harbormaster's wife being in the worst condition. Kelian did her best to keep the captain alive, but he slipped too far beyond her reach. He died late that night. Even as she helped her assistant roll the body into a tarp to be taken away, the healer realized her own throat burned with a fierce thirst. When morning came, her face was marked with livid blotches, and by noon she was delirious.

* * * * *

"Keep your hands up. Keep them up! Protect your face," bellowed the weapons master for the tenth time that morning.

Linsha obeyed by lifting her elbow higher than it should have been, leaving her chest exposed. As she guessed he would, the weapons master threw up his arms and stamped over to rearrange her defensive posture.

"You are a master with a sword," he complained. "How can you be such a dolt in hand-to-hand fighting?"

"Because I've never let anyone get this close!" she replied testily.

In truth, Linsha was an expert in two forms of martial arts—also the dagger, the short sword, the rapier, and assorted weapons from other cultures. But Lynn would not be. Lynn of Gateway was a sell-sword with no formal training, which meant Linsha had to disguise her abilities and pretend she knew few of the advanced moves in the strategy of self-defense.

"Lynn, by the gods, I don't know how you've survived as long as you have."

"I'll take that as a compliment." In one flowing movement, she slid her dagger from its sheath, flipped it in the air, caught it by the hilt, and slid it neatly back into the sheath at her belt.

The corners of his mouth turned up in a half-smile. The master's head was level with her own and bore a long braid of graying black. His arms and legs were muscular but trim as those of a runner or wrestler, and he walked with the slow grace of a panther. He pointed to a straw target against the wall of the training hall and said, "You may not be able to fight with a dagger, but I'll wager a steel piece you can throw it."

Linsha's dagger left her hand before the words died in the air, and before he noticed what she was doing, she snatched his blade out of his belt sheath and threw it, too. Both daggers penetrated the black center of the target and hung there quivering. She turned and gave him a demure smile. "You'd win. Like I said, I don't let people too close to me."

"In that, you are quite skilled. Still, young woman, there will be times when an opponent slips past your guard and moves closer than you want." So saying, he took a quick step behind her, struck with his foot to knock her off-balance, and flipped her over his back to the dirt floor.

Ruefully Linsha tried to take a deep breath. As she stared up at her instructor, her chagrin turned to embarrassment. Commander Durne had joined the master and leaned over to examine her. He flashed one of his glowing smiles and offered her a hand. Her face hot, Linsha accepted his hand—it would have been rude to do otherwise—but she dropped it the moment she bounced to her feet.

Durne's cool blue eyes actually twinkled. "Does she pass muster?"

"She'll do," the master said, crossing his arms. "She is superb with a sword, but as expected with one of her background, she is weak in the arts of personal defense. We will concentrate on that."

"Excellent."

Linsha allowed herself a mental sigh of relief and got busy dusting off her pants and new tunic. She walked to the target and retrieved the two daggers. With a bow, she returned the master's blade to him and pushed her own back in place.

"Have you attended the horse master yet?" Durne wanted to know. When she shook her head, he gestured to the entrance. "Then if you are finished here, I will walk with you."

The weapons master saluted the commander, nodded to Linsha, and left to attend to other duties.

Durne fell in beside Linsha as they walked into the blazing heat outside and moved toward the stable. At first he said nothing.

Linsha glanced up at his handsome profile so close by and swiftly tore her eyes away. She hated the way her heart was beating.

Finally he spoke, and his voice was very different from the brusque, powerful speech he used with other men. "I admit I was reluctant to accept you into the guards when Lord Bight told me he wanted to give you a chance. I didn't think you were equal to the duty." He chuckled and unconsciously rubbed the newly healed scar on his forehead. "You are proving me wrong."

Linsha felt her heart contract from the warmth in his voice. Yet another voice, a silent knell of reason deep in her head, sounded a warning. She couldn't let him get too close or see beyond her mask; she could never reveal her unexpected attraction to him.

"Glad to do so, Commander," Linsha said with a mischievous smirk. She added a bit of swagger to her walk. "So you and Shanron having a bit on the side?"

The words flew out of her mouth before Linsha knew what possessed her to say such a thing. The question was certainly in keeping with Lynn's crude persona, but Linsha's face flamed to her auburn roots, and she was so astonished by her temerity she nearly stumbled over her own feet. Commander Durne slowed, his face filled with displeased surprise. Angry at herself, Linsha scrambled to think of something to say.

Before she could apologize or make any move, he said, with an edge as sharp as a sword blade, "By the staff of Hiddukel, you are an impertinent wench."

Wench? Plenty of men had called her that in the past, but she'd never grown used to it. She hated that patronizing appellation, whether it was spoken by a half-drunk Khur in a tavern or by the commander of the Governor's Guards. Linsha jumped on the opportunity to hide behind her chagrin and anger. Her green eyes turned to green fire, and the red of embarrassment on her face faded to a fiery clay of outrage. She planted her hands on her hips and said tightly, "What I said was out of line and I regret it, but don't call me "wench" again, or I'll rip your tongue off at the root."

Several guards grooming their horses nearby turned around in surprise and stared at the sight of a new recruit yelling at the commander like a back-street ruffian.

Commander Durne's brows rammed together. His lips thinned to pale lines. When he spoke, his voice was quiet, implacable. "You are no longer on the streets of the waterfront. Do not use that tone with me again. Nor will you issue threats against a commanding officer in this unit. If you do, you will be dismissed from service and removed from this city. Is that clear?"

Not one word was spoken above a calm, moderate tone, but Linsha felt as if she had been punched. Her mouth opened, then closed with a click. She knew she had gone too far. It was time to beat a hasty retreat. Taking a step back, she snapped to attention and brought her fingers to her chest in a crisp salute. "I apologize, Commander," she said, loud enough for the other guards to hear.

He directed a soul-freezing glare at her, then turned on his heel and marched away, his back as straight as a board under his scarlet surcoat.

A sigh, soft as a whisper, escaped Linsha as she watched him go. Well, if her rudeness didn't alienate him, nothing would, she thought. He would probably report her offensive behavior to Lord Bight and avoid contact with her from now on. Linsha sighed again. She allowed her heart to indulge in self-pity for just a moment. It wasn't fair. It wasn't fair that the first man she liked and respected and felt any desire for in too many years would have to be someone she dared not have. The Clandestine Circle would have her sword if they knew.

Linsha ignored the smirks on the faces of the watching guards and went sadly into the stable to saddle Windcatcher and report to the horse master.

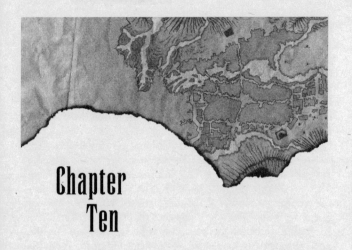

Chapter
Ten

Mount Thunderhorn did not blow "at any moment" as Elder Chan Dar had predicted. Instead, the dome near the summit of the volcano slowed its growth and festered like a huge, steaming boil on the face of the peak. Since it showed no immediate inclination to burst, Lord Bight took advantage of the respite to do a complete inspection of the lava dike encircling Sanction. For a full day he rode with a squad of his bodyguards and a team of dwarf stonemasons, examining the entire length of the fiery moat.

Linsha rode with them, a squire in training, observed, and kept her mouth shut. She hadn't paid much attention before to the maintenance of the moat and its retaining walls, and she stared, fascinated, while Lord Bight and the dwarf engineer, Chert, studied the walls and the sluggish flow of the red-gold molten stone and made their decisions on what sections needed repair and which ones could wait for another time. A few places had eroded dangerously close to the softer earth and needed immediate attention.

At these points, Lord Bight stood close to the fiery moat, drew on his power, and diverted the lava long enough for the dwarves to remove the failing slabs of rock and replace them with new slabs skillfully cut to fit neatly into place. Then Lord Bight smoothed over the new wall, casting a spell to help seal it from the intense heat and friction of the flowing lava.

Although Linsha witnessed this process twice that day, try as she might to understand what the governor was doing, she couldn't discern how he drew on his magic. It was widely believed among the Solamnics that he was a powerful geomancer, yet he did not verbally invoke any words of power or use complicated spells. All through the long, hot afternoon, she racked her thoughts to decide if he was drawing on the ancient magic that fueled the sorcery her father taught at his academy, using the mystic energy of the living spirit, or using some hidden item charmed with the old high sorcery of the gods. Magic was difficult to use in any form, and as far as anyone knew, Lord Bight had never trained at the Academy of Sorcery or at the Citadel of Light. Nevertheless, he wielded his power with subtle effectiveness and enigmatic strength.

When the inspection was complete and the lord governor and his guards rode back late that night, Linsha was perplexed and impressed, but no closer to understanding the secret of Lord Bight's power.

The following morning, the day after the death of the captain of the *Whydah* and the announcement of the governor's decree, Lord Bight rode out to check the progress of the aqueduct and to meet with the tax collectors to establish the tax rates for the approaching harvest season and make provisions for hardships resulting from the hot, dry weather. To her disappointment, Linsha did not go with him this time, for she was ordered to attend her training and learn more of her new duties at the palace. She reported as ordered to the weapons master and the master of recruits and hoped she wouldn't draw the attention of Commander Durne. The commander, she was told, was busy with the City Guards in the harbor district. May he stay perpetually busy, she thought, and forget all about me.

That hope was banished the fourth day of her service.

As soon as she finished her noon meal, Commander Durne was there barking orders for her to don her full uniform and attend a meeting of the Governor's Advisory Council as an observer. As silent as a statue, he waited for her, then escorted her to the large audience hall in the palace and positioned her by a window and a wordless guard.

"Do not talk. Just pay attention. Lord Bight will be here shortly," Durne said before he left the chamber.

Linsha could only salute and obey.

Patiently she balanced her weight on both feet and prepared to wait for a long time. She did not try to talk to the motionless guard across the window from her. He did not speak, move, or even glance her way. His hand rested on a light spear at his side, and a sword hung at his waist.

To her right, the long, narrow window was open to catch a slight breeze, and if Linsha leaned back a little, she could see the hazy, hot sky and, in the distance, the trailing plume of smoke from Mount Thunderhorn caught on an westerly wind. The guard softly cleared his throat in warning, and Linsha straightened in time to see the first of the officials arrive for the meeting: Chan Dar, the leader of the newly organized Farmer's Guild, accompanied by his assistant. Both men were lean and baked brown from days of hard work in the fields, and both looked slightly uncomfortable in the long, flowing robes adopted by the city's elders. They glanced around the hall, perhaps surprised that they were the first to arrive.

A long table with cushioned chairs set around it had been arranged in the center of the hall. A servant, arrived bearing a tray with a pitcher of cooled wine and plates of honey cakes, plums, and date bread. He showed the two elders to their places at the table, laid the tray before them, and left them to fetch more trays.

Chan Dar had no sooner poured himself a cup of wine than Lutran Debone, head of the City Council, bustled in with two assistants, a scribe, and a small boy bearing a fan.

Linsha saw Chan Dar roll his eyes in such an exaggerated expression of dislike, she had to stifle a smile.

"Ah, good day to you, Chan Dar," Lutran greeted heartily. "I see your fields are still free of the burning rivers of lava from Mount Thunderborn."

The farmer snorted. "Not that it makes much difference. The heat and the lack of rain are shriveling our crops as surely as a volcano's eruption," he replied, his long face morose.

The portly elder took his seat across from the farmer. He did not make a reply while his boy poured wine and fetched cakes and arranged the cushions just so. When at last he was comfortable and the scribe had settled himself on a bench nearby, Lutran clucked his tongue. "What about your new irrigation system you pushed through council last year? Is it not finished yet?"

Chan Dar steepled his fingers and cast a withering glance at his colleague. "You know well it is not. Not after your ploys delayed the money to pay the wages of the laborers. Thanks to your petty interference, the canals weren't finished in time to catch the spring runoff."

"My petty interference?" Lutran looked shocked that anyone would think such a thing. "If I remember correctly, it was one of your farmers who brought up the land dispute and your engineers who bickered over the layout of the canals."

"Problems that were quickly settled, but the laborers—"

"Are you two worrying that same bone again?" said an unfamiliar voice from the door.

Linsha turned her head just enough to see a woman enter the hall. She recognized her immediately—Asharia, the priestess of the Temple of the Heart. Although Linsha had never had the opportunity or need to meet Asharia, she knew the middle-aged priestess by reputation. Not one to be content to stay in her temple, Asharia organized the refugee camp north of the city, ran a small temple school for those who wished to study the mystic arts, kept a regular schedule of healers available to help the citizens of the city, and served on the City Council. She admitted forthrightly that she was not an exceptional healer, but any lack she had was more than compensated by her organizational skills and her enthusiasm. Linsha suspected the lord governor had her on his council to act as a buffer between the bickering elders.

Asharia walked sedately to a chair beside Elder Lutran and smoothed her long gown before she sat down. The men glowered at each other but let their argument slide away. The priestess was known to have a sharp wit and a scorching tongue.

As soon as Asharia seated herself, the rest of the Governor's Advisory Council arrived. Mica the dwarf, with an armful of scrolls, parchments, and books, stamped to the table and dumped his burden on the polished surface. He straightened his garments and flicked off some lint from his sleeve before he sat beside the priestess. Vanduran Lor, head of Sanction's powerful Merchants' Guild, came with the chief magistrate for the city. The new harbormaster, looking young and ill at ease, walked in next, followed by Lord Bight's treasurer, the governor's scribe, and last of all Ian Durne, Commander of the City Guard.

They took their places around the table while servants brought more wine and finger foods and served the refreshments. Only Lord Bight's chair remained empty. The company made small talk in hushed tones among themselves while they waited. Even Lutran stopped annoying Chan Dar and concentrated on his wine and cakes.

Linsha tried not to fidget, but she was hot in the new uniform and unaccustomed to standing still for so long. Sweat trickled down her lower back and itched maddeningly around her waist. When she shifted slightly to scratch it, she caught Commander Durne's warning eye on her and froze in place.

Bootsteps echoed in the hall, drawing her attention, and Lord Bight entered from a separate doorway. The council members rose to their feet and bowed as one. Linsha studied Lord Bight appreciatively as he strode to the large chair at the head of the table. The governor had put aside the simple clothing he preferred to wear and was dressed in a formal robe of the finest linen and silk, dyed a rich golden brown. Thick gold threads embroidered the hem of the robe and its sleeves, and a gold belt hugged his waist. He wore a heavy collar of gold, studded with tiger's eyes and topaz, and a simple gold circlet in his thick blond hair.

The governor inclined his head to the council and asked them to sit. He remained standing at the head of the table and leaned forward, his hands resting lightly on the wood. "I've called this special session of the Governor's Council to discuss the disaster that is building in the harbor district. For those of you who do not know all the details, Mica will tell us about the contagion and how it is spreading."

The dwarf pushed aside a pile of papers and scrolls and drew out a list. "From the reports I received this morning, there are now thirty-five people stricken with the disease at the sick house, and there are rumors that the disease is starting to break out in the Street of the Courtesans and the northern neighborhoods. Besides the entire crew of the death ship, there have been nineteen deaths that we know of. That includes most of the crew of the *Whydah*, the harbormaster and his wife, and the serving girl from the tavern where the last sailor died. Worst of all, there doesn't seem to be any protection from it. Once a person becomes ill, he or she usually dies within two days."

"Two days!" repeated Chan Dar in dismay. The farmer had been busy outside the city in the farms of the vale and had not, until today, learned of the virulence of the disease. "What is this plague?"

Mica tossed his list down and leaned back in his chair. "I don't know. I have found no records of anything like it. We have had agues that are similar and plagues of buboes that are as deadly, but I've never seen a sickness with this combination of symptoms. The skin discolorations are very unusual. For lack of a better name, we have been calling it the Sailors' Scourge."

Lutran had been nervously sipping his wine while Mica

spoke, and he gestured to his boy to pour some more. "But what about the healers?" he asked as the boy splashed the light white wine into his goblet.

Asharian answered for Mica. "Our healers are doing what they can. Unfortunately, this disease drains a great deal of energy to bring it under control. I have sent more healers to the sick house, but . . . even healers are not immune. Already two of our healers have died."

"Are there any persons who have had contact with the death ship or the sick crew who have not become ill?" Chan Dar wanted to know.

Mica nodded. His broad fingers drummed on the table as he thought. "Apparently some kender shared an ale with one of the *Whydah's* crew. They reported to the sick house but have not become ill. They're driving the healers crazy trying to help. And two full-blooded dwarves. It could be that human blood is the most susceptible to this sickness. Interestingly, only two of the minotaur crew that repaired the *Whydah* are sick."

Lutran groaned. "Human blood. That's most of our population."

"Lord Governor," Vanduran spoke up. He shifted in his chair to face Lord Bight. "I, too, have heard the rumors that the disease is spreading into other areas. Not everyone is obeying the law of quarantine. The merchants are getting worried, not only for their own safety, but for the health of Sanction's economy. Already we've had several ships turn away before they loaded their cargoes. Other shipments are sitting on the wharves and rotting. Half of the dockhands did not come to work today. They are terrified of catching this plague. What can we do to stem this disease before the news leaks out to the rest of Ansalon and we are ruined?"

Lord Bight stood and paced slowly back and forth. The council watched him quietly, for he appeared to be deep in thought and no one wanted to interrupt him. To Linsha's surprise, he walked over to her window and stood beside her, looking out, yet his mind was far away, and his golden eyes looked deep into visions only he could see.

Ignoring Commander Durne, Linsha turned her head and looked directly at the lord governor's profile. She wondered what was going on inside his head.

"Much and little," he said, so softly only she could hear.

She started and stared at him, astonished. Had he understood her thoughts? No, that was impossible . . . she hoped. He cocked his head slightly, one eyebrow raised. "First it's pirates and volcanoes, then it's the Dark Knights at the back door, the Legion at the front door, the Solamnics at the side door, and the black dragon next door. Then it's taxes, clean water, farmland, refuse disposal, just laws, security, shipping rights, and refugees. Now it's a plague. What next—the return of the gods? You know," he said to Linsha as if he was about to impart a long-kept secret, "it's not easy being lord governor."

And by Paladine, if he didn't wink at her!

In spite of the tension and the seriousness of the situation, Linsha wanted to laugh. That, she thought, was one of the things she liked about him, the self-confident rascal in him that could not take things too seriously because he was convinced he could handle any crisis, no matter how small or large.

Linsha lifted her chin a little and said in her most serious tone of voice, "Aye, Lord. But you're so good at it."

"Yes," he said, grinning at her. The glint of humor was still in his eyes when he turned back to the puzzled council and resumed his pacing. "This plague," he said, raising his voice so they all could hear, "is threatening to destroy everything we have built here." He took three long strides back to the table and banged his fist on the wood. "We have put too much into this city to let this plague rip it out of our grasp. We will find a solution no matter what it takes or how bitter it is to swallow. That means," he added with a meaningful look at Lutran and Chan Dar, "that we will have to work together, without the usual bickering. I expect total cooperation from everyone here."

Chan Dar rubbed his chin thoughtfully. "Does that mean from the volcano, too?"

The others stared at him to see if he was serious. The

farmer was usually so pessimistic and humorless they never expected him to try a joke.

"Absolutely," Lord Bight replied, deadpan. "Thunderhorn has already agreed not to blow his dome until this crisis has passed."

The farmer nodded. "That's a relief."

Asharian burst out laughing and the others followed suit. The image of a volcano promising to be agreeable was ludicrous, but they had all seen enough of Lord Bight's power to know anything was possible when he put his mind to it, and that thought was reassuring.

Lord Bight sat down in his chair, poured some wine, and lifted his goblet in a silent toast to the farmer. Chan Dar's lips lifted in a slight smile and he returned the gesture.

The tension broken, the council immersed itself in the business of helping its city. It took several hours of discussion, of poring over lists and examining different ideas, but by late afternoon, the governor was satisfied that his council was prepared to handle the crisis. The most difficult part, they all knew, would be convincing the people that some of these emergency plans had to be enforced for their own good. Supplies had to be hoarded, water had to be stored and rationed. The work on the aqueducts would have to be pushed ahead, at the expense of other projects. The sick needed care, and the dead had to be cremated as soon as possible. Normal commerce would continue as long as the health of the city allowed.

However, for the sake of incoming vessels with cargo to unload, the new harbormaster suggested isolating the end of the long southern pier. Ships could moor there, unload their cargoes, and leave without endangering their crews. It would slow work considerably, but he reasoned, it would reassure ships' captains and help prevent the spread of this strange malady outside Sanction.

Priestess Asharia straightened up at that. "How do we know the disease hasn't struck somewhere else? Where did the crew of the galley pick it up?"

"I've read the ship's log," Mica said, sounding irritated. "There is no indication of what happened. Everything was normal up to four days before they reached Sanction. After that, the log is blank. Listen." He yanked a leather-bound logbook out of his pile and opened to a page marked with a scrap of fabric. " 'Fourth day of Fierswelt'—that's twelve days ago," he added with a slightly patronizing tilt of his nose. " 'Two days out of Haligoth. Brisk winds. Clear skies. Logged twenty miles by midwatch. Lookout reported seeing a blue dragon, but no one else confirmed.' " He laid the book down. "That is the last entry."

The harbormaster waved a hand toward the harbor. "But where were they?"

"Somewhere in the Newsea," the dwarf said.

"That's helpful. The Newsea is rather large," Lutran grumbled.

The priestess laid a firm hand on Mica's arm before the dwarf said something rude. "That still doesn't answer my question," she pressed. "Has the disease struck somewhere else? Perhaps someone has found a cure for this."

Vanduran rubbed his hand down his gray beard. "Our merchants haven't heard of a plague anywhere else this summer. And with their nose for profits, they would be some of the first to know."

Linsha listened thoughtfully and pondered how much of this tangled mystery was truth and how much was evasion. Any of these people could be misleading the council for reasons of his own and using the citizens of Sanction as pawns in a deadly game of power. Even the Clandestine Circle told her they knew nothing about the plague, but she knew all too well they didn't disclose information when it suited their purposes. Perhaps they were aware of other outbreaks and concealed it from her.

"Check with your contacts again, Guildman Vanduran," Lord Bight suggested. "We must examine all possibilities, no matter how vague."

"There is another contingency we should discuss before we end the meeting." Commander Durne leaned forward in his chair, his features set in a grim expression. "What if the plague spreads out of control in the outer city? Do we bar the gates to protect the inner city?"

"No," said Vanduran forcefully.

"Yes," said Lutran and the treasurer together.

The others looked at their nails or at the tapestries on the walls.

Lord Bight tapped his fingers on the table. "That is an option we will discuss later. Such an act could overly alarm the population and cause more harm than good. The city should not be divided. It needs to work as a whole to halt this plague now, before it spreads out of our control."

One after another, the council members nodded and made their assurances, and the meeting came to an end. Armed with plans and the support of the other advisers, they bade farewell to the governor and went out the door talking among themselves. At last only Lord Bight, Commander Durne, and the silent guards were left in the large hall. Late afternoon sunlight slanted through the tall windows and splashed on the sea-green floor. A breeze, strong from the west and the open waters of the Newsea, blew through the open windows and made the tapestries ripple like living ribbons of color.

Lord Bight rose slowly to his feet, his gaze lost in some inner contemplation. "I will be gone for two days, Commander. Do not alert anyone. I leave you in charge."

Concealing his surprise, Commander Durne stood, too. "May I ask where you are going? I will arrange a unit of guards to go with you."

"You may ask," Lord Bight responded lightly. His eyes snapped back to the present. He picked up his goblet, drained the last of the wine, and waved to his servants to approach and clear off the table. When he was ready he said, "I am going to contact one of my sources. I will not need guards."

"Your Excellency," Durne said, looking alarmed, "you shouldn't be gone at a time like this without some protection."

Bight shrugged. "Fine. I'll take her." And he pointed to Linsha. He turned his back on the room and strode out, effectively cutting off any argument.

Linsha's jaw dropped.

The guard beside her shifted on his feet but said nothing.

Beside the table, Commander Durne made a few choice comments under his breath. To Linsha, he seemed more annoyed than worried. "Squire!" he snapped. "Be ready to attend Lord Bight at his convenience. You are dismissed."

Linsha made a salute to Durne's stiff back and hurried out of the audience hall as quickly as she dared. Outside in the hall, she paused in the corridor while her speculations ran in a dozen different directions. It was known that Lord Bight occasionally took brief mysterious trips, sometimes alone and sometimes with a chosen guard. So far the Clandestine Circle hadn't been able to discover where or why. Now she had an opportunity to find out, and yet she couldn't help but wonder why he would take her. Was his choice meant to be an insult or a supreme compliment? And why would he go at this time? It was little surprise the commander was so angry. Perhaps she should flee before Lord Bight trapped her in an undesirable situation. No, that wouldn't do. She had to go with him. It was the opportunity of her career in Sanction!

She pressed her palms against her temples. The heat and the tension had given her a terrific headache. Her head felt as tight as the ropes on a wine press. Lost in her thoughts, she began to walk down the corridor.

When in doubt and confusion, Linsha usually sought solitude and quiet to think things through. That afternoon was no different. She found herself outside in the courtyard, heading for her cubicle on the top floor of the barracks.

The room was stuffy and hot, for her window faced away from the breeze, but she pulled the heavy door hanging close behind her and removed the outer surcoat of her uniform. She rummaged in her bag until she found her three leather juggling balls. She had to juggle to allow her mind to settle down from its wild pacing and to put aside her frustrations.

One after another, she set the balls in motion, up and down, back and forth, in a steady beat as rhythmic as her heart. Keeping her eyes on the balls, she turned her mental focus inward to the beat of her heart. Just as Goldmoon had taught her, she concentrated on the power within her spirit

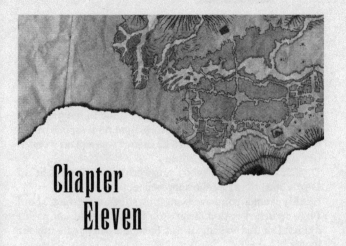

Chapter
Eleven

ootsteps pounded in the hall outside
and startled Linsha awake from a
sleep she never meant to take. She reared up, her heart
pounding, and stared around at her darkened room just as
Shanron stuck her head past the curtain.

"There you are! I've looked everywhere else. Come on.
Lord Bight is waiting for you!"

Linsha jumped to her feet and rubbed her eyes. She was
still groggy and furious that she had been caught so unprepared. It was already night. She hadn't eaten, or warned
Varia, or changed her damp shirt. She didn't know if she
should have packed supplies or saddled her horse.

She raked her fingers through her mussed hair, strapped
on her sword and daggers, and snatched her uniform tunic
off the bed. Then she ran downstairs behind Shanron.

The lord governor and Commander Durne waited for her
in the courtyard next to the barracks entrance. Linsha forced
back a groan at the sight of displeasure on Durne's face. She

didn't want to face him any more that day, or for several years to come.

He glowered at her, taking in her disheveled appearance and harried expression.

However, Lord Bight didn't seem displeased. He had changed his robes for a pair of smooth, leg-hugging pants, supple climbing boots, a long-sleeved tunic in his preferred color of gold, and a leather vest. He bore no weapons save a long dagger at his belt, and all he carried was a plain wooden box the size of a jewelry chest.

"Lord Governor, I really must protest—" Linsha heard Durne start to say as she approached.

"My friend, you have been protesting all evening," Lord Bight returned with a laugh. You know I would not go if I did not feel this was important. Sanction will be safe in your hands."

Durne didn't respond. He gestured toward Linsha with a stiff hand. "But why take only one guard? And why this one? She hasn't even taken the oath of loyalty. Take Shanron. Or Morgan. Or myself!"

"I need you here. As for the woman, she interests me. I might have a use for her, and this journey will give me a chance to learn her true mettle." He calmly accepted Linsha's salute and said to her, "Go to the kitchen. The cook has prepared a pack and some water bags for us. That is all we'll need."

Linsha hurried to obey, wondering just what he meant by "I might have a use for her." Shanron went with her and helped her collect the pack of supplies and the water bags from the cook. The guard didn't seem at all surprised that Lord Bight had chosen Linsha to go. She thumped the new recruit on the back and wished her a safe journey back. Shanron even promised to take fish scraps to the cat in the stable and to exercise Windcatcher. Linsha thanked her warmly before they returned to Lord Bight. It would be easy, she thought, to make a friend of this southern woman. Even if it proved they did share an interest in Ian Durne.

Shanron gave her a quick farewell and disappeared into

the barracks to enjoy the rest of her off-duty time. Linsha tucked her surcoat through one of the straps, hoisted the pack to her back, and hurried to catch up with the governor, who was already walking toward the open gate. She could only hope Varia was watching from the stable and would understand her absence.

"Keep a close eye on the council," Lord Bight advised Durne. "Don't let them weasel out of their responsibilities. Especially Vanduran. He tends to put his guild ahead of the city. The merchants must adhere to the new work schedules and stay off the southern pier. Make sure the new crews are added to the aqueduct site. We must get that finished as soon as possible."

"Yes, Your Excellency," Durne said reluctantly. He regarded Linsha for a moment, made as if to speak, then changed his mind. At the gate, he bowed to Lord Bight and stepped back while they passed through.

Linsha cast one glance back to see him standing alone in a pool of torchlight, the wavering light glinting on his dark hair and casting his face in shadow. She almost lifted her hand to wave good-bye, then caught herself before she did something so foolish. He wouldn't care. He disapproved of her.

She bent her shoulders to the pack and walked briskly after Lord Bight. The night was full about them, heavy with heat and moisture. A veil of clouds hid the stars and obscured the single pale moon. The wind of the afternoon had blown itself out, and now the darkness crouched down, breathless and still. Below them, the lights of the city glittered through a thin pall of smoke and dust.

Abruptly the lord governor veered off the main road and took a footpath that plunged down the hill into the trees.

"Where are we going, Excellency?" Linsha panted as she pushed to keep up with him. As dark as the path was, he followed it as swiftly as a hound on the blood scent.

"Patience, my young squire," he replied softly. "With patience all will be revealed."

The footpath could hardly be seen in the dense shadows

under the trees, yet Linsha realized it wasn't that difficult to follow. It ran straight as an arrow's flight between the trees down the hill, across a narrow vale, and up another hill. She soon guessed where the path led. The only thing in this direction that deserved a path such as this was the Temple of the Heart on the neighboring hill.

They broke through the trees onto a broad, grassy lawn, and Linsha saw that her assumption was right. The temple lay before them on the brow of the hill, its white stone shape a ghostly gleam against the black bulk of Mount Grishnor towering behind it. Torches burned on sconces at the front entrance, but Lord Bight avoided the lighted door and, hugging the shadows, made his way around to the rear, where the dormitories and outbuildings clustered under a grove of tall pines. Curious, Linsha followed. The night was still early enough for people to be busy, and many lights burned in the windows of the dormitories or passed among the trees as students, mystics, and servants went about their evening tasks.

Lord Bight ignored them all. With the wooden box still tucked under his arm, he crouched in a concealing clump of shrubbery and concentrated on the back of the temple.

The ancient temple, Linsha knew, was shaped by three rectangular blocks forming a **U** around a central, square-shaped room whose roof line soared high into the trees. Centuries ago, before the First Cataclysm, the central room had been used as an altar room for the worship of the gods of Good. It had been left empty during Queen Takhisis's rule, abandoned to neglect and decay and shrouded with tales of vengeful spirits. Now the temple was totally repaired and refurbished to serve the mystic missionaries from the Citadel of Light. If there were any angry spirits left, they did not seem to mind the intrusion.

Linsha waited with the lord governor without asking questions for what seemed a long time, until at last he tapped her on the arm and hurried out of his hiding place. She moved after him as silently as possible, since secrecy seemed to be what he wanted. Although why he should be sneaking around a temple where he was favored was beyond her ken.

The grounds were empty at the moment; there was no one in sight on the paths or near the temple. The lord governor dashed across the open space to a door in the back of the temple and froze in the shadow of the building. A detached kitchen stood nearby, its lights still glowing in the windows for the cooks who worked late cleaning the pans and pots from the day's meals. The smell of wood fires, roast fowl, and cooked vegetables still lingered in the stagnant air.

Linsha kept a wary eye on the kitchen while she ran after Lord Bight across the grass and gravel paths to the door. Briefly she wondered if it was locked, but it slid open easily under his hand, and the two eased into the darkened room beyond. She saw it was a dining room, set with trestle tables and cupboards stacked with dishes.

Lord Bight bypassed the tables, went to the front of the long room, and ducked into an alcove, where another door stood in black shadow. The governor, Linsha mused, seemed to know this temple as well as his own palace. This door, too, gave way to gentle pressure and opened to reveal a stairway leading down.

Closing the door behind her, Linsha walked blindly down behind the lord governor and hoped fervently that her faith in him was not misplaced.

A small white light flared in front of her, and she saw Lord Bight standing at the foot of the stairs, holding a small hand lamp.

"There are torches farther on," he said in a whisper, "but this will do for now." He suddenly grinned at her, his handsome face illuminated with pale light. "This is where it gets interesting. Are you still curious? Afraid? Do you think this is a trap?"

Linsha felt a jolt of alarm. Gods, this man was too intuitive for her liking, but she couldn't back out now. A flood of excitement washed through her, and the blood of the Majeres sang in her veins. "I'm with you, Lord Governor."

"Good." With the lamp in one hand and his box under his arm, Lord Bight led her into the basement of the temple.

This lower level seemed to be little used for anything but storage, for all it contained were rooms full of crates, old furniture, piles of moldering rags and rotting fabric, all coated in a thick layer of dust and mildew. The lord governor made his way through the clutter and mess to a room on the southern end of the building that Linsha estimated was directly below the old altar room.

Without pause, Lord Bight moved an old worm-eaten table aside, inserted his fingers into a narrow crack in the wall, and pulled hard. The crack widened and lengthened until it reached the ceiling and the floor, then suddenly an entire section of the wall swung back and a black opening gaped before them.

Linsha took note of the fact that there was little dust on this strange door or on the doorframe around it. The door had been used before, and fairly recently.

"Be careful. The steps are steep," he warned her, ducking through the opening.

He wasn't kidding. Linsha stepped through the opening after him, expecting the top of a stairway, and nearly slipped off into the bottomless dark. This doorway opened into the *middle* of a stone stair so steep that it was almost like a ladder, and so narrow that she bumped her head on the opposite wall. Fighting to regain her balance, she planted both hands on the walls beside her and carefully pushed herself back upright. She drew a deep breath and let it out in a rush of relief. Above her, the black stairway continued up to what was probably a hidden door in the altar room above. Far below her now, the little light in Lord Bight's hand lured her downward on a steeply curving spiral stair, down to what she could only guess.

"Close the door!" Lord Bight's voice rose up to her from the depths of the stairwell.

She cautiously reached through the opening to grasp the stone door and pulled it tightly shut behind her. Keeping both hands firmly pressed against the damp stone walls, she went down step by step after the lord governor. He was far ahead of her by now, his light like a tiny star in the Stygian darkness. Shortly it disappeared down the curve of the spiral and left Linsha in total darkness. She tried to hurry, but her boot slipped on a particularly slick step and nearly threw her down the stairs. After that she picked her way down carefully, mostly by feel, and hoped Lord Bight would be waiting for her at the end. She couldn't hear anything beyond her own breathing and the thud of her boots on the stone, and occasionally her sword would bang on the walls. Beyond those noises, there was nothing else to interrupt the heavy silence.

The air turned steadily colder the deeper she descended, and the odors of dust and old basements gave way to the dense smells of ancient stone and old air. The first warning she had of the stair's end was a cold draft that swirled up the funnel of the stairwell and raised goose bumps on her bare arms. She took two more steps down and landed heavily on a stone floor. The sudden transition from steep steps to flat floor threw her forward, and she would have fallen if two strong hands had not caught her arms and pulled her upright almost into a tall, solid body.

The warmth of his hands on her chilled skin and the strength of his grip took her by surprise. Although she couldn't see an inch in front of her face, she could identify the man who had her by the feel of his sleeves brushing her arms and the warm, almost spicy scent of his body. What she didn't know was what he planned to do next, and she tensed her muscles and prepared to fight if need be.

A deep, throaty chuckle rumbled near her ear. "Be careful of that bottom step," Lord Bight said belatedly. His hands released her, but his fingers sought hers. "Squire, you are amazing. Most people would have screamed if someone grabbed them in the dark."

"You forget, Your Excellency, I used to do the grabbing in the dark before I mended my evil ways."

His lips twitched at her saucy reply. "Come on. I don't want to lose you in this place." His fingers tugged her along what seemed to be a narrow tunnel.

Her mind sensed the oppressive weight of thick layers of

rock above her head and the closeness of the stone walls on either side. Fortunately they didn't have to go far. Lord Bight rounded a corner, and Linsha saw his lamp burning low on top of the wooden box.

"The torches are here," the governor told her. "I left the lamp here when I came to get you because it's almost out."

"You can see that well in the dark? I can hardly find my feet, let alone the floor."

He shrugged, letting go of her hand. "I've been down here before." He reached into a small alcove and pulled out a bundle of torches. "These won't last that long, so we'd better take several. Do you mind carrying them?"

"Not if it means we have light," she said with conviction. She pulled off her pack to add the bundle to her load while he lit two of the torches from the dying lamp. Light flared up around her, golden and welcome. She glanced around and, squinting in the sudden brightness, she saw Lord Bight stand upright, a torch in either hand. His muscular body was bathed in the firelight, and his eyes flickered bronze, then gold, from the torchlight reflected in their depths.

There was a powerful majesty about him that reminded her of her father, Palin Majere, when he stood on the pinnacle of the magnificent Tower of the World at his Academy of Sorcery. These men were much alike, she decided, powerful in their determination to succeed, passionately devoted to their causes, wise and often remote. Their differences lay in their perceptions of themselves. Although he founded the renowned academy, Palin still considered himself a student of magic, and there was a gentle humility about him that allowed him to deal gracefully with even the most difficult sorcerer. Lord Bight, on the other hand, was one of the most confident, self-satisfied people Linsha had ever known. Pugnacious, tough, and often the rogue, he ruled his kingdom as if ordained by the gods before they left. He gave her the impression that he found the world and its people endlessly amusing, and only a veneer of civility kept him from laughing at everything.

Lord Bight interrupted her musings. "You should put

your tunic on. Your skin is chilled already, and we have long way to go."

Linsha took his advice and pulled on her uniform tunic before she lifted the pack to her back. He handed her a torch. "Will you tell me now where we are going?" she asked, holding the torch up to see his face.

"As I said earlier, I am going talk to one of my sources."

That didn't exactly answer her question, so she tried another tack. "Why didn't you bring your other guards?"

He eyed her knowingly. "I only need the guards in Sanction, where there are too many people to distract me. Down here I do not need them."

"So why did you bring me?"

"You heard what I said to Commander Durne. I have something in mind for you, but I need to know you better before I put you to use."

Linsha eyed him from beneath her arched brows for a long minute. While he seemed to be telling the truth, his answers had little substance. She crossed her arms. "I suppose you won't tell me what you have planned."

"Patience," he said in a soft voice.

"Fine," she replied disgustedly. "If you won't tell me where we're going, will you at least tell me where we are?"

"Beneath the temple," he replied blandly.

She glared at him. "You know what I mean, Your Excellency."

"Come. Let me show you. There is a whole layer of Sanction most people know nothing about." He continued through the tunnel, away from the stairs and the outside world.

Linsha realized immediately this tunnel was no lava tube or natural crack. The passageway had been made by skilled hands. Its walls were smooth and its floor carefully leveled, and it was wide enough for two people to walk abreast. Unconsciously she lengthened her stride until she walked by Lord Bight's side. Her eyes probed the blackness ahead, and her hand rested lightly on her sword hilt.

He watched her with a sidelong glance, a half smile

hidden behind the neatly trimmed beard. Only loyal body-guards or friends were allowed so close, but Lord Bight let her stay. The tunnel twisted around a few turns, then it went on before them in a southerly direction, dropping continuously deeper beneath the city. There were no side openings or intersections with other tunnels. It appeared to be a passage with a definite objective, but who made this tunnel, and where did it go?

Linsha wanted to ask, but didn't. Apparently Lord Bight planned to keep her in suspense. He said nothing to her to break the deep and profound silence around them. He seemed to be listening for something, for he held his head slightly cocked to one side, and his gaze was intent on something she could not see.

Ahead, the torchlight gleamed on lighter rock at the edge of its luminosity. As they drew nearer, the light revealed a wall across their path. On the wall was a lintel carved from a pale stone into an arch of delicate grace and simple beauty, a lintel that framed a door of smooth stone. The door, if it was one, had no handle, no lock, and no sign of any line, crack, or opening. It blocked the end of the tunnel as surely as the solid wall around it.

Unperturbed, Lord Bight handed his torch to Linsha and placed his right palm flat against the middle of the door. "There are magic wards inserted into the stone," he explained to her. "They're as old as the tunnel around you. Without the key words, nothing short of an earthquake would open this entrance."

"And, of course, you know the words," she muttered.

He made three sounds, almost like animal grunts and whistles, and the door moved beneath his hand. "Of course," he said, giving the door a light push.

Before she had time to comment, Lord Bight plucked his torch out of her hand and ushered her through the doorway. There he stopped on the threshold and held his torch high. Linsha lifted hers as well and gasped in surprise. They were in a chamber, high and broad and divided by a natural formation of stone pillars created when the Lords of Doom were young. The pillars stretched from ceiling to floor and had been polished by loving hands so their colors of white, gray, and black glowed like smoked glass in the light of the torches. Large chunks of granite had been carved into benches and scattered around the cavern. A thin stream of water flowed from somewhere above and fell in a long, silvery ribbon to a clear pool below.

"It's beautiful," Linsha breathed.

"This is a shadowhall," he said quietly.

Of course.

Like a sluice gate opening in a canal, the word 'shadowhall" triggered a flood of long-forgotten memories in Linsha's mind, memories of an elf woman, Laurana, a friend of her grandparents, sitting by a fire and telling stories of her brother.

"Gilthanas." The name broke from her lips so softly she didn't realize she had said it aloud. Gilthanas and his love, Silvara. They had been here, in these tunnels, so many years ago. They had seen the Dark Queen's Temple of Luerkhisis on Mount Thunderhorn, with its sulfurous caves and its pillars of fire. They had found the hidden chambers and the stolen dragon eggs with the help of the elusive shadowpeople.

Lord Bight turned to her, his hand clenched around the torch, his face as hard as granite. "You know the story, then. You have heard of Takhisis's foul experiments and the oath she broke to the Dragons of Good."

Linsha's words were steely. "I heard it. I also heard many shadowpeople were killed for helping the elves and the silver dragon."

"They were," he said, his voice grim and sad. "But not all. When I came down here for the first time to obliterate what was left of the Temple of Luerkhisis, I found a few survivors. We reached an agreement, they and I, and they stayed to rebuild their realm."

"Where are they now?"

"Wait," he said softly.

They started on their way again across the cavern, alert for any danger. They hadn't gone far when a slight noise stopped them in their tracks. A scratching noise, like claws on stone, came from the darkness overhead, and a dark shadow moved across the ceiling of the chamber. It flitted sideways so quickly that Linsha almost missed it. Then another form, black and shapeless, darted behind a pillar not far ahead. Something growled menacingly.

The governor stopped Linsha with his arm and quickly said, "Don't move. Don't draw your weapons. They're here."

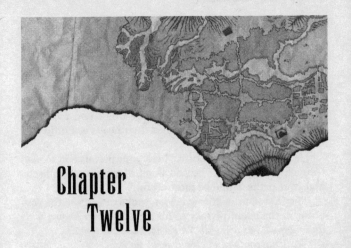

Chapter
Twelve

Linsha's eyes widened. To the surface dwellers of Krynn, the shadowpeople were creatures of myth and legend. Shy and elusive, they lived below ground in subterranean communities rarely seen by other races. They were believed to be benevolent and deeply loving within their own clans, but they could be fierce defenders of their realm when threatened. She remembered, too, that the shadowpeople were capable of telepathic communication. Deliberately she moved her hand away from her sword and held both arms outstretched in a gesture of peace.

Three shapes separated from the darkness and moved slowly to stand at the farthest rim of the torchlight. Although they were manlike in shape, they were not tall by human standards, being nearly a head shorter than Linsha. Smooth fur, in shades of brown and grizzled black, covered their bodies, and a thick gliding membrane connected their arms to their legs. Their large heads had flat, upturned noses, wide flaring ears, and huge eyes that glowed with an eerie green luminescence.

One male, slightly larger than the other two, stepped farther into the light, and Linsha saw he had long claws on both his hands and feet and a pair of fangs that gleamed on the edge of his upper lip. He looked her over carefully before he hissed softly to his companions. The other two moved in behind him, and all three inclined their heads to Lord Bight in a sign of recognition.

He returned their gesture. "I ask your permission to pass through your caverns," he said aloud. "I am in need of haste, and your paths would be most useful."

The first male, a grizzled elder, spoke directly to the governor in the silent privacy of his mind. *You are known to us and may pass as you will. We do not know the female.*

She is my companion. I will speak for her.

The batlike creatures focused on Linsha for a disconcertingly long time, then they growled among themselves before responding.

We sense she is loyal to you, but she guards too many secrets.

I know.

As you wish. We do not sense evil in her, so she may pass as well.

"Thank you," Lord Bight said out loud, but the shadowpeople had already vanished between the thought and the spoken word.

"What was that all about?" demanded Linsha, who hadn't been included in the telepathic conversation.

"They gave us permission to use their tunnels," Lord Bight said, moving forward once more.

Linsha looked nervously around at the chamber of stone and everlasting night. "You do not govern down here?"

"Only through cooperation and respect. That is all they want, to dwell in this place in peace. They have been here since ancient times. They are as much a part of Sanction as the merchants who barter or the gully dwarves who help pick up refuse, and I am pleased to have them."

A resonant tone in his voice caught Linsha's attention, a

tone of pride and attachment she had heard before in her grandfather's voice when he talked about his inn or her father's voice when he discussed his academy. "You truly are devoted to Sanction," she murmured, intrigued by his unexpected sentiment.

"It fascinates me." He halted in front of her so abruptly she had to slam to a stop and fling her arm aside to keep from hitting him with the torch. He loomed over her, his powerful form menacing in the flickering battle of shadow and light.

A low, rumbling laugh brought goose bumps to her arms. At once wary and alert, Linsha held still and regarded the governor inquiringly as he circled slowly around her and came to rest in front of her again, so close she could feel the heat of his body. It took all her hard-learned self-control to master the impulse to leap back and draw her dagger. Instead, she lifted her brows and tried to breathe normally.

"People fascinate me, too." he spoke softly, like a whisper of steel. "I like to know who they are and why they do the things they do. Especially those I allow close to me."

"It is a wise man who knows his friends and enemies," Linsha quoted pontifically from a long-dead philosopher whose name she could never remember. She heard another low laugh that reminded her of the rumbling of a lion about to charge.

"Which will you prove to be when the time comes to decide?"

Linsha felt a chill that had nothing to do with the temperature of the air. She opened her mouth to protest, only to feel him place a finger on her lips.

"Words prove nothing," he admonished. "It is your deeds I will watch."

He turned on his heel as abruptly as before and strode off, leaving Linsha mentally gasping. Doubtfully, she trailed after him while her mind replayed that brief confrontation again and again. By the powers of Paladine, she thought, what did he mean by that? Was he trying to catch her off guard, or did he know more about her than he was telling? Had she revealed more than she intended?

Lord Bight gave her not a glance but continued walking rapidly across the great cavern. At the far end, he ducked through another opening into a tunnel similar to the last. Beyond the shadowhall, though, the single tunnel broke off into a labyrinth of tunnels, passages, and halls. To the left and right, arched doorways opened into tunnels going in every direction. Half-seen stairways dropped away into gaping blackness, and countless turns and junctions left Linsha totally bewildered. It was good she had a guide who seemed to know where he was going, and she hoped in the back of her mind that he wouldn't leave her down there to rot. She had no doubt she could never find her way back by herself.

The air was cool and damp in the tunnels, and sometimes they passed deep chambers that smelled strongly of mushrooms. Several times they crossed over shallow streams where blind fish swam in the crystal clear waters. Although they didn't see another denizen of the shadowpeople's realm, Linsha sensed the creatures were close by. She had an eerie impression of watchfulness, and once in a while she would hear faint voices growl in the gloom or the distant scratch of claw on stone.

They had walked for nearly two hours through the maze of tunnels before Lord Bight broke the silence. "We are under what is left of the Temple of Duerghast. From here the going becomes more difficult."

To Linsha's embarrassment, her stomach chose that moment to rumble a loud protest at her lack of supper.

Lord Bight shook his head. "I suppose we'd better rest so you can eat. I'd hate to have my bodyguard faint from hunger." He jammed the end of his torch into a crack in the wall and sat on the stone floor, the box between his knees.

Still dubious of his intentions, Linsha sat out of arm's reach. Her own torch guttered a few times and went out, leaving them in the feeble light of just one torch. Hurriedly she lit another one, then delved into the pack for food. Lord Bight sat wordlessly and watched her, his eyes half amused, half knowing.

She managed to eat a slab of bread and cheese and some

figs before she lost her patience. "Why are you staring at me?" she demanded.

"You're prettier than the stone wall," he replied reasonably.

She snapped a few waterfront oaths, then lapsed into silence. There was no arguing with him. He was as good as Ian Durne at keeping her off-balance. What was it about these two men that made her act like a tongue-tied maid? She downed a mouthful of water, shoved everything back in the pack, and jumped to her feet in one fluid, angry motion. He followed more slowly, looking amused, and took the lead once again.

The passage they were in ran due south, then curved to the east under the flanks of Mount Ashkir. Other junctions and tunnel openings dwindled in number until the path ran on alone and gradually left the Shadowrealm behind. The feeling of watchfulness faded from Linsha's awareness, and the echoes of voices vanished into the dark depths of the earth. The only sounds left were the dull thud of the travelers' footfalls and the subdued swish of their clothing. The tunnel itself degraded from a smooth path to a rough opening that was barely more than a wide crack in the mountain. The walls pressed closer, and the floor became uneven and more difficult to cross. Rockfalls and boulders lay on the trail. Fissures opened up before them, some smoking with sulfurous steam. The air grew noticeably warmer. When Linsha put her hand on the walls, she could feel a quiver in the rock like a distant tremble that shook the bowels of the volcano.

Mount Ashkir was still an active volcano, and years after its primary eruption, it still belched steam and ash and an occasional stream of lava. But its main force had been dissipated, and the lava river that once threatened to engulf the south side of Sanction had disappeared, largely due—at least, so they said in Sanction—to Lord Bight's magic. All that remained on the surface of Ashkir's slope was a narrow flow on the eastern side that fed into the defensive dikes that protected the city from invasion from the East Pass.

Linsha tried to keep all of that in mind as the path worked deeper and deeper into the interior of the peak. Lord Bight was with her and he could handle a recalcitrant volcano, but Mount Ashkir was quiet these days; there was nothing to worry about. It didn't matter that the air had become uncomfortably hot and heavy, and the quivering had strengthened to a continuous low-pitched rumble that Linsha could feel through her boots with every step. Everything would be all right.

She wished she could remove her tunic again, but Lord Bight didn't stop or slow down, and Linsha kept doggedly at his heels. Soon the path entered a long, narrow cavern that sloped upward on a steep incline. The rumbling was louder still, echoing through the passage with a dull roar like distant thunder.

They scrambled up the black slope, using both hands and feet to fight for balance on the broken rubble. At the top, the trail plunged into another opening that Linsha recognized was an old lava tube. Although old beyond measure, the tube was still passable enough to crawl through, and it bore straight and true for several hundred feet.

At the mouth of the tube, Lord Bight tossed aside his used torch and faced Linsha with a feral grin of anticipation. "You won't need your torch here."

Linsha followed suit, trying to ignore the nervousness that gnawed in her belly. When she climbed into the tube behind Lord Bight, she peered past his shoulder and saw why the torches weren't necessary. At the opposite end, the opening of the tube glowed with a pulsing reddish glare that flickered with tongues of yellow. The rumbling she had heard for so long thundered down the tube to pound at her ears. Linsha's mouth went dry; her face shone with sweat. She crawled rapidly after Lord Bight, ignoring the sharp flakes of rock that cut her hands and gouged her knees. The light intensified, and the heat beat at her face like an opened kiln.

The governor looked back once to see if she was still following. When his gaze found hers, he nodded once and pushed on without a word.

All too soon for Linsha, they reached the end of the tube and crawled out onto a wide ledge in the largest cavern Linsha had ever seen. It was immense, a vast chamber beneath the mountain, where the liquid lava rose from the depths through an unseen chasm. The molten rock gathered at the bottom of the cave in a seething, bubbling river that filled the chamber with lurid light and heat.

Fumes, acrid and bitter, burned Linsha's throat and brought tears to her eyes. She reeled back in shock from the fiery heat. Swiftly she tore a strip from her tunic, doused it in water from the bag, and tied it across her mouth and nose. Lord Bight did the same.

Gesturing to her to follow, he made his way carefully to the right along the path that followed a narrow shelflike ledge. Rough and uneven, the ledge tenaciously clung to the upper wall of the great cavern for its entire length, snaking above the slow-moving river of lava until the stream cascaded down again out of sight into another chasm beyond sight and knowledge.

Linsha clamped her hand over her mask and moved after the governor. She kept her eyes on the ledge in front of her feet and tried to disregard the dizzying drop only a step away from her path. The intense heat made her feel sluggish and slow, but she crept on, knowing that to stop meant certain death. She thought she knew now what it felt like to be a fly trapped in a fireplace.

They were nearly three quarters of the way along the length of the cave when Linsha finally saw a narrow, dark opening at the end of the trail. She wiped her sleeve across her streaming eyes to look again and knocked her mask askew. It had dried in the intense heat, so she fumbled at its knot to untie it and drench it with water again. A wave of dizziness engulfed her, causing her to stumble into the wall. Her elbow crashed into a sharp projection, and pain lanced through her arm. Half-blind, choked with fumes, and dizzy with heat and pain, she tried to right herself, only to lean too far in the other direction. Her boot came down heavily on a cracked edge of the stone, and before she could regain her balance, the crack gave way and her left leg plunged over the edge of the shelf.

Frantically she threw her body forward to hug the ledge. The impact of her fall knocked the air from her lungs, and the pack on her back slipped over to her side, tipping her weight even more off-balance. Her fingers scrabbled on the crumbling verge, but her arms were too weak to stop the momentum of her fall. Her right leg and hips rolled over the edge and her grip failed.

"Help!" she cried to Lord Bight. In her desperate struggle to retain her place, she couldn't see him, and in her mind she was alone as her upper body slid completely off the shelf and her arms slid inexorably toward the brink.

A hand clamped on her wrist and brought her fall to a wrenching stop.

"Hold still," Lord Bight hissed as he grabbed for her other arm.

Linsha's slide downward abruptly stopped, and, lifting her head, she stared upward into his golden eyes. "Don't drop me," she begged. "Please don't let me go."

A strange emotion flitted across his face, but her eyes were still too blurred to see it. He shook his head, as if to rid himself of an irritant, and said in mock severity, "Squires. You just can't take them anywhere."

Bracing his feet against the solid stone, he gave a tremendous heave and hauled her body up and over the edge and onto the shelf. Without giving her time to recover, he pulled her to her feet, lifted her arms across his shoulders, and took her weight on his back.

"Come on. A little farther and you can rest where the heat is not so great."

Linsha didn't answer. She closed her eyes and put her trust completely in the man who had saved her. She didn't really have the strength to do anything else, but surely if he had meant for her to die, he wouldn't have bothered rescuing her from the lava.

With a slow, cautious tread, Lord Bight carried her along the last length of the ledge to a wide crack in the cavern's wall. Below them, the fiery river of lava curved away and vanished into the bowels of the mountain. Blessed coolness flowed over Linsha's face and filled her grateful lungs. The air was still hot and acrid, but after the deadly atmosphere of the cavern, the air of the stone passage was a relief. He carried her through the crevice into another, much smaller, cave that wound on, dark and still, beyond the fire and thunder of the lava hall.

When he reached several large chunks of fallen rock, he loosened his hold and let her slide down to a sitting position on the stone. She tore off her mask, leaned forward, resting her elbows on her knees, and tried to regain her breath. Lord Bight, to her disgust, hardly looked weary.

He sat down beside her and untied the water bag for her. "Let's rest here for a while. It's very late, and we both could use some sleep."

"I'll keep watch," Linsha said automatically, fumbling with the pack. The fumes in the cave had given her a ferocious headache. She doubted she could sleep even if she wanted to.

The governor grunted and lay back on the flat rock, his head resting on his hands. "Suit yourself. I don't think that's necessary here. I need you fresh in the morning, so get some sleep if you can." His eyes closed.

Linsha tried to stay awake. For a while she was able to concentrate on the pounding in her head and on the faint red illumination still visible from the distant crack. Lord Bight looked content on his rocky bed, and all was peaceful. As time passed, the pain in her head mercifully loosened to a dull throb. Her eyes grew heavy. She leaned back against the rock wall, feeling as weary as a storm-tossed swimmer. Listening to the subdued thunder of the lava, she hummed some tunes to herself that seemed to blend with the steady rumble in the background. Eventually the words were forgotten and only the music played softly in her mind like a shepherd's pipe on a windblown hillside.

Linsha's eyes drifted closed. Her hand slumped away from her sword. The music played on in gentle, lulling melodies until at last it faded away altogether, and Linsha slept.

Lord Bight opened his eyes cautiously, took note of her

soft breathing and relaxed posture, and then swung his legs around and moved to sit beside her. He studied her closely for a minute. Gently, almost like a caress, his hand brushed those crazy curls off her forehead and came to rest lightly on her skin. He concentrated on her sleeping face and deftly extended his power around her to examine the nature of her aura.

A satisfied smile curved his full lips. Almost reluctantly he withdrew his hand and allowed the mystic power to recede back into his being. Pleased, he returned to his position on the rock, and soon he, too, was asleep.

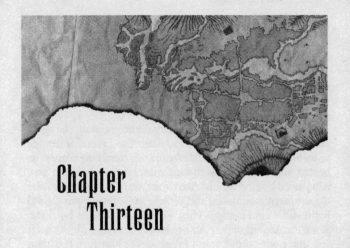

Chapter Thirteen

Perhaps two hours later, Linsha woke with a start. Although they were still entombed by stone and darkness, her internal clock told her it was close to morning in the world outside. She sat up, stiff, sore and disgusted with herself for failing in her duty. She had fallen asleep on watch, a punishable crime in many orders, and certainly in the elite corps of Lord Bight's bodyguards.

She climbed to her feet and scrubbed her face with one hand. It surprised her that the hand hurt. A tinderbox in the pack lit a spare torch and gave Linsha light to examine her hands. Both were scraped and lacerated from her fall, and further examination revealed a tear in the leg of her new pants and bruises on her legs and abdomen.

"Great," Linsha grumbled to herself.

"What is?" asked the governor, sitting up. "This rock bed that has disagreed so strenuously with my back?"

Linsha sniffed. At least he had the decency to be stiff this morning. His endurance and strength were beginning to make her feel like an old woman. "I've torn my uniform already," she said irritably and pointed to the damage. "And worst of all, Your Excellency, I fell asleep on duty."

Lord Bight lifted his shoulders in a shrug, although he was secretly pleased she had confessed. "I told you to, remember? Don't sweat it." He didn't tell her about his small part in helping her to sleep.

They ate a quick meal, lit a second torch, and set out again on the faint path under the mountain. The cavern of fire fell away behind them, its rumble fading to a trembling silence, its heat giving way to bone-chilling cold. Linsha estimated they had passed beyond Mount Ashkir and were somewhere under the southern mountains, and yet where they were going, Lord Bight still would not say. They walked and climbed for hours along the underground path in a steady march south. At what felt like noon, they took a break to eat and rest and then pushed on again harder than before. As if he sensed a deadline approaching, Lord Bight set a fast pace, and from the ease that he found his way through the bewildering passages and caves, Linsha realized he had been this way before, probably many times.

It was nearly sunset when Lord Bight struck a passage that sloped steadily upward and led Linsha toward the surface. They entered a long, flat-roofed cavern with a broad floor, and they saw a slit of daylight gleaming at the far end. Both of them hurried forward, eager to be out of the oppressive darkness. The light grew brighter the closer they drew, and they tossed their torches aside and began to run. Their run turned to a sprint, and, laughing in relief, they plunged into the sun and wind of early evening.

Linsha threw her arms wide and collapsed on a sward of grass. She inhaled the perfume of sun-warmed grasses and wild flowers and the tang of pine and cedar. A breeze stirred among the trees, and insects trilled noisy songs in the grass.

The cave exited into a narrow valley strewn with broken rock and copses of mountain pine. The valley ran roughly north and south down the flanks of a reddish peak that still gleamed a fiery bronze in the ruddy light of the setting sun.

Linsha didn't recognize the peak, but she judged from the distance they had traveled that they were on the south side of the range that hemmed in Sanction. And the only thing on this side of the mountains was the swampy domain of the black dragon, Onysablet.

Her delight evaporated. A cold lump of apprehension settled in Linsha's belly. She shook off the bits of grass on her clothes and climbed to her feet. Lord Bight had walked to an outcropping and stood looking south.

"Your Excellency, why are we here?" she ventured.

He continued to look south. "To meet a contact. Do not fear. As long as you are with me, you will go unharmed."

"What contact?"

He turned around, the pleasure turned to ashes in his eyes. His broad face was set in a grim mask. "I am going to summon a dragon. One who considers herself a scientist of sorts."

"Sable," hissed Linsha. Instinctively she scanned the southern horizon for a sign of the monstrous black.

The man, still carrying his wooden box, began striding down the valley. "Leave the pack and come. We need to hurry."

"Lord Bight . . . this is stupid. Even if the black comes, she won't help us," Linsha yelled after him.

"Young woman," he shouted back, "trust me!"

Linsha hesitated for a few heartbeats, long enough for several alternate courses of action to run through her mind and be rejected in the face of too many truths. He had brought her this far, he had saved her life, and she was still his bodyguard and honor bound to defend him no matter how stupid he was behaving. Not to mention the fact that the Clandestine Circle would sell its collective soul to know how Lord Bight managed to fend Sable off his territory. Witnessing this meeting could be the chance she'd been waiting for.

Muttering under her breath, she tossed the pack and the spare torches into a clump of bushes by the outcropping and sped after him. He marched downhill at a ground-eating pace for over a mile while Linsha jogged to keep up with him. She spent the time pondering the possibility that he had suddenly suffered a mental breakdown. Summon Sable? That was lunacy.

The valley ended abruptly on the flat head of a broad, treeless plateau. Lord Bight crossed it and came to a quick halt at the rim, where the ground dropped away in a breathtaking cliff. Several hundred feet below, the base of the cliff formed the wall of a small canyon that contained a dark, brackish stream.

Linsha, coming up beside Lord Bight, looked down and saw where the stream meandered out of the canyon into a low range of hills. Dusk approached, and the sky was filled with mellow light that cast a pale glow on the murky terrain below. The governor pointed south. She followed his motion and stared out beyond the hills to the sunken fringes of the watery realm of the dragonlord, Onysablet. The largest black dragon left after the Purge, Sable laid claim to this land that had once been the foothills and verdant grasslands of Blöde, and she reshaped the landscape to fit her will, crushing the level of the land and bringing in the waters. The ogres who lived here had been driven into remote mountain strongholds in the southern Khalkists, and now, more than twenty years after her arrival, only a few scattered high points of land remained dry above the largest swamp on Krynn, and the once high foothills of the southern Khalkists were nothing more than rocky points jutting out of the drowned land.

Linsha shuddered. The destruction and waste of such a huge area filled her soul with rage. She crossed her arms and glared at Lord Bight. "So how do you call a dragon who is probably miles away and busy making more swamp?"

"Like this." He pulled a thin chain out from under his tunic and palmed a slim silver whistle. His eyes closed, and his face took on a tense mask of deep concentration. He took a few deep breaths then blew a long note on the whistle.

At least Linsha assumed there was a note. She did not hear a thing. "You're joking."

He glanced at her, his eyes crinkling at the corners, and blew more air through the instrument. "There is more to this whistle than meets the eye. Now, look that way," he told Linsha, a finger pointing southeast.

The sun's red disk slipped to the horizon on their right, and shadows crept out of the stagnant swamp. The wind blew stronger over the plateau, burdened with the smells of rot and mud and marsh grass.

Linsha waited, her heart pounding, her eyes fastened on the darkening skyline. The sun slipped lower, and a few stars, like tiny shards of crystal, peeped through the dusky twilit sky.

A small black dot appeared just above the hazy dark line of the swamp's horizon. Linsha had to look twice to see it. It looked like a bird in the distance, but as it sped nearer it grew larger and larger until the black shape became a dragon that roared over the swamp like a storm cloud. Monstrous and dark as the bog she sprang from, Sable flew past the boundaries of her watery realm, over the barren line of hills, and swept over the plateau. She circled overhead, her great head swiveling to stare at the humans who had the audacity to disturb her. The wind of her passing flattened the grass on the plateau and sent dust and grit swirling.

Linsha clenched her hands at her sides and resisted every instinct she had that screamed at her to draw her sword. Against that ebony monster, she knew her tiny blade could do no damage, and it would probably only irritate Sable. She could only pray fervently that Lord Bight knew what he was doing.

The governor stood motionless, his head tilted up to watch the dragon, his hands and the wooden box in plain view.

Sable circled around again, then banked her great wings and landed on the flat plateau. The ground trembled under her massive weight, and her huge body blocked the light of the setting sun. She settled her wings close to her dusky body and surveyed the two people not more than twenty feet away. Her yellow eyes gleamed like twin fires in the twilight.

"Hogan Bight," she hissed. "Aren't you dead yet?"

He laughed and sketched a bow. "Onysablet, how pleased I am to see you."

The dragon lowered her long head close to Linsha. Her ivory horns twitched in irritation.

The lady Knight froze. The reek of decay and foul muck filled her nostrils, and the heat of the dragon's breath blew over her like a hot furnace. But she refused to move or react to the dragon, even though it took everything she had to resist the dragonfear.

"Who is this worthless bit of refuse? I hope this is another addition for my zoo," Sable said maliciously. "I'm rather short of females."

A shudder shook Linsha from head to foot, and she almost bolted. Sable's zoo was nothing but a collection of hideous creatures created by her revolting experiments with parasites, slaves, swamp creatures, and anyone unlucky enough to be caught in her domain.

Lord Bight shook his head. He put his hand on Linsha's shoulder, and she felt reassurance in his touch and strength in his nearness.

"Sorry, Your Mightiness," he said lightly. "This one is not available. However, I have brought something I think you will appreciate more." He unfastened the catch on the wooden box, lifted the lid, and carefully withdrew a glass jar that rested snugly in a nest of cotton. He held up the jar for Sable's inspection. The jar held some dirty water that partially obscured a loathsome creature that swam about within.

Sable dipped her neck to peer closely at the thing. "What is it? I can barely make it out."

"A cutthrull slug," he announced with visible pride.

The dragon's head shot up and her eyes flared in excitement. "From the caverns of Mount Thunderhorn?"

"The same. The shadowpeople found this for me. I've been saving it for a special occasion."

Stunned, Linsha tore her eyes away from the dragon to stare at the man, wondering if she understood him clearly.

"And what makes this a special occasion, little man?" Sable purred, her yellow eyes greedily fastened on the jar.

"I wish to appeal to your scientific nature," Lord Bight replied. "I have come across an interesting disease, and I thought perhaps, with your vast knowledge and years of research, you might be able to identify it."

Intrigued and a little flattered, Sable crouched closer to the ground. She crossed her forearms and looked down her long snout at Bight. "Describe it."

He did so, in clear and precise terms, without once mentioning the fact that the disease was imperiling Sanction.

Sable's expression turned contemplative—an effect that Linsha found disconcerting. "Where did you witness this disease?"

"On a ship from Palanthas. Most of the crew had died from it."

The dragon curled a lip thoughtfully. "Since you rarely leave that ridiculous little lair you call Sanction, it must have come into your harbor." She paused as if dissecting this information. "I'm surprised the ship made it past those dark ships near the bay. Pirates are always on the lookout for an easy prize. Hmmm . . . let me think." She gazed sightlessly into the distance, oblivious to the drops of acid that fell from her teeth to the ground. "It sounds similar to a plague I noted before the last Cataclysm. Killed mostly humans. Unfortunately it died out before I grew interested enough to study it."

"How? How did it die out?" he asked, trying not to sound too insistent.

"I don't remember. Some thought it was induced by magic because it flared up so quickly." Sable suddenly snorted and sprang to her feet. "That is all I remember. I have talked enough, Bight. May I have the jar, or do I melt you and your female into an insignificant puddle?"

He laughed. "You can try, Sable, and I will never bring specimens for your collection again."

"Ha! Most of them are worthless anyway. I don't know why I bother coming."

In spite of her words, she watched avidly while Lord Bight placed the jar and its creature back in its packing and fastened the lid. With a delicacy Linsha wouldn't have believed possible for such a large dragon, the black clamped three claws around the box and lifted it carefully. She executed a little run toward the edge of the plateau before she jumped skyward and her wings took their first great sweep downward. The force of the air thrust beneath her knocked Linsha and Lord Bight to the ground. Without a final word or farewell, Sable glided into the approaching darkness and passed away on silent wings.

A very long moment of silence followed.

Linsha was so flabbergasted she didn't know what to say. She climbed to her feet and stared at Lord Bight, who appeared deep in thought. Emotions seethed within her: disbelief, amazement, disappointment, relief, awe, confusion.

"Is that it?" she finally exploded with the first thought that came into words. "We left Sanction in the middle of a crisis and walked for an entire day to give a jar of waste water to a dragon? For what?"

He rose and answered calmly, "Actually that was not just dirty water. It was a cutthrull slug, a very rare and particularly viscous little parasite that Sable has wanted for her collection."

"Is that how you bribe her to stay away from Sanction? An odd parasite here, a slave there? I can't believe she accepts it. There has to be something more."

"Why?"

Linsha heard the sharp edge of his query and realized her questioning was pushing the limits of her position as squire. She toned down her inquisitor's voice and returned to being Lynn. She lifted her hands in a careless gesture. "Sorry, Your Excellency. The dragon scared me witless. I guess I just overreacted."

"She does have that effect."

"But I still don't understand how a dragon overlord like Sable doesn't just melt you and take Sanction for her own."

Lord Bight cocked one eyebrow and flashed his enigmatic smile. "Sable and I have a diplomatic relationship. The creatures I bring her are only a small part of it."

A diplomatic relationship. The Clandestine Circle would love that ambiguous response. In fact, Linsha couldn't wait to tell them. For years the Knights of Solamnia had thought it strange that the lord governor seemed to devote most of his efforts toward foiling Sable while the Dark Knights continued to camp at his back door. Why, they wondered, didn't he do something to rid Sanction of them permanently? Some in the Circle feared he was secretly laying the groundwork for a profitable treaty with the Dark Knights.

Except, Linsha thought, what good did it do to rid yourself of one enemy when a more powerful one could just move in and turn all your hard work to swamp? Lord Bight was not all-powerful, despite how he acted sometimes, and his resources were not limitless. Perhaps he decided to resolve his problems with the worst enemy first and merely keep the others at bay until he was ready to give them his full attention. She couldn't believe that he would willingly relinquish control of the city to anyone, dragon, or Knight, or even volcano. Lord Bight would deal with the Knights of Takhisis when he was ready. Unfortunately, none of this explained why Sable respected his presence in Sanction.

Linsha pulled in a deep breath. She still felt shaky and confused, and she wasn't sure what Lord Bight had learned from the conversation with Sable.

When she asked him, he rubbed his beard and answered dryly. "Sable knows not to lie to me. It would dry up her source of specimens. But she rarely tells me anything directly. That reference to dark ships and pirates, for example. There could be one, or there could be many. There have been no pirates in Sanction Bay for many years, but she wouldn't have mentioned them if there hadn't been some kernel of truth in her words. When we return, I intend to send some scouts to find out."

He began walking back up the plateau, and Linsha fell in beside him.

"What about the disease?" she asked.

"Oh, she knows what it is. That's why she left so quickly, so she wouldn't have to tell me. But she did drop a few useful hints. There *is* a precedence for this plague; maybe we can find it in the old records. And the theory that it was started by magic. That's interesting. I need to talk to Mica about that one."

"All right," Linsha sighed. "I'm just glad that's over. Where to now?"

"Back to Sanction."

"Back the way we came?" she groaned.

"Unless you'd rather climb over the mountains. That takes about three more days."

Linsha thought about Varia and Windcatcher, her bed in her small chamber, the bathhouse in the garden, and in the back of her mind came a teasing reminder of Ian Durne. "No, thanks," she said. "I'm with you, my lord."

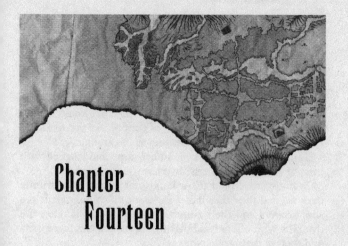

Chapter
Fourteen

The journey back to Sanction was as long and arduous as before, and yet, for Linsha, it was easier in some ways. She knew what to expect and how to pace herself, and she could prepare herself both mentally and physically for the dangerous crossing of the lava chamber. She made the return trip through the fire cave without a stumble and suffered only a headache from the heat and fumes.

Lord Bight was more at ease, too, and talked with her for hours through the dark and endless passages. He loved to tell stories about Sanction in the early years, when the citizens were becoming accustomed to his ways and the town was being rebuilt.

"A shipload of gnomes wandered into Sanction Harbor," he said, his voice full of amusement. "They had the biggest, most complex hunk of machinery mounted atop this flat-decked boat that had no rudder and no anchor. That thing crashed into the southern pier just two days after we finished rebuilding it." He laughed quietly at the memory. "They were so upset, I couldn't stay angry with them for long, so I put them to work to pay for the damages. We were trying to clear out the slums to the north, and I asked them to build some construction equipment to help with the task. They were so excited, they tinkered and experimented for days, and when they finally completed a machine—I still don't know what it was supposed to do—it ran out of control, set fire to an old building, and burned half the slum to the ground."

Linsha imagined the scene in her mind and laughed with him. "I suppose that's exactly what you intended."

"Of course. I paid them handsomely, and in gratitude they burned the other half." He went on to talk about the shopkeepers and their running feud with the kender, the dwarves who offered to build the aqueduct, the merchants and their shipping companies.

In a voice full of memories, he talked about his friend, the harbormaster, who boldly walked up to him on the water-front many years ago and told him the docks were a disaster and what did he intend to do about it?

"I hired him on the spot," Lord Bight said, a hint of sadness in his voice.

Linsha listened, fascinated, to every word. She learned as much about Sanction's history, its people, and its governor in that one journey as she had in all her years on the streets. Lord Bight's stories, as well as the ring of sincere pleasure and fascination in his voice, only confirmed her belief that he would never betray himself or the city by turning over control to anyone else. She wished fervently the entire Clandestine Circle could have been there to hear his stories. Maybe after listening to him, they would realize the truth and leave him alone. Then again, probably not. The Circle was suspicious by nature and required overwhelming amounts of evidence to change their minds. A few stories told in the dark by the man they disliked and distrusted wouldn't budge them from their belief in his inherent evil.

Linsha and Lord Bight made one stop that night and another during the long, dark day to rest and eat. They made good time and were past the volcano and close to the halls of the shadowpeople soon after sunset.

They were nearing the tunnel beneath the old Temple of Duergast when Lord Bight said, "I've had enough of stone tunnels. Let's go see Sanction in the open air."

At Linsha's willing reply, he led her into a different passage and eventually to another stone spiral staircase. This one led up to a secret door in the ruins of the black temple once dedicated to the worship of Queen Takhisis. The temple sat alone, abandoned and ignored, on a high ridge in the shadow of Mount Ashkir.

"The only reason I leave the temple alone is that it makes a good disguise for the secret door." Lord Bight told Linsha. "It also has a spectacular view of Sanction."

After exiting through the hidden door, they picked their way through rubble and piles of windblown debris in the temple's main altar room and found their way outside. The day's light had faded completely, and night held sway over the Vale of Sanction. A thin veil of clouds covered the sky, and a warm wind blew from the west. After the cold of the subterranean tunnels, the heat of the summer night almost felt good.

The governor was right, Linsha saw. The view of Sanction was spectacular. From the high ridge, they could see the harbor spread out to their left and the lights of the long southern pier laid out like a string of jewels. Before them and to their right stretched the city, bustling with lights and moving traffic as the citizens took advantage of the break from the fiery daytime heat. The lava dikes gleamed like a red-gold ribbon across the velvet darkness of the valley.

Although they were too far away to hear the general hubbub of the city, one noise, long and strident, penetrated the humid darkness: a signal horn blown from the southern end of the harbor district.

Lord Bight snapped an oath.

"Where? Can you see it?" Linsha asked. She knew the City Guards' horn signals well and recognized the call as a signal for fire.

"There," he said and pointed to a large warehouse near the southern pier. Smoke, barely visible against the city lights, was just beginning to curl upward from the roof.

"Gods," Linsha breathed. "At least it's not close to the quarantine hospital. But if that fire gets out of control . . ."

She didn't have to finished the sentence. They both reached the same dreadful conclusion. Lord Bight broke into a jog down an old stone road that snaked along the ridge. The road had been paved at one time, but nature and farmers scavenging for building stones had left the road weedy and full of holes. It doubled back along the ridge several times, then curved down past several new farms where grape arbors grew in neat terraces. The road quickly improved here where local use was heavier, and cottages and small buildings grew more numerous the closer Linsha and the governor came to the city.

Soon they reached another road that led to the southern bridge over the lava moat. City Guards stood by the high, arched bridge and crossed their spears to bar the way. Lord Bight snapped an order, and the startled guards hurried aside.

Linsha hardly noticed the increased heat and the stink of molten rock as she ran behind the lord governor over the bridge and through the common meadows. Beyond the meadows, they reached the heavily populated neighborhoods just to the west of the new city wall.

Linsha, more familiar with the back streets and alleys, led the way now with her sword loosened in its scabbard and her eyes searching for trouble. They reached a small postern gate in the city wall where a squad of the City Guard stood nervously. Strangely, the gate was closed and barred.

"What is the meaning of this?" Lord Bight demanded, walking out of the darkness into the light of a dozen torches.

Linsha had to give them credit. The startled guards snapped to attention and saluted the lord governor without falling over themselves or asking a lot of stupid questions. Their sergeant stepped forward to present himself.

"Your Excellency, we were not expecting you. Commander Durne said you were detained at the palace."

Lord Bight grunted a noncommittal response, then said, "Why are the gates closed?"

The sergeant looked surprised that Lord Bight did not know. "Orders, sir. The disease has spread so far, the City Council decreed that the city gates were to be locked and barred last night when the city was quiet. Folks haven't liked it one bit, I can tell you, sir."

The governor's eyes narrowed and the lines of his face hardened to stone.

"But what of the City Guards that patrolled the waterfront and the harbor district?" Linsha asked.

"Those that were not sick or dead were withdrawn under Commander Durne's orders," replied the sergeant. He recognized Lynn and nodded to her. "The west side of the city has been pretty much left to its own, and people are scared."

"There's a fire in the warehouse district," Lord Bight said angrily. "Is there anyone left to put it out?"

"I don't know, Your Excellency. The volunteer fire brigade should answer the summons, but whether or not there are enough men left able to fight a fire, I don't know."

"Then I'd better go check on it. Come on, Lynn," the governor ordered.

"Your Excellency, wait!" protested the sergeant. "You need to get in behind the wall. The plague is rampant in the outer city."

"That fire is more dangerous at the moment," Lord Bight replied, turning away.

"Then let us go with you, your lordship. You will need all the help you can find," offered the sergeant.

Lord Bight answered in midstride. "Thank you, Sergeant. I appreciate your offer. However, until I know more about the situation, you should obey your orders and guard this gate. Later I may need someone to let me back in."

The sergeant and his men saluted. They took Linsha's pack for safekeeping, gave her a small wine sack, and watched worriedly as the two hurried back into the darkness of the streets.

Linsha gratefully sampled the wine as she followed Lord

Bight. It was a white of local vintage, light and refreshing on a hot night. She passed the sack to the lord governor, who took a long swallow before he passed it back. Linsha slung it over her chest for later.

Although she would have liked more, she needed to stay alert. Something wasn't right in these streets she knew so well. The taverns and shops were open but were nearly empty, and every house she saw was closed and barred, despite the hot night. There were the usual gully dwarves and stray dogs rooting about the refuse heaps and some groups of happily chattering kender, but there were very few people of any race outdoors. She noticed, too, a faint stench of death on the wind that had not been there a few days ago.

Shortly, another smell masked the scent of death, smoke thick and black. It boiled out of the burning warehouse and clogged the streets downwind with a choking, blinding haze. Linsha decided she'd had enough of hot fumes for one day and tugged the governor in another direction. She brought them around through the warehouse district so they could approach the burning building from the north, where the smoke wasn't so thick. A few other people, mostly men, hurried in the same direction.

By the time Linsha and Lord Bight reached the warehouse—a two-story structure of timbers and stucco—the fire was out of control. A desultory bucket line made some attempt to keep it from spreading to a neighboring warehouse, but the fire was so intense, the wall of the neighboring building was starting to smoke. The wind didn't help either, for it whipped the fire into a conflagration and blew sparks and embers onto other buildings. The summer had been too hot and too dry, and the city was like a tinder pile waiting to burn.

The lord governor made a quick assessment of the emergency. Before he could take action, however, a tall, smoke-covered man recognized him and burst out of the bucket line. "Lord Bight," the man cried frantically. "You've got to help us. That warehouse is empty, but the one about to catch fire is filled with barrels of wine and lamp oil." It was Vanduran

Lor, head of the Merchants' Guild. His long face was streaked with oily sweat and flushed from the heat of the fire.

The governor rolled his eyes. Could there be a warehouse in the district any more volatile?

"Vanduran, what are you doing here?" Lord Bight growled. "I thought the council voted to shut the city gates. Shouldn't you be in the inner city?"

The merchant drew himself up. "I didn't vote for that, Your Excellency. My business and my workers are here. I stayed to look out for them." He leaned forward, his hands clasped in supplication. "Please, we had to move the sick house this afternoon to that larger warehouse on the next street. It's in the direct path of the wind and sparks."

"Why was it moved?" Lord Bight demanded, his eyes lost in the shadows of a frown.

Vanduran looked puzzled that the lord governor didn't know. "The previous house was overwhelmed," he told Lord Bight. "The healers there died, and the plague has spread through the harbor district so fast we can no longer control it."

"In two days?" Linsha said, appalled.

The merchant nodded sadly. "The disease flared up like . . . like that." He pointed to the fire. "Once the gates were locked, there was no one to enforce the quarantine, so we just packed up everyone in the hospital and moved them to a larger building. At least the people who want care can go there and receive help. We have volunteers taking care of the sick, keeping the delirious away from others, and a few healers are there." He paused again, his eyes haunted. "But it's dreadful."

At that moment, everyone's attention was drawn to a clatter of horses' hooves, and a contingent of City Guards and the Governor's Guards turned a corner and rode into the street where the bucket line struggled to hold back the fire. Commander Durne rode at their head. He spotted Linsha and Lord Bight, and his face split in a grin of relief and pleasure.

"Lynn," Lord Bight said to Linsha, taking her arm. His

voice was low and urgent." There's something I want to do, but it requires time and concentration. I cannot be constantly interrupted. Tell Commander Durne to keep the bucket line moving and do what he can to keep the fire from spreading. I will be back."

"Where are you going? Let me come with you," she insisted.

"Not this time. I won't be long." He gave her arm a slight squeeze, and as the guards rode toward them, he faded back into the milling crowd of helpers and onlookers.

Vanduran turned around to say something more to the governor. "Lord Bight, I—Where is he?"

Linsha, aggravated that she couldn't follow the governor, pretended not to hear him. The roar of the fire was increasing by the moment, making any conversation difficult.

Commander Durne and his men rode over to where Linsha and the guild merchant stood across the street from the fire.

A flush of pleasure warmed Linsha's face and took her by surprise. For two days, she had been gone from Sanction and inundated by the magnetic presence of Hogan Bight. She had deliberately tried not to think about Ian Durne in the hope that she could forget her senseless infatuation for him. But the moment she saw his long, lean figure sitting so easily in his saddle, the yearning came washing back, and she caught herself staring at his face.

To hide her discomfort, she didn't give the commander a chance to start demanding answers. She saluted to him as he dismounted and focused on the emblem of the burning sword on the chest of his uniform coat. She brusquely said, "Sir, Lord Governor Bight asks that you organize the fire fighters as best you can. He will return shortly."

Durne nodded as if used to such requests. "Good evening to you, too, squire. I am pleased to see you returned safely."

An unexpected warmth in his voice pulled her gaze back to his face, and their eyes met in a brief moment of silent union. He lifted a devilish eyebrow and grinned.

"Commander Durne," an insistent voice demanded loudly. "Lord Bight has slipped off again! Would you please do something before the other warehouse goes? There's a street of apartment buildings right next door." Vanderan waved an agitated hand in the general direction of the conflagration.

"And the sick house," Linsha added, having to shout now over the noise of the raging fire.

Her words were lost in a sudden roar as a section of the roof collapsed into the building in an explosion of sparks and flames. Burning debris fell on buildings close by and threatened new fires. She heard the rumbling groan of tortured timbers in the dying warehouse.

"Let's go," Commander Durne bellowed. Swiftly he organized his men into two more bucket lines and commandeered the use of every barrel, bucket, box, or container he could lay his hands on. Spectators were pressed into service, either manning the public water pumps or carrying buckets. Other volunteers wielded shovels to put out ground fires or to smother burning debris.

Another crash signaled the fall of the rest of the roof in a shower of burning embers. The smoke and the heat grew worse. Suddenly someone shouted and pointed toward the roof of the wine storehouse. The eaves on the corner nearest the fire were scorched and smoldering. As people turned to look, the roof burst into flames. Guild Master Vanduran gave a horrified shout and swiftly led a small group of helpers into the smaller warehouse. Moments later they were rolling barrels of wine out of harm's way.

Linsha found herself in the bucket line, frantically passing buckets back and forth to douse the flames of the second fire. She wondered briefly where Lord Bight had gone and why, then her mind returned to the threatened building and the desperate need for water.

"Lynn, thanks be, You're all right. Where have you been?" a familiar voice murmured beside her.

Linsha glanced sideways. Lady Knight Karine Thasally stood in the line beside her, her face begrimed with sweat and soot, her pale hair speckled with ash. She exchanged an empty bucket for the full one in Linsha's hand.

Linsha turned her head so only Karine could hear. "Lord

Bight took me to see Sable," she answered as softly as she could over the uproar of the fire.

Karine nearly dropped her bucket. "What?"

The expression on her leader's face was worth the trip under the mountains.

"You'd better report this in person. The Circle is starting to question your silence."

Linsha ignored that. "Are you doing well?"

Karine grimaced. "So far. But we've lost two others. Good men. Lynn, be very careful. There are ugly rumors spreading in the outer city that blame Lord Bight for this catastrophe. The citizens here are outraged about the closing of the city gates. They fear the city council is leaving them out here to die."

"That's preposterous," Linsha snapped, passing on a bucket.

"You know that and I know that. But everyone is terrified. They want someone to blame. Rumors are rampant."

Linsha remembered the man who incited the boys to throw bottles at Lord Bight and the crowd. "Is there a possibility these rumors are linked to one person or a group of persons?"

Karine was surprised by the suggestion. "Not that we know of. Why?"

"Just a thought." She started to ask Karine to have someone look into it, but an ugly thought stopped her. The three leaders of the Clandestine Circle wanted Lord Bight discredited. What was to stop some of their other operatives from making a few well-chosen comments, opinions, or hearsay rumors in some busy tavern or crowded street? No one would know the source of the rumors. She wondered if Varia had had any luck finding the man with the strange gait. A talk with him could be very interesting.

Another thought, a safer one, occurred to her, and she asked, "Have you heard anything about Elenor? I'm worried about her."

"Not yet," Lady Karine said. "If I can, I'll send someone to check on her."

They worked in silence side by side, passing buckets until their arms and backs ached and their eyes and throats stung from the smoke.

" 'Ware the walls!" someone shouted.

Everyone turned to stare at the first warehouse. Its roof gone and its interior gutted with flame, the warehouse looked like a burning shell, and the outer walls, weakened by heat and a lack of support, began to sag. The danger lay in the fact that no one could be certain which way the walls would fall. Two appeared to be sagging inward, but the other two bulged out over the streets, crowded with volunteers and onlookers.

Linsha felt a strange trembling in the soles of her feet. It reminded her of her passage under Mount Ashkir when the earth shook from the power of the volcano. But she wasn't near a volcano vent now. The trembling increased dramatically until her legs were shaking. Other people noticed it, too. Voices broke out in cries of fear.

Commander Durne identified it first. "Earthquake!" he shouted. "Earthquake! Everyone away from the buildings."

Shouting and screaming, people tried to run as the shaking became stronger. The fire fighters staggered away from the burning buildings. The first warehouse shivered violently, its walls swaying, then it collapsed in a blazing heap of timbers and rubble. The fire in the second warehouse abruptly leaped skyward as the structure cracked apart, allowing air to rush into the interior. The fires roared, their ruddy light stark against the night sky. The earth groaned and shook like a thing in pain.

Linsha and Karine threw down their buckets and turned to run. Suddenly Karine grabbed Linsha's arm and pointed with a shaking finger. "Lynn, look!"

Not more than five paces away from the two women, the paving stones in the street started to shake so hard they vibrated loose from their places. Linsha looked closer and saw the worst of the tremors radiated out from the center of the block containing the two burning warehouses. Everything within the roughly oval area shook as if battered by a giant, while the earth outside the affected area seemed only to tremble in shock. Beset by the unending tremors, the ground became like quicksand, unstable and hungry.

With sudden ferocity, a massive sinkhole yawned open beneath the two warehouses. Rubble, flaming timbers, masonry, wine barrels, oil kegs, and the burning remains of two buildings collapsed into the gaping hole in a rending, sliding crash. Smoke and dust roiled up into the night sky.

Deeper into the hole slid the wreckage. Street pavers, hitching posts, buckets, and a freight wagon trembled on the edge of the monstrous hole, then slipped over into the churning flames and debris.

Karine and Linsha stood awestruck, gazing at the sinkhole so close to their feet, until someone drew them away.

"I'd hate to see you two fall in there," Commander Durne shouted over the cacophony of the collapsing buildings.

Karine shot Linsha a quick glance, nodded her thanks to the commander, and hurried away.

Durne remained standing by Linsha, his pale eyes glinting in the reflected light of the fire.

By now the wreckage of the two buildings had slid out of the sight of the stunned spectators on the street, and the fires, smothered by earth and rubble, died out. Darkness, hot and steaming, closed down over the block, broken only by a scattering of torches and smaller debris fires.

The shaking slowed, and the tremors finally ceased. The earth settled quietly back to normal.

Into the sudden, shocked silence, one voice said loudly, "Suffering shades of perdition! That's one way to put out a fire."

Scattered laughter helped ease the frightened tension.

"Broach the wine casks," Vanduran Lor shouted. "Let's drink to that."

There was a ragged chorus of cheers and a rush to the small pile of salvaged casks. The guild master stood aside and let the fire fighters have their reward.

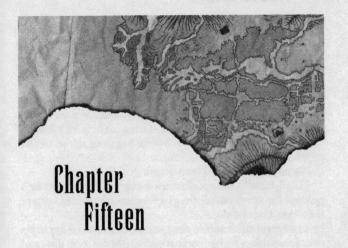

Chapter
Fifteen

Commander Durne put his men and Linsha back to work smothering the remaining fires before another one went out of control. A small group of people gathered at the rim of the sinkhole to stare down.

Linsha took a minute to snatch a look and saw the hole was not as deep as she imagined. The building debris filled the bottom, and earth had collapsed over and around the pile. Anyone with a little determination could fill in the hole, level the lot, and build another warehouse. There was plenty of determination in Sanction.

Then she overheard a man say, "At least we now have somewhere to put the bodies." And her heart turned cold. She could hardly bear the thought that the spirit of the city she admired so much had been forced, almost overnight, to shift from looking for possibilities to looking for mass graves.

"I heard someone say this fire was started deliberately

to spread into the infected district," a man said in a cold, penetrating voice that drew people's attention.

Linsha stiffened, her ears pricked to listen.

"They're all infected," a sailor snorted. "All but the inner city."

The first speaker pointed eloquently at the smoldering remains in the sinkhole. "He wanted to burn out the infection at the hospital. So they start it here, make it look like an accident so no one will know. Maybe burn out the rest of us in the process."

"Who does?" a third man asked.

"Lord Bight!" the speaker cried angrily. "I've heard he's ordered his guards to set fires in warehouses like this where they won't be obvious."

Linsha sidled nearer to the speaker. She crossed her arms over the emblem on her surcoat and hoped the soot, dirt, and darkness would hide the color of her uniform. Although she had not seen the man who caused the boys to pelt the guards with bottles, she had Varia's description of a man with a strange gait. This man she watched now was slight, dark-haired, narrow in the face, and had a twisted foot. She didn't recognize him, but she would wager a steel coin he was the same troublemaker.

So why was he here, agitating the people, now? Linsha dearly wanted to know if he just carried a giant grudge, or if he was in someone's pay.

A few of the spectators had left once the fires were out, but the guards, the volunteer fire fighters, and many stragglers remained to finish the wine and gawk at the sinkhole. The group by the speaker near the pit was growing into a crowd as more people, drawn by the gathering and the loud voices, pressed around to listen. Linsha could hear other people in the crowd pass on the overheard rumors. The story grew with every telling. Faces already strained with fear turned hard in anger. A few tried to argue for Lord Bight's sake and were shouted down.

Linsha tried to think of a way to extricate the speaker from the mob without attracting attention, but nothing creative came to mind. She was about to summon Commander Durne for help when she saw Lord Bight walk slowly out of a darkened alley. For the first time since she had known him, he appeared tired and sapped of his usual boundless energy. Commander Durne hurried to his side, and they conversed quietly.

A small light clicked in Linsha's mind. Now she knew why the sinkhole appeared so conveniently under the warehouses. I must be really tired not to have thought of it sooner, she grumbled to herself. Then anger welled up in her soul. These people knew their lord governor wielded magic that could control the earth. Why couldn't they understand that now?

Later she realized what a risk she took, but at that particular moment, exhausted, sore, thirsty, hungry, filthy, and angry, she let go of her common sense and marched into the thick of the crowd like an avenging spirit.

"Are you fools that you listen to such drivel?" she shouted furiously at the mob around her. She stamped up to the dark-haired man and shoved her face close to his. "Who do you think formed the quake and the sinkhole and put out the fire? Have you forgotten the man who tamed your volcanoes? Who preserved your peace? Who dedicated his life to saving this pathetic city? Lord Bight isn't going to burn something he has worked so hard to build."

The speaker's eyes glittered feverishly. "Why should he worry about us when he has the fat, wealthy merchants and the elders in the city to protect?" he yelled back at her.

"*You* are the city, all of you. He is doing his utmost to save everyone he can. Merchant, sailor, baker, or laundress."

"And who are you?" the man snarled, pointing to Linsha's uniform. "His guardian whore? Of course you're going to speak to save him."

Linsha turned livid. "Save him from what? The likes of you? He doesn't need me to speak for him. His actions should be all you need to remember his devotion to Sanction."

"What devotion? He's probably hiding in his palace behind the city walls."

"No! He's—" But her words were cut off by a barrage of questions.

"Then why has he ordered the gates locked against us?" a woman shouted.

Another sailor cried, "Why has the harbor been closed down?"

Linsha threw up her hands as if to ward off the verbal blows. "To slow the spread of the plague until we can find a cure."

The suggestion of such a possibility brought a storm of response. Questions, statements, angry curses, and hopeful shouts erupted from the crowd as everyone voiced his or her opinion.

The dark-haired man's strident voice rose above all others. "Lord Bight's only idea of a cure is to burn down the harbor district. He burned the ships and the inn, didn't he? That's his answer to a cure. Burn us to the ground and use the merchants' money to rebuild! That's why the gates are locked!"

"I've had enough out of you," Linsha muttered to herself. She raised her voice over the clamor and bellowed, "Have any of you stopped to think that gathering close together like this could be what helps spread the disease? Look at the crew of the *Whydah* and the people they touched. How many of you are already infected?"

That silenced them. The terror of the plague was more effective than dragonawe to break up the shouting mob. Everyone looked askance at those around to look for the telltale blotches, the flush of fever, or the blank-eyed look of delirious terror. The crowd abruptly fractured as most people thrust their way out and hurried away. A few moved farther away from each other and waited to see what would happen next.

In the jostling and shoving press, the dark-haired man tried to sidle away from Linsha. Someone banged into her back, and she snatched the opportunity to fake a fall forward. Her hand shot out and grasped the man's arm as if to save herself. Her other hand flashed into her coat and pulled a slim knife from her waistband. When she straightened, she had the blade pressed firmly into his back and his arm bent at an uncomfortable angle.

"We need to talk. In private," she hissed in his ear.

His eyes rolled back at her, and she felt his muscles tense. "Don't try to fight me. I can break you in half."

She saw Commander Durne and several guards deliberately move her way through the dispersing crowd. Her eyes narrowed and she looked for a path to slip out of sight. She didn't want to interrogate this fellow in front of the man she suspected he almost killed.

But there was nowhere to go. The sinkhole was to her right, and a mass of people behind her might spot her dagger and try to relieve her of her prisoner. The guards and the commander were closing in on her.

Instead she tried a desperate ploy. Hauling the man closer, she shoved her dagger through his clothes and into the skin of his back. He gasped and stiffened in fear. "I saw you at the south pier," she said fiercely, close to his ear. "You are the one who told the youths to throw the bottles at the Governor's Guards."

The man sneered. "So what of it? Seemed a good joke at the time."

Linsha smiled inwardly. So she was right. Now to take it a step further. "No. You meant more. You wanted to cause trouble for Lord Bight. You've been all over the waterfront stirring up trouble and spreading rumors. Who do you work for?"

"No one!"

"Do you see that man walking toward us? That's the man who fell in the harbor after the bottle hit his head. I'm going to tell him it was your fault."

The crowd was rapidly thinning, and Durne was clearly headed in their direction, his brow lowered and his hand on his sword. Her prisoner saw the commander and visibly blanched. A strange curse burst from his lips, and he tried to squirm out of her grasp. Linsha twisted his arm tighter and pushed the blade deeper into his muscle until he clenched his teeth and stilled his struggles. They both were breathing heavily from their quiet, intense struggle.

"Who paid you?" Linsha tried again.

"Get me out of this and I'll tell you," he whispered, almost frantic.

"Tell me now and I'll let you go to fend for yourself."

"The Knights," he gasped. "An agent for the Knights."

"*Which* Knights?" Linsha breathed.

But she was too late.

A Khurish trader, huge, swarthy, and tipsy on the free wine, swaggered up to see the sinkhole. Suddenly he staggered and banged into Linsha's arm. Her grip on her prisoner slipped. He snaked out of her grasp, whipped out his own dagger, and leaped at her.

At the man's violent move, the Khur turned in surprise, his big arm sweeping around to stop the man he thought was attacking him. In the same instant, Commander Durne sprang after the dark-haired man. The Khur's huge forearm swept over the shorter man's head and caught the side of Linsha's face, knocking her down heavily. Durne reached them just as she fell. Propelled by his angry momentum, he slammed into the dark-haired man and they both fell backward into the Khur. In the blink of an eye, the three men tottered on the crumbling edge of the hole. Then, in a tangle of arms and legs, they toppled over the rim into the blackness of the pit.

Linsha tried to sit up. Her head rang from the Khur's accidental blow. She sensed someone come up behind her, and without looking around, she knew it was Lord Bight. His hand steadied her and his quiet strength helped her to her feet.

"Lord Bight! It's Lord Bight," people cried around them. "He's here!" Overcoming their fear of the plague, people came forward to gather around their governor. The Governor's Guards hurried forward, too, and swiftly took their places around Lord Bight to keep the crowd at a safe distance while he talked to the citizens and tried to allay their fears and answer their most desperate questions.

Meanwhile, Linsha recognized one young guard and called him over. "Morgan, come help me. Commander Durne fell in the hole."

Together they climbed carefully over the edge and down the steep slope. Tendrils of acrid smoke rose to meet them. Dirt and debris slid under their boots, making their footing unstable. They found the Khur first, flat on his back and grinning at the night sky. He was unhurt and unperturbed by his predicament, so they left him where he lay and searched deeper for Durne and Linsha's prisoner. The pit was hot and treacherous, with hidden holes and shattered debris.

A faint groan led them to the commander, who was sprawled on his back against a large pile of street pavers. The speaker lay on his chest close by, his legs still tangled with Durne's. Morgan scrambled over to his commander and examined him as best he could without moving him.

Linsha slid over to the other man. He remained motionless and limp, his arms flung out. She tugged him free of the commander's legs, then pulled him over. He rolled, gurgling, onto his back to reveal a dagger buried in his chest. Muttering several highly suitable epithets, she pulled the knife out of his body. It was an old one, plain and well used. Probably his own. Disgusted, she laid it on his chest and turned back to Commander Durne.

Morgan had the commander sitting up and trying to get his breath.

"Had his wind knocked out of him," the guardsman grinned, obviously relieved.

Commander Durne drew a gasping breath and winced.

"Are you hurt?" she asked.

"I hit my back on the stones. I think he fell on me."

They all looked at the body.

"Who is he?" Morgan wanted to know.

Linsha shook her head. "I don't know. I thought I recognized him from the incident at the south pier, but he wouldn't talk to me. I was hoping we could arrest him and make him talk. He must have fallen on his dagger." She decided it would be better not to say any more, even to Commander Durne.

"Too bad," Morgan said and immediately dismissed the dead man from his thoughts.

The two of them eased Commander Durne to his feet, but when they tried to help him climb the slippery slope, he groaned in real pain and nearly fell again.

"Morgan, we're going to need some help to get the commander and that Khur out of here. Go see if you can find some rope and some extra arms."

The good-natured guard didn't mind taking orders from a squire when they made sense. With an easy punch to Linsha's arm, he climbed up the side of the sinkhole and out of sight.

Commander Durne sank thankfully to a sitting position on a heap of dirt. Linsha squatted beside him to wait. Despite her efforts to ignore him, she found her eyes drawn inevitably to his face, and she saw his pale gaze studying her. A delicious warmth stole over her, and she indulged in a visual appreciation of his handsome features: his wide mouth, the long, straight nose, the slight indentation in his chin.

He endured only a moment of her silence before his words came tumbling out. "I do not have and never have had a relationship with Shanron," he said abruptly.

Startled, Linsha lowered her eyes. "Even if you had, it is none of my affair. You are my commander. You made that very clear."

He sighed. "I am well aware of that. Yet I find myself drawn to you. I hoped I could put you out of my mind during your absence. . . ." His voice trailed off. His hand cupped her chin and gently tilted her face up to look at him. "Even in this reeking darkness, you're beautiful," he whispered. "What is it about you I cannot resist?"

Usually so confident and self-assured, Linsha trembled. She tried to say something, but nothing even remotely coherent came to mind.

"Commander Durne! Lynn!" Morgan's voice called above them. "Here comes a rope."

The moment of privacy was gone. Linsha felt rather than

saw Durne withdraw from her, and although disappointment cut her, she understood. He couldn't reveal his feelings or even show favoritism for her in front of his guards and still remain an effective leader. She gave him a small smile, then scrambled to her feet to fetch the rope.

With the help of willing hands above and a strong rope, Commander Durne climbed up the sinkhole. Linsha managed to urge the Khur to his feet, tie the rope around his middle, and help him out of the hole as well. The dead man was left where he had fallen.

He wasn't alone for long.

True to the needs of that disastrous week, workers soon set about filling the sinkhole with dead victims of the plague. When it could hold no more, the bodies would be covered with lime and buried under a mound.

Linsha was the last one out of the hole. She climbed out gratefully and withstood a bearish hug from the drunken Khur. She watched him walk unsteadily away. "Thank you, Morgan," she said to the guard as he coiled up his rope.

"Good work, you two," Lord Bight said, joining them. "Now, if the fires are out and everyone is finished playing in the hole, we must go."

A crowd of people still hovered around, and they followed the governor and his guards as the group mounted the horses. Lord Bight was given Morgan's horse, and Morgan and Linsha doubled up with other riders.

"Lord Bight," someone called. "Would you open the city gates? We have friends and family behind the walls. Some of us have jobs. It's too late now to stop the spread of the sickness in the inner city, so let us go in."

Guild Master Vanduran joined the governor by his horse. "The City Council acted in what they thought was the city's best interest," he tried to explain.

Most of the people wouldn't accept that. "They never asked us!" another man shouted.

"That's right!" called a woman. "When they closed the gates and the fires started tonight, we thought you intended to burn the harbor district."

The lord governor looked out over his citizens and raised his hand for silence. "I did not order the gates to be barred, and I never considered burning the sick house or any part of the city." His voice took on the same hypnotic, reassuring tones he had used at the gathering on the south pier. "The closing of the gates was a misunderstanding between myself and the council. The fires were not of my doing, but I promise you I will investigate these rumors of arson. Do you believe me?"

A murmur of cautious satisfaction met his question.

Led by Lord Bight, the company rode forward slowly, so the trailing crowd of Sanction's citizens could keep up with them. More people—men, women, kender, dwarves, elves, and a scattering of other races—joined the march through the hot, dark streets toward the city wall.

Torches were burning beside the huge double doors that stood closed and barred against the city's own populace. City Guards paced the walls and watched nervously as the crowd approached. They didn't recognize Lord Bight in the dim light until he raised his hand to stop the procession.

As soon as the riders and the whispering, expectant crowd halted behind him, he rode forward into the torchlight, accompanied by Commander Durne.

"Who dares bar the gates of this city against me?" he shouted.

Agitated voices called from the wall walk, and there was the sound of running footsteps.

Captain Dewald's fair head appeared over the wall. "My lord! I did not know you were out there. I'm sorry. We were told to allow only Commander Durne and his men to reenter." He snapped orders to someone below, and a postern gate was thrown open.

Lord Bight did not move. The crowd watched their governor hopefully.

"Captain, who ordered these gates to be locked?"

"Your Excellency, the City Council demanded that we lock the gates, and in your absence, we had to obey," Dewald shouted.

"You did as you were required, but I am now counter-manding that order. It is too late for such a measure to be effective. This city will have to stand or fall as a whole. Open the gates and leave them open."

A heavyset figure robed in dark robes pushed his way through the postern and stood blocking the smaller gateway. It was Lutran Debone, the city elder. "My lord, is that wise?" he cried. "We have not yet had any outbreaks in the inner city. Why risk those people to certain exposure?"

Lord Bight urged his horse forward a few steps. "Have you closed the city market? Did you forbid the merchants from visiting their offices or warehouses in the harbor district? Did you shut down the houses on the Street of the Courtesans? Or forbid entrance to anyone from the water-front in the previous days? Have you kept the City Guards apart or forbade their patrols on the waterfront? The disease is already out of control. Since we cannot stop it, we must join together to find the best ways to fight it. Now, open the gates."

Shouts of agreement rose up behind him, and the throng of spectators pushed forward toward the wall.

Alarmed, Lutran turned, hurried back inside, and slammed the postern shut behind him. But louder than the slam of the smaller door came the grinding of gears as the great gates were pulled open.

A cheer rose from the watching crowd as Lord Bight, Commander Durne, Linsha, and the guards rode in through the gate. Satisfied at last, the people walked in through the gates after the governor. There they halted, gathering in chattering groups on the street to enjoy their victory. They knew now their governor would stand up for them.

There was no sign of Lutran Debone.

Captain Dewald met Lord Bight and Commander Durne beside the guards' hall. He saluted his leaders, the relief plain on his face.

"You were right, Your Excellency. The Sailors' Scourge has already started among the courtesans and in the guard camp. I had not had a chance to tell the council."

171

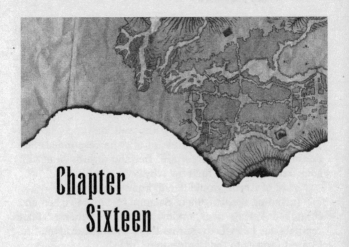

Chapter Sixteen

As soon as the guards' horses had been unsaddled and tended and the guards had trooped off to the dining hall for a well-earned meal, Linsha dashed up the ladder into the hall loft. Her head had no sooner cleared the opening when a winged shape dived out of the darkness and dropped onto the floor beside her. Linsha cleared the ladder, scooped up the owl, and groped her way into a darker, more private corner of the barn. She flopped down on the hay and buried her face in the owl's downy feathers.

Varia cooed with delight. "I missed you! Where did you go? What happened?" she hooted.

The lady Knight lay back in the scented hay, and while Varia perched carefully on her knees, she told the bird the whole tale of her journey under the mountains with Lord Bight to visit the black dragon. Varia listened intently, her head tilted slightly forward and her eyes stretched wide. She commented on each new event with chuckles and clucks and hoots and growls. Although she was used to Varia's talkative nature, Linsha couldn't help a smile. Telling the owl a story was like talking to a crowd.

The owl listened carefully, though, and when Linsha was finished, she wanted to know more.

"So you think Lord Bight has traded with the dragon before?"

"Absolutely. He knew the paths well and knew how to summon her. Most incredible of all, she responded. She doesn't like him, that's certain. But she regards him with some respect. I'd like to know why."

"Most of Krynn would like to know why."

"Including the Knights of Solamnia." Linsha sighed and scratched Varia's neck under her warm fathers. "That reminds me. I saw Lady Karine this evening during the fire. I have to report to the Clandestine Circle."

"What fire?"

"Well, when we got back—" and Linsha launched into the rest of the story of the warehouse fire, Karine, the sinkhole, and the death of the dark-haired man with the clubfoot.

Varia *hoo-hoo*ed softly. "The description fits the man I saw. It probably was the same one."

"It galls me that he died before he could tell me which Knights. I hate to even think it, but I wouldn't be surprised if the Clandestine Circle had something to do with this," Linsha said.

Varia fluffed her feathers in agitation. "Spreading lies and unfounded rumors about your opponent just to create trouble is not honorable."

"Neither is trying to dispose of your enemy by discrediting him. That kind of deceit was never covered in the Measure." She threw her arms up over her head and groaned. "So what am I doing? Deceiving two of the finest men I've ever met . . . after my father and grandfather, of course. Gods, I hate this!"

Immediately Varia's feather "ears' perked up. "Two?" she squawked. "I know you admire Lord Bight. Who is the second?"

Linsha was silent until the owl hopped down onto her chest and stared her straight in the eyes. "All right, all right. I meant Commander Durne. I like him, all right? He's handsome and intelligent and—"

"And he's your commander! And a stranger. What do you really know about this man? What if he's a spy himself?"

"He can't be a spy. He's been at Lord Bight's side for years," Linsha said softly. "But I do know the danger. I just can't stop how I feel about him. Nor can I stop the guilt I feel for deceiving him like this. He doesn't deserve it."

The owl bobbed worriedly up and down. "Now, don't you do something stupid like telling him who you really are. Even if he isn't anything more than a loyal officer in Lord Bight's court, he could still betray you, even unintentionally, to others."

"I know. I'll be on my guard."

Her voice was so sad, the owl rubbed her face against Linsha's cheek. "Do you love him?"

"I don't know." Her answer was a sigh. "Mother used to say, 'Since love concerns the heart, how can the head understand it?' I wish I could talk to her now."

"Your mother would say, Be careful."

Linsha laughed softly. "Yes, Mom."

For once the owl had no further comment. They sat together in companionable silence for a while until Linsha asked, "Have you seen Calzon or Elenor? I worry about them."

"Calzon is still alive and well and selling his tarts in the market, although he has also been spending some time in the refugee camp. There are many sick there, and the rats are plentiful. I do not know about Elenor. I flew by her house yesterday, but I saw no sign of her. I hope she is well."

Linsha stretched out in the hay. Drowsiness stole over her, and she felt her eyelids droop. "So do I," she replied slowly. Then she added, "Why do you suppose the Circle leaders hate Hogan Bight so much?"

"He is an enigma to them. They cannot predict what he

will do and they do not know where he gets his power. That frightens them."

"He doesn't frighten me." She chuckled sleepily and snuggled deeper into the hay. "I think the Circle has seriously underestimated his ability to survive and adapt. He's not going to be so easy to remove."

The owl looked at her curiously. What a complicated weave this woman was! She declared her attraction to one man, and yet the nuances in her voice and the subtleties of her body language revealed a deep respect and devotion to another man. Varia hooted softly. Life had certainly been less complicated when Linsha was a mere alley-basher. Not as interesting, but definitely simpler.

"Where is your cat?" Linsha asked, her voice thick with approaching sleep.

"She's over there. Your friend brought her so much fish, she has been too stuffed to hunt for me." The owl flapped over to the other side of the hayloft and came back urging along the tortoise-shell ship's cat. The graceful feline saw Linsha, meowed, and dropped beside her in the hay. She didn't seem at all frightened of Varia.

Linsha stroked the cat's soft side and rubbed her ears. The cat purred softly. Linsha listened to the gentle sound and to the other contented noises that filled the barn with tranquility: the movement of tired horses eating their grain, the rustle of mice in the hay, the faint flutter of the bats in the cupola, the sighing of the wind in the eaves. One by one she drew her mind away from each sound until there was nothing left in her ears but the thud of her own heartbeat. Before long that, too, faded, and there was only the silence of sleep.

Varia found a place to perch on a roof rafter just above Linsha's nest in the hay. She tucked one foot up into her feathers and settled down to wait in contemplative peace. Suddenly her eyes opened wide and the feathers on her head flared up. She heard movement in the stable below. It sounded like a male human, perhaps a groom checking on the horses one last time. A heavy step passed through the aisle and came to a stop by the ladder to the hayloft. Varia tensed, listening. Nothing happened. The man didn't walk away, but he didn't climb the ladder either. All she heard were the night noises of the barn.

Something moved by the ladder. A small dark shape leaped gracefully into the loft and padded across the floor. Varia stared down at it. It was another cat, a big orange tom, and one she had never seen in the barn before. The owl hunched over, ready to dive on the cat if he offered trouble.

The big tom sensed the owl's presence. He sat down in the hay near Linsha and looked up into Varia's round yellow gaze with his own golden eyes.

Varia straightened abruptly. Understanding, fresh and titillating, filled her mind. She started to hoot with laughter and nearly fell off her rafter. Remembering the sleeping woman below, she toned her amusement down to throaty warbles and watched in good humor as the orange cat sniffed Linsha's face then lay down close to her side, across from the other cat. The calico lifted her head once, meowed, and went back to sleep.

The animals in the barn settled down for the night.

* * * * *

By the time dawn filtered through the barn's windows, the orange cat was gone. Varia did not mention him, for she loved a good secret, and the calico cat remained inscrutable.

The sound of banging lids on feed bins and the neighs of hungry horses brought Linsha wide awake and made her aware of her own hunger. She used her fingers to comb the hay and dust out of her hair, brushed off her dirty uniform, and hurried down the ladder in search of breakfast.

Shanron met her in the courtyard and greeted her with cool pleasure. But she took one look at Linsha's uniform and marched her back to the barracks, where she thrust clean clothes in Linsha's hands and ordered her to the bathhouse. "If you go into the dining hall looking like that, you'll have kitchen duty for a week," Shanron told her.

"Leave your uniform in the bathhouse. The attendants will wash it for you."

The day was already sultry and windless. The bathhouse stood alone in its shady grove like an oasis of relief, and Linsha decided that Shanron had the right idea. She peeled off her filthy uniform—still stained with dirt, soot, blood, and sweat—tossed it to a bemused attendant, and plunged into the pool like a three-year-old.

Shanron appeared a few minutes later with a flagon of cooled ale and a plate of bread, meat, cheese, and two plums. "I told the cook you were back and had missed dinner, and he nearly fell over himself finding things for you to eat. I think someone has been talking to him about you. He's usually not so solicitous."

"Thank you," Linsha said appreciatively. "Thank you, too, for feeding the cat."

Shanron smiled with a softness that was unusual to her hard features. "She's a dear. I can see why the captain wanted her saved. May I continue to feed her? She and I and the cook have formed a routine now."

"Of course. Just don't feed her so much. The stable attendant was complaining that she wasn't catching mice." Linsha left out the fact that the attendant was an owl.

"I hadn't thought of that," the woman guard said. "Well, enjoy. I can't stay. Commander Durne told me to tell you that you are to report to the weapons master. You still have your training to complete. I'm off to sentry duty at the front gate." She waved a hand and strode out.

Although the cool water felt delightful, Linsha decided not to overextend her time in the bath. She ate quickly, scrubbed clean, and put on a clean tunic and pants. She had a second uniform tunic, but it was hot and she draped it over her arm and decided to let the weapons master tell her if she needed to wear it. With her sword at her side, she went to the training hall and reported for duty.

The rest of the morning she spent with the weapons master practicing close-order defense and the use of a short pike, a weapon she was not familiar with. At lunch she ate in the hall, and in the afternoon she stood sentry duty at the back gate with another squire and worked in the stable. She didn't see Lord Bight or Commander Durne that day, and she was surprised to discover that she missed them both. When she asked, she was told Lord Bight had taken a squad and left to monitor the lava dome on Mount Thunderhorn, while Commander Durne was busy setting up a sick house in the guard camp.

By evening Linsha was weary to the bone, but she finally had a few hours of free time, and she decided to fulfill her duty to another organization. Saddling Windcatcher, she told the stable groom she planned to ride out to exercise her mare. Although she wasn't supposed to leave the palace grounds unattended, she hoped to slip out of sight for a brief while into the trees above the palace riding fields and make her way to the safe house. By her estimation, the small croft was only a few miles away.

* * * * *

"Bight gave her a what?" asked one of the Circle leaders with quiet incredulity.

"A cutthrull slug," Linsha repeated. "He brings Sable specimens for her collection in exchange for information." The lady Knight clasped her hands behind her back and gazed at the three Knights in front of her. They sat at the small table again, like magistrates in court, and even Linsha had to admit they looked as sweaty and tired as she felt. Lady Karine had warned them Linsha would come, and they had been waiting most of the day to hear her report about Lord Bight, but it was not at all what they expected, and the interview had not gone well. Linsha had told them and retold them her tale of the journey to see Sable, and still they could not seem to accept it.

They bent their heads together, murmuring among themselves for a minute. Then the elder Knight turned to Linsha. "We find it difficult to believe that Bight controls Sable with only a few specimens. Are you certain there was nothing else mentioned or alluded to?"

"*Lord* Bight," Linsha replied with a sharp emphasis on the "Lord." She was growing tired of the Circle ignoring his title. "And he does not control the black dragon. I believe they have some sort of agreement, but what it is based on, I do not know yet. I can tell you, though, I am convinced Lord Bight will not willingly relinquish control of Sanction to anyone, and that includes the Dark Knights and the Solamnics."

"We didn't expect it to be easy," one Knight snapped. His face was flushed and he appeared unwell. "Have you found any weakness? Anything we can exploit?"

Linsha eyed him thoughtfully and wondered if the leaders had been in the city. She knew they traveled to other clandestine groups in the area and moved frequently, but only they knew where they went. Perhaps, she thought bitterly, if they had spent more time in Sanction, they would have come to understand better the complicated character of the city and its leader.

She drew a long a deep breath and tried to put her thoughts into words. "My lords, I beg you to think long and carefully before you do anything to undermine Lord Bight's authority. Sanction is a unique place. It has its own problems and factions that are not found anywhere else, and while Lord Bight may be dictatorial and heavy-handed at times, he is the best one to manage its affairs. He controls the volcanoes, he knows the city from the underground up, and he holds a deep respect for its citizens. If you try to control Sanction at this time without Lord Bight, you could be opening yourselves up to disaster." She stopped on that word, seeing in their stony faces a total unwillingness to bend. She wondered if they had heard anything she said.

The elder Knight shook his head. "It's clear, Lady Knight, that your appraisal of the situation in Sanction does not agree with ours. Bight is no longer necessary to the government of Sanction."

She opened her mouth to protest, but the first Knight cut her off with a chop of his hand. "We would relieve you now if you were not the highest placed operative we have. It is our intention to remove Bight to make way for a Solamnic government that will further our interests in this region and drive a powerful wedge into the side of the Knights of Takhisis. We need you to do your part."

Sanction doesn't *need* a Solamnic government, Linsha wanted to shout. Instead, she simply stood, her fingers clenched behind her back, and tried to look penitent. The threat of removal shocked her to the core.

"One more thing," continued the second Knight. "We think a Dark Knight may have successfully infiltrated Bight's inner circle. Unfortunately, we don't know who it is or what position this Knight holds. Be wary. As you know, the Knights of Takhisis were granted control of Sanction nearly thirty years ago. The longer Bight holds them off, the more they want it. The Dark Knights will stoop to anything to regain control of the city and, if possible, destroy Hogan Bight."

"But we won't," Linsha said, half in earnest, half in sarcasm.

"We do what is necessary."

Linsha nodded a short jerk of the head that held little agreement, then stiffened her arm into a salute. "My lords, you have my report. May I have permission to withdraw and return to the palace before my absence is noticed?"

The first Knight rose to his feet and came to stand in front of her. His rugged face softened into an expression of impersonal compassion. "Lynn of Gateway, we know you are in a difficult position in the city. Remember your Oath and your duty, and you will do what needs to be done. You may go."

It took all of Linsha's self-control to contain her dismay, turn on her heel, and march out of the croft. The tendril of frustration that took root during her first meeting with the leaders plunged deep into her angry thoughts and sprang forth into a tangled vine of emotions and confused loyalties.

Brooding behind her silent mask, she rode Windcatcher back to the riding fields and the palace courtyard. She spoke to no one, not even Varia in her loft, while she curried the mare, forked hay into her manger, and bedded her down for the night. Although the evening was still early, she avoided the dining hall and went directly to her room.

But it was a very long time before she found rest.

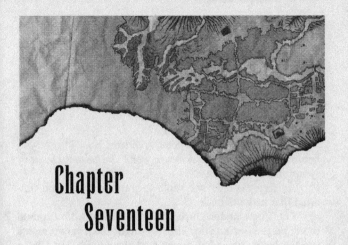

Chapter
Seventeen

The next morning, the twelfth dawning since the merchantman had sailed blindly into Sanction Harbor, the sun rose hot and brazen, and the wind died before midday. The heat grew steadily until the streets became like furnaces and even the shade offered by buildings or trees gave little relief. To the west, a pall of smoke and haze draped the shoulders of Mount Thunderhorn where the lava dome slowly grew like a deadly boil on the volcano's slope. The city's harbor remained eerily quiet.

Linsha expected to return to the training hall as before, but Commander Durne found her in the court and told her to report to the governor's audience hall to stand guard through another council meeting. The commander spoke to her formally and turned away as soon as his orders were issued, and yet she saw the pleasure in his eyes and recognized the way his lips tried to turn up in a smile.

Something fluttered in her stomach as she watched him stride away.

Resigning herself to a tedious morning of standing still in a hot uniform, she pulled on her tunic, strapped on her sword, and went to the lofty audience hall where the table and chairs had been set up once more for a meeting of the Privy Council. When she walked in, she was surprised to see the room was empty except for a man sitting in the great seat of the lord governor.

She bowed. "Your Excellency."

Lord Bight inclined his head. "Squire. I hoped to see you before the others arrive. Are you well? You have no fever or symptoms of the disease?"

"I'm fine. So far," she replied, both surprised and flattered that he would ask.

"You, Commander Durne, and the others were exposed to the plague during your efforts to fight the fire two nights ago. I have commended them for their courage, but I have not had a chance to tell you. I appreciate your efforts to help this city." His lips quirked up in a half-grin. "Thank you, too, for your company under the mountain. It was very informative."

Linsha hesitated. She wasn't sure how to interpret that last statement. "I hope you were satisfied with my 'true mettle,' " she said finally.

"More than satisfied. I have no doubt that you will do well."

A blush crept up her cheeks, and she bowed again to hide her embarrassment. There it was again, that stab of guilt. Lately her feelings of inadequacy and disillusionment had become a painful canker in her mind, but the knowledge that she was deliberately misleading Lord Bight, and Ian Durne, burned in her belly like acid.

"I have something to give you," Lord Bight continued. "Before our visit to Sable, I watched you and wondered if you would become ill after your work with the guards and on the ships. When you did not, I was pleased. Still, I do not want to trust to luck or fate much longer. I want you to have this." He reached into his robes and drew out something fastened to a slim gold chain. The chain slid through his fingers like a golden stream as he held it up just high enough for Linsha to see.

She drew in a sharp breath. A bronze dragon scale hung from the chain. The scale was about the size of her fist and gleamed with translucent shades of deep bronze. Its sharp edges had been filed off and rimmed with polished gold.

"I found this years ago and have kept it, waiting for a good use for its beauty and potency. It has been enchanted with protective spells that I believe—after hearing Sable's tale—will protect you from this contagion. Will you trust me and try it? If its magic works for you, we might be able to find a way to adapt its power for all of us."

Linsha quirked a brow at him and said, "Is this because you do not want to lose a useful pawn?"

His gold eyes flickered with a strange light, but his face showed no expression and he didn't seem angry at her temerity. "Of course."

Slowly she held out her hand. She hadn't been able to say no to him yet. "If it doesn't work for me, I'll come back from the dead and lodge a complaint."

He chuckled and slid the gold chain into her hand. "Fair enough."

Hanging the chain about her neck, Linsha tucked the scale under her tunic, saluted the governor, and took her place by the window just as Commander Durne, the dwarf Mica, Chan Dar, the master of the Farmers' Guild, and the new harbormaster entered the great hall. The four quietly took their seats as servants arrived with refreshments.

A second dwarf—Chert, the engineer, dressed in dusty leggings and leather vest—arrived and plumped down on the chair beside Mica.

The group was subdued. They paid more attention to the wine and fruitcakes than to each other. A few more minutes passed before Priestess Asharia came into the hall and took a seat beside Lord Bight.

Linsha was stunned by the change in the vivacious woman. Asharia's boundless energy had reached an end, leaving behind a woman pale and haggard and mantled in exhaustion. She sipped a glass of wine given to her by Lord Bight, but she made no effort to eat or speak.

Lutran Debone came next, followed by a second man wearing the colors of the Merchants' Guild. Lutran, too, was subdued and didn't even bother to irritate his nemesis, Chan Dar. He sat at the far end of the table and looked everywhere but at Lord Bight.

The final man, in the merchant's robes, bowed to the lord governor. "Your Excellency, I am Wistar Bejan. My master, Vanduran Lor, sends his regrets. He is unwell and cannot attend. He has asked me to come in his place and give you what aid I can."

Lord Bight looked troubled. "I hope he is not ill with the scourge."

A younger man than Vanduran, Wistar appeared uncomfortable in the presence of these august people. His head drooped. "I am afraid he is. He would not leave the harbor district where his ships lie moored and his warehouses sit full of goods he cannot move. He is at home now, but his family holds little hope."

The governor turned to look at the priestess with a silent question.

She shook her head. "Most of my healers are dead or dying, Your Excellency. This disease is too powerful, too devastating. I will try to find someone to go to him, but unless we can find stronger tools to fight this plague, it will defeat us."

Lord Bight leaned forward, his hands clenched to the arms of his chair. A light like hot fire was behind his golden eyes. "I will not accept defeat," he said in a fierce voice. "Not from the plague, nor the volcanoes, nor fires, nor any of you."

His last words caught the council by surprise, and they swiveled in their chairs to look at him.

"As you know now," he went on, "I was gone for two days conferring with a source I know well. The information I gained has been passed on to Mica, and we are making every effort to find those stronger tools. Since my return, I have discovered that too many things have gone wrong. For example, the supplies I ordered from the farms were not delivered to the city. Why not?" He pinned his raking gaze on Chan Dar.

The farmer nervously shifted in his seat and replied, "We are still taking an inventory, Your Excellency. Many of the crops have failed this year because of the hot, dry summer and the lack of water for the new irrigation project." He paused for a moment to glare at Commander Durne. "We were also raided by the Knights of Takhisis two nights ago. They swept out of the northern pass, burned some barns, stole our food, and disappeared before anyone could stop them. I mentioned this to the commander, but he has been busy."

"We have all been busy," growled Durne. "Your problems are only two among many. I don't have the manpower to spare to chase stray Knights back into the mountains."

"The guards have been trying to help us," Chert spoke up for the first time. He put his fists on the table and frowned. "One of the reasons you don't have water yet is that the construction sites for the aqueduct have been sabotaged. The destruction is childish. Tools and plans stolen; measuring lines misaligned; mortar ruined. Simple things. But they have all added up, and we cannot find the culprit. Or culprits. Someone is trying to hinder us, to delay the completion of the aqueduct. It is stupid! Why would anyone do such a thing when our wells are going dry and there is such a need for water?"

Why indeed? wondered Linsha.

"Lord," Wistar spoke up. "We think the fires in the warehouse district were deliberately set."

"Explain"

"Vanduran wondered about it earlier. There were two or three smaller fires set in other places, but those were quickly put out by nearby residents. Only the warehouse fire went out of control. He found a witness who saw someone in the warehouse only a short time before the fire started. The warehouse was supposed to be locked and empty."

187

"Did this witness have a description of the intruder?" asked Commander Durne.

"Unfortunately, no. It was too dark."

"So," Lord Bight's voice grated. "We have raids, arson, sabotage. What else?"

"Your Excellency, if I may speak." Linsha stepped forward. At Lord Bight's nod, she moved closer to the table. "I think you could add inciting to riot to your list. The man I tried to capture the night of the fire was spreading rumors that you had ordered the fires to be set."

"Why?" Asharia said, horrified.

"He claimed the lord governor wanted to burn out the contagion by burning the hospital and the harbor district. He said the gates were locked to save the rest of the city. Many of the people there believed him. I think he could have started a full-blown riot if we had not been there to stop him."

"What happened to this man?" asked Chan Dar. "Did he also start the fires?"

Linsha's mouth tightened in disgust. "I don't know. He tried to escape and fell down the sinkhole. Apparently he fell on his own knife."

"How convenient," the farmer said snidely. He turned to looked at Lutran. "It was your council that ordered the gates shut. Did you also send this rumormonger to cause trouble?"

Lutran Debone leaped to his feet, his expression livid. "Of course not! The entire City Council debated the closure of the gates and voted to lock them. We did not intend to start any trouble."

"But you did not carefully think this through, did you?" Lord Bight said coldly.

The elder finally met the gaze of the lord governor. "No, Your Excellency. We did not. We did not consult with Commander Durne either. I admit we were frightened and overwhelmed by the disaster. You were not here to accept the responsibility, so we took it upon ourselves."

Lord Bight ignored the insinuation about his absence and gestured to Lutran to sit down. "I understand why you would want such a plan to work. I wish it would, too. I would lock those gates in an instant if I thought it would save our people." He leaned back in his great chair, resting his head on the silken pad behind him. His face lost all expression, and only his burning eyes moved to study each member of the council in turn. "Unfortunately, our enemy is within, and it is not something we can lock out."

"Lord Bight," said Asharia, speaking for them all. "Do you suspect one of us is responsible for these crimes?"

If he didn't, Linsha thought, he ought to. According to the Clandestine Circle, one these people close to Lord Bight was an infiltrator from the Knights of Takhisis, and after hearing the list of things that went wrong in the governor's absence, Linsha was inclined to agree. The problem was finding the traitor. All of these people had been in Sanction for years and had been advisors to Lord Bight for as long as she had been there. Where had the Circle gotten its information?

"I do not suspect anyone yet. But I will not let this continue. I am declaring martial law for the city to go into effect immediately. The older residents will remember the laws from the early days, but for the newer inhabitants, my scribes will make copies and post them on the news boards. Alert your own people. The guards have resumed patrols in the harbor district to control the looting. Second, the City Council is to go into recess until this crisis passes. If you have a problem, bring it directly to me. Third, we will double the guard on the construction sites, and I will send riders to guard the shipment of food into the city. Is there anything else?"

"We could use laborers to dig more graves in the outer city," Asharia suggested.

"Unless the families object, take the bodies to the lava dikes. The lava will be quicker and cleaner."

They talked for a while longer of rationing food supplies and water, of setting watches for more fires, and of sending patrols to search houses for dead bodies. Their mood was grim and their optimism languished in the face of such difficulties. Lord Bight soon called an end to the meeting and told them to return the next day.

Commander Durne hurried out to organize guards for the construction sites and to strengthen the watch on the walls. The others left more slowly in ones and twos until only Mica and the harbormaster were left.

Lord Bight beckoned to the harbormaster to stay and walked slowly with him close to the window where Linsha stood. Without mentioning his source, he told the harbormaster about the rumor of pirates and dark ships near the mouth of the bay.

The harbormaster glanced out the window toward the harbor. "I haven't heard that, but I will send scout ships to investigate."

"As soon as possible. And when they return, tell no one but me," Lord Bight ordered.

When the harbormaster had bowed and left, the lord governor turned to Linsha. "Now, squire, I have a task for you."

Linsha tried to hold on to her bland expression. The last time Lord Bight said something like that, she'd found herself facing a lava river and a black dragon.

"Are you able to read? Enough to identify labels and titles?" he added.

Her eyebrows lifted. This sounded a little safer. "Yes, Your Excellency."

"Excellent. Mica is going into the harbor district to retrieve some records from an old priest. I would like you to go with him, help him find the place, and bring the records back to the Mystics' temple. He has a great deal to sort and catalog, so help him with that, too."

"My lord," Mica said, the annoyance plain in his voice. "I can do this myself. I doubt an alley cat is going to be much help."

Lord Bight swiped his hand to one side. "I think you'll find this one is different. Take her with you. She knows that area better than you do."

"But she's human. If she's exposed to—"

The lord governor cut him off. "She's been exposed indirectly several times. She may be immune to it by now."

"Immune? I doubt it!" grumbled the dwarf. "If she isn't, then it's on your head."

The lady Knight jerked her chin up in a knowing nod. So that's why Lord Bight gave her the dragon scale—to send her out into the plague-ridden city. How kind. Still, the scale beneath her tunic lay warm against her skin and took away the worst of her inner dread.

With a salute to the governor, she joined Mica by the table. She smiled sweetly at him and said, "Meow."

The dwarf had no sense of humor. He stood and glowered at her. "Come on. Let's get this done," he said with poor grace.

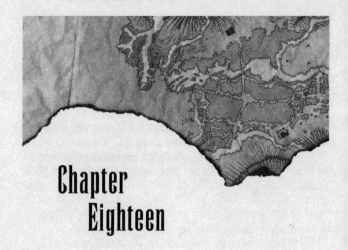

Chapter
Eighteen

For the fourth or fifth time since they left the palace, Linsha swatted away a swarm of flies from her face and glanced at the silent dwarf walking his horse beside hers. He hadn't said a word as they traversed the length of the road into the city. His deep-set brown eyes stared straight ahead; his bearded face registered no emotion. She noticed he was as fastidious about his appearance as ever, for his hair was combed, his clothes were immaculate, and his heavy boots were new. He carried no weapons, only a leather pouch filled with things that left lumps and bulges. She wondered if he had trained at the Citadel of Light with Goldmoon or at one of her mission schools. She wondered what had brought him to Sanction. His stony silence discouraged conversation, and his brooding gaze seemed far away.

They took the Shipmaker's Road and passed easily through the city. Wheeled traffic was very light and few pedestrians were out. The Souk Bazaar was almost deserted.

At the West Gate, City Guards held a strong presence.

A sergeant Linsha didn't know halted them and requested to know their business. Mica told him gruffly, and because he was well known to the guards and Linsha wore the uniform of the governor's bodyguards, they were quickly passed through.

"Sorry," the sergeant apologized. "The gates may be open, but we're trying to restrict traffic to only what is necessary. Most people are cooperating."

At that moment a heavily loaded freight wagon rumbled through without stopping. The two drivers merely waved.

Linsha pointed at the tarp-covered load. "Why didn't you stop them?"

"They've been by here twice today. That's the dead wagon, carrying bodies to the lava moat."

Mica shrugged at her expression. "You had to ask."

They left the gates and hurried on into the outer city.

"Where do you need to go?" Linsha inquired.

"Watermark Street. The man is a scribe and has a shop there," Mica said.

"Then we need to turn left here."

"No, we don't. Watermark Street parallels the harbor. We'll just go straight and meet it," he growled.

"If you go straight along this road, expecting to find Watermark, you'll end up in the harbor. Watermark dead ends in a fish market a block before Shipmaker's Road. Besides, I know the shop you want. He's the only scribe on that street and his shop is in a tiny alley."

"Fine," he said in annoyance. "You lead the way."

Linsha was pleased to do just that. She trotted Windcatcher ahead of the grouchy dwarf and let him worry about keeping pace with her. She relaxed into her saddle, glad to be back on familiar streets in the daylight, to see favorite landmarks and old scenery. The problem was that, while the streets and buildings looked unchanged, the atmosphere was radically different. The bustling energy and verve she was so used to feeling in the streets were gone. The harbor district seemed virtually empty. Only a few people were outdoors, mostly dwarves or kender or those without human blood, and they hurried by with tough expressions, as if driven by some grim purpose. Houses were boarded shut; taverns were closed. Here and there a few stores were open for business, while others were locked and shuttered. Some had even been looted. Abandoned dogs roamed about, looking for food.

The stench of death Linsha had noticed two nights ago was still present and even stronger in the heat of day. She noticed also many of the houses they passed had yellow paint splashed on the doors.

When she asked Mica about the paint, he unbent enough to answer. "The paint is to mark homes where all the inhabitants have died." Linsha fell silent. Worry for Elenor preyed on her mind, and she wondered if she could talk the dwarf into taking a small detour to Elenor's little house to check on the old lady. She glanced back at the dwarf's stony face and decided probably not. But maybe she could confuse him in these back streets enough to lead him by Elenor's house. It wasn't that far from Watermark Street.

Casually she pushed Windcatcher into a faster walk and turned the corner at the public water pump, where a few children played in the trickle of water that still flowed. Mica duly followed, making no comment. Linsha led him on past empty inns and gaming houses, where desultory music echoed into the streets to lure customers inside. She took several more side streets and turns and soon came to the street she knew so well.

Mica rolled his eyes. "Either you have no idea where you are going, or you are deliberately trying to mislead me."

Linsha turned in her saddle and said, straight-faced, "I'm deliberately misleading you so I may check on an old friend. We aren't far from Watermark. I'll have you there in five minutes."

"You didn't need to sneak around like this," he sniffed. "All you had to do was ask."

"Oh, sure," she muttered. And give him the satisfaction of saying no?

They passed a small grove of sycamores drooping in the heat, several silent houses, and a small bakery before reaching Elenor's house. Linsha noticed the ladder still leaned against the chimney and a few windows were open to the slight breeze blowing in from the harbor. There was no yellow paint on the door.

Before Mica could protest, Linsha leaped off Windcatcher and flew to the door. "Elenor?" she shouted. She shoved open the door and dashed inside.

"Oh, by Reorx's Beard," Mica grumbled. After dismounting, he tied both horses in the shade of a nearby tree and stamped into the house after the infuriating woman. He found her in the back of the house, in a small kitchen, bent over the still form of an old woman sprawled on the floor.

Linsha raised a tear-streaked face. "She isn't dead yet. Please help me, Mica."

The dwarf laid a gentle finger against the woman's jugular. Her pulse still beat steadily and there was no sign of the tell-tale blotches, but her skin felt hot and dry.

Together they lifted Elenor and carried her to the bed in her small room. Linsha went to fetch water while Mica examined Elenor. It took a while for Linsha to find a bowl, a pitcher, cloths, and water, so by the time she returned to the room, Mica was already finished.

"She doesn't have the plague yet," he announced. "She's dehydrated and there's a lump on her head. She must have fainted and struck her head on the floor."

"I'm not surprised about the dehydration. There's no water in the house. I had to get some outside."

Using the cloths, Linsha bathed Elenor's face in the tepid water and trickled water down her throat. Mica found the lump on her head and, using his power of healing, repaired the bruising and strengthened her diminished system.

Elenor's eyes fluttered open. She saw Linsha first, and a smile shone on her withered face. "You're back!"

"Hello, Elenor. I came to visit and what do I find? You flat on the floor. What were you doing, chasing ants?"

The woman's face screwed up in bewilderment. "No, I . . .

Let's see. I was looking for a bottle of cherry cordial I had hidden somewhere. I was thirsty. There's not much to drink."

"Elenor, when was the last time you fetched water?"

"Just before you left," she replied. "You told me not to go out until you came back."

Linsha shook her head in disbelief at her old friend's confusion. "That's not what I said. Elenor, I asked you not to go back to the Dancing Bear or down to the waterfront. I didn't mean you had to lock yourself in the house."

"Oh," said the old woman weakly.

"Who knows? Maybe it saved her life," Mica put in.

The two women looked at him in surprise. Linsha hastily introduced him. "Elenor, this is Mica, the governor's healer." Then, to him, she asked, "What do you mean?"

He lifted his shoulders slightly. "If she didn't leave, she probably wasn't exposed to the disease. I believe it spreads through some kind of contact. Perhaps skin to skin."

Linsha thought about that. It made sense. Such a reason could explain why she had not yet caught the disease, for even though she had been on the ships and around the harbor district, she had not touched anyone that was ill at the time.

Elenor nodded. "He's right."

The dwarf crossed his arms and looked away, obviously dismissing the old woman.

Linsha gave her a glass of water to sip and said, "Why do you think so?"

Much of Elenor's spirit was returning, for she leaned across the bed and lightly poked the dwarf in the stomach. "I may be old, but I am not entirely befuddled. I remember an epidemic like this. So many years ago. My grandfather and grandmother died of it."

Mica's attention returned with a snap. "When was this? Where?"

Elenor's hand fluttered. "Nigh on sixty years ago, I'm thinking. I was just a little thing."

Mica looked skeptical. "Then how do you know it's the same thing, if you were young then and you've locked yourself in now?"

"The Kellen boy came to help me for a day or two. He brought me news and fetched water and helped me in the garden. But . . ." Her face screwed up in worry. "I haven't seen him for a few days. I hope he's all right."

"So do I," Linsha said soothingly. "We'll look for him when you're feeling better. Now, please, Elenor. Tell Mica about the plague."

"It happened around Kalaman."

"That territory was controlled by the Dark Knights during the war," Mica observed.

"I know that! Now, do you want to hear or not?"

To Linsha's surprise, Mica bowed politely and sat on the corner at the foot of Elenor's bed, his mouth shut.

"The plague came out of nowhere," Elenor went on. "It nearly wiped out our village and several more besides. I remember my grandma was so sick. Same symptoms, if Kellen was right. Fever. Dark red blotches. Running bowels. Terrible dreams. My grandma died in two days. Even the healers couldn't cure her. They were horrified." Her voice faded away, and she stared into the distance of old memories.

"Do you remember how the disease was stopped?" Linsha quietly prompted.

Elenor lifted her hands in an apologetic shrug. "I don't know. It left the valley as quickly and mysteriously as it came. Our priest of Mishakal blamed it on evil magic, but he died before he could learn the truth of it."

Mica made an inarticulate sound and bounced to his feet. "Fine. Thank you for your tale," he said to Elenor, then he spoke to Linsha. "Please finish here, squire. We still have our task to finish. Today." And he stamped out of the room.

"Stiff-necked, insufferable old stick-in-the-mud," muttered Linsha.

Elenor laughed softly and patted her arm. "Don't take him seriously. He's not as stuffy as he acts."

"How do you know?"

"Look at his eyes. They aren't hard and cold and shifty. He's being careful about something, but he cares more than he reveals."

Linsha exhaled in a snort. "If you say so."

Since Elenor felt stronger and able to cope, she convinced Linsha that she was well enough to be left alone. Linsha brought her some tea and filled every pitcher, bowl, and bucket in the house with water. She promised to return as soon as she could and left Elenor sitting comfortably in bed with her tea, some oat cakes, and a ewer of water close at hand.

Linsha finally came outside where the horses were tethered in the shade and Mica stood, tapping his foot impatiently.

She held up a finger to forestall any complaint. "Thank you very much for helping my friend. Whether or not you care, it means a great deal to me."

The dwarf hesitated and glared at Linsha, who kept her expression benign. "You're welcome."

Linsha remembered Sable's scrap of news about a past plague and wondered if there was any connection to Elenor's story. Perhaps Mica knew, since Lord Bight had told him what the dragon said. Thoughtfully she asked, "Did Elenor's story mean anything to you?"

Mica snorted through his large nose. "The ravings of a sick old woman. Now, unless you have any more old friends to visit, let's go."

Linsha decided not to waste her time by responding to his bad temper. She swung into the saddle and led the healer through several more streets to Watermark Street. The road was an old one, one of the originals from Sanction's early days. The buildings were of old weathered timber, darkened stone, and crumbling brick. Shops, houses, and workplaces crowded haphazardly on both sides of the road and along narrow alleys. Usually, this time of day, the street would be lively with pedestrians and conveyances alike, but on this day, the area was nearly deserted, except for a few people clustered in the shade of an outdoor patio beside a tavern and a few carts and wagons in the street. A cat, perched on a low stone wall, watched Linsha and Mica ride by.

They walked their horses several blocks north until Linsha came to a halt in front of a small group of shops bisected by an alley. There she dismounted and, after tying Windcatcher to a hitching post by the board sidewalk, waved at Mica to follow. The shop she wanted was in the alley. She turned into the side street and nearly walked into a nondescript work horse facing out toward the street. The horse was hitched to a wagon that sat parked close to the left side of the alley.

Linsha's suspicious were not aroused until she glanced in the wagon bed. Then her eyes narrowed and her hand automatically loosened the strap on her sword sheath. The wagon had been loaded carelessly with a variety of things: clothes, furs, bolts of cloth, bags of salt and spices, boxes, personal items, weapons, a money box, and half a dozen new pairs of boots.

Wordlessly she held up her hand to Mica to stay back, and she glided like a cat toward the scribe's shop. A wooden sign decorated with a relief carving of a quill pen and a scroll hung above the shop door. The door stood wide open. She pressed back against the wall and slid a look around the corner. The front room was a wreck of torn maps, spilled ink, and scattered parchment. Inside, she could hear muffled voices—two, she guessed—and a mix of cracks, thuds, breaking glass, and slammed doors.

Suddenly a short muscular man came hurrying into the front of the shop carrying an armload of blankets, hangings, and woven rugs. Grinning, he hauled his load out the door and came face-to-face with Linsha's steel.

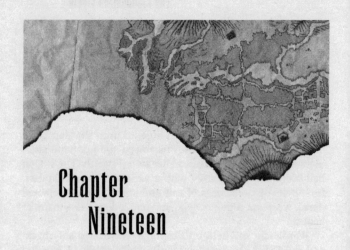

Chapter Nineteen

He opened his mouth to yell. Linsha waved the tip of her blade an inch from his eye and shook her head. The sound died in his throat.

Mica swiftly dragged the man out of the doorway, and while he bound and gagged the first looter, Linsha weaseled into the shop to find the second. She followed the sound of breaking wood into the back rooms and to a small storeroom. The second man was there, bent over an oak chest that so far resisted his efforts to open it with a pry bar.

She studied him carefully from the hall before she attempted to approach him. This man was different from his companion, for he had smooth muscles, a slim build, and the lithe grace of a predator. Linsha had seen men like this before, and they were always as fast to strike as a snake. She didn't want to give him the opportunity to attack first.

"Drego!" he suddenly shouted. "What's taking you so long? Get your carcass back in here and load up these wine bottles."

Linsha saw a stool lying on the floor, probably kicked aside by the looters. She noiselessly picked it up and pressed back by the door to wait. The sound of splintering wood came from the storeroom, followed by a chuckle of glee.

"Hey, Drego, I got it." The voice approached the door.

Linsha mentally counted the paces to the door—one, two, three—and out of the room he stepped, just as she swung the stool around, aiming for his head.

But the intruder was as fast as she feared and suspicious of his friend's silence. He had already drawn his knife and came out the door looking for trouble. He saw Linsha before he saw the stool, and he instinctively twisted aside and flipped the knife in her direction just as the stool caught him on the shoulder. The stool and the looter fell to the floor in a heap.

A tearing pain caught Linsha in the muscle between her neck and shoulder just above the collarbone. She started to reach for the embedded knife, but the intruder, although dazed by the blow, squirmed to his knees and threw himself at her. Linsha barely managed to fend him off with a kick to his face. The effort cost her balance, though, and she crashed into the wall and slid to the floor. She cried out as the impact jarred her wound.

Her opponent was tough and furious in spite of his pain. Blood streamed from his broken nose, and he favored his left arm where the stool struck him, yet he pushed his body up and dived after the knife stuck in Linsha's shoulder. His weight fell on top of her, pinning her to the floor. His fingers snatched for the knife, causing it to tear deeper into the muscle.

Linsha gritted her teeth. With one hand, she struggled to fight him off, and with the other, she groped for her own blade in its sheath at her waist. They writhed, tangling their legs and banging into the wall.

Someone stamped loudly into the hallway. "Lynn!" Mica snapped. "What are you doing? Quit fooling around and subdue the scum."

The looter lifted his head in surprise and saw the stocky

dwarf standing a few feet away with a large cudgel in his hands. He hesitated, and Linsha could imagine the thoughts running through his head: take his chances with two opponents here or be hanged by the City Guard for looting. She recognized the flickering change in his eyes and sensed the abrupt tensing of his body just before he struck. This time she was ready for him.

She threw up her arm and blocked his second grab for the knife. Giving a tremendous heave with her lower body, she threw the man off-balance enough to give her a chance to wrench her own blade out.

He grabbed her hair and slammed her head into the wall. His fingers closed about the leather handle of his knife and wrenched it out.

Burning pain seared across her neck and chest. Furiously Linsha brought her dagger close by her side and drove it upward. She felt the blade puncture flesh, glance off bone. Hot blood spilled over her. The man's weight sank slowly down on top of her until she couldn't breathe.

Suddenly she was free of the looter's weight. Mica heaved the body off her.

"Are you hurt? Dragon's bones, answer me."

Linsha tilted her eyes down to looked at the tears and the blood soaking into the scarlet and gold tunic. "Damnation. Look at this. Another uniform ruined. They're going to start making me pay for these." Frowning, she pushed herself up the wall to a sitting position. "Oh, and thanks for your help," she added sarcastically.

The dwarf leaned his cudgel against the wall. "You're the sell-sword bodyguard. You're the one paid to do the fighting."

"Why are you so bloody patronizing?"

"Why are you so self-serving?" he retorted.

"Arrogant!"

"Insolent!"

"Sulky, grouchy, and a pain in the butt."

"Shallow, meddlesome, and a pain in the butt."

The absurdity of their argument suddenly struck Linsha, and she began to laugh. "See? We do have something in common," she said before her laughter turned to a grimace of pain and fresh blood darkened her scarlet tunic.

Mica shook his head. "Here. Let's get you cleaned up. I'll take care of that wound," he said gruffly.

He gently pulled away her tunic and the cotton shirt beneath to reveal the wound on her neck and shoulder. The wound was messy and deep but mostly superficial, and he quickly cleaned it and pressed a soft cloth against the torn skin and muscle. He paid no attention to the gold chain about her neck.

"You saw me heal Commander Durne's head wound. I'll heal your injury the same way."

"I may be a sell-sword but I'm not stupid. I know the mystic power of the heart," she murmured irritably.

"Good." He closed his eyes and pressed his fingers against her skin. Humming to himself, he concentrated to draw his power from his inner being through his arm, his hand, his fingers and down into Linsha's knife wound.

A tingling heat spread over Linsha's shoulder. It warmed her blood and went tingling up her neck, along her arm, and over her breast. The pain retreated until it was little more than a gentle ache. She relaxed, musing over the unique feeling of someone else's power healing her body.

Mica blew out a long sigh and sat back on his heels. "There. The skin is closed. The muscle will be sore for a few days and you'll have a scar, but it's healing."

"Thanks, Mica," she said. She sat for a few more minutes and drank a cup of water he brought her, then she climbed carefully to her feet. The loss of blood made her weak and a little dizzy, but she pushed the fatigue aside and went to work. While she searched the house, Mica dragged the looter's body outside, where the guard patrol could pick it up. They met back in the front room where the old priest sold his work.

Silently they looked around at the devastation. The room had been trashed by the looters as they searched for things of value. Scrolls, parchment, vellum, and delicate sheets of handmade paper lay strewn everywhere, torn and shredded or lying in pools of spilled ink. Quill pens had been torn and bent and scattered over the counter. Old maps were ripped from the walls and torn to pieces. A broken shelf spilled its books on the floor, and a smashed lamp lay in a puddle of oil that seeped into the wooden floor.

"Well," said Linsha, gazing at the mess, "I hope his records weren't in here."

"I doubt it. They're probably with his personal things. So where is he?"

The lady Knight grimaced. "In his bed. He's been dead for a day or two. The entire place is a wreck. The looters have been here for a while."

Mica snatched a broken quill off the counter and tossed it to the floor. "Blast it! I really needed to talk to that priest."

"I'm sure he would have preferred that, too," Linsha said dryly.

Ignoring her remark, Mica left the shop to search the rest of the priest's residence. Linsha went outside to bring their two horses into the shaded alley. She took off her blood-soaked tunic and tossed it over her saddle horn. Her shirt was bloody as well, but not as bad, so she dabbed it off as best she could with some muddy water from a public pump and left it to dry. Unwilling to listen to Mica's irritations, she started to straighten up the shop. Ostensibly she did it to look for the records. Internally she wanted to do something for the dead scribe within. She didn't know him, had never been in his shop, yet he had died alone and lay unburied and vulnerable to scavengers. The least she could do to honor the dead was fix some of the dishonor done to him.

For nearly an hour she labored to clean the floor and counter and put things back in order. She was kneeling beside the counter, picking up broken glass, when the sound of heavy boot treads interrupted her quiet thoughts.

"On your feet! Who are you, and what are you doing in here?" demanded a harsh voice.

Linsha snapped out of her reverie and came alert. As she slowly stood upright, her sharpened attention picked out something in the big wooden counter she hadn't noticed before. But there wasn't time to investigate. Two City Guards, both dwarves, stood by the door, their swords pointed unwaveringly at her. She saw with some amusement that their eyes widened at the sight of the bloodstains on her shirt.

"I am Lynn of Gateway," she answered. "Squire in the service of the lord governor. I am, as you can see, trying to clean up this mess."

The second dwarf started forward. "Lynn. I've seen you before." He lowered his sword. "She was in the guards until the governor picked her out," he told his companion.

The first guard sheathed his weapon. "Sorry. We've had reports of looters in this area. We saw the horses and the wagon—"

"And the man tied to the wagon wheel," added the second dwarf. "That got our attention."

"I would worry if you didn't investigate," Linsha said. She explained her mission to the shop with Mica and told the guards briefly what had happened. Mica, hearing the voices, came out to join her. He was empty-handed.

The guards stayed for a few minutes then left, taking the prisoner and the wagon with them. The dead priest and the looter they left for the dead wagon to retrieve.

Mica took in the changed state of the shop. "Looks better," he admitted.

"Did you find anything?"

"Not yet."

"Then look at this." She bent over and pointed under the counter. The counter was a large, heavy fixture made of oak stained and aged to a deep, rich brown. The front, facing the door, was trimmed with simple panels; the top was flat and featureless, save for the nicks and stains of steady use. In the back lay a trove of shelves, cupboards, drawers, and slots. Linsha had already refilled some of the shelves with the salvageable parchment, scrolls, and sheets of valuable paper. But on the end abutting the wall was a narrow drawer built into the bottom of the countertop. Linsha hadn't noticed it until the guards disturbed her and she looked up at just the right angle. It didn't have an obvious handle or lock, only a finger-sized indentation at the top edge. When Linsha tried to pull it open, it remained firmly in place.

Intrigued, Mica moved in for a closer look. He poked and prodded, tested every inch of the visible drawer front, thumped and pushed until at last a pleased smile creased his bearded face. He pulled a slender silver pin out of the side of the drawer, slid the top panel sideways out of its slots, and pulled out a drawer. The compartment within was deceptively large and, to the delight of both Linsha and Mica, it was filled with four large folio books, leather bound, hinged with steel, and embossed with symbols of the god, Mishakal.

Mica grinned in delight as he reverently lifted the books from their storage place. "Nice work, squire," he told Linsha. He laid the books side by side on the counter and opened the first one. "These are records from a temple here in Sanction. They begin before the invasion by Highlord Ariakas and the dragonarmy. Apparently the priests taught minor healing arts there."

"Would they have known of a plague up near Kalaman?" Linsha asked, eyeing the books dubiously.

"Maybe. If it was brought to their attention in some way. Hmmm . . . this is interesting." The dwarf's attention became locked on the book before him.

When he made no effort to share his observations or invite her to look at one of the books, Linsha drifted away. She was too tired to make the effort anyway. Working so hard in the heat of the day combined with the effects of her blood loss had sapped her strength away. She felt like a candle left too long in the sun. She wandered over to a corner away from the spilled pools of ink, propped her back against the walls, and slowly let her knees bend until she was sitting on the floor. Her head sank back and her eyes closed. Exhaustion overwhelmed her.

She lost track of the time as she dozed. Dreams came and went, fleeting images plucked from her subconscious that tickled her fancy or tore at her emotions. They came and went and came again, whirling around and around, like her juggling balls, in an endless circle. She dreamed of a strange orange cat and a black dragon, of a ship that burned without being consumed, of her mother dying of the plague while she sat helplessly by. She saw Varia's moon eyes staring at her from the night and she heard the owl say, "You will follow your heart." The words echoed and reechoed into another vision of Lord Bight, laughing softly at her in the darkness, "Which will you prove to be when the time comes?"

She heard more voices: Sir Liam Ehrling, the Grand Master of the Knights of Solamnia, whispered the Oath in her ear; a faceless Knight of the Clandestine Circle repeated over and over, "At all costs," until she thought she would scream. Other voices came, voices she did not know, and they talked over her and around her in an endless bedlam of sound that thundered in her head and drove all the other dreams back into the dark recesses of her mind.

All at once one familiar voice called her name softly, insistently. The tones titillated her heart, sending it tripping over its own beat. The nuances of his words warmed her with pleasure. The other voices faded into reality, and Linsha realized she was awake. There were other men in the shop, and one in particular was very close to her.

She opened her eyes, looked up, and fell into Ian Durne's blue gaze. Without conscious effort, her face ignited in a dazzling smile that warmed her skin to roses and lit her eyes like jade touched with sunlight.

She saw him respond in kind, simply and with delight. Their eyes locked in a rapt gaze that excluded all but the tantalizing attraction they saw in each other.

Neither one of them realized how long they stayed there, staring at each other, until the two Governor's Guards who came with the commander elbowed each other and loudly cleared their throats.

Commander Durne stood up and quelled them with one raised eyebrow. He offered a gloved hand to Linsha to help her up.

Trembling inside, she took it and let him pull her to her feet. She wasn't certain she had the strength to make it on her own anyway. Her knees felt wobbly and her heart was pounding. But whether it was the waking from her dreams or the unexpected presence of Ian Durne that caused her weakness, she did not know.

"Two City Guards told me you had run into some trouble," the commander said.

"A couple of looters," Mica replied, still engrossed in a book. "The squire took care of them."

Durne turned back to Linsha and indicated her torn, bloody shirt. "You were injured."

"Yeah. The dwarf took care of that," Linsha retorted.

The commander's lip twitched in a controlled smile. "Are you well enough to continue your duties?" he asked Linsha.

"Of course. I'm fine," snapped the dwarf. At the startled silence that followed, he lifted his head, looked at the four guards staring at him, and belatedly realized the commander wasn't talking to him. He grumbled something and went back to reading.

"I'll be all right," Linsha answered. "I was waiting for him to finish."

"It's getting late," the commander observed. "If you wait for him to finish, you could be here for several days."

A glance out the window showed Linsha he was right. The shadows had grown quite long since she sat down, and the sun was settling low in the western sky. She rubbed her forehead. She had obviously slept longer than she thought.

Commander Durne studied her pale face and remembered the state of his body after the dwarf healed his head injury. The mystic healing sped up the process of recovery nicely, but the body still had to recover from the shock of injury and blood loss. He made up his mind. "We were going back to the palace. Pack your books, Master Dwarf, and we will ride with you to the temple."

Mica recognized an order when he heard it. Reluctantly he closed the book he was reading and piled the four together. He and the guards wrapped the volumes in blankets and bundled them together with rope. They loaded the books on the back of Mica's horse. When they were finished, Linsha closed the shutters in the shop window, bade a silent farewell to the dead priest, and pulled the door shut behind her.

In a group, the guards and the healer rode back to Ship-maker's Road and turned east toward the city gates and inner Sanction. They saw very few people. The sick lay in their beds and ranted and died in the frightful heat; the well stayed indoors, either hiding or caring for their loved ones. The harbor and the city lay in a stupor of late afternoon heat and malaise that showed no sign of relenting.

At this rate, Linsha thought, the city would be easy pick-ings for the first enemy who dared risk Lord Bight's wrath. She sighed.

Commander Durne heard her and turned his head to see her. He slowed his stallion until Windcatcher walked by his side. "What are you thinking?" he asked softly.

Linsha liked his voice. She liked his nearness and the way he spoke to her as if he genuinely wanted to know what was on her mind. She couldn't imagine that a man like him would be interested in a sell-sword with Lynn's dubious history, and yet his eyes devoured her and the vein in his neck seemed to throb with the same nervous pounding hers had.

"I was thinking that Sanction is dying," she finally answered. "If this plague doesn't ease off soon, it will deci-mate the entire population and leave the city vulnerable to attack. I'm not sure even Lord Bight has the strength to defend Sanction alone . . . if he survives."

"I hope the plague doesn't last that long!" he said fer-vently. "But you're right to worry. The City Guards have been hit hard, particularly those who patrolled the harbor district, and the plague is spreading through the eastern guard camp." He paused and glanced at her thoughtfully. "Did Mica find anything in the records he was so anxious to read?"

"I don't think so. They're from a temple in Sanction. I can't imagine that they will include anything from as far away as Kalaman."

Commander Durne surprised her by visibly starting. The movement was spontaneous and immediately controlled, so she wasn't certain what she had seen in his face. Did he already know about the earlier outbreak? No, how could he? Surely he would have told Mica or Lord Bight. She was just letting her suspicious nature read more into this than was there.

"What does Kalaman have to do with this?" he asked, his voice faintly curious.

"We learned there was an earlier plague there that was similar to this one," she answered.

"Where did you hear that?"

Linsha made it a policy never to reveal her sources unless directly ordered. "From an old resident who was ill."

"Was this resident lucid at the time?"

Linsha pretended to study the stone flagging beneath Windcatcher's hooves. She heard a note in his voice she could not clearly identify. Was it excitement or alarm? "I don't know. Seemed lucid enough, but you know how fevers can affect people. It seemed a good lead at the time."

"What did Mica make of this lead?" Durne persisted.

"Very little. He doesn't hold out much hope of finding something useful." She shook her head, trying to be tolerant. "But then he doesn't hold out much hope for anything. Especially me."

Durne chuckled. "Nor any of us. Mica is a superb healer, but he cares more for the process than the patients." He shot a look over his shoulder to the dwarf, who rode silently at the end of the group. Mica's eyes were elsewhere, his thoughts probably lost somewhere in the text he had read. Durne leaned slightly closer to Linsha and lowered his voice. "Watch your back around him, Lynn. Lord Bight is not entirely certain of his loyalties."

Linsha started to say some trite remark, then closed her mouth. She didn't really know what to say. Or what to think. There were so many possible players in this game of intrigue in Sanction, it was almost impossible to be certain of who everyone really was. There was an alleged Knight of Takhisis in the government somewhere, but for all she knew, the Legion could have infiltrated the governor's inner circle, or the Knights of Solamnia could have slipped someone in and not told her. There could even be a spy with his own agenda who wormed his way into the court, or a disgruntled advisor who was spreading rumors. The possibilities were endless and too much for her tired brain this evening. She nodded her thanks to Commander Durne and lapsed into a pensive silence that lasted long after they left the harbor district behind.

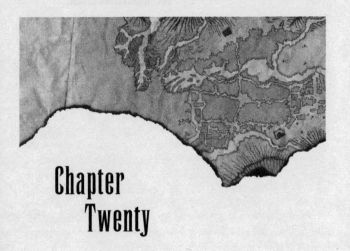

Chapter Twenty

The party of red-clad guards rode through the city gates just as the merchant guild's clock rang five. The city guards at the gate saluted their commander and waved the group through. They were past the Souk Bazaar and had made the turn on the road to the Governor's Palace and the temple of the mystics when a clatter of hoofbeats caught their attention. Lord Bight, mounted on his sorrel, came trotting down the road at the head of a troop of heavily armed Governor's Guards. He saw Commander Durne and rose in his stirrups.

"I've had a report that the Dark Knights are going to raid into the northern Vale tonight," he shouted. "Bring your men and come with me."

Linsha automatically reined Windcatcher around to follow the commander, but he stopped his horse in front of her. "Not this time, squire," Durne said. "One injury a day is our limit. Escort Mica back to the temple, then return to the barracks and get some rest. There will be other times."

Linsha turned to Lord Bight to appeal the decision, but he took one look at her bloodied shirt and snapped, "Obey your orders." Then he wheeled his horse away, and the company cantered after him along the road to the east.

Linsha watched them go. Although she loved a good fight against the Knights of Takhisis, she felt like a limp rag tonight. Commander Durne was probably right to send her back. She wouldn't be much use to them. Reluctantly she turned and followed the dwarf.

The healer paid no attention to the absence of the other guards or to Linsha's continued presence. He rode on toward the temple, humming to himself and staring at something only he could see between his horse's ears.

At the fork of the road leading to the temple, he turned in his saddle and said, "You don't have to trail me up to the temple. I think I can find my way from here."

Linsha ignored his sarcasm. "I was told to escort you to the temple. I will escort you."

His lips pulled down in an irritated frown, but he said nothing more. They rode in silence through the trees and up the hill to the green lawns of the temple grounds. Mica didn't bother to say good-bye or invite her in. He simply reined his horse in the direction of the temple stables and left her behind.

Linsha glared after him. If there was anyone in Lord Bight's court who should be the Dark Knight spy simply by measure of his unpleasant attitude, it should be that dwarf! She hoped Lord Bight or Commander Durne would find something else for her to do tomorrow besides help the ungrateful lout.

Rather than backtrack the way she came, she decided to take the trail through the woods that Lord Bight had showed her the night they entered the passages under the city. Wearily she turned Windcatcher down the hill and toward the trail to the palace. The mare's hooves stepped soundlessly on the thick grass of the lawn. The light of early evening was gold and hazy around them. She found the trail easily enough and reined the horse into the long shadows under the trees. The woods lay still around her, for there was no wind to stir the leaves.

An owl hooted a long, angry cry in the trees ahead.

Linsha started upright in her saddle. Owls did not usually call in daylight. If there was one out in these woods, then it could only be . . . The lady Knight dug her heels into the mare's sides. Windcatcher sprang forward.

"Varia!" Linsha called. The owl cried again, a long, shivering note of anger and sadness.

Windcatcher cantered down the trail between the trees and through the undergrowth.

A brown shape swooped out of a large sycamore and soared by Linsha's head, wailing softly. "Linsha, I hoped you would come this way. Follow me!" the owl cried. She banked to the right, away from the path and toward a copse of smaller, denser pine. Linsha had to slow the horse to a walk in the thick growth of vines, shrubs, and small trees. When she reached the copse, she had to dismount and tie the mare to a tree limb, then continue on foot. She pushed into the thick stand, and the dark evergreens closed in around her.

"There, under that young pine. Do you see him?" Varia directed her.

Linsha shoved a branch out of her face and came into a slight clearing in the middle of the pine trees. Evening sunlight barely penetrated the heavy growth and the deep shadows that cloaked the forest floor, but there was just enough light to gleam on a patch of bright red, a red that had no place among the stand of trees. Linsha hurried forward. She came to two black boots lying among the crushed grass. Her gaze followed the boots up to the red breeches trimmed in black and the red tunic of a Governor's Guard. A man lay on his belly in the shade of the pines, a man who looked unnaturally still.

Linsha took in his dark blond hair and strong build, but she didn't recognize him until she rolled him over and saw his face. "Captain Dewald," she gasped. Commander Durne's lieutenant stared up at the sky with clouded, sightless eyes.

"What happened to him?" she asked the owl as she knelt beside the body.

"I don't know," Varia hooted. "I came to the woods, hoping to meet you. While I waited, I did a little hunting and there I found him. He has been here a while, for ants have already discovered him."

Linsha pulled her hands away and used only her eyes to examine the body. She tried to disregard the lines of ants that crawled around his open eyes, nose, and mouth. "Oh, wait. There." She pointed to a dark stain and two small rips on the chest of his tunic. "He's been stabbed twice, by a stiletto, I'd wager, but there's no blood on the ground. He was probably killed somewhere else and dumped here. No one but an owl could have found him in this undergrowth."

Varia sat on a branch close by and craned her neck to see the man clearly. "Linsha, I know this man," she said.

"Really. How?"

"I have seen him with Lady Annian."

Linsha's anger boiled up. "What? He's a Knight?"

"No, no," the owl hastened to reassure her. "I think he's only a paid informant. I have seen him with Lady Annian in the streets. Enjoying the taverns . . . and things. I think he was her contact in the court."

"She knew I was joining the guards. Why didn't she tell me?" Linsha said furiously.

"Maybe she didn't want to jeopardize his safety by putting him in contact with you. He wasn't a trained Knight, remember."

"I'd say his safety has been jeopardized with or without me." She brushed the ants off Captain Dewald's face and closed his eyes. Not that the closed lids would stop the ants and flies for long, but it seemed a respectful thing to do. "I wonder who caught up with him, and why."

Varia fluffed out her feathers and hooted softly. "I will tell Lady Karine tonight. She can tell Annian. The news will grieve her." She sidestepped along the branch until the limb drooped under weight, bringing her close to Linsha. "Tell me what happened to you."

"Looters," Linsha sighed. "One caught me with a knife." She rubbed a finger over Varia's brown and white barred wing.

The owl hopped gently onto Linsha's wrist. "I am glad you were not seriously hurt. A healer closed the wound?"

"Mica. He and I were collecting records to take to the temple."

"Ah, the grumpy dwarf."

Linsha's face became thoughtful. "Commander Durne said something to me that I thought was strange. He told me to watch my back around Mica, that Lord Bight doesn't trust him."

"Doesn't trust his own healer?" Varia repeated dubiously.

"Yes." She pursed her lips. "Keep a watch on Mica when you can. If you see him leave the temple at odd hours or do something out of character, let me know."

"As you wish. What are you going to do about him?"

"Mica?"

"No. The captain."

Linsha sat back on her heels and said, "I can't lift him onto Windcatcher alone. He's too big. I'll have to report this. Commander Durne may want to see this place before they move the body."

She carefully rolled his body back the way she had found him. Feeling tired to the bone, she climbed to her feet and, still carrying Varia, returned to her horse.

"You came out to meet me," Linsha remembered. "Was there something else you wanted to tell me?"

Varia bobbed her head. "Lord Bight heard from one of his spies that the Dark Knights are going to raid the farms again. He took off like an avenging dragon with most of his men."

"I saw them on our way back. Commander Durne wouldn't let me go with them."

"He cares about you. I suppose that is one thing I like about him."

"You don't like him?"

The owl turned huge eyes on her. "I did not say that."

"But you don't like him," Linsha persisted.

"I do not know him well enough to decide," Varia replied. "But I do not trust him. I cannot see past his facade, and that bothers me."

It disturbed Linsha, too. Varia was a superb judge of character and preferred to spend her time with creatures who were generally good. If Varia couldn't look past Ian Durne's social masks to read the makeup of his character within, she would never come to like him. It bothered her also that Durne shielded himself so well that even Varia's perceptions couldn't sense him. What did he have to hide?

She tucked the thought away in her memory for later and led Windcatcher back to the trail. "I will come to the barn tonight if there's time."

With a powerful thrust, the owl launched herself off Linsha's arm and winged into the trees. "Until then," she called and was gone, a whisper on the wind.

Heavy of heart, Linsha rode to the palace and reported to the officer of the watch. The lieutenant's face paled, and his hand worked, open and shut, on the pommel of his sword while he shouted orders and organized a squad to investigate the murder.

When they were ready, Linsha led them back to the captain's body and explained how her normally staid mare had bolted from a snake and charged into the undergrowth close enough to the grove of pine for Linsha to catch a glimpse of red.

The lieutenant, a stranger to her, eyed her suspiciously, paying special attention to her bloody shirt. She told him about her duty in the harbor district and the run-in with the looters. She suggested he talk to Mica and Commander Durne.

Still, the lieutenant took no chances of making a mistake in this murder of one of their own. He ordered Linsha to stand by until Lord Bight returned, then he posted guards by the body and Linsha and sent to the temple for Mica.

The dwarf, he was informed, had gone back to the city and was not available.

When she heard this, Linsha clenched her teeth and suppressed the oaths she wanted to utter. Maybe Varia had seen him and was following.

The nearly full moon rose and sailed placidly to its zenith before Lord Bight and his men returned from the farmlands in the vale. They rode slowly, bringing many wounded and three riderless horses with them. The officer of the watch met them at the front gate. He quaked inside, seeing Lord Bight was already in a towering rage, but he stood straight and delivered his bad news.

The lord governor reined his horse aside and rode down the hill without a word. Commander Durne waved the company on, then he and a squad trotted after Lord Bight into the trees and followed the flickering light of torches to the copse of pine and the body of Captain Dewald.

"Oh, no," Durne breathed. He threw himself off his horse and knelt beside the body of his friend and aide. He bowed his head and covered his eyes with his gloved hand. Lord Bight squatted down on the other side of the body and, like Linsha, brushed away the ants and flies from Dewald's face. After a moment Durne collected himself and, with Lord Bight's help, tipped the captain's body over. Together they examined it as thoroughly as they could in the light of torches.

"Who found the body?" Lord Bight demanded.

One of the guards pointed to Linsha, who sat under a nearby tree with two more guards in close attendance.

"Why are you under guard?" Commander Durne sprang to his feet and strode to her.

She stared up at him in weary resignation. "The officer of the watch didn't like the stains on my shirt. He was just trying to be careful."

"You may release her," he ordered, and the two guardsmen saluted and moved away.

Once again she explained how she had found Dewald's body on her way back to the palace. Lord Bight listened carefully, although his eyes burned with an inward fury that Linsha sensed had little to do with this incident. Commander Durne studied the ground around the body, noted the lack of blood and the drag marks in the grass, and came to the same conclusion Linsha had.

"He was killed somewhere else and dumped here," he told the lord governor.

Lord Bight merely nodded, containing his anger like a volcano about to erupt.

Silently the company of guards gathered around their fallen comrade. They laid the captain's body on a litter and escorted him through the veil of silver moonlight to the palace on the hill. There they wrapped him in a linen shroud, placed him on a bier, and set him to rest in the great hall until his burial in the morning. Guards stood at his head and feet, and his sword rested at his side. Commander Durne knelt by the bier for a long while, his head bowed and his hands resting on the shrouded arm of the dead.

Linsha, meanwhile, found herself free at last to seek her rest. After feeding and rubbing down Windcatcher, she retrieved a loose caftan robe from her quarters and made her way to the garden bathhouse. The courtyard was quiet, and the few men that were about were subdued and grim. She knew the foray that night had been a disaster, but no one had given her the details and she hadn't asked. It seemed too much to face on top of the untimely death of Captain Dewald.

In the bathhouse, she handed over her bloody tunic and shirt to the ever-present attendant, who merely shook her head at Linsha's carelessness with uniforms and bore them away.

Linsha's bath was prolonged and delightful. When at last she was finished, her skin was wrinkled and scrubbed clean and her muscles no longer ached. She pulled the caftan robe over her head and walked outdoors, barefoot and dripping wet. A passing breeze drifted through a trellis of twining moonflowers, bringing a delicious scent to the night. She wandered along the paths in the back garden beside clumps of gardenias, peonies, and hibiscus. The wind cooled her wet skin and stirred her damp curls.

A faint splash reached her ears, and she wondered if Shanron had decided to use the bathhouse at this late hour. She hadn't seen the barbarian woman that day. Maybe Shanron would like some company. But when she walked out from between a corridor of shrubbery into the open place where the reflecting pool sat, she saw it wasn't Shanron who had come to enjoy the garden. It was Lord Bight. There, in the rectangular stone pool, lay the lord governor of Sanction, reclining in the water and the silver light of the moon's rays. He stretched out full length, still completely clothed. Only his boots lay on the ground where he had dropped them. His head rested on the stone wall, his hand idly stirred a floating water lily. The small fountain played over his face in a shimmering shower of white droplets.

Fascinated, Linsha walked to the side of the pool and stood studying his face. He didn't hear her over the splash of the fountain, and since his eyes were closed, he didn't notice her either. He looked utterly serene. The lines of care and anger were erased from his face, replaced by an aura of contentment and quiet joy that even the gray-white light of the moon couldn't disguise.

She reached out to touch him, then checked and slowly withdrew her hand. Moments of peace such as this had to be rare for him these days. She didn't want to disturb it. She turned silently to go.

"You're not disturbing me," his deep voice said above the music of the fountain. "Please stay."

She halted a step away from the pool and smiled down at him. His eyes stayed closed, but he grinned back at her. "What are you doing, Your Excellency?" she had to ask.

"Swimming," he replied without opening his eyes. "I try to swim every night. It helps me relax. It was too late to go to the harbor tonight, so I came here."

"Your Excellency, there is a perfectly good bathhouse over there. If you use it, you won't come out smelling like fish."

"The bathhouse was occupied. Besides, my excellency likes fish," he announced. "Fish and water and flowers and moonlight and night wind and beautiful wet women." He patted the stone rim of the pool, inviting her to sit down.

"I'm not wet anymore," she teased.

His hand snaked out, snatched the hem of her robe, and pulled hard. With a squawk, she toppled into the pool, sending waves of water and lilies sloshing over the rim. He laughed as she surfaced, soaked and bedecked with pond plants. "Now you are," he gasped and laughed again.

Linsha swatted him with a handy lily pad. He roared and splashed water at her. They fought their mock battle from one end of the pool to the other until the pool was a mess of plants and mud and the fish were hysterical. At last they staggered out and collapsed, drunk with delight on the grass lawn.

The lord governor sighed and lay on his back. "Thank you, Lynn. I haven't laughed like that in days."

"Any time, my lord." Linsha was surprised to realize she meant it. She had admired and respected Lord Bight for some time. Now she could add the truth that she genuinely liked him, arrogant rascal that he was. "But you don't need to thank me," she went on, primly wringing out her robe. "You were the one soaking himself in a fish pond like a decrepit sea elf."

"Decrepit!" he bellowed. "I'll show you decrepit." He lunged to his feet and snatched her before she could run. Throwing her over his shoulder, he marched to the bathhouse and tossed her in the bath, robe and all.

Linsha hadn't grown up with an older brother for nothing. Shouting a war cry, she boiled out of the water, grabbed his muddy tunic and hauled him in after her. His weight fell on top of her, and for a moment they thrashed intertwined in the water.

Abruptly he pushed away from her and climbed swiftly out of the pool. Panting and dripping, he gazed down at her for a long moment, his expression unreadable in the shadows.

Linsha perceived his withdrawal immediately, and she was flooded with embarrassment and remorse. In the pleasure of the moment, she had let herself forget her adopted place and character. She was not a Lady Knight worthy of his attention. Here she was only Lynn, a squire in his court, and she had no business cavorting with him in the bath.

"Your Excellency," she said nervously, "I'm sorry. I didn't mean to offend you." She groped her way out of the pool across from him and pulled her wet robe closer around her. Her curls lay plastered to her head.

"You didn't," he said. "You have reminded me that even

lord governors should play once in a while." He handed her a towel. "It's late. I still have duties to attend to. Good night, squire." Still soaking wet, he turned on his heel and strode out of the bathhouse.

Linsha watched him go, worried by the sudden change in his demeanor. Her hand automatically clutched the dragon scale under her wet robe. Had she offended him that badly? All of her pleasure evaporated in a sense of dismay and confusion. She dropped her towel on a rack and said softly, "Good night, my lord."

Outside in the hot darkness, Linsha walked quickly through the garden toward the barracks. Head down, her thoughts elsewhere, she didn't see the dark figure detach itself from the garden gate and slide out of sight into the shadows of the courtyard.

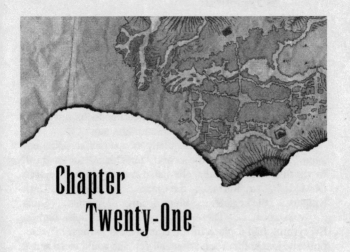

Chapter
Twenty-One

The moon hung low in the western sky and shed its light through the open loading door and ventilation windows in silvery beams that barred the velvet darkness of the hayloft. In the patch of light that gleamed on the hay-strewn floor, Linsha spread out a blanket and settled down to wait for Varia to return.

Although the night was waning, Linsha was still pent up and agitated from her time with Lord Bight. She had wanted to leave him in peace and instead he left irritated and affronted by her presumptuous behavior. At least she guessed that is what had forced him to withdraw from her. Since he hadn't explained, she could only assume he was displeased by her conduct, and yet if he didn't want to participate in such horse-play, why had he started it? There were other possibilities, of course, but none that seemed likely. Perhaps the tensions of the day had caught up with him and haltered his exuberant play. She hoped he would eventually accept her apology, for she couldn't stand the thought of his rejection.

There was just enough illumination in the stable loft to see what she was doing, so Linsha pulled out her leather juggling balls. Often the disciplined spin of the balls helped her put her thoughts in order, and tonight she needed all the help she could get. She sent the juggling balls sailing in a slow circle from hand to hand and up and down. As the balls traveled through her hands, she turned her focus inward to the people who occupied her thoughts the most.

"Lord Bight," Linsha said quietly as one ball smacked her palm. "Mica," she said to the second. "Ian Durne," for the third. In rhythm with the balls, she listed more names. "Captain Dewald . . . Lady Karine . . . the Circle . . . Solamnics . . . Dark Knights . . . the Legion . . . Sailors' Scourge . . . pirates . . . Sable . . . volcanoes . . ." There was a pattern to all these names. Everything had a place in the complicated pattern of Sanction, she just hadn't found them all yet. She could feel a sense of urgency building like the dome on the volcano. Time was slipping away from her. The Clandestine Circle would be expecting action, yet she didn't have all the answers to make the right decisions.

"Lord Bight," she murmured again. Even after days in his personal guard, she was no closer to knowing the truth of his power or his origins. If he was a trained sorcerer, he must have taught himself, for he had never set foot in her father's academy and had been using sorcery long before Palin founded the school. So where did he learn to use the power? Only a handful of people understood and practiced the ancient magic as well as he.

"Ian Durne." Now, there was a conundrum. Cool, efficient, capable. Yet Lord Bight left him in charge while he went to see Sable, and everything went from bad to worse. Did he botch the job, or were things simply beyond anyone's control? Now his aide was dead and the night's raid was a disaster. What was happening here?

"The Circle." They wanted Lord Bight discredited and removed from his position of power. Were they working under orders from the Solamnic Council or from their own secret agenda? Did Sir Liam condone their desire to be rid of

Lord Bight? Why couldn't she convince the Circle that Hogan Bight was the best leader for this complicated, temperamental city?

She murmured the names again, around and around in her mind like the balls in her hand. "How do they fit together?"

"How does who fit together? You and me?" asked a man from the darkness.

The balls fell from Linsha's hands as she spun around to face the ladder, her dagger already in her grip.

"It's all right, Lynn," said Ian Durne. "It's just me. I didn't mean to startle you."

By all the absent gods of Krynn, she thought, slowly dropping her blade. How long had he been out there? She slid her dagger back in place and, still keeping an eye on him, knelt to retrieve the balls.

The commander walked between the stacks of hay to stand at the edge of the moonlight. "I didn't know you could juggle. Where did you learn to do that?"

"I taught myself. It helps me think," she replied in soft tones. She noticed he carried a bottle of wine and two stemmed cups.

He held up the wine like a peace offering. His eyes were like glass in the moonlight, his face stern and sad. His usually immaculate uniform was dusty and rather disheveled, and his weapons were nowhere in sight. Linsha thought she had never seen him look so weary and forlorn.

That warm flutter started again in the pit of her stomach. She tried to ignore it, to remember Varia's advice. He was a stranger. What did she really know about him? "What are you doing here?"

"I saw you cross the courtyard, and I thought I'd join you."

She stood up, uncertain how she felt about that. "Can't sleep?"

"No." He looked up at the roof wrapped in darkness, at the timbers and the piles of hay. "So, why are you up here?"

"It's peaceful. I like the animals."

"It helps you think," he finished for her. "Ah, may I sit down?"

She nodded and smoothed out a corner of her blanket with a bare foot.

He lowered himself to the blanket in stiff, slow movements, then he uncorked the wine and poured a generous measure in both glasses. Sampling it, he sighed with pleasure. "A nice red. One of the new local vintages. It's pleasantly soft, with a fine, lingering finish." He glanced up at Linsha, still standing by the edge of the blanket. "Oh, please, sit down. I hurt my neck tonight and I don't want to look up."

Linsha hesitated, torn between being discourteous and on guard, or polite and vulnerable. Did she really want to put herself in this position? She could just take her leather balls and go. Varia would find her. She wouldn't have to stay here, alone with this man who awakened such an attraction in her. She could say "thank you" and "no" and leave him to the blanket and the wine and the darkness.

"It is said, 'In delay there lies no plenty,' " he murmured.

"It is also said, 'If you leap too soon, you can lose all,' " she quickly retorted.

He grinned. "Ever the cautious alley cat. Always sniffing around corners before you enter the street."

"Of course. A cat can never be too cautious when there are big toms around."

As if on cue, a large orange tomcat strolled out of the darkness, his tail held high. "Where did you come from?" Linsha asked. The cat twined around her legs and purred, but when Ian reached for him, his ears flattened on his skull and he hissed at him.

The commander grumbled, "That's why I don't like cats."

A laugh welled up in Linsha's heart. She scooped up the cat and sat cross-legged on the blanket across from Ian, the cat curled up in her lap.

"You are so beautiful when you smile," Ian said, his voice a haunting whisper. He poured a glass of wine, black-red in the moonlight, and handed it to her.

She saw him wince from the movement. "Tell me what happened tonight."

He passed a hand over his eyes and stayed silent for a long

while before he spoke. "It was a fiasco. We were ambushed by the Dark Knights on a farm in the northern vale."

Linsha sucked in a breath. "How?"

He gulped his wine and poured another measure. "Lord Bight's informer betrayed us. Instead of catching the Knights off guard, we were attacked by a full company of their horsemen lying in wait for us. We lost five men, and ten more were wounded before we could fight our way out."

"Ye gods," Linsha breathed. "No wonder Lord Bight was so upset." The orange cat bumped his head against her hand to be petted, and she automatically began to stroke his soft fur and rub his ears. "Then to lose Captain Dewald to murder . . ." Her voice faded.

"It hasn't been a good night," he groaned in understatement. He finished his second helping of wine, poured a third, then pointed to her cup, still untouched in her hand. "You haven't tried the wine."

She sampled the wine, letting it trickle down the back of her throat. He was right; it was very good. "What happened to the informer?" she asked.

"We haven't found him yet. If I have my way, he'll be drawn and quartered."

"How did you get hurt?"

His smile flashed again in the pale light. "Some big Knight sideswiped me with a short lance and knocked me out of the saddle. I nearly snapped my neck." Switching his cup to his right hand, he gingerly reached out and touched Linsha's shoulder.

To her astonishment, the orange cat snarled at him and lashed at his hand with a clawed paw.

Ian jerked back. "All right, all right, you stupid cat. Lynn, tell your guardian there to relax. I just wanted to know if your injury was doing well."

She stroked the cat until he subsided, but she made no effort to move him. She glanced up at Ian from under her dark brows. "It aches and burns at times. Other than that, it's fine."

Ian's third cup of wine disappeared and was replaced.

Linsha watched him worriedly while she sipped her own wine. She had never seen his control slip like this before.

"I'm sorry you were the one to find Captain Dewald in the woods," the commander said apologetically. His words were coming out slower than normal and a little rough around the edges.

"Do you have any idea who would want him dead?"

Ian swept his free hand through the air. "Any number of people. Solamnic Knights. Dark Knights. A jealous competitor. A jealous husband. The captain was my right hand. Maybe he was killed to strike a blow at me."

"I'm sorry. I know he was your friend."

"He was a good man." Suddenly he started chortling. "You know, he used to tell this awful joke about an elf, a kender, and a draconian." He fell back in the hay, laughing so hard he spilled wine over his tunic. He tried to tell the joke to Linsha and lost the punch line somewhere in his hilarity. His laughter gradually subsided, but his verbosity did not. He talked to Linsha about Dewald and his exploits, about the men in his command who died that night. He told her funny stories about Sanction and told more jokes than Linsha could ever remember while she listened and laughed and tried not to yawn too much. Through it all, he drank steadily, first from the wine bottle then from a flask he brought out of his tunic.

After nearly an hour, to judge from the lengthening angle of moonlight, Ian sagged back into the hay. He fell quiet so quickly that Linsha stared at him, wondering if he was ill. She lifted the protesting cat from her lap and crawled across the blanket to his side. He was lying on his back with his eyes wide open and staring at the roof. Slowly they slid from the roof and fastened on her.

She gazed down at him from his broad forehead down along the line of his cheek and jaw to his full lips and the small cleft on his chin. Her appraisal offered an invitation, and he took it.

His fingers touched her nose, her eyelids, and caressed the side of her face. They slid through her curls, curved around the back of her neck, and pulled her head down to him. Softly, gently his lips curved over hers, and he kissed her long and deep and passionately.

Linsha's will to resist lasted perhaps two heartbeats before her resolution melted like an old candle. It had been too long since she felt this way. He woke in her a need she thought long dormant, one she could not honestly call love. Perhaps what she felt for him was just lust or infatuation. She didn't know—not yet. But at that moment, she didn't care. All that mattered was his closeness and their need for each other.

Smiling, she traced his hairline with a finger that curled sensuously along his ear and across his strong neck. She delighted in the warm, masculine feel of his skin, in the musky wine-splashed scent of his body. She kissed him again.

He buried his face in her neck; his arms wrapped around her. As soft as an owl wing, she heard him mumble, "I love you." Then his body went slack and his breathing slowed. His arm dropped away. He slipped beyond consciousness into a sleep induced by too much wine and too much weariness.

Linsha leaned away, her heart sore and her body disappointed. Only her common-sense mind seemed to heave a sigh of relief. It was then she became aware of the orange cat crouched on the blanket, uttering a most obnoxious noise somewhere between a growl and a yowl. The moment she moved away from Durne, he stopped, making his point obvious even to Linsha's tired mind. For some cat reason, this tom did not approve of the commander. Linsha pushed herself up to a sitting position and sighed a long, heartfelt breath.

"Who are you, cat, to question my judgment? What are you doing up here, anyway?"

The cat merely blinked his yellow eyes in the darkness and watched her every move.

Linsha sat back on her heels and found she was swaying with exhaustion. The events of the long day had caught up with her at last and wore away every trace of strength she had left. Yawning hugely, she straightened Ian's limbs to a more comfortable position. He looked boyish in his sleep and so helpless lying there. His vulnerability touched her.

But it did not erase her professional sense of an opportunity to be had. While the cat watched, she laid her fingers on Durne's temples and summoned her power from the core of her soul. With a deft touch, she extended it around the man and the telltale colors of his aura. As she hoped, his outward nature was a decent blue, tinged only with small red taints of evil. It was when she probed deeper into his mind that she touched a barrier that resisted her even through a wine-induced sleep.

"Varia was right," she muttered to the cat, who studied her intently. "He is strongly shielded. Why does he feel the need to do so?"

Her power faded and the ensorcellment was broken. Ian stirred in his sleep until Linsha brushed a kiss over his mouth.

"I am such a fool," she muttered to herself. "I am living a lie that I hate. I have fallen for a man I do not trust, and I am deceiving another man I count as a friend. Every day that he calls me Lynn, I pray that one day he will call me Linsha and not hate me."

The cat meowed softly.

"I live for honor and yet I have none. What am I going to do?"

Perhaps in response to the sadness in her voice, the cat padded over beside her, rose on his hind legs, and patted her cheek with a delicate paw. The unexpected gesture comforted her. She scooped him up and carried him to the other side of the blanket. She could go no farther. She sagged down onto the hay and stretched out in the warm darkness. Sleep took her in moments.

The orange cat did not settle down at once. He circled her twice, sniffed her face and hair, and gently nosed her hands. One paw found the chain and the hard edge of the dragon scale still tucked beneath her tunic. Satisfied, he curled up against her, putting himself between her and the man who slept nearby. Soundlessly the cat watched through the remainder of the night.

At dawn, a newborn light worked its way into the barn and eventually woke the commander on his bed of hay. He groaned and rubbed his face. Painfully he pushed himself upright. His head was a leaden weight, his side was sore, and his neck felt as if someone had replaced the bones with a hot iron rod. And what was he doing in this hayloft?

A small, angry sound caused him to turn around, and he saw Linsha asleep on the blanket, curled on her side, her back to him. Memory returned, blurred and reluctant. What had he done? More to the point, seeing a fully clothed woman sleeping close by, what hadn't he done? The noise, he realized, came from the large orange cat crouched at Linsha's back. He was staring at the man with undisguised dislike.

"Blasted cat," Ian muttered. He thought of waking Lynn and perhaps continuing what he apparently missed last night. Then he decided to let her sleep. His body was battered, in pain, and in need of a healer's touch. He wouldn't be much good to her like this. He scratched the stubble on his chin. A shave would help, too. Besides, he could hear the horses stirring below and knew the grooms would be along soon. It wouldn't be appropriate for the governor's Commander of the Guard to be found in a hayloft with the newest squire.

He shook his head to help clear the cobwebs in his brain and climbed to his feet. He should never have had so much wine. "Sleep well, fair lady," he said to her supine form. Gathering up the empty wine bottle and the cups, he paused to glare at the cat. "Begone, or I will deal with you later."

The cat curled his lips and hissed an angry, defiant warning.

Hurrying now, Commander Durne climbed down the ladder and left the stables.

Only after the stable door closed and the sound of his footsteps faded away did the owl step out of the shadows in the roof and come drifting down on open wings. She came to rest on Linsha's hip and peered down at the cat. "You're here again? Have you been here long?"

The cat meowed in response. *Long enough.*

"Good," chirped the owl. "I just wish you'd show up in your other form and dispose of that cad before he hurts her."

Not yet. She can hold her own with him for a while. He

flicked a piece of hay off his paw and yawned. *I must go. Long day ahead.*

"Come back anytime," Varia hooted, her moon eyes bright with amusement. "Not that I heartily approve of you, but you're an improvement over that other man. He's dangerous. I just wish Linsha would see that."

"See what?" The lady Knight stirred and stretched sleepily, forcing the owl to hop off to the loft floor. "Would see her way to waking up. I have news," Varia trilled.

Linsha yawned and stretched again and threw an arm up over her eyes. "I'm awake now, so tell me. Did you see—"

"Yes," the owl interrupted abruptly. "And I followed Lady Karine when she told Annian. The news upset her as I expected. The captain was supposed to meet her yesterday to give her some important piece of information."

"But he never showed."

"No."

Her memory of the night before belatedly returned, and Linsha sat up, looking around for Durne.

"He left," the owl told her, the disapproval plain in her musical voice. Her statement was seconded by a meow from the cat.

Linsha frowned at them both. First the cat, now the owl. She found their joint dislike of the man she loved very irritating. What did they know? Then she grew annoyed with herself for even caring what two animals thought about Ian Durne. Oh, gods of all, she was tired. She rubbed her temples and tried to recall what Varia had been talking about. "What information did the captain have that was so important someone killed him?" She asked rhetorically.

The owl eyed the cat thoughtfully before she continued. "There's more. Mica did not go back to the temple last night. He stayed in town."

Linsha's interest piqued. "Where?"

"I don't know. He met someone, and they went in the direction of the refugee camp. I lost them near the wall."

"Could he have been going somewhere in his capacity as a healer?"

"Perhaps. If he was, he was going armed. He wore a sword."

Linsha was amazed. "Mica?" She couldn't remember seeing the dwarf bearing any kind of weapon besides his surly personality. "Is he still there?"

"I have been watching the temple. He has not returned."

"Perhaps I can find him. I would like to know what he is up to," Linsha said, thoughtfully chewing on a piece of hay.

The owl stared at her, unblinking. "May you leave the palace?"

"I was ordered to attend him with his work."

"That was yesterday," Varia pointed out.

"Maybe the guards won't know that. I'll tell them I am going to the temple."

Varia tilted her head and fixed a yellow eye on the cat. They stared at each other for so long that Linsha wondered petulantly what they were plotting. She knew Varia was telepathic at short ranges if she wanted to be; were cats, too?

"Fine," said the owl, breaking the silence. "You may try that. But if you go to the camp, be careful. The plague has hit hard there."

"Are you speaking to me or the cat?" Linsha said, her voice peevish.

"You," the owl responded, as if to a small owlet. "The cat has other places to go."

Linsha's brow furrowed in perplexity, but she didn't ask for an explanation. Varia often spoke of things Linsha didn't understand, and while she could have used her mystic abilities to talk to the cat, talking to animals was something she did only when she had time and a great deal of patience. This morning she had neither.

She yanked her blanket off the floor, upsetting the cat, and jumped to her feet. "I'm going to change. I'll leave you two to your private chat." Shaking her head, she climbed down from the hayloft.

Cat and owl watched her leave. A growling purr, almost like laughter, rumbled from the cat's chest.

"Yes, she is stubborn," Varia agreed. "And she gets mean as a gorgon when she hasn't had enough sleep."

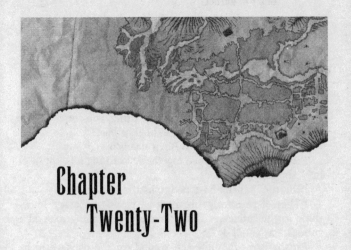

Chapter
Twenty-Two

The sentries at the back courtyard gate had received no orders about the squire, Lynn, and after seeing her in a proper uniform and listening to her explanation, they let her pass. They watched her proceed down the hill and onto the path that led to the Temple of the Heart and were satisfied.

To appease her conscience and to be sure the dwarf had not yet returned, she went to the temple first to inquire about Mica. The stately white building gleamed pale gold in the rising sun, and its windows were thrown wide open to catch the morning breeze. Despite the hour, the temple grounds were nearly empty and unusually quiet. Linsha walked up the path from the woods, across the neatly tended lawn, and up to the front portico before the door porter saw her and welcomed her inside.

Priestess Asharia overheard her inquiries to the door porter and, drawn by the red uniform of the Governor's Guards, came to see the visitor for herself. Although her face was drawn and thin from overwork, she smiled pleasantly at Linsha. "Mica has not returned yet. He went to the refugee camp last night to check on some patients."

Linsha let her face fall, and she shuffled her feet indecisively. "I have an important message for him from Lord Bight. I need to deliver it in person."

"Oh. Well, if you want to risk the camp, you could deliver it there. I just don't know when he'll be back."

"Perhaps I'd better. Lord Bight needs him."

Asharia's hands clasped together. "Lord Bight is not ill, is he?" she asked worriedly.

"Oh, no," Linsha hastened to assure her.

"Then if you are going anyway, could you carry something to the infirmary there for me? I was going to send a runner, but you'll do."

Linsha agreed. While she waited for the package to be brought, temple servants served a glass of wine, since the meager supply of water was for medicinal purposes only. She sipped it slowly, and she had just finished when the priestess returned lugging a large pack with straps. "I'm sorry to keep you waiting," said Asharia. "The extract of lupulin had not been bottled."

Linsha dredged her mind for that familiar name and came up with memories both uncomfortable and unpleasant of her grandmother forcing the stuff down her throat after she fell ill from a bad meat pie. "Cinnamon, hops, and yarrow for stomach cramps and diarrhea."

Asharia nodded, impressed that Linsha recognized it. "With a touch of valerian to relax the patient. It's an old remedy for grippe and dysentery. It isn't widely used, but we're trying anything. We've discovered most of our patients die from loss of fluids, so we're hoping to slow down the dehydration and maybe give the people a chance to fight the illness."

That sounded logical. "Treat the symptoms," Linsha said.

"For now. Until we can stop the cause." Asharia paused and laid a hand on Linsha's arm. "Be careful, young woman. Do not enter the camp. We have guards and runners on the roads, so give your load to one of them and have him find

Mica for you. If you do go in, touch nothing. Mica thinks the plague may be spread by touch."

The lady Knight nodded. "He told me that already," she said as she hefted the bulky pack. The bottles of extract had been so well packed, she didn't hear any clink of glass. She bowed a farewell to the priestess and took the dirt road down to Asharia's refugee camp on the hill just to the west of the temple.

Unfortunately the busy camp, due to its proximity to the temple and the healers, had naturally evolved into a hospital camp and had been one of the hardest hit areas of the city. As soon as Linsha crested the slope near the camp, she saw two large dirt mounds at the side of the road, mass graves for the victims of the plague. A third hole had already been dug, and a row of bodies lay wrapped and waiting to be placed within. Linsha held her breath as she passed. In the intense heat, bodies deteriorated rapidly and the flies gathered in dense clouds. There was a light wind from the west, but all it did was stir the dust on the well-beaten tracks and spread the stench of illness from the camp.

Before her, the road wound along the hill and plunged into a complex of tents, huts, and permanent wooden buildings. She could see only a few people moving about. Many more lay on pallets inside the tents, in the shade of awnings, or under the few scattered trees. If the stench was bad, the sound was worse—worse than bedlam, worse than anything she had ever heard. An endless drone of mingled groans, moans, and soft sobbing filled the air of the camp like the aftermath on the field of battle, and over that rose a babble of shouts, rantings, and screams from those patients trapped in the nightmares of delirium.

Linsha's footsteps slowed at the edge of the camp. Her hand went unconsciously to the dragon scale beneath her shirt. She looked around for a guard or runner in Temple robes, but everyone still upright was busy in other parts of the camp. She saw only a short gnome sitting on a stool by the roadside. He was busy with pen and paper balanced precariously on his knee.

"Excuse me, " Linsha said. "I'm looking for Mica. Is he still here?"

The gnome scratched his head with end of the quill pen, smearing some ink in his white hair. "Uh, no." He went back to his sketching.

Linsha tried again. "Sorry to bother you, but I need to know where he is. And I also have this pack of bottles from Priestess Asharia. It is to be delivered to your infirmary."

The gnome sighed at her interruption. He carefully laid his paper aside and hopped off his stool. "I'll take the pack to the infirmary. We're not supposed to let anyone pass inside."

Linsha looked dubiously at the gnome, for he hardly looked bigger than the pack itself. "It's heavy," she warned.

He smiled for the first time. He was a young gnome, Linsha realized, with unlined brown skin and brilliant blue eyes, and he proved quite capable of lifting the pack to his back and carrying it. "Mica left early this morning. He said he was going back to the temple," he said, turning to go.

Linsha waved her thanks and gratefully turned away from the camp. Now she didn't know what to do. Mica hadn't returned to the temple, and he wasn't in camp. He must be in the city. The only problem was where. . . . She knew she shouldn't be absent from the palace for long, nor could she search the entire city, but she didn't want to give up the hunt yet. Maybe, she thought, he went back to the scribe's house to look for more records. She could look through that neighborhood and hope for a bit of luck.

Setting off at a trot, she followed the track along the outside wall down past outlying cottages and businesses and into the heart of the outer city. She saw signs of the ravages of the plague everywhere she went: barricaded houses, yellow paint splashed on doors, grim demeanors of the people who ventured out, and here and there hastily dug graves in gardens and small parks. The stench of death and sickness fouled the air. Many of the people she did see wore masks or veils to help filter out the dust and smell.

It didn't take her long to find Watermark Street and the scribe's shop. To her disappointment, there was no sign of

Mica. The shop was shuttered and locked as before; the only difference was a splash of yellow paint on the doorframe. Linsha looked up one side of the street and down the other to no avail. With nowhere else in mind to check, she was about to turn back to the palace when a soft rustle warned her of Varia's approach. The owl landed on the edge of a roof nearby.

"He is two streets over, in an outdoor tavern," the owl hissed with excitement, and she winged to another roof across the road. Linsha hurried after her.

From her days patrolling this district, Linsha knew which tavern Varia meant, for it was one of only a few that offered tables set outside in a small garden. Apparently the tavern keeper was either desperate or overly optimistic to have opened his bar this day. Striding with purpose, Linsha took an intersecting street over three blocks and worked her way back through a shaded alley to come upon the tavern from the rear. The outdoor portion of the establishment lay at the back on a bricked patio shaded by a large latticed roof hung with a thick canopy of vines. As Varia reported, Mica sat at a round table, facing Linsha. A human man sat across from him, listening to his hushed talk. Because he had his back to her, Linsha couldn't see the man's face, but something about his grizzled hair and the angle of his shoulders looked vaguely familiar.

Linsha knew her red uniform made her too conspicuous to simply ease into the small number of tavern patrons, nor was there enough cover to get close enough to hear what Mica was saying. She had to content herself with a shaded corner behind a pile of empty crates and a framed view of the dwarf and his companion through a gap in the stack.

Varia flew silently across the rooftops and landed with a faint rustle in the foliage of the lattice. She, too, hunkered down to watch and listen.

While she waited, Linsha studied the man with Mica. She had seen him before, she knew that. At the moment, his head was bent over a mug, so the only part of him visible was his hunched back and shoulders and his long, gray-black hair pulled back in a leather thong. Just then a barmaid walked out the door with a tray of mugs, and the man looked quickly around, giving Linsha an unencumbered view of his profile.

A spark of recognition electrified her. By the gods, it was Calzon, the Legionnaire who sold his turnovers undercover in the Souk Bazaar. He looked younger than his usual disguise and better dressed, but Linsha could recognize his aquiline nose and strong chin anywhere. Linsha thought she knew most of the Legionnaires in Sanction, but if Mica was meeting with this member of the Legion of Steel, then he was probably either an informer or a member himself of the Legion. It was possible this meeting was nothing more than a friendly get-together between friends, but Linsha doubted it. Not here; not in the middle of this crisis. She would bet any number of steel coins that Mica was a Legionnaire. A Legionnaire placed undercover as the lord governor's healer. Linsha wanted to laugh. This is what the Clandestine Circle deserved for disregarding the Legion of Steel.

For one mischievous moment, she thought about sauntering over and renewing her acquaintance with Calzon. Fortunately her better sense convinced her not to. It could jeopardize her cover, and possibly Mica's as well. No, it would be better to keep this secret in her back pocket for future reference. She settled back in her hiding place to observe what would happen next.

A short while later Calzon finished his drink. He clapped Mica on the shoulder and exited toward the street. Mica watched him go. He fiddled with his drink for a while longer, then smacked a few coins on the table and strode out. Linsha kept him in sight and followed as best she could in her red uniform in the light of day. Yet the dwarf made it easy. Looking neither left nor right, he stamped single-mindedly to Shipmaker's Road and headed directly back to the temple.

When they neared the city gate, Linsha signaled to Varia and waited for the owl to find a perch. "Did you hear anything?" she asked hurriedly.

Varia chortled. "He was talking about you. He was telling the man he thinks you are an agent for the Solamnics. Apparently you talked in your sleep yesterday."

"Wonderful. Well, I guess we're even," Linsha remarked thoughtfully. "I think he's a Legionnaire. He was meeting with one of the men I know."

"He also thinks there is a traitor in Lord Bight's council, but he did not want to say more until he has more evidence."

Linsha scowled after the dwarfs retreating figure. "Did he mention what evidence he wanted?"

"No. He was very agitated about something, and he was very annoyed that you were following him around yesterday."

A quick smile lit Linsha's pensive gaze. "He'd better get used to it. If he discovers who this traitor is, I want to be there." She wiped the sweat on her brow and went on. "Follow him to be sure he's going to the temple. I'm going to get ahead of him and meet him there."

"Linsha, I think he is being followed by someone else."

The lady Knight stiffened. "Are you sure?"

"No," said the owl, bobbing her head, "but there is a man in plain clothes ahead of you. I just saw him again. I don't think he is aware of you yet because he is concentrating on Mica."

"All the more reason to vanish. Can you watch them both?"

"If the man continues to follow, yes."

"I'll see you at the temple," Linsha said softly. Turning left, she broke into a jog again back to the northern neighborhoods, up the road past the refugee camp and its sad mounds, and along the track to the temple. Panting and drenched with perspiration, she arrived at the temple doors two minutes ahead of Mica.

The porter was explaining to her that Mica had not yet returned when the dwarf stamped up the walkway and brushed past her. His bearded face was red from his brisk walk. He gave her an irritated glance and demanded, "What are you doing here?"

Linsha rolled her eyes. "I've been looking everywhere for you," she said, breathing hard. "The priestess even sent me to that ghastly camp so I could find you."

"What for?" he asked in a tone that doubted her intelligence.

"She has a message for you," the porter put in to be helpful.

Oops. Linsha forgot about that. Thinking fast, she pulled the dwarf into the foyer away from prying ears. "Lord Bight has been trying an experiment that so far has been successful, and he wanted me to inform you for your research."

"Why you?" He curled his lip in tolerant mockery.

Linsha kept her expression blank, her tone matter-of-fact. "Because I am the experiment."

The dwarf examined her with keen eyes, then indicated she was to follow him. He led her down a flight of stairs to a lower level and a large room filled with shelves of books. A worktable stood in the middle of the room, half buried under stacks of scrolls, books, and old manuscripts. Linsha recognized the bound records of the priest-scribe stacked at one end.

Mica lit several oil lamps hanging on chains from the ceiling. He crossed his arms.

"Explain," he demanded.

Linsha walked to the table. She didn't know if Lord Bight wanted this known or not, but surely he hadn't meant to keep it from his healer. "The lord governor told me he suspects the plague may have a magical origin. He has given me a talisman to protect me."

"Huh. So that's why he sent you with me into the city. I thought maybe he was hoping to be rid of you," Mica said, his words snide.

Linsha ignored that. Now that she had a strong suspicion of Mica's identity, she was more willing to overlook his grouchy personality. Any operative who had made it this far in Lord Bight's court and survived more than two years like Mica had to be good. "No," she said lightly. "He sent me to help you because I can read and wield a sword. The talisman was an addition."

Mica cast an eye over her, as if looking hopefully for signs of fever. "Is it working?"

"So far."

He snorted. "What is it?"

"A bronze dragon scale."

Mica was startled into saying, "A what?"

In reply, Linsha pulled the gold chain out from under her tunic and showed him the bronze disk. In the light of the oil lamps, it gleamed with a cool fire.

"I'll be a gully dwarf's squire," he exclaimed, leaning forward to see it better in the light. "Did he say where he got it?"

"He said he found it. It's supposed to be ensorcelled with protective spells." She turned it over in her hands. "It looks so new. I'd like to know where he found it—considering he's been here for thirty years and has forbidden the Good dragons to enter the city, to appease Sable."

"I daresay that edict is freely ignored by those metallics who can take the shape of a person." He waved a hand at her to put the talisman away. "For now, keep that scale safe, Alley Cat, and don't show it to anyone else."

Linsha tilted her head and looked sidelong at him. "Anyone in particular?"

He leaned forward, his expression serious. "If you have the favor of Lord Bight, it would be wise not to make it known, or the knowledge could be used against him . . . or you."

"The lord governor has been good to me," she replied, pushing off firmly the idea of any special preference, "but he is using this only as an experiment, not a mark of favor."

"So you think. Just follow my advice."

Her eyes lit with a sparkle of fun, and she grinned. "Why, Mica, I didn't know you cared."

A frown crossed the dwarf's face. The grump was back to normal, Linsha thought.

And yet somewhere in the conversation a small advance had been made and accepted. Without words or conscious effort, the secret knowledge each had of the other had altered their perceptions and reactions. Their different orders were not allies, but they were not enemies either, and some time or some where in this deadly game of intrigue, they might need one another.

"Can you really read?" Mica asked, pondering the stacks before him.

"Common Tongue, Solamnic, Plains Barbarian, and Abanasinian," she answered bluntly.

"Impressive."

She shrugged, bringing a twinge to her healing shoulder. "I get around. I know the thieves' hand talk, too, but that won't be found in any books."

He picked up a large pile of record books and tomes. "Good. You start with these," and he dumped them in front of her.

Linsha picked up the first one, an old treatise on common herbal remedies. "What are we looking for?"

"Anything having to do with a disease like our scourge or any mention of magic being used to create a widespread illness." He settled down in a chair and selected another book. "I suspect Lord Bight is right, but I can't fight something I don't know."

"Are you sure there was nothing in the ship's log from the death ship?"

"I read it cover to cover."

Linsha pulled up another chair, sat down, and opened the book. Her attention wandered into the pages. "Hmm," she said as she read. "It's a pity we couldn't talk to the ship's captain before he died."

A strange, speculative light flickered in Mica's eyes when he considered her words. "A pity," he murmured.

* * * * *

The captain of the black ship, *Lady's Sword*, unrolled his map on the chart table and looked up at the other captains gathered around. The map at his fingertips was a new one, richly inked and carefully drawn. It showed the eastern half of the Newsea, marking in the swampy realm of the black dragon, Sable, the diminished lands of Blöde, and the holdings of the Knights of Takhisis based in their city, Neraka. Sitting like a blot in the middle of it all was Sanction, a rich jewel perched at the toe of Sanction Bay on the easternmost point of the Newsea.

"Plans are well under way," the captain said, pointing a callused finger to Sanction. "Our informants say the plague has decimated the lower city and seriously weakened the guards. As soon as we receive the signal, we will sail for the harbor."

One captain, a tall fair-haired man, tapped a finger on the western side of the peninsula separating their ships from Sanction Bay. "Our fleet is scattered in all these coves and inlets. Will there be time to reassemble?"

"If all goes well, the volcano's eruption will be visible enough to give us time before our contact's signal arrives. If not, we'll try to regroup as we sail. The harbor's entrance is narrow anyway, so we will have to enter in groups of three."

A loud commotion on deck interrupted his words, and all heads turned to the door just as it crashed open. Three muscular sailors shoved a pair of young fishermen into the captain's cabin. The two men were forced to kneel before the assembled captains. Fear and recognition shone like sweat on their faces.

"Who are these men?" barked the captain.

One of the sailors grinned nastily. "We found them snooping around the cove. They spotted the ships before we caught them."

"Unfortunate," the captain commented. He turned cold eyes on the fishermen. "A little far from your fishing grounds, aren't you?"

"Oh, no, sir," one of the young men hastened to explain. "The heat has driven the fish from the shallow waters. We were just out looking for some deeper holes where the fish might have fled."

"They were carrying nets on their boat, but they didn't have so much as a baitfish on board," a sailor said.

The captain lifted a dark eyebrow. "Scouts? Has Bight heard rumors of us?" When no one answered, he moved swiftly to the front of the fisherman who spoke and clamped his hand over the man's face. Muttering under his breath, he drew on the power of his dark mysticism and projected it into the mind of his victim. He used neither gentleness nor patience, and the force of his will ripping into the man's mind brought forth a shriek of agony and terror from the prisoner.

The other captains looked on impassively, but the second captive stared with bulging eyes and a face filled with mingled anger and horror.

After a minute or two, the captain broke the link and withdrew his magic. The fisherman slumped to the floor, his eyes rolled up into his head, his body already slack in death.

"Bight is only guessing," the captain told the others. He turned to the sailors. "Dispose of these two. Double the guard and bring any more spies you capture to me."

The sailors gave a salute and dragged the prisoners away.

"Now, gentlemen," the captain said in satisfaction. "Let us discuss the order of battle."

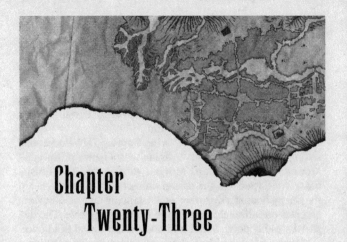

Chapter
Twenty-Three

Linsha worked with Mica in silent companionship until midafternoon before her stomach and a messenger from the palace interrupted her concentration.

"Commander Durne orders you to return, squire," the messenger told her. "I don't know why I'm the one who always has to come and get you."

"You're just privileged, I guess," she teased the young guard. Morgan had enough sense of humor to take it.

He grinned. "You'd better not dally. Word is, the commander isn't happy with you. Squires do not leave the palace without permission."

"I had permission!" she said indignantly.

"And," he overrode her protest, "without checking with the Officer of the Watch."

"Oops," Linsha admitted.

"You'd better go," said Mica dryly.

She closed her book, bowed to Mica as a squire should to

acknowledge the governor's healer, and followed the guard outside. They followed the path through the trees, passing the place where she had found the body of Captain Dewald. She slowed involuntarily to look at the trampled grass and the signs of many horses in the grove.

Morgan slowed down beside her. "They buried him in the crypt beneath the palace this morning. I wish I could find the scum that did this to him."

Linsha silently agreed. A living Captain Dewald happily selling information to Lady Annian was a better prospect all around, in her opinion. Morgan moved on, and Linsha quickly followed. As she passed one scraggly pine, she heard the sleepy hoot of a disturbed owl. Glancing up, she saw Varia perched on a branch close to the trunk of the tree. The owl gazed steadily down at her and nodded her round head once.

Linsha scratched her cheek to acknowledge the signal and hurried on. So Varia confirmed it: Mica had been followed. Who else was interested in the dwarf's activities? She could only hope for now that he would take his own advice and be careful.

Morgan took her through the courtyard gate and into the palace and led her directly to Commander Durne. The commander was with Lord Bight, the harbormaster, and several other officers in the governor's office on the third floor, all bent over a map spread across the large worktable. The young guard gave her a wink, pushed her in, and closed the door behind her. Nervously Linsha stiffened at attention

"Indications are the volcanic dome is going to blow soon, Your Excellency," one of the officers was saying. "The dome is growing larger again, and the smoke has increased. The camp has been bothered by tremors for two days. We recommend these areas in the camp, here and here," and he pointed to spots on the map, "be evacuated to a safer distance until you are able to bring the flow under control."

Lord Bight studied the map for a minute. He wore robes of black silk belted with gold that subtly altered the coloring of his face. His sun-bronzed skin seemed shadowed on the planes of his cheeks and jaw, and his deep-set eyes looked thunderous. "No. The dome should last for two or three more days. The Knights of Takhisis have been putting pressure on us in the north. After the debacle last night, they may want to take advantage of this distraction to the east, and I don't want to give them the idea we are relaxing our vigilance."

Another officer suggested, "Could you destroy the dome now, before it erupts?"

Lord Bight looked up, his eyes hooded. "I could level the dome now, but it would be premature. I want to wait until the pressure within is strong enough to blow itself out and push the lava in the direction I want it to go."

Even though the captains did not completely understand what he meant, they nodded and looked as if they agreed completely.

"Commander Durne, until I lance that boil on the mountain, you can pull the men back from the wall closest to the dome. Just be sure you increase the guard in the observation towers."

From her quiet post by the door, Linsha observed the commander, who stood beside the lord governor, his red uniform a sharp contrast to Lord Bight's black robes. To her disgust, her heart beat faster as she watched him, and her skin grew warm.

"My lord," Durne replied, "the City Guard is already stretched thin in the harbor district due to losses from the plague. What if we pull all patrols back to the city wall? That would give us the extra guards we need for the eastern perimeter."

Something about that suggestion niggled in the back of Linsha's mind. Commander Durne had pulled the City Guard out earlier, only to have Lord Bight reinstate them. Why was he so determined to have the guards out of the harbor district?

The harbormaster was aghast. "And leave the outer city open to looters, arsonists, and pirates?"

"Pirates?" Durne repeated derisively. "What pirate in his right mind would approach a plague city?"

"A nonhuman one," the harbormaster pointed out, and

then he blurted, "Or maybe the ones in those black ships lurking outside the harbor."

A shock-laden silence suddenly fell on the room. Lord Bight closed his eyes and seemed to be counting to ten.

"What ships?" an officer asked.

The harbormaster belatedly remembered he wasn't supposed to be discussing this news with anyone but Lord Bight. He tried to look unconcerned and failed miserably. "We had a report of a black ship out in the bay, so I sent some scouts to take a look. Routine."

"You said ships," another captain pointed out.

Linsha looked curiously at Commander Durne and thought it rather strange that he wasn't saying anything. He stood bent over the table, his palms flat on the table top, his eyes staring into nothing.

"Look," the harbormaster said quickly. "I spoke out of turn. I don't know if the ships are there. I haven't heard back from my scouts. I just don't believe the outer city should be left without its guard."

Lord Bight opened his eyes and, after giving the harbormaster a scathing glance, agreed. He tapped the map with a stiff forefinger to get his men's attention. "Leave the watch in the outer city, Commander. We'll use Governor's Guards to stand watch in the towers while the City Guards continue their patrols of the camp and outer fortifications."

"Yes, my lord," Durne finally responded, although Linsha noted the tension in his jaw and around his mouth. She wondered if he had a headache from all the wine he'd drunk the night before. "Lord Bight," he continued, "even though the construction of the aqueduct has slowed somewhat, it is still advancing. Do you wish us to keep guards posted there as well?"

The lord governor pursed his lips in thought for a moment, then answered, "We need the guards, but we need the water more. Elder Lutran tells me the city wells are going dry. Yes, keep the guards on the aqueduct as long as possible." He stepped back from the table and crossed his arms. "Gentlemen, you are dismissed."

The captains filed out in a group until only Commander Durne, the harbormaster, and Captain Omat, the officer of recruits, were left in the room with the lord governor.

Lord Bight beckoned to Linsha. When she approached and saluted, he sat in his chair and eyed her quietly, that oddly knowing flicker in his deep gold eyes.

"Squire Lynn," Commander Durne's voice cut through the stillness like a whip. "The officer of the watch told me you left the premises of the palace without permission."

Linsha bowed her head. Even Lynn would know when to act contrite. "I apologize, sir. I thought I was supposed to help the healer, Mica, at the temple today, and I didn't think about the rules."

"Start thinking about them, squire. Memorize them. Drill them into your head until you live and breathe the structure of this company. It may save the governor's life."

"Yes, sir," she answered firmly.

The commander turned to the officer of recruits. "Captain Omat, I want you to clearly explain the rules governing the lives of squires to this recruit and have her memorize them while she polishes armor in the training hall. Tonight she may stand watch in the observation towers."

Captain Omat saluted briskly. Linsha silently groaned.

Lord Bight leaned forward in his chair. "Before you go, squire, did you and Mica find anything useful in the books?"

"Just hints, your Excellency. Some herbal remedies he wanted to try. A few hints about similar illnesses. Mica is still looking." She saw his gaze search for the gold chain around her neck and knew he was making sure she still wore the scale. Since she had carefully hidden it under her linen shirt where it could not be seen, she caught his eye and dropped her chin in a single nod. He understood.

Captain Omat escorted her from the office and followed his orders to the letter. He took her to the training hall in plain view of many of the guards, placed her in an obvious position, and gave her a stack of breastplates to polish. For an hour, while she rubbed polish into the steel and buffed it to a silvery sheen, he read her the rules and regulations and made her memorize them. Guards in the hall would come by and order her to recite a rule or offer criticism on her work, but while this happened frequently, Linsha sensed no maliciousness in their attention, only humor and the shared knowledge that they had all been there before. Linsha didn't mind. It was all part of the experience and a small price to pay for the information she had gained that morning.

The captain left her after an hour with orders to continue until the evening meal; after her dinner, she was to report to the Officer of the Watch—properly this time—for her sentry assignment.

Linsha returned an armload of polished armor to the armory. When she came back with more, Shanron was sitting on a stool waiting for her, her long face downcast, her arm in a sling.

"I didn't pull my shield up fast enough," Shanron said when she noticed the look of concern on Linsha's face. "Thankfully, Mica came by late last night to set it." She hefted her arm a bit and grinned ruefully. "It still aches. How's your shoulder? I heard you had a run-in with some looters."

"I didn't move fast enough either. In fact, the weapons master was just here telling me exactly what I did wrong. I let him get too close."

Shanron crooked a smile. "Who? The weapons master or the looter?"

"Both," Linsha laughed.

They chatted for a time about the guards and polishing armor, about Shanron's home and the character of cats."

"Have you seen a large orange tomcat in the barn with the ship's cat?" Linsha asked at one point.

"Not one like that," Shanron said. "There are a few gray tabbies who hang around the feed room and a black who rules the aisles, but no orange tomcat. Why?"

"I've seen one twice now. At night."

"Maybe the ship's cat is in heat."

"I don't think so. He stays with me."

"I can't help you." Shanron lapsed into silence and stared moodily across the room.

Still bent over her polishing, Linsha lifted her eyes to watch her friend worriedly. Shanron's eyes glistened with unshed tears, and her nose was turning red. Her face seemed paler than normal. "Is something wrong?" Linsha asked in a voice just above a whisper.

A tear slipped down Shanron's cheek, only to be wiped savagely away. She seemed to be wrestling with a dilemma, for her mouth opened and closed and her eyes fastened on Linsha, then slid away before she could decide to say anything.

After a very long silence, she said quietly, "Lynn, does the word 'chipmunk' mean anything to you?"

Linsha felt a shock surge through her. "Small, stripy rodents?" she replied guardedly.

"Nothing else?" her friend asked in a small voice.

"It could be other things, I guess. Why do you want to know?"

Shanron sighed a long, sad breath of air and explained. "Captain Dewald was my friend, my . . . well, we were very close. Close enough that I was considering leaving the guards so I could marry him."

Linsha's mouth fell open. "Shanron, I'm so sorry. I didn't know." She wondered if Lady Annian knew.

The tall blond warrior blushed self-consciously. "No one did. We tried to be very discreet. Anyway, the day before he was murdered, he came to me very agitated, frightened even. When I asked him what was wrong, he only said, 'I think they know.' He wouldn't explain what he meant. He told me if anything happened to him, I was to ask you about a chipmunk." Her last word rose in a note of disbelief.

The whole tale sounded unreal, and yet, if there was no truth to the matter, how would Captain Dewald have known that chipmunks had any significance to her if Lady Annian hadn't told him? She thought quickly over her options, then decided to trust in Shanron. "A dead chipmunk left on a certain windowsill is a signal that means 'Come at once. Most secret.' "

A sound, somewhere between a gasp of disbelief and a

laugh of incredulity, burst out of Shanron's lips. She leaned forward, pulled a small packet out of her sling, and slipped it into Linsha's lap. "Don't tell me more. What I don't know can't be forced from me. Just take care of yourself." She wiped her sleeve over her eyes and stood up. "I have sentry duty tonight, too, so maybe I'll see you later."

Linsha grinned and waved to Shanron as she sauntered away, then neatly slid the packet under her waistband. Curiosity consumed her, but she could do nothing about the packet until she was finished with the armor and could leave the hall. Impatiently she polished and buffed and hauled armor back and forth until the bell rang in the courtyard for the evening meal and she could gratefully put away the rags and the polish. She walked out of the training hall with the intention of slipping up to her room to open the packet and was intercepted by Captain Omat. The captain's face was adamant as he led her into the dining hall and supervised her meal. She made a loud comment about baby-sitters, but he ignored her and waited for her to eat. As soon as she was finished, he escorted her to the Officer of the Watch.

"This recruit," he told the officer, "is still learning the rules. Make sure she knows the regulations for sentry duty backward and forward."

"Asleep fall not do," Linsha responded promptly. The Officer of the Watch, a dour man with too many positions to fill and not enough guards, promptly sent her to the farthest observation tower in the eastern fortifications.

The blood-red sun eased below the horizon while Linsha and a squad of Governor's Guards marched through the city to the guard camp. Darkness crept slowly out of the east to meet them. High haze and thin clouds obscured the sky, and only a slight wind stirred the dust and wood fire smoke above the city. The camp was busy with the changing of the guard and the return of the day patrols. At the easternmost end of the camp, before the squad reached the earthworks, Linsha saw a huge tent set aside as an infirmary. Here in the camp, the plague had struck hard, but sick guards were immediately quarantined, and unlike the harbor district where the Sailors' Scourge spread out of control, the plague in the camp had remained within limits.

As ordered, Linsha reported to the northeastern tower and, with another Governor's Guard, relieved the sentries on watch. The two City Guards showed them the signal flags, a farseeing glass, and the torches they might need.

"Keep a close eye on that beast," one guard said. She pointed to the mountain. "Lord Bight instructed us to watch the dome for signs of molten lava, increased smoke, and any explosions."

"Oh, fun," Linsha remarked in a dry tone. "How do we let him know the peak is about to blow?"

The other guard indicated a round glass ball nestled in a box of cotton fluff. The ball contained a bright orange liquid and a wick that extended out of the ball. "His lordship said to light the fuse, throw it as high in the air as you can, and duck. But don't touch it until it is needed," he warned.

The City Guards departed for their meal and a needed rest, leaving Linsha and the second guard by themselves in the tower. The other guard was a middle-aged man, slim, capable, and utterly devoid of conversational skills. Linsha's few attempts to talk to him were quietly rebuffed until she took the farseeing glass and retreated to the opposite end of the tower.

There was just enough ambient light left to use the glass, so, leaning on the parapet, she trained the long glass on the volcano. It loomed, stark and black in the gathering twilight, a sleeping giant about to awaken. Smoke wreathed its shoulders like a cloak. She looked for any signs of the infamous Temple of Luerkhisis that had once sat upon the western side of the mountain, but the hideous dragon-headed temple had been razed to the ground, and any remains were long gone. She lifted the glass a little higher to locate the cave where the red dragon, Firestorm, had her lair during Sanction's occupation by the Knights of Takhisis, and that, too, seemed to be gone. Either it had been destroyed or it was obscured by the shadows of night.

She turned to the right and swept the glass over to the

distant hills that led to the entrance of the East Pass. Tiny flickers of light marked the fortified camp of Governor General Abrena's Dark Knights, who waited, ever ready to attack at a moment's notice. Between them and the vale burned the golden dikes of lava, wide and deadly and more effective than any wall.

The hours passed uneventfully. The mountain remained impassive. The Dark Knights stayed in their eastern camp. If they sallied forth from the North Pass, Linsha didn't see any indication of it. She hoped all was quiet in the city as well. After fires and raids and ambushes and sick civilians, both groups of guards needed a peaceful night.

Two hours after midnight, two new guards came to relieve them. They had no news to report and simply told Linsha and her companion to return to the palace. Linsha was happy to obey. The packet from Shanron still lay under her waistband, waiting for her to open it in a moment of privacy. She and the guard rejoined the others, and as a squad, they marched out of guard camp and moved toward the palace.

At the East Gate, the City Guards passed them through, all but Linsha.

"Squire Lynn?" called the officer on duty. "You are to wait here for further orders."

The veteran guards laughed among themselves at the hapless squire and went on without her. Linsha watched them go in dismay. It was probably the doing of that blasted Captain Omat. She'd bet he had some other onerous duty for her this night.

But it wasn't Captain Omat. Minutes later, a tall, familiar shape walked out of the darkness into the light of the gate's torches. Unconsciously she straightened her shoulders and stared eagerly at his face while he had a few quiet words with the City Guard officer. The officer saluted his commander, and Ian Durne came to where she was standing. "Come with me, squire," he ordered.

Curious and pleased, Linsha followed him at the proper distance along an empty street. As soon as they were out of sight of the gate, Ian ducked into a shadowed doorway and pulled Linsha in with him. His arms gathered her close, and his mouth closed hungrily over hers. A fire ignited in her body, and she pressed against him, meeting his kisses eagerly.

He broke off at last and clasped her face in his hands. "I've wanted to do that all day," he gasped in her ear.

She laughed and kissed him again until their knees trembled and their bodies ached for each other. "Is there somewhere we can go?" she murmured.

He took her hand and pulled her along the sidewalk. "I was hoping you'd ask. I have a friend who has a house near the bazaar. He has kindly lent it to me tonight."

Linsha said nothing more. She held his hand and ran beside him along Shipmaker's Road to a large house set flush with the sidewalk. The ground floor held a tailor's shop, but Ian led her to an outside staircase that led upstairs to a comfortable apartment. A small lamp glowed on the fireplace mantel in the front room, and several candles burned on a table set with plates of food and a flagon of pale white wine. In the back, Linsha could see another room with a large bed and more candles gleaming by the bedside.

She looked around with delight. "You planned all this?" she breathed. His only answer was another long, delving kiss.

They saved the food for later. He led her to the bed, and the last coherent thought she had was to secretly pull the packet and the dragon scale out of her clothes and tuck them out of sight in her boot.

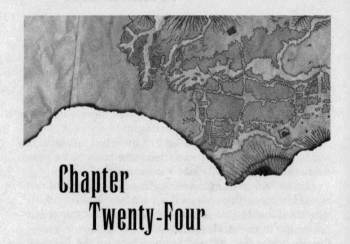

Chapter
Twenty-Four

They left the apartment shortly before dawn and unwillingly closed the door on the privacy they had so enjoyed.

"Maybe tonight," Ian murmured into her hair, "if the volcano stays quiet and the city doesn't burn down."

"I look forward to it," she replied, stretching languorously against him. He kissed her again in the warm darkness, and she almost gave in to the temptation to open the door and push him back inside. But Commander Durne was due back at the palace, and Squire Lynn was expected to report for duty at daybreak. Reluctantly they assumed their roles once more and walked back to the palace, Squire Lynn keeping the proper pace behind her commander.

As soon as Commander Durne left her in the courtyard and disappeared into the palace, Linsha ducked into the stable and ran up the ladder to see Varia.

The owl was in a huff. "Where have you been?" she cried angrily. "I was so worried I was starting to drop feathers."

Linsha flashed a cake-eating grin that Varia understood perfectly. "You were with him," she squawked in dismay. " Oh, Linsha, I hope you don't regret that!"

"I'll try not to," Linsha said flippantly. "But look at this. Captain Dewald gave it to Shanron to give to me if he was killed." She pulled out the packet and showed it to the owl.

Varia shuffled from foot to foot, wanting to say more, but she knew the lady Knight enough to know she wouldn't listen. Linsha had made up her mind, and for good or ill, she had made her love known to the commander. Only time would tell if it would be a blessing or a curse. Varia put her worry aside and let her curiosity take over. She watched as Linsha carefully unwrapped the thin packet.

The outer wrapping was just a worn piece of scrap parchment torn from the back of an old book. Inside was another piece of paper and a scrap of red fabric that matched the fabric of her uniform. Linsha turned the paper over and saw a letter hastily scrawled on its worn surface.

Skull Knight killed informer. I fear I am next. Knight in Gov. Guards, but don't know who. Found scrap in dead man's hand. Dark Knights to attack after volcano blows. Warn Annian.

"Oh, my," whistled Varia. "No wonder they killed him."

A cold, sick feeling crept into Linsha's awareness. There was a Skull Knight in the Governor's Guards. That explained a great deal. How many things had gone wrong, how no one had found him. Skull Knights were Knights of Takhisis trained in their dark mysticism to manipulate minds and shield themselves from other mystics, to use the power of the heart to corrupt and spread evil. She closed her eyes and breathed a small prayer that she would not meet this Knight and know his face.

"Who do you suppose it is?" Varia asked.

"I don't know!" Linsha said in a hoarse voice. "It could be any of the captains. Or the weapons master, or the horse master." She couldn't go on, and Varia didn't press her.

"Do you want me to take this to Lady Karine?" the owl asked.

Linsha shook her head. "Not yet. First I ask a favor, a big one, because I know you don't like to fly in the daylight. Would you please fly out past the bay and see if those black ships are there? The harbormaster said he hasn't heard from his scouts, but if this note is right and the Dark Knights plan to attack when the volcano blows, the ships may already be grouping for an attack."

"That will take all day. I won't be back until after nightfall," warned the owl.

"I know." She stroked her fingers down Varia's velvety head. "Just be careful. I'll try to meet you back here tonight."

"What are you going to do?"

"Try to find a Skull Knight before he finds me."

The owl hooted farewell, and the two went their separate ways. Linsha reported for duty as ordered and spent the day reciting rules, polishing armor, working with the weapons master, and studying every guard in sight for some telltale sign that would reveal him as the Dark Knight. Interspersed in her tangled thoughts were memories of the night before, and in those brief moments, she could relax and remember a few hours of uncomplicated pleasure and happiness. She wondered, too, what Lord Bight was doing and why she hadn't seen him that day, or what luck Mica was having with the records. She had hoped to be sent to the temple to help him, but her officers had other plans.

Commander Durne stopped by the training hall in the midmorning and watched her practice with the weapons master. He shared a smile with her and made a comment or two about her stance. As soon as the weapons master was distracted, he bent over and murmured, "Tonight. Same place," then hurried away to his duties. She watched him until the weapons master drew her attention back to her work by kicking her feet out from under her.

Linsha was also concerned she would be given sentry duty in the night watch again and wouldn't be able to meet Varia or Durne until late in the night, but Captain Omat posted her to the afternoon watch in the hottest hours of the day. Linsha couldn't decide whether to be happy or disgusted at his timing.

Once more she traipsed out to the guard camp with a squad of guards and was sent to the northeastern tower. She climbed up the stone stairway behind her companion guard and came out into the fiery sun. The two guards on duty hastily showed them a barrel of warm water, turned over the watch, and vanished down the stairs.

Linsha sighed. Surely someone could have built a roof over this tower. She leaned on the stone parapet and quickly changed her mind. The stone felt like a baker's oven.

Restlessly, she paced from one side of the tower to the other. Her companion, the same dour man from the night before, settled himself in a corner and pretended she wasn't there. Linsha curled her lip at him and continued to pace. After a while, she picked up the farseeing glass and studied the volcano. She found the dome immediately, like a huge boil near the crater of the mountain. Smoke and steam poured from cracks along its surface, and Linsha fancied she could see it pulsate and heave from the tremendous forces building beneath it.

Several horsemen arrived at the base of the tower and dismounted. Peering over the wall, Linsha recognized Lord Bight and his sorrel. Her heart suddenly contracted in a pang of guilt and nervous anticipation. He had said very little to her since the incident in the bathhouse. Was he still angry with her? Or worse, had he found out about her night with Commander Durne? That possibility, while remote, was the most painful to examine. She had an odd feeling he wouldn't approve.

The packet, tucked into her waistband, poked her skin and reminded her of its presence. The information in the letter was another dilemma. Should she tell him of its contents and warn him of the possible attack? If she did, such an action would be a certain violation of her orders from the Circle. She was supposed to discredit him, not help him. On the other side of the coin, wasn't she obligated to do everything in her power to stop the Knights of Takhisis from gaining control of Sanction? Telling the Circle about an imminent attack wouldn't help. The only one strong enough to stop the Dark Knights was Lord Bight.

Linsha's hands clenched into fists. Oh, Father, she sighed to herself. I wish you were here to talk to me.

When Lord Bight stepped onto the tower heights, Linsha and the other guard stood at attention and saluted. The lord governor had come alone, leaving his other men to wait below. He acknowledged their salutes and moved to the wall to study the volcano.

The second guard moved back to his corner and resumed his silent watch.

Linsha shifted back and forth on her feet, uncertain what to do. She wanted to talk to Lord Bight, but she hesitated to approach him without some sign that he was willing to listen.

"Squire," he called. "Come here."

Linsha's fingers clenched again. How did he do that? Could he read her mind or he was he just incredibly intuitive? "Yes, my lord," she answered, joining him by the wall.

He dropped his voice so the other guard couldn't hear and said, "I wasn't offended by you the other night. The problem was with me."

Linsha looked away. All at once she realize she had received something rare and almost unheard of in Sanction, the governor's apology. Just as suddenly her spirits lifted and she turned back to him, a smile on her lips.

Her relief was so obvious to him, his hand went out on its own accord and gripped her arm.

Although startled by his touch, she didn't flinch or move away. Her green eyes regarded him steadily while she sorted through what to say. "Lord Bight, yesterday you said the Knights of Takhisis might take advantage of this distraction. It is in my mind that you are right. What better time to attack the city than when it is weakened by disease and its governor is busy with a volcano?"

"That has been on my mind as well, Lynn," he replied.

He dropped his hand to his side and turned back to look at the volcano. "The dome is almost ready to blow. I can hear the lava rumbling deep within the cone. Tomorrow I will go to the mountain to work my spells. I have to exert much of my power to release the pressure and send the ash and lava where I want them to go, and there are times during the working of the magic when I am vulnerable. I want guards I can trust to be with me. Will you be one?"

Linsha caught her breath. She was honored beyond speaking that he would ask her, would put his welfare and safety in her trust. Then her thoughts darkened, and her face grew pale under her tan. What of the Clandestine Circle? What of her vows to the Knighthood? She was under orders to help dispose of the lord governor. But by the gods, she could not agree to that course. She found his eyes on her again, and this time she couldn't meet them.

"The time is coming, Lynn," he said in a voice so soft she could barely hear him, "for you to decide. Friend or enemy." Turning on his heel, he left the tower and left Linsha in a whirlwind of emotion. She pressed a hand over the dragon scale under her shirt and felt its hard, comforting edges. If only the scale had a magic spell in it to protect her from folly.

For the rest of her watch, Linsha stood by the wall and stared blindly at the mountain while she fought a battle within. This time she didn't even want the distraction of her juggling balls. Over and over in her mind, she replayed the events of the past sixteen days, examining and considering every face, every conversation, every nuance of feeling she could remember. Somehow she had to find a path through the complications that would allow her to help Lord Bight without incurring the wrath of the Clandestine Circle. There had to be a way! He meant too much to Sanction to lose. By all the stars of Chaos, she finally admitted to herself, he meant too much to *her*.

But so did the Knights of Solamnia. For as long as she could remember, she had listened to the tales of her grandparents and parents, of their deeds and their friends' deeds. Their courage, honor, and devotion to good had been imbued in her since childhood. The Knights of Solamnia caught her fascination after she heard her grandmother talk about her uncles, Tanin and Sturm Majere, who became the first non-Solamnics to enter the Knighthood. If they could do it, Linsha determined, so could she. After that, she had asked for the tales of Huma Dragonbane, Riva Silvercrown, and Sturm Brightblade again and again, until even her patient mother grew tired of them. Her beloved parents had not been enthused about their daughter joining the Knights of Solamnia, but they didn't try to dissuade her either, and eventually, with her parents' and grandparents' blessing, she became the first non-Solamnic woman to ascend to the Order of the Rose among the Solamnic Knights. It was an honor she didn't take lightly. Although she hated the deceptions of her mission in Sanction, she still belonged heart and soul to the Order of the Rose and all it stood for. Honor and justice.

The problem now was to find a solution that would allow her to serve justice without losing her honor.

By the time the brazen sun finally touched the horizon, Linsha had a raging thirst and a bad headache and was no closer to a resolution than when she started. The relief watch came promptly at sunset and told her all was quiet in the city. She and her silent companion rejoined the squad and began the march gratefully back to the palace for an evening meal and a long, cool drink of anything but tepid water from a barrel.

As they approached the East Gate, Linsha felt her hopes rise, and she scanned the area for the familiar tall figure of the commander. There he was, waiting with the City Guards posted at the gateway. He nodded once to the officer in charge, then beckoned to Linsha.

"Squire, attend me," he ordered.

The squad moved on, leaving Linsha behind. She waited patiently in the shade of the wall while he spoke to the guards on duty, and while she felt anticipation for the coming hours, something of the innocent joy was gone, destroyed by the simple packet in her waistband and its scrawled warning.

The Skull Knight was in the Governor's Guards. Oh, please, she begged silently, don't let it be Ian.

Twilight fell over the city as they walked down Shipmaker's Road toward the house near the bazaar. Ian didn't try to kiss her or touch her while there was still light in the streets and people to see. He waited until they had climbed the stairs and walked into the front room of the apartment.

The room was dim with evening and hot with the summer's heat. Swiftly Ian closed the door behind her and gathered her into his arms. "Come here, Green Eyes," he whispered.

Linsha's reservations faded to distant heat lightning, and she gave in to the desire of his embrace. Their lips met and they shared a kiss, timeless and prolonged, that led to more until their hands and tongues couldn't get enough and their clinging turned to need. Laughing, Ian hooked an arm under her knees and shoulders and carried her to the bed in the next room.

* * * * *

Hours later, Ian Durne kissed Linsha softly on the cheek and carefully rose from the bed. She slept lightly on her side, her hand close to her face, her red curls springing everywhere across the pillow. He watched her for a moment and felt regret like a knife blade in the gut. Moving silently, he picked up his uniform and boots and carried them to the front room, where he dressed as fast as he could. He opened the door. The night was full and hid the streets and alleys in dense darkness, but across the street, a tiny light flickered once in an alley. Commander Durne beckoned.

Two men dressed in black loped across the street and met Durne at the foot of the stairs. "I want her out of this," he ordered. "Restrain her, but don't kill her. Do you understand?" His hand shot out and grabbed one man's arm in a painful grip. "And, Jor, if you lay a hand on her beyond what it takes to tie a rope, I will flay you alive."

"Yes, sir," both men grumbled.

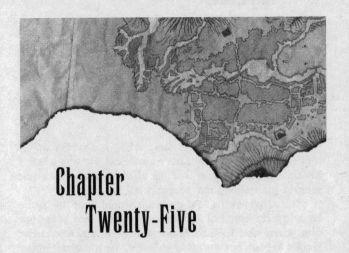

Chapter
Twenty-Five

The first sign of danger Linsha became aware of was a soft creak of the floorboards near her side of the bed. The unexpected sound brought her wide awake, and her eyes opened to see two black figures lunging toward her. Automatically her hand reached for a dagger, but she had no clothes, no weapons, nothing. Hands reached for her. She erupted out of the bed in a tangle of limbs and bedclothes, screeching with fury.

The sheet pulled tight around her legs and threw her off-balance. She fell into the first figure and felt powerful hands grab her arms above the elbow and force them back until she moaned with pain. Without saying a word, the second figure clamped a hand like a steel trap over Linsha's nose and mouth. A wad of rough fabric scratched her face and shut off her air.

She fought desperately to escape, but the two silent men were strong and efficient. A strange smell filled her nose from the fabric. It clogged her nose and drifted into her lungs. She choked and coughed and only succeeded in inhaling more of the noxious smell. All at once she became dizzy. Her strength drained away and her eyesight faded.

Where is Ian? she thought briefly before the world went black and she knew nothing more.

* * * * *

Mica closed the book he was reading and rubbed at the dull ache in his temples. This was useless. He was wasting his time trying to plow through all these books for some scrap of information that probably did not exist.

He had hoped the lord governor would send the squire back to help him, but apparently she had been kept busy somewhere else. Too bad. She was irritating and a Solamnic Knight to boot, but she could be useful. He thought it rather poor planning that the leader of his cell hadn't bothered to tell him of the presence of a good Knight in the Governor's Guards. While it was true the Legion and the Solamnics had little to do with each other if they could help it, he knew Calzon had a contact in the knightly order and it could have been useful to know who that contact was. Not that it mattered now. One way and another, Lynn's identity had been revealed to him.

His biggest concern now was finding the key to the Sailors' Scourge. He believed the disease was induced by magic, but now he had to prove it and, if possible, find something that would break the vicious cycle of the contagion. That was easier said than done. Mystic magic, his specialty, had very little effect on the disease, so it was probably based on something from the old magic of the gods, the magic that no longer existed on Krynn except in old artifacts and talismans of power.

He stretched his arms and neck. He was getting stiff from so much sitting. As he stood up, his eyes fell on the spine of a book half buried under a pile of tomes and scrolls. A ship's name flashed into his mind. He snatched the ship's log out of the pile and opened it to the first page that listed the galley's crew. Lynn said it was a pity they couldn't talk to the captain before he died.

Mica's finger found the right name: Captain Emual Southack. "Well, Captain, maybe we can talk to you now," the dwarf murmured.

He blew out his work lamp and went up the stairs two at a time. He sketched a wave to the porter, and before the man could ask questions, he hurried down Temple Way toward the city and the harbor.

In his rush, he didn't pay attention to the trees around him or the road behind him. If he had, perhaps he would have noticed the furtive figure that followed him carefully through the shadows.

* * * * *

A dull, throbbing pain beat in Linsha's head in time with the steady rhythm of her heartbeat. As consciousness slowly returned, she tried to groan and discovered the sound was muffled by a wad of fabric in her mouth. When she tried to spit it out, it remained held firmly in place by a strip of leather tied around her head. That fact surprised her. Opening her eyes, she saw little but darkness, yet the room and the vague shapes within it were familiar. Warily she lay still for a time and took inventory of her predicament.

She was lying, still unclothed, on the bed she had shared with Ian. A sudden thought occurred to her, and she looked frantically around for him. There were no bodies; she was alone. Did that mean he had done this to her and left her? Or had he been taken against his will?

She found her hands were tied together and fastened to the bedstead so tight she could barely move. There was no possibility of pulling or tearing or breaking those ropes. Her legs, too, were bound at the knees and ankles. Someone had even wrapped the sheet tightly around her. She was trussed like a fowl and left here. For how long?

For that matter, how long had she already been here?

Linsha closed her eyes, fighting to hold back the tears of

rage and frustration. She was a trained Knight. How could she have let herself get into this? And Ian, where was he? What was happening while she lay here tied to the bed like a sacrificial virgin?

She couldn't cry out for help. She couldn't move or reach her weapons or do anything to get herself out of this mess. She needed help . . . and fast.

Varia, her mind thought wildly. Had Varia returned yet? She knew the owl was telepathic at short distances, but she didn't know if Varia was clairvoyant enough to receive a cry for help from a long distance. It was worth a try.

She relaxed her body, letting each muscle ease into loose stillness until she could feel only her heart beat, slow and soothing, in her chest. She focused on the heartbeat, on the power within its steady rhythm, and slowly she began to pull that power to her will. Warmth pervaded her limbs, driving away the pain in her head and hands. Energy flowed through her in a tingling, invigorating surge.

She stretched out with her mind, sending her power outward in a call to Varia. *I am here. Bring help.* She repeated the words over and over, like a litany, and projected them as best she could in the direction of the palace and the barn. As time passed and nothing happened, her desperation grew stronger and her power responded, rippling out from the house in a steady flow like the beacon light at Pilot's Point.

What felt like hours passed, and there was no sign of the owl or anyone else. Despair coiled around Linsha's heart, and her hope began to wane. *I'm here,* she tried one last time. *Please come.*

* * * * *

The waterfront was nearly deserted at that time of night. Even the gaming houses were quiet and the taverns were closed. A few lights burned in windows where families nursed their sick or guarded their homes. The City Guard patrols passed silently through the streets and every now and again chased looters out of stores or houses.

Mica paid little attention to the city around him except for landmarks he used to find his way in the dark. His one drawback as an operative for the Legion was his tendency to be single-minded when he was possessed with an idea. This night, his idea led him directly to the end of the long southern pier. He bypassed several piles of crates and barrels to be hauled into the city in the morning and found a seat on the very edge of the long pier. His legs dangled into darkness, and beneath his feet, the restless water surged about the pylons.

Out in the bay, he saw three galleys swinging peacefully at their moorings and a flock of smaller fishing craft and pleasure boats scattered across the harbor. A number of freighters rode high in the water near the northern pier, waiting for life to return to normal in Sanction and shipping to resume.

Mica lifted his eyes and looked far out in the bay, where the guards had burned the *Whydah* and the ill-fated merchantman. There. Out there. He closed his eyes now and made himself comfortable. His mind relaxed and emptied of all thoughts but one, Captain Emual Southack. The captain's spirit was probably close to the ship he loved, and using the power of his heart, Mica hoped to summon him long enough to answer a few questions.

Spiritualism, one of the paths of mysticism, was not something Goldmoon encouraged, for it could be dangerous and often tempting, but Mica had tried it before successfully and felt he could attempt it tonight. The only drawback was it always left him drained and exhausted for several hours afterward. Still, Mica decided that little side effect was worth the effort if it led him to some answers. He focused on his heartbeat and murmured a few dwarvish phrases he liked to use to settle his concentration, then he slowly let his senses drift outward toward the place where the ships and their dead lay beneath the water. He shaped his magic into a call and sent it rippling outward from this world into the world beyond in a summons that opened the door and invited the captain to answer.

Nothing happened at first, and Mica directed more energy

into the enchanted plea. He reached his senses deep into the water, where the darkness was impenetrable and the rotting bones of dozens of ships lay in the mud of the bay. His mind touched the charred remains of the *Whydah* and the ship from Palanthas, and he felt a connection made.

Captain Southack, he called again.

A hushed sound, like the summer wind, blew past him. *I am here.*

Mica caught the faintest scent of salt water and charred wood. He opened his eyes. In front of him hovered an image of a man dressed in dark pants and a short coat over a vest of red silk.

Captain Southack? I need to ask you something.

* * * * *

I am coming! The cry echoed so faintly in the recesses of Linsha's tired mind she did not recognize it at first. It came again, a little louder and a little closer.

The lady Knight lifted her head. *Varia? I am here. Upstairs.*

I am coming came the call, as clear as the courtyard bell.

Footsteps pounded up the stairs, and Linsha heard a familiar voice ask, "In here? Are you sure?"

She struggled wildly to answer, but she didn't need to. Varia's voice hooted and cried and trilled in an ecstatic response.

"All right, all right," said Shanron's puzzled voice. "I'll get it open."

The old lock on the door was no match for the determined kick of the guard woman's boot heel. The door crashed open, and Varia flew arrow-straight into the bedroom and circled over Linsha's bed. Shanron followed a little more slowly as if she still wasn't convinced anyone was there. She stepped into the bedroom, saw Linsha, and bolted to the bed.

"By the gods, Lynn. Who did this to you?" she cried, kneeling by the bed. With her dagger, she hacked through the bond around Linsha's hands and legs and carefully cut the leather gag.

Linsha wrenched off the ropes and slammed them to the floor in a burst of pent-up fury. Clutching the sheet, she tried to stand up. But her legs had been tied too long and were numb from the ropes. She staggered sideways as feeling rushed back into her limbs in a burning, prickling cascade.

Shanron caught her and pushed her down to sit on the edge of the bed. "Slow down," she admonished. "Take a deep breath and let the blood back into your feet."

Calmer now, Varia came to land on the headboard. She leaned over, her eyes huge, her feathers fluffed to twice their normal size. "What happened? What are you doing here?" she hooted loudly.

Feelings of anger, relief, and self-recrimination poured out of Linsha in a spate of words while she told her friends what had happened.

Shanron flipped her long braid over her shoulder and gave her a lascivious grin. "Ian Durne, huh?"

Varia refrained from saying "I told you so" only because she didn't know where the commander could be. She was willing to accept the possibility he was a victim of foul play, but she wouldn't believe it until she saw his body.

"We've got to get out of here," Linsha said when she finished her tale. She tried her legs again, and this time she could stand upright without help.

Her clothes were still on the floor, but her sword and daggers were gone. Stabbed by worry, she thrust her hand into her boot and found, to her relief, the dragon scale and packet still inside. She hung the scale back around her neck and sighed in relief. She had grown used to the scale and the smooth feel of it against her skin. She vowed she wouldn't take it off again for anyone until it was time to return it to Lord Bight.

As she hurried into her clothes, Linsha looked curiously at Shanron. "How was it you came with Varia?" she asked.

Shanron glanced at the owl and laughed. "That bird nearly scared the wits out of me."

Varia shrugged her wings. "I was a bit abrupt."

"Abrupt! I was in the hayloft giving the cat a midnight

snack when out of nowhere this hysterical owl dropped like a missile into the hay and started screeching something about helping you. Well, the cat ran like a fiend, and I nearly bolted up the rafters. I've never had an owl yell at me. What kind of an owl is this, anyway?"

"I was not yelling. I was trying to make you listen." Varia hopped off the headboard and walked deliberately over the bed to Linsha's side. "You scared me. I did not know you could summon me like that."

Linsha gave her boot a last tug, then gently scratched the owl's neck. "Neither did I," she said softly. She clasped Shanron's arm with painful urgency. "Thank you, both of you. I'm afraid I still need you. Something evil is going to happen, and soon. That packet you gave me warned that the Dark Knights would attack the city when the volcano erupts. I think we'd better find Lord Bight."

Varia bobbed her head. "You were right about the ships. There is a fleet gathering at the mouth of the bay. They're decked out like pirate ships, but if those are pirates, I'm a pigeon."

Linsha held out her forearm for the owl to ride, and the three left the apartment, closing the door firmly behind them. Night still ruled the streets of Sanction, and all was deathly quiet. The moon had risen, casting its waxing light on the world below.

"Do you know where Lord Bight is?" Linsha asked Shanron as they hurried through the dark streets.

Shanron thought a moment, then answered, "No. I just got off duty an hour ago. He may be at the palace, but I'm not sure."

"We'll try there first. They'll know where he is."

The two women walked faster, past the bazaar and onto the road that led toward the two hills. Varia flew ahead from trees and rooftops and kept a close watch on the road ahead and behind. They left the streets and the big houses behind and entered the wooded strip of road leading up to the palace. The moonlight was dim there, little more than speckled patches of quicksilver on the path. The woods thinned, and Linsha and Shanron could see the torches on the walls of the palace flicker through the trees ahead.

Out of the shadows in front of them, they heard Varia's blood-chilling screech of anger. The scream shocked them both and sent their hearts racing. Linsha reached for her sword and grabbed only her belt.

"What was *that?*" Shanron exclaimed.

Without answering, Linsha hurried off the road to a small clearing nearly lost in the night-dark shadows under the trees. Varia screeched again: "On the ground in front of you."

Linsha's foot snagged on something solid and heavy that tripped her forward. She caught herself on a sapling before she fell, sprawling, and dropped down beside the thing. Her hands reached out, touched fabric, leather, and something warm and wet. She couldn't see who it was in the thick darkness.

"What is it?" Shanron hissed. She groped across the uneven ground to come up beside her.

"Not what. Who!"

"Oh, no," mourned the guardswoman. "Not again."

A voice, barely above a whisper, spoke out of the darkness. "Alley Cat?"

"Mica?" Linsha cried out. Shaken, she touched his face and felt his bearded jaw. "Mica, oh, gods of all. Hold still. Let me help."

"No time," he groaned. "Too late. No strength left to heal." His words came out forced and so hoarse she could barely understand him.

"No, I can—"

But he didn't hear her. His hand groped out and she took it, pressing it tightly in her hers. His skin was surprisingly cold.

"Listen," he struggled to say. "Captain Southack told me. Ship captured by . . . Dark Knights. Crew deliberately poisoned . . . arcane magic spell. Passed by touch of skin on skin. Need—" He broke off in a long racking spasm.

"Mica, please," Linsha begged. "Let me—"

His hand tightened around hers. "Need old magic to cure.

Find dragon." His words grew more labored.

"Who did this to you?" Shanron asked.

Mica waited so long to answer that the women almost despaired. Then he gathered the strength from somewhere and managed to find an answer. "Skull Knight. Careful, Alley Cat. He plans to kill . . . Lord Bight at volcano . . . then signal ships. Stop him."

Linsha sat back on her heels. She understood now. Her eyes hurt with tears unshed as she stroked his cheek. "It's all right, Mica, you can rest. Thank you. I'll take care of it," she said, quiet and reassuring.

Her fingers felt his lips move in a slight smile. "Not bad . . . for a Knight," he whispered.

She sensed his mind gradually fading until there was only emptiness. The tears slid down her cheek unheeded. Varia keened above his head.

Shanron shuddered at the sound. "Is he dead?"

"He was already dead. Only the vestiges of his mystic power kept his spirit here long enough for someone to find him." She looked up at her friend and said as a tribute, "He was a Legionnaire."

Shanron flung herself to her feet, propelled by driving emotion. "That's enough! I'm up to my breastplate in whatever this mess is, so will you please tell me what is going on? What do you mean, he's a Legionnaire? Who is Captain Southack? Who is the Skull Knight? Why would anyone kill Mica?"

"Have you got a light?"

The reasonable question took Shanron by surprise and quieted her barrage of questions for a moment while she thought. Then she pulled a flint and steel out of her pocket and dropped them in Linsha's hand.

Using the tools and a pile of tinder, Linsha was able to light a tiny fire and put together a makeshift torch. Shanron watched in silent speculation.

With the feeble light, Linsha was able to see Mica more clearly and examine the dampness on his chest. She felt sick. "Not much blood," she pointed out, opening his leather vest.

"Look. He's been stabbed twice, just like Captain Dewald. Probably the same weapon."

"Probably the same man."

Linsha nodded. "Your captain was selling information to the Knights of Solamnia and got too close to this Skull Knight. Just like Mica." She jerked his vest closed again, her grief and dismay plain in her voice. "Captain Southack was the captain of the Palanthian ship that brought the plague. My guess is, Mica used spiritual mysticism to summon the captain's spirit, and he asked for information that wasn't in the ship's log. The Dark Knight must have ambushed him on the road to the palace."

Shanron ground her heel into the dry grass and earth. "So who is this Skull Knight?" she insisted.

"I don't know. All Captain Dewald knew was that he was in the guards." Small tendrils of dread curled up her back.

"Poor Alphonse. He really went in over his head," Shanron said mournfully. "So why did he give the packet to you, and what did Mica mean when he said, "Not bad for a Knight"? Who are you?"

Linsha knew revealing her covert status as a Knight with the order was a violation of her vows, but at that moment, she didn't hesitate. Shanron was a friend and an ally and had already heard enough to put it together anyway. "I am a Knight in the Solamnic Order. I took the position of guard to monitor Lord Bight's activities." She leaned forward to look her friend in the eye. "But things have gone horribly wrong. Shanron, now I fear the lord governor is in danger, and I need someone I can trust to help me."

Shanron didn't reply at first. She stared, deep in thought, at Mica's body. But Linsha guessed she saw another man lying there. "Will we find the Dark Knight that did this?" she asked at last.

"I hope so," Linsha said fervently. She hoped there was no quaver of nervousness in her voice. While she was prepared to meet most Dark Knights, a Skull Knight trained in the evil arts of dark mysticism was a fearsome opponent and one she was not confident about facing alone.

"Count me in," Shanron finally agreed. "Although this could be misread as aiding and abetting a forbidden order, I am technically protecting the lord governor."

"Exactly." Linsha closed Mica's eyes, gave his hand a squeeze in farewell, and stood up. From the position of the moon, she estimated the night was three or four hours past midnight. There was little time to waste. Lord Bight had already made it known when he planned to remove the dome on the volcano, so it was logical to assume the Skull Knight knew of the decision and had already passed the word to the forces of the Dark Order. The ships Varia had seen could already be massing outside the harbor. Linsha rubbed her wrists where the rope had chafed the skin. Ian, where are you? she wondered, half afraid to know the answer.

Her eyes went to the palace, where torches burned at the pylon gate, then switched to the darkened, beleaguered city. Although she wanted to find Lord Bight, she knew where she had to go.

"Shanron," she said, leading the other woman back to the road. "Take word to Lord Bight. Tell him about Mica and the ships. Warn him of the possible attack."

"Where are you going?" Shanron demanded.

"To get some help. I hope," she finished under her breath. At the look of doubt in her friend's face, Linsha clasped her arm. "Trust me. I will not fail you . . . or Lord Bight."

The guardswoman hesitated only a heartbeat. "All right. But when this is over, we're going to have a long talk about secret identities and lying to friends."

Linsha gave her a half smile and held up her hand as if giving an oath. "I promise." She waited while Shanron waved and broke into a run toward the palace, then she turned and headed the other way.

"Come on, Varia. It's time to put a chipmunk of our own on Lady Karine's windowsill."

The owl hooted a laugh and led the way back toward the city.

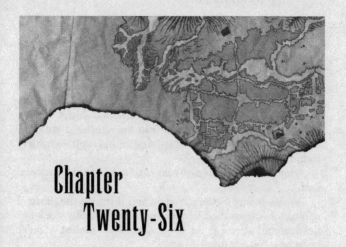

Chapter
Twenty-Six

The Souk Bazaar was closed for the night, and the streets were deserted by everyone but the roving patrol of City Guards. Many of the booths sat empty, abandoned after their owners left the city or died, or the merchandise became scarce. The bazaar had a forlorn look about it that even the night couldn't hide.

Linsha hurried after Varia to the shop of a small weapons merchant on the south side of the bazaar. Lady Karine ran the shop as her cover and lived in a small house behind it. She couldn't be certain Karine was here this night, but it was the best place to start. As she expected, the shop was locked and barred, so she knocked discreetly.

She had to knock for several minutes before Karine's apprentice shuffled into the showroom in a nightshirt, carrying a hand lamp.

"We're closed!" he yelled across the shop.

Linsha peered through the little window in the door and tried to say, "I need to talk to Karine—"

"We're closed," he bellowed again.

She moved to the louvered shutters across the large window and shouted, "Look. It's Lynn. I need to come in."

"Go away. We're closed."

Linsha abandoned politeness. A crude but sturdy bench sat against the wall of the store next door and, being the property of a trusting sort, was not nailed down. Linsha hefted it once and smashed it into the shuttered window. The glass behind made a satisfying sound as the shutters slammed into it.

"Hey!" came a protest from inside, followed by several oaths.

Linsha swung the bench again and this time the shutters sprang loose from their latches and flew open. She stuck her head in and glared at the flabbergasted apprentice. "You're open now," she informed him.

Before he could stop her, she threw the bench through the window and climbed in after it. "I am Rose Knight Linsha Majere, and I want to see Karine. Now!"

The young man crossed his arms and looked obstinate. "It's late. She's asleep."

Linsha's anger flared from a slow burn to a crackling blaze. This young Knight may be Lady Karine's bodyguard, but he was carrying things too far. "Then wake her up. Tell her to come at once. Most secret."

He snorted at her impatience. "Is this some sort of emergency?"

She took a long, slow breath and enunciated each word very carefully. "Yes. Please get her here before the Dark Knights burn this town down around your imbecilic head."

He threw up his hands. "All right. All right." He turned to go, then glared back at her. "But you're paying for that window."

Linsha made a face at his back. As soon as he was out of sight, she rummaged through the shelves and stacks until she found two daggers and a sword to her liking. Armed now, she paced back and forth across the room, feeling tense and edgy. She found a small lamp and lit it, and in the golden glow of its illumination, she continued to pace while she thought about what she would say to her commander.

She was apprehensive about reporting to Lady Karine, who would pass everything on to the Clandestine leaders, for her behavior in this had not been exemplary. She had not discredited Lord Bight in any manner, she had not sent any reports beyond a brief description of their meeting with Sable, and she had grown too enamored of the commander of Lord Bight's guards. Moreover, she had grown too fond of Lord Bight. The Circle would not be pleased if they knew that.

Nevertheless, she hoped Lady Karine would look past her failings for now and do what she could to muster their forces to help Lord Bight and the city. The Circle could reprimand her later if they would just see past their hidebound, self-serving prejudices and— Linsha caught herself in mid-thought. She was letting her anger over her entire situation escape again. She couldn't let her emotions command her or reveal her true thoughts.

Hurried footsteps drew her out of her ponderous thoughts, and she stopped and stood at attention as Lady Knight Karine Thasally entered the room.

The tall lady Knight nodded once to Linsha, then waved her guard out of the room and closed the door behind her. Karine glanced around the room, taking in the bench, the broken window, and the daggers at Linsha's belt with phlegmatic eye. She had dressed hurriedly, although carefully, and was ready for whatever emergency she might face, but she was a little surprised by Linsha's vehemence. "What's wrong, Lynn?" she asked, her tone cool. "You aren't usually so agitated."

Linsha heard a note of displeasure in her commander's voice that set off a small alarm in her mind. Lady Karine was a half-elf, tall and fair and totally competent, and she usually worked quite affably with Linsha. But there was an undertone in her voice tonight that Linsha hadn't heard before, an underlying vibration of tension and aggression. Perhaps it was due to the fear of living among the ravages of the plague, or perhaps it was simply irritation at being awakened in the middle of the night and finding her window smashed. Whatever provoked it, Linsha decided to tread carefully.

Linsha moved to the center of the room and made her report as unemotional and concise as she could, telling Karine the facts she felt were important for her to know. She told her about Captain Dewald's death and the packet he passed on to her, about Mica's information from the spirit of Captain Southack and the dwarf healer's murder at the hand of the Skull Knight. She went on to explain Lord Bight's plan to relieve the pressure within the volcano and remove the threat of the volcanic dome.

Lady Karine's fair eyebrows drew together. "As I understand you, the Dark Knights introduced this plague into the city to weaken its resistance, ordered their covert agent to assassinate Lord Bight, and they plan to attack the city the moment they know he is dead."

Linsha nodded, shifting her weight from foot to foot. She had not talked directly with Lady Karine in months and had no feel for what the commander thought about her superiors' desire to replace Lord Bight.

"The plan is well conceived," Karine admitted thoughtfully. "Defending this city against a seaborne invasion could be difficult at this time." Linsha went on hurriedly. "Thanks to Mica, we have information that could help us find a cure for the plague and stop the Dark Knights. But much time has passed. We need to move quickly—summon the others, alert the City Guard. Please, I need your help."

"Have you told anyone else your information?" Karine asked.

Linsha thought of Shanron and checked what she was going to say. "No, not yet," she said instead.

"Good. The less interference, the better."

A feeling of futility crept in and fueled Linsha's anger. "We can't just sit by and do nothing," she insisted. "We must help Lord Bight."

"Lynn, I can understand your outburst because you are not aware of our designs. We do not intend to save Lord

Bight. It is our desire that he be removed from his position so a more suitable leader can be placed there."

Linsha felt her frustration boil over. Lady Karine sounded just like the Circle leaders. "More suitable!" she exploded. "There is no other man more suited to be Lord Governor of Sanction. He loves this city, and he's tough enough to keep it in line. He would rather bury it underground with the shadowpeople than allow any order or usurper to change this city. He isn't going to deal with the Knights of Takhisis, Sable, or anyone else, so why can't the Solamnics just try to work *with* him?"

Karine didn't move. "You do not know enough of the workings of the Circle to comprehend what is happening," she said stiffly.

"Don't patronize me!" Linsha shouted. "I understand my assignment perfectly well. What I do not understand is why all of you insist Lord Bight must be removed." A terrible conclusion came to life in her thoughts, and she asked herself, why do they say "our" and "we" so much when it is the Solamnic Council who governs the Circle's activities? "Is this decision condoned by the council? Does Grand Master Ehrling know what the Circle is trying to do here?"

Karine's slender face was unreadable. "It is apparent you have become too emotionally involved to be effective," she said, sliding past Linsha's question.

A cold burst of apprehension slid over Linsha like a bitter draft. Lady Karine, as well as the Circle leaders, had enough seniority to remove her from duty, and at the worst, to disavow her, or even strip her of her Knighthood if they chose. If they were scheming without the knowledge or permission of the order's Grand Council, they could make her vanish and no one would ever know the truth. Fiercely she drove her anger to a deep chamber in her heart and forced herself to bow.

"Lady Knight, I apologize for my doubts. I am tired and concerned for our people. I came here only to warn you of the possible attack and to seek your advice."

"Then listen well," the commander said coldly. "I order

you to stand down. Do not go back to the palace or seek out Lord Bight with your information. Report to Lady Annian and stay with her to help organize a move against the Dark Knights. Do nothing more."

Linsha felt her face grow hot. Her breathing turned harder and faster, and it took all her self-control to keep her voice even and calm. "What about Lord Bight?"

"The Skull Knight will take care of that problem for us. We will send our Knights to stop him before he can signal his forces."

Linsha silently thanked whatever powers that be she had not mentioned Shanron. If all else failed and she was forcibly detained, Shanron still had Mica's information about the Dark Knights, the plague, and its cause. "And the city? Do you plan to just let Sanction die of this plague and the Dark Knights' swords?"

"Of course not. We will do what we can to help. If all goes as planned, the city will survive."

But Lord Bight will not, Linsha told herself. This could not be right! There was no honor or justice in this action. Nowhere in the Measure did it suggest Knights of Solamnia could stand by and allow their enemies to assassinate a lord governor while they move in and take over his city for their own machinations. Surely, Grand Master Ehrling never condoned this.

But, oh, Paladine, what if he had?

Linsha stood still, her mind in a turmoil, her loyalty torn in two. There was nothing more she could think to say or ask, no more arguments she could put forth to Karine's implacable countenance.

The commander raised her arm and pointed to the door. "You are dismissed. Report to Lady Annian," she said in a voice of adamant.

A salute was almost more than Linsha could manage. Somehow she got her arm up in a crisp salute, then turned on her heel and marched out the door, her head up, her face deadpan, and with a feeling of finality, she closed the door behind her. No matter what she did, she knew Lady Karine and the Circle would not trust her for some time to come. Now she had to decide how much *she* trusted the Clandestine Circle.

Varia flew out of a shadowed garret and landed on Linsha's shoulder. The lady Knight began to walk in the direction of Lady Annian's perfume shop.

"I have been stood down," she told the owl in a strangled voice. "They are going to hide until Lord Bight is dead, then sweep in and snatch the city out of the grasp of the Dark Knights."

Varia uttered a strange noise like a smothered squawk. "Where are you going?"

"I am to report to Lady Annian."

The owl was quiet for a moment, her head turned sideways to gaze solemnly at Linsha's face. "You have a good heart, Linsha. You must follow it."

Linsha's eyes hurt with threatened tears. She made a face. "My heart has led me into one quagmire already. I don't want to follow something so flawed."

"Your affection for Ian Durne is only a small part of your spirit. Maybe I should say you have a good soul. Let it guide you."

"It could guide me into exile or dismissal from the Knights. I don't think I could bear to bring that kind of dishonor on my family."

"What about the dishonor you could bring on yourself?"

"What are you, my conscience?" Linsha said it lightly, but in truth Varia was only vocalizing the sentiments another small voice whispered in her mind.

The owl did not answer. She regarded Linsha through her moon eyes for another moment or two, then she shifted her gaze to the streets behind them.

Linsha continued to walk, although by now she paid little attention to where she was. A faint light, yellow and orange, lined the eastern mountains, and the stars retreated before the approaching sun. She looked to the east and saw Mount Thunderhorn illuminated with a dawn light that lit its smoke-crowned peak with fire and glowed on its rugged inclines. Up there, she knew, Lord Bight would soon be walking to stand on the boulder-strewn slopes and face the power of the volcano. He had asked her to be with him and protect him during the execution of his spells. Had he known of the presence of an assassin? How would he feel when she did not appear?

It was time to choose. Would she be his friend or his enemy? Either choice bore a great cost. If she chose to believe in the integrity of the Circle, to blindly follow her oath and return as ordered to Lady Annian, she would turn her back on Sanction, on Lord Bight, a man she deeply admired, and on Ian Durne, the man she wanted to love. They would be condemned to whatever fate befell them without warning, without help, without support from her. She would betray Lord Bight's faith in her, Shanron's trust, and her own promise to Mica and follow a course of action she did not believe to be right or honorable. Nor could she willingly put the entire responsibility on Shanron. While it was true Shanron had heard Mica's message and was capable of defending Lord Bight from most men, she was no match for a Skull Knight.

If, however, Linsha chose to disobey the Circle and help Lord Bight, she could face punishment and possibly the dishonor of exile and disgrace. There was no time to present her case to the Solamnic Council; she would have to act on her own, and in doing so, she could lose her place in the order, in her very world. Part of her thoughts wished fervently Caramon or Palin could be here to help her sort through this dreadful maze and to give her their blessing on whatever decision she made. She had tried for so many years to make her parents and grandparents proud of her. How would they understand this?

Yet, another part of her knew this resolution was hers alone. She could seek sanction from no one but herself. It was her sense of honor and justice she had to satisfy, her conscience she had to live with.

Linsha came to a stop. In surprise, she looked around and saw she was nowhere near Lady Annian's shop. She had walked in circles and was close to the West Gate in the city wall. The coming morning light was stronger now, and the city was beginning to stir. A light breeze rustled the flags and banners that hung on the towers. The horn would soon be blown to signal the change of guard.

Linsha twisted her neck to look at Varia and found the owl regarding her again with wide, round eyes. "How do you feel about exiled Knights?"

"It depends on why they were exiled."

"For following their hearts."

Varia tilted her head and blinked. "It is your inherent goodness that drew me, young woman. Not your status."

A faint rumbling reached her ears, and she looked up to see a laden baker's cart coming over the cobbled road toward her. An old man with graying hair and a shuffling gait grinned at her from between the shafts of his cart.

"Mornin', Gorgeous. I see you've managed to survive so far. Where'd you get the owl?"

"Calzon," she cried, unaware of the raw emotion in her voice.

Twenty years seemed to drop from his body as he suddenly straightened. "What's wrong?" he asked with more compassion than Lady Karine.

Linsha's hand tightened around her sword hilt. "Mica's dead," she said. "A Dark Knight killed him last night." Several choice curses exploded from the Legionnaire, and his face darkened with rage. "How? Where? Did you find him?" he demanded in one breath.

Linsha told him quickly how she had found Mica in the woods and the last words the dwarf tried so hard to say. "The Knights of Takhisis have planned an attack to take place while Lord Bight is distracted by the volcano," she went on. "I believe a Skull Knight assassin will attempt to kill him so the Dark Knights can invade the city virtually unopposed."

"Have you told your superiors yet?" Calzon asked.

Linsha answered simply, "Yes." She wanted to warn the Legionnaires, but she would not discuss her problems regarding the Circle with an outsider.

Calzon's eyes narrowed, as if he sensed more in her words than she intended, and he was about to say more when a slight tremble shivered through the ground and quivered up their feet and ankles. Both agents looked down, startled, and felt it again. All at once three or four dogs bounded out into the street and began barking. A flock of birds burst out of a nearby tree. Varia hooted a warbling cry. A deeper tremor rattled the buildings and shook up a cloud of dust. People shouted in alarm.

"The volcano. Look!" Calzon cried out.

Far in the distance, against the brightening sky, the red cone of Mount Thunderhorn belched out a billowing cloud of smoke, and a low, continuous thunder shook the morning air. Suddenly a bright orange light trailed up from the distant fortifications, and it shot up into the sky like a shooting star and exploded in a brilliant burst of orange and gold light.

"The signal from the tower," Linsha exclaimed. "The dome has already started to collapse. I've got to go!"

Calzon grasped her arm and gave it a squeeze. "Thank you, Lynn. The Legion will be ready." He dumped his cart beside the road and dashed back the way he had come, his long hair flying behind him.

Varia waited until he was out of earshot, then sprang aloft. "I will get Windcatcher," she called, and she flew, swift as a hawk, for the city gate.

Linsha broke into a run.

At the West Gate, the City Guards on duty stood looking east, worriedly watching the volcano. The pounding of Linsha's footsteps drew their attention back to the gate, and they raised their spears, wary of her precipitous approach.

"Do not look to the east for danger," she shouted to them. "Keep your eyes to the west. We have had word the Knights of Takhisis are massing ships for an attack."

The Officer of the Watch stood in the middle of the gateway and eyed her scarlet uniform. "We received no word of this. Who are you?"

Linsha skidded to a stop. "Governor's Guard, Lynn of Gateway. Late of the City Guards. We just learned this news.

They may attack the harbor this morning."

"How do you know this?"

"Mica, the healer. Didn't he come through here earlier this night?" The guards glanced at each other and nodded. "He told me," she said.

"Why didn't he tell us?"

"I don't know. I think he was in a hurry to reach Lord Bight. But he didn't make it. A Dark Knight murdered him. I reached him just before he died."

Gasps of surprise and outrage met her news. The guard officer slapped the signal horn hanging at his side. "I will put the City Guard on alert," he said, his face filled with anger.

"And warn the harbormaster. He can post watchers at Pilot's Point," she added, then she turned on her heel and ran back the way she had come, east on Shipmaker's Road.

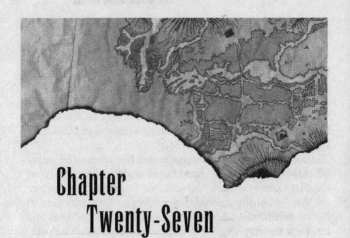

Chapter Twenty-Seven

Linsha passed by the bazaar again and was hurrying through a small suburb of walled houses and well-trimmed gardens when she heard hoofbeats behind her coming at a fast pace. She moved to the side of the road and saw Windcatcher cantering toward her. The bay mare wore only a halter and trailed a broken lead rope. Her eyes rolled in excitement; her coat was damp with sweat. Varia flew above her head, warbling a wild song.

A nearby watering trough provided a convenient mounting block. Linsha climbed swiftly on Windcatcher's bare back, snatched the rope, and urged her into a canter toward the East Gate and the guard camp. She didn't stop at the gate but pounded through, past the astonished guards and on toward the camp.

The volcano was clearly visible now. A loud rumbling issued from its throat as smoke, steam, and ash poured forth, swelling into the air in shapeless gray and white masses. The dome could not be seen behind its cloak of smoke, but every now and again flashes of red and orange gleamed upward in the gloom.

The camp was in an uproar when Linsha arrived. Horns blared from every corner. Men hurried back and forth. Officers shouted orders as the guards pulled back from the northeast fortifications and hurried to strengthen the southeast walls, facing the East Pass and the camp of the Dark Knights. Mounted men rode by in squads toward the northern defenses.

Linsha slowed Windcatcher to a walk and moved out of the way. "Where is Lord Bight?" she shouted to the sentries at the main entrance.

"On the volcano," came the reply.

"Was anyone with him?"

"He had a few guards, but he sent most of his company to help man the siege works in case the Dark Knights try to attack from the passes."

"Only a few," Linsha repeated worriedly. "Was Commander Durne with him?"

The sentries traded questioning looks. "He came by here, but we don't know where he is now," a sergeant answered.

The hope that Ian was not responsible for leaving her bound and gagged in the apartment diminished. If the sentries saw him here, he was certainly still alive and moving under his own free will. She swallowed hard against a sudden hard lump in her throat. She was about to urge Windcatcher forward when she thought of one more question. "Did the woman guard, Shanron, accompany Lord Bight?"

"No," the sergeant answered again. "She arrived later and followed him toward the mountain. In a great rush, she was."

Linsha's call of thanks flew behind her as she pushed the bay mare into a canter again. They followed the edge of the camp toward the northeast observation tower and the great earthen ramparts of the siege works. Linsha didn't see Varia, but she knew the secretive owl was close by and would fly to her aid if the need arose.

The horse flew over the paths, past rows of tents and the

crowded infirmary, past the open practice fields and the empty horse corrals, Linsha clinging to her bare back like a burr. A few guards called out to her, but Linsha ignored them and concentrated on finding the quickest path to the mountain.

They came at last to the tower, and Linsha saw several Governor's Guards still manning it in spite of the grit, ash, and smoke that drifted down on the wind. The men leaned on the crenellated wall and gazed toward the burning mountain.

The possibility occurred to Linsha that if one Dark Knight could hide as a Governor's Guard, so could others. What if these were henchmen of the Skull Knight, positioned there to protect his rear? Without a word, she sped by the tower and, ignoring the guards' shouts, guided Windcatcher over the rim of the wall.

Thirty feet down plunged the mare, her haunches tucked under her, her forelegs driving into the dry, grassy incline. At the bottom, she lunged forward across the open moat. The next fortified wall stood about a hundred feet away, rising like a huge brown ridge before the horse and rider. A set of stone steps had been set in the wall for the aid of the defenders, and Windcatcher clattered up them two at a time.

At the top of the second wall, the mare had to stop, for there was no apparent road for a horse. The defenses had been arranged to thwart not only siege engines and ground forces but mounted cavalry as well. Rows of sharpened spikes had been planted on the far side of this wall like a tilted forest of spears. Only a narrow footpath wound down between the spears toward the heavily fortified trenches, the moat of lava, and the volcano.

Reluctantly Linsha slid off and left her mare on the berm. She paused for a minute or two to study the lay of the land. Every moment she delayed could risk Lord Bight's life, yet she couldn't rush out there alone and unprepared. She could get lost on the wrong path or stumble into an ambush. As far as she could see, this section of the fortifications was deserted because of the risk of pyroclastic flow from the collapsing dome. Beyond the line of trenches lay a wide strip of no-man's-land and the sullen, reddish yellow flow of the lava in the wide moat. A slender stone bridge arched over the slowly moving river of molten rock to the stony ground beyond.

The hot rim of the sun had lifted above the peaks and now slanted its light on the face of the mountain. Looking up the slope, Linsha saw no movement or sign of any person among the rocks. However, the angle of sun revealed to her a large crevice partially concealed by a protruding ridge of stone halfway up the mountain. Perhaps that was the lair of the infamous red dragon, Firestorm. Higher still, Linsha could see glimpses of the lava dome through the shapeless masses of steam and smoke that roiled out of its heart. Like a gigantic boil, it had swollen to the size of a coiled dragon and was beginning to burst apart from the internal pressure of the rising lava.

At that moment Linsha caught a glimpse of something red moving near the base of the peak. It was impossible to see who it was, but the sight was enough for Linsha. Loosening her sword in its sheath, she ran down the inclined wall through the forest of stakes. Her feet carried her nimbly down into the trenches, past empty guard posts and fortified bulwarks. The slender path continued up and over the trenches, then into the wide, barren strip of land before the moat. Linsha hurried faster over the level ground toward the bridge over the moat.

The bridge was little more than a stone footpath that arched over the lava. It had no handrail, no walls, and was barely wide enough for one person. Linsha shivered when she saw how narrow it really was, but others had crossed it, and so must she.

She was almost to the bridge when another patch of red caught her notice. This one lay huddled to the side, at the foot of the span, and did not move. Her heart pounding, Linsha rushed forward and found the body of one of Lord Bight's guards. He lay on his side, his back to the siege works, his face gray with death. Muttering an oath, she sprang onto the bridge.

Beneath her, the lava moved sluggishly. Semi-hard plates of superheated rock floated on a current of brightly glowing crimson lava. The heat was ferocious, and the air tasted bitterly metallic on Linsha's tongue. She gasped for breath and felt her throat ache for water. She walked purposefully up the arch, keeping her eyes firmly on the stone at her feet, and started down the other side.

"That's far enough, Lynn."

Every hope, every imagined excuse withered and died at the sound of that voice. Feeling sick, she looked up and saw Ian Durne standing at the foot of the bridge. He grasped Shanron by the neck and held a knife to her throat. The guardswoman's face was furious, but she stayed frozen in place.

"Oh, Ian, why did it have to be you?" Linsha cried. The only satisfaction she found was the genuine look of regret that crossed his handsome face.

"I tried to keep you out of it, Lynn. I don't want to kill you. Or her," he said, pushing Shanron closer to the edge of the moat. "Just back away. Return to the tower and I will leave her here, alive."

Shanron dug in her heels and yelled, "No, Lynn! He means to kill the lord governor."

Linsha looked at them both—her friend, her lover. A sense of betrayal rose in her like gall. "You know I can't do that," she said loudly.

"I know. Ironically, that's why I fell in love with you," he replied, his voice tinged with sadness. "Tell me, before we end this, who are you?"

Linsha slowly drew her sword and rested it point down on the stone. Sweat poured from her face and stung her eyes; her lungs ached. She felt dizzy and sick, but she stood firmly on the bridge and replied, "I am Rose Knight Linsha Majere."

"Majere!" He gasped and gave a sharp laugh. "What a twist, to fall in love with one of the Majere clan. By Takhisis, Lynn, you are a marvel. I only wish we could have met under different circumstances."

"You don't have to do this either, Ian. Just let Shanron go.

You can leave, go back to the Dark Knights at the East Pass."

"You know I can't do that," he said, copying her words. "We're too alike, Lynn. We love our orders more than each other." The last word was barely past his lips when, in one violent move, he cut Shanron's throat and pushed her into the lava river. The guardswoman's body struck the lava, burst into flame, and sank beneath the scarlet surface.

Linsha started forward in horror. "No!" she screamed at him. "You didn't have to do that!"

He drew his own sword and stepped onto the bridge. "Now we're alone again, Lynn. Just you and me. Come kiss me, Green Eyes."

Just then, in a blur of motion, another creature joined the confrontation. A cream and russet bird dropped with the speed of a hawk out of the sun and clamped her dagger-sharp talons into the right side of Ian's face. He bellowed in surprise and pain and fell back off the bridge.

"Run, Linsha!" Varia screeched.

The lady Knight needed no urging. Anger and revenge could wait; she still had her duty to do. She bolted off the bridge, away from the killing heat and lava. She dashed past Ian's struggling form and up the trail toward the volcanic peak. Lord Bight was still up there, working his magic, expecting her to come. She had to put herself between him and the Dark Knight.

"Come on, Varia," she yelled back.

The owl winged past her, chuckling like a madwoman, blood staining her talons. "He follows, but slowly."

Linsha nodded grimly and pushed herself on. The trail crawled up the mountain through fields of volcanic rock and broken boulders, apparently heading toward the crater at the peak. The daylight dimmed around her as the boiling smoke covered the sun. The thundering grumble of the mountain shook the ground beneath her feet.

Looking up, Linsha realized the trail led not to the peak but to the large crevice she had noticed earlier. There was still no sign of Lord Bight.

"Lynn," came a cry from below.

She hesitated and glanced back. On the trail behind, Commander Durne came after her, as inexorable as the volcano. Blood stained the right side of his face, and his visage was dark with fury.

Linsha looked quickly around. She wanted to choose her place to make a stand where the advantages would be in her favor. She had neither helmet, mail, nor shield, only her sword and her athletic ability to keep her alive. This was not a good place, for it was steep and slippery, with beds of gravel and scree. She hurried higher, but nothing offered itself to suit her purposes.

Finally the trail reached the crevice and widened out into a broad, level ledge almost like a porch. She ran across the ledge and entered a huge cave. Far back, at the very edge of the cavern, she saw a bright yellow glow flicker and gleam against the black rock. A figure stood silhouetted there, dressed in long robes, his arms held high over his head while he chanted his spells to the erupting power of the mountain.

"Lord Bight!" she shouted, but there was no answer. She thought she saw him move, but she couldn't be sure, and there was no time to find out.

Commander Durne caught up with her at last. Panting, he charged up the path and onto the ledge.

Linsha whirled to face him, her sword raised and ready. She slid a dagger out of its sheath and tried to will her muscles to relax.

"Oh, my beautiful Lynn, why can't you just stand aside? What does that man mean to you?" He advanced toward her, his own blade poised.

The lady Knight refused to answer. She could only stare at his face. Varia's talons had scored across his cheek and forehead and had torn his eyelid. That side of his visage was a mask of blood, and she doubted he could see through the gore that covered his right eye. She drew a long, quavering breath. "Oh, Ian," she sighed, and she walked to meet him.

Their swords clashed, steel on steel, in the first tentative test of each other's skill. At first glance, it looked to be an uneven contest. Durne was a head taller than Linsha, broader, older, with height, reach, and weight all on his side. But he was blind in one eye, and she had the speed and agility to hold her own.

Back and forth across the ledge they fought with deadly concentration, their swords and daggers rasping and clashing together as they struggled. The sun had risen higher and poured its relentless heat on the ledge. The volcano belched its fumes and smoke into the air they breathed. Both suffered, but both fought on with relentless care, conserving their strength and using their skill to prolong their endurance. At times, when their eyes met across the braced blades of their swords, there was no love left, only the inflexible determination to fulfill their purposes: she to save the lord governor, he to kill him.

At one point, Linsha drew back, panting, and Durne followed her example. In that brief respite, Linsha had to ask, "I know why you killed Captain Dewald. Were you also the one who stabbed Mica?"

He laughed at the timing at her question. "Since you're going to die, Lady Knight, I will tell you. Yes. I met Mica on the road back to the palace. He started to tell me what he had learned and I was forced to kill him." He shrugged and wiped some blood and sweat from his face. "We are not yet ready for Sanction to find a cure."

"So you knew about the poisoned sailors and the magic plague. That's why you wore gloves all the time."

"Of course. It was my idea."

By the gods, Linsha marveled. What a cold, callous, bald-faced statement. How could this man have deceived her so thoroughly? "Was the dark-haired rabble-rouser one of yours, too?"

"Actually, yes. The irony of it was the bottle striking me in the head and you diving into the water to save me." He chuckled and shook his head. "I think I fell in love with you then."

Linsha went white-hot with fury, and she leaped back into the battle, her sword arching toward Durne's right side. The Dark Knight barely blocked her blow. He aimed a punch at her head, but she slid sideways out of his reach. The duel continued.

From her vantage point on a high rock, Varia watched and waited for her opportunity. She wouldn't interfere as long as Linsha held her own, for Varia was terrified of swords, but she might spot another chance to could take out Durne's remaining eye, and she didn't want to miss it.

For over an hour the two combatants fought in the sun. Both bled from minor wounds, and both were struggling with exhaustion and dehydration. Here and there, blood splattered on the rocks.

Although neither one noticed it, the volcano was quieter now. Its steam and smoke drifted to the southeast to irritate the Knights of Takhisis, and the lava that spilled from the dome followed a simple course down the volcano's side in a direction that would bring it directly to the existing lava moat.

It was about midday when the shell of the dome collapsed and the pyroclastic flow everyone feared began its charge down the mountainside in a roiling, lethal cloud of black ash and gas that boiled outward at the speed of a flying dragon.

Both Linsha and Durne froze in place and looked up at the approaching flow in horror. On it came, a black storm that burned and buried everything before it. They were about to bolt for the slim protection of the cave, when the flow suddenly lost its power and collapsed. To their amazement, the grit, ash, and gas subsided into a mere cloud that drifted southeast on the wind.

It was Durne who recovered first. He pressed Linsha hard and drove her back with a sudden lunge. Her foot slipped on a bloodstained rock, and she fell hard to the stone. He rammed his blade toward her throat.

Frantically she raised her arm to parry the thrust but succeeded only in pushing the tip toward her chest. The sword point struck her on the breastbone, and to his amazement, it skittered sideways and slashed across her shoulder and sank into her forearm. Linsha cried out in pain, nearly as surprised as he at her reprieve. She managed to pull herself free and slither out of his way. Bleeding heavily, she struggled back to her feet.

He drew back, panting, and demanded, "What armor do you wear beneath that shirt?"

Hunched over her wounded shoulder, she slowly drew out the dragon scale and let it shine in the sun. Her throat burned from thirst and her limbs quivered from her exertion. Pain flamed in her shoulder. But somehow the scale gave her strength and eased her pain.

She was in the act of straightening up when Durne launched himself upon her in a ferocious leap. Throwing his sword down, he battered into her, slamming the air out of her lungs. He wrapped his arm around her neck and shoved her sword aside. For a moment they heaved and strained, but then his weight bore her down, and they fell heavily onto the stone only a few paces from the ledge. Linsha's sword slid over the rim of the ledge and dropped out of sight.

"I want you to die in my arms," he hissed in her ear. "I want to be the last thing you think about." He pressed his lips to hers even as he tightened his arm across her throat. Summoning his dark mystic power, he poured his last strength into his arm muscles and tendons and pulled them tight around her neck.

Linsha felt as if a steel band was squeezing her head off. Her blood roared in her ears as her veins were compressed, and her vision turned black and red. Her heels drummed on the rock, and her lungs wanted to explode. She tried to pull her own power from her heart, but the strength that crushed her throat seemed to drain her body of any spark of mystic energy. She groped for the dragon scale, and as her mind fell spiraling into darkness, she inexplicably thought not of Ian Durne, but of Hogan Bight.

Then the pressure on her neck suddenly released. She gasped and coughed, trying to pull air into her lungs past her abused throat. Something seemed to be happening to Durne just above her, but she was too shocked and fighting too hard for breath to understand what he was doing. Desperate to save herself, she pulled out from under him and rolled away from his struggling body. As her breathing returned to some semblance of normal, her head began to clear, and she groped for her second dagger hidden in the side of her right boot.

A curse of enraged pain brought her fully alert. She focused on Durne and saw for the first time that he was fighting Varia. The owl swooped and dived just above his head. Her talons had torn his scalp and his face, and her fierce attack drove him away from Linsha. But it also brought her close to his sword.

Triumphantly he snatched it off the ground and brought it up in a wide swing toward the owl.

Linsha could not utter a sound. In a frantic effort, she launched herself at Durne's body and slammed her good shoulder into the small of his back. Her dagger punctured his right side. The impact sent a wave of intense pain through her wounded shoulder and arm. A cry tried to escape her strangled throat and came out only a wheezing gurgle. The world spun around her. She had no strength to regain her balance, and she crumpled to the ground. Her fall brought another fresh explosion of pain. Try as she might to see what happened to Varia, her consciousness faded to hazy darkness.

The impact of her attack knocked Durne's aim off, and instead of slicing the owl in half as he hoped, the blade turned sideways and caught the owl on her wing with the flat edge. There was an audible snap, and Varia tumbled to the ground on the very lip of the rock.

At the same time, Durne was thrown off-balance by Linsha's tackle. He staggered and nearly fell off the ledge, and only a monumental effort of will kept him on his feet. Somehow he hauled himself upright and stood cursing at the dagger wound in his back. The slash was shallow but painful, and blood spread in a dark stain across his scarlet tunic. He blinked through the blood in his eyes. He caught a glimpse of the owl flapping pitiably on the ledge.

"Blasted bird!" he swore under his breath. He started forward, intending to kick her over the edge.

Something large and heavy moved at the mouth of the cave. He heard the noise and turned toward it, but he couldn't see well enough to identify it. All he saw was a gleaming flash of bronze in the sunlight.

Suddenly a shadow fell over him.

Commander Durne rubbed his left eye with a sleeve just enough to wipe the blood off his lashes. Wondering, he tilted his head to look up at the thing looming over him. A scream ripped from his throat.

It was the last sound he ever made.

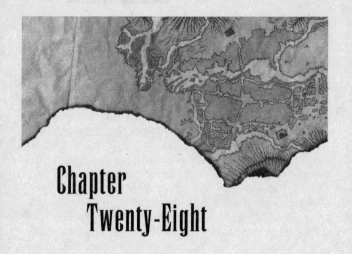

Chapter
Twenty-Eight

T he lookout stationed at Pilot's Point
was the first to spot the fleet of dark
ships sailing north into Sanction Bay. He raised a red flag of
warning and blew his horn until he was scarlet in the face.
Across the broad harbor, another red flag was raised in reply,
and a second horn blew its warning to the city. Fishing boats
and small craft scurried out of the way as best they could.
The City Guard blockaded the streets and set men to defend
the piers. Although the guards were few, other men and
women joined them with weapons in hand and grim determination in their faces. The guard officers didn't ask who
these people were; they were just glad for the help.

Dark and menacing, the ships came three abreast into
the tranquil blue waters of the harbor. The standard of the
Knights of Takhisis—the death lily, the skull, and the
thorn—flew above the black sails. The first three ships
steered immediately for the southern pier and the two
smaller northern piers to capture the important landing

sites, while the rest of the fleet blockaded the entrance to the bay and disposed themselves around the harbor. A large, flat-hulled barge was rowed into position directly across from the waterfront and anchored in place. Swiftly engines of war were set up on the deck, and catapults began to launch flaming spheres into the buildings behind the docks.

The defenders on the piers and docks and in the streets watched breathlessly as the first wave of shore boats loaded with armored men were launched toward the city. The largest of the attack vessels reached the southern pier, slid smoothly alongside, and even before the ship stopped, the invaders were firing a swarm of arrows at the defenders on the pier.

Everyone was too busy at first to notice the shining dark creature winging out of the smoke and reek of Mount Thunderhorn. Over Sanction he flew, glittering and magnificent, hot with the furious heat of the volcano still in his veins. He spread his wings to their full length, and his shadow soared across the waters. Someone shouted, and the cry was taken up from one end of the harbor to the other.

"A dragon! A dragon comes!"

Bronze in hue, long and lean, he flew over the ships in the harbor, his scales gleaming bright in the noon sun. He winged southward over the blockade, then tipped his wing and circled back. As he passed over the ships blocking the harbor, lightning erupted from his jaws and seared down into the wooden hulls of the black ships. Fire sprouted on the masts, sails, and decks of every ship he struck. The terrified crews jumped overboard.

Without a backward glance, the bronze tucked in his wings and dived into the water, his weight and speed sending a huge ring of waves flowing across the harbor. For a heartbeat, he was underwater, out of sight of the black ships. Then he erupted to the surface beside the catapult barge and, with one swipe of his massive tail, crushed the hull to splinters. The barge sank out of sight in moments. The dragon moved on to the ship by the southern pier and sank it, too, with his tail. Roaring gleefully, he charged out of the water and dispatched more ships with his lightning breath.

The black fleet, or what remained of it, tried to flee in

panic, but the dragon would have none of it. Ignoring spears and arrows fired at him, he attacked each ship and crushed it or burned it until there was not a ship left in Sanction Harbor flying the standard of the Knights of Takhisis.

The city defenders stood on the docks and cheered.

The dragon winged lazily around the harbor once, then turned back to the east and disappeared into the clouds of Mount Thunderhorn as quickly as he had come.

* * * * *

Linsha hung suspended in a shadow realm of darkness. She struggled to focus her mind enough to discover what was happening outside her body. What happened to Varia? Where was Ian? But she couldn't get through the darkness. It clung to her, thick and cloying, and cocooned her in a drifting web of lethargy. She could sense pain, but not really feel it. She could sense heat and thirst, but not enough to pull aside the cloak of darkness.

Something touched her forehead. Cool and gentle, it stroked her skin in a soothing caress. Healing power radiated out of the touch. It wasn't the mystic power of the heart. It was something far older, more wild, yet it touched the center of her own heart and revived her exhausted reservoirs of energy. The pain subsided to a distant ache. Gratefully she followed the gentle touch out of darkness and slipped into a restoring sleep. In time, the dreams came in slow and vivid visions.

She became aware of standing on the ledge on the side of the mountain. The sun was shining, but the breeze was cool, and the volcano sat quietly in the afternoon light. Behind her, the Vale of Sanction opened its arms to the blue waters of the bay, and cradled in its midst, the city of Sanction sprawled in peaceful repose.

Yawning in front of her, the wide crevice loomed like an orifice into the heart of the mountain. Once it had been the lair of a red dragon. Now it was believed to be empty and abandoned. Or was it?

A large shape moved out of the cave's entrance and came to stand in the sunlight. It was a bronze dragon, eighty feet if he was an inch, from scaled nose to pointed tail. His huge body took up most of the ledge.

Awestruck, Linsha gazed up at him. She felt no fear. Bronze dragons were allied with Good and were known for their inquisitive natures and senses of humor.

This one tucked his wings carefully about his sides and settled down on the ledge, curling around Linsha so she stood in the protective encirclement of his tail and body. Sunlight shone on his rich bronze scales and beamed in his deep amber eyes. He blinked down at her.

Linsha stared back. "Who are you?" she breathed.

"You could say I am the Guardian of Sanction." His voice was low and resonant.

"Does Lord Bight know about you?"

"Of course." The hidden smile in his tone was obvious to the perceptive.

Linsha heard it and couldn't help but grin. "Are you the secret of his influence over the other dragons."

"Let's say we help each other once in a while."

Her face lit up with hope. "Oh! Then, please, maybe you can help us now." She told him about the plague and Mica, the dwarf's search for a cure and his death before he could find the full answer. "He said the old magic spell needed more old magic to break it. He said to ask a dragon. Does this make sense to you?"

The big bronze tilted his horned head in thought. "Actually, I think it does. I will study this. Perhaps Bight and the temple mystics could use my help."

She smiled up at him. "Thank you." Her awe was slowly fading in the face of his friendliness, replaced by an instinctive trust and liking.

The dragon lowered his head and looked her directly in the eye. "Before we go any further," he said seriously, "I want to know who you are."

The lady Knight nodded. She felt totally at ease with the dragon. It was like being with an old friend she hadn't seen in years, and it seemed reasonable she should tell him the truth. After all, she had broken her vow twice this day. Why not a third? So she told him, and before long, she found herself sitting on the dragon's leg, explaining a great many things. She certainly hadn't meant to say so much, but he was interested and friendly, and he chatted to her in his own turn about other dragons and pirates and Sanction's fragile survival. In some small corner of Linsha's awareness, she knew this was just a dream, hatched from her imagination and fueled by her wounded heart. So what difference did it make how much she talked? This was one of the best dreams she'd had in years, and she was in no hurry to see it end.

Eventually their talk turned to the Knights of Takhisis.

"Why is it you do not fly against the Dark Knights and drive them from the passes?" Linsha wanted to know.

"No one but Bight knows I am here. He has arranged a tenuous treaty with other dragons, both good and evil, to stay out of Sanction Vale. If I fly against the Knights outside of Sanction, they will bring their blue dragons, which will infuriate Sable and others and break the treaty. We will deal with the Dark Knights when the time is ripe."

A belated thought occurred to Linsha and she suddenly sat up straight. "The black ships. I was supposed to warn Lord Bight."

"He knows. The ships made the mistake of sailing into Sanction's harbor. Once there, they became fair game." The dragon clicked his claws in satisfaction.

She subsided back to her seat. The mention of the Dark Knights awakened memories she preferred to let sleep, and an abiding sadness seeped into her soul. "Do you know where Ian Durne is? The last thing I remember is knocking into him to save Varia."

She was surprised to see the dragon look rather smug. "The commander is dead," he answered. "I am sorry if this hurts you, but he did not deserve to live."

Linsha said nothing. She wasn't ready to talk about Ian yet or to delve into her feelings and motives to understand why she had loved him, nor was she ready to fix honest eyes on the countenance of her failures. In time, if she was allowed time, she would face her memories of Ian Durne and try to put them to rest.

The dragon, sensing her sadness, curled his neck around her and rested his head on his foreleg. His movement nudged Linsha from her seat on his leg. Without resistance, she slid to a sitting position on the ground by his head. Unshed tears ached in her eyes as the grief of lost friends, the pain of failed love, and the fear for the days ahead bled from her wounded soul.

"I am with you," the dragon whispered.

She wrapped her arms around his neck and sobbed as if her heart would break.

* * * * *

The next thing Linsha became aware of was darkness, the simple darkness at the edge of sleep. Slowly it unraveled around her until it was merely a haze. Through the haze, she heard someone say, "Will she live?" Varia.

"Of course." A deeper voice, familiar and welcome. Lord Bight.

Linsha's eyes slowly opened and focused on a bed curtain suspended above her. Dim golden light from a single lamp wavered on the material in dancing patches.

"Linsha . . . welcome back," the lord governor said.

She turned her head and saw him sitting beside the bed. His tanned face looked haggard and tired, but his eyes gleamed with success. "You called me Linsha," she said, or at least tried to say. Her voice came out hoarse and barely audible. She realized her neck was swollen and her throat bruised from Durne's attack.

"A friend told me," he said. He reached over and gently touched her throat to still any more talking. "Just rest. Priestess Asharia was here a little while ago. We have closed your wounds and tended your body. Tomorrow will be soon enough to finish your healing."

She nodded, but she had to ask, "Varia?"

The owl cooed softly from the bed stand. She sat ensconced in a nest of blankets with a sling supporting her newly set wing. "All is well for now," she hooted. "It is night. The volcano sleeps. The Dark Knights have been routed."

"Go back to sleep," Lord Bight said. "You are safe here in the palace."

Linsha sank deeper into the clean sheets and cozy pillow. She smiled sleepily. "All I need now is the orange tomcat from the barn," she whispered before she slid back into the recuperative darkness of sleep.

Varia looked up at Lord Bight. He flashed a conspiratorial grin and rose to his feet. "Good night, owl," he said, his voice quiet.

Sometime later, Linsha woke again to darkness. The lamp burned low beside the bed, and Varia slept. The room was quiet about her. Yet some small sound or movement had awakened Linsha. She lay still and listened, waiting for a repetition. Then it came again, a soft meow. Small feet padded across the room. She felt a weight land on the bed near her feet, and the orange tomcat appeared in the dim light. His purr thrummed in his chest as he blinked at her.

Smiling, she patted the bedclothes beside her. She didn't wonder how he had found her or why he was there. It was enough that he had come. She rubbed his ears and fell asleep to the music of his purr.

* * * * *

Linsha remained in the room in the palace for two days as her body healed and her voice and energy returned. No one but Lord Bight knew she was there, for he told his guards that the guardswomen, Shanron and Lynn, had died defending him from the traitor, Ian Durne. The guards were stunned by the duplicity of their commander and by the deaths of Mica and the two women. News of the tragedy spread through town faster than a swarm of locusts.

Meanwhile, city folk breathed a huge sigh of relief that Sanction had been spared an invasion by the Dark Knights.

That was the last thing they needed. No one knew where the big bronze dragon had come from, and no one knew where he went. They were just grateful he had come to their aid when they needed him most.

The people of Sanction had other things to think about as well. Word came from the Temple of the Heart that, thanks to the efforts of the governor's healer, Mica, a possible cure had been found for the Sailors' Scourge. Using the fragments of information from Sable and Mica, and a few donations from the elusive bronze dragon, Lord Bight and Priestess Asharia concocted an infusion made from dragon scales and restorative herbs. A call went out to volunteers to try the new antidote, and in a few hours, a line stretched out of the temple and down the road. Asharia gave some to anyone willing to try the concoction and then went to the refugee camp and the Guard camp to dose those already sick. She spread the news as well that the disease was spread by touch and recommended gloves be worn by anyone caring for the sick. Gloves sold out in the city shops in less than a day. Although Asharia and her surviving healers wouldn't celebrate yet, she told Lord Bight the results looked promising.

The lord governor told Linsha this later that night and pointed to the scale she still wore on the golden chain. "You were our first successful experiment," he said, grinning.

She fingered the scale and felt the slight scratch where Durne's sword had gouged the gold rim. "It protected me in more ways than one," she said. Reluctantly she pulled it off and held it out to him. "I should give this back before I go."

He took the chain, but instead of keeping it, he hung it back around her neck. "It's yours. A favor from an admirer."

"Won't you need it for the cure the mystics are making?"

"We have a few more where that came from."

Pleased she could keep it, she looked down at it and remembered Mica's words: the favor of the lord governor. Perhaps Lord Bight favored her enough to help her with a request. They were silent for a time, contemplating each other in the yellow light of the lamps. There were things they needed to discuss, but neither one was willing to break these brief moments of companionship.

At that moment, Varia flew in the open window and landed on the chair arm beside Linsha. Her wings had healed under Linsha's care, and this evening she had taken her first easy flight. She cocked an eye at Lord Bight but said anyway, "I flew by a certain croft tonight and found it occupied."

Lord Bight raised one eyebrow.

A haunted looked passed fleetingly over Linsha's face. "Did you stop?"

"Yes. You won't like this. I overheard the men in question vote unanimously to have your name dishonorably removed from the order's lists."

"Thank you, Varia," Linsha said sadly.

Lord Bight leaned over and rested his elbows on his knees. His eyes looked hooded in the dim light. "What will you do now?"

"This only strengthens my resolve. I must go to Sancrist Isle. I will plead my case, and yours, to the Solamnic Council. They must know what is going on here."

"You don't have to go. You could stay here, in my protection."

"Thank you, my lord," she replied, more touched than she would have thought possible. "But I cannot stay. The Knighthood means too much to me. I have to clear my name and try to make the council understand how important you are to this city." She had already told him the gist of the Circle's latest activities in Sanction without naming names or specifics. "All I ask," she went on, "is will you help me leave the city undetected?"

He gave her a half-smile, his eyes reflecting the sadness in hers. "That's the least I can do for the squire who defended my life."

"Anytime, my lord. I'm sorry I cannot stay to do whatever task you had in mind when you chose me for your guards."

Lord Bight straightened, his mouth quirked in an expression of humor. "Oh, but you did. Ian Durne. I suspected there was a traitor in my circle, but he kept himself well guarded. What I needed was someone like you to drive him into the open."

Linsha stared at him, her eyes wide. "Someone like me?" she repeated. A thousand and one speculations ran through her mind.

Lord Bight just gave her an enigmatic smile.

The lord governor was true to his word. On a dark night, three days later, he escorted her and Varia out of the palace to the Temple of the Heart. There they slipped into the underground passages of the shadowpeople and made their way south toward Mount Ashkir. They came out into the ruins of the Temple of Duerghast. Linsha was delighted to find Windcatcher tethered inside the old altar room. The mare was saddled, bridled, and carried two saddlebags packed with supplies.

Lord Bight stood apart while she checked the girth and admired the new cloak tied to the saddle. He cleared his throat. "I cannot stay. I am sending someone who will carry you and the horse out of here and will take you to Schallsea." He gathered her into his arms and held her. "I will miss you," he said gruffly.

"I am such a fool," she murmured into his chest. "I wasted so much time and love on a man I knew was not right."

His arms tightened around her. Gently he pushed the auburn curls aside and kissed her forehead. Then he silently walked out the door into the hot summer night.

Numb, Linsha leaned against Windcatcher and watched him go. At last, she untied the mare and led her outside. She and Varia and the mare stood on the hillside and looked down over Sanction, glittering with lights as life rekindled in the city with new hope. The sight helped renew Linsha's exhausted spirit. After all, if a stubborn, fractious town like Sanction could pull itself up by its bootstraps, so could she. And someday, when she had restored her honor within the Knighthood and could walk the streets of Sanction without pretense or secret, she would come back. She wasn't finished with Sanction yet.

The sound of large wings drew her eyes up to the dark

sky, and she saw the bronze dragon come winging out of the night. He landed in the tall grass, being careful not to frighten the mare.

"I'm glad you came," she said. "I thought you were a dream."

He winked at her and shook his great head. "Good. Then maybe I will stay in your dreams until you return. Are you ready?"

She patted Windcatcher and mounted the mare. "She's never done this before, but I think Varia will be able to keep her calm."

The owl hooted and hopped onto the saddle horn in front of Linsha.

Gently the big bronze clutched the horse in his front legs and took three running leaps downhill. Even with the weight of the woman and the horse, he went airborne easily and soared out over Sanction Bay. He circled once over the city before he turned south for the Newsea. The city lights dimmed into the darkness behind him.

Classics Series

Classic tales from the heart of the DRAGONLANCE saga.

Dalamar the Dark
Nancy Varian Berberick

As war simmers on the borders of Sil-vanesti, Dalamar will find a way to become a wizard. His quest will take him along dark paths toward an awesome destiny.

Available January 2000

The Citadel
Richard A. Knaak

Against a darkened cloud it comes, framed by thunder and lightning, soaring over the ravaged land: the flying citadel, mightiest power in the arsenal of the dragon highlords.

An evil wizard learns the secret of creating these castles in the air and seeks to use them to gain power over all Krynn. Against him are a red-robed magic-user, a cleric, an ancient warrior, and—naturally—a kender.

Their battle shakes the skies of Krynn.

Available August 2000

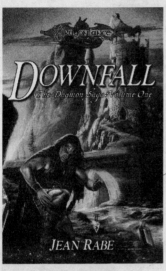

Downfall
The Dhamon Saga
Volume One
Jean Rabe

How far can a hero fall?

Far enough to lose his soul?

Dhamon Grimwulf, once a Hero of the Heart, has sunk into a bitter life of crime and squalor. Now, as the great dragon overlords of the Fifth Age coldly plot to strengthen their rule and to destroy their enemies, he must somehow find the will to redeem himself.

But perhaps it is too late.

Don't miss the beginning of Dhamon's story from Jean Rabe!

Available May 2000

Dragons of a New Age

The Dawning of a New Age
Great dragons invade Ansalon, devastating the land and dividing it among themselves.

The Day of the Tempest
The Heroes of the Heart seek the long-lost dragonlance in the snow-covered tomb of Huma.

The Eve of the Maelstrom
Dragons and humans battle for the future of Krynn at the Window to the Stars.